# over the
# MOON

USA TODAY BESTSELLING AUTHOR
# K.K. ALLEN

# Over the Moon

# COPYRIGHT

To my first reading buddy and BFF since we were 12, Tasha. And to her momma in heaven who used to laugh at us kids for sitting on the couch all day reading Sweet Valley High during our sleepovers. Happy Birthday, Anna. XO

# PROLOGUE

## SYLVIA

S team from my shower envelops me as blood washes off my skin and circles the drain. I'm not sure how long I stand there and watch the crimson swirl like an endless ball of unraveling string. I'm not even certain how much, if any, of the blood belongs to me. While my skin is welted and bruised and a permanent knot continues to tighten in my gut, I don't see or feel a single open wound on my body.

The desperate need to scream claws up my throat, and tears prick the backs of my eyes as they threaten to burst all over again. The anger comes in waves, pushing me toward the riptide, no matter how hard or fast I fight to swim away. It's the darkest battle I've ever faced, yet somehow, I know it's only the beginning.

When the red finally fades, I tear my eyes from the drain and shut off the water. I reach for a folded towel, and my injured arm screams in pain at the simple motion. Still, I manage to get the stiff fabric around my body before daring a look into the mirror. Fog over the glass blocks my view, but that doesn't matter. I can still feel the map of scars that cover my body.

Seventy-two hours have passed since I ran away. It's been bus stop after bus stop, evidence of my injuries cloaked under a big gray hoodie and baggy sweatpants. Now, I need to figure out my next move. While leaving was always the plan, I didn't expect it to go down like that. Still, running away from home was easy. Settling into somewhere new... That will be the challenging part.

After easing my aching body into a fresh set of clothes, I open the bathroom door and am instantly blasted with icy-cool air and a brightly lit hotel room. I'm alone, and everything is where I left it, save for the manila envelope that's currently sliding through the crack at the bottom of the hotel door. I hurry over to the envelope and stuff it inside my duffel bag—there's no need to look inside since I already know what it contains. I lift my bag over my shoulder, wincing through the pain, then head for the door, stopping only long enough to catch a glance at myself in the long mirror.

The girl staring back at me isn't the same one that walked into this hotel room hours ago. Not a stitch of makeup appears on her face. Her once-brown long locks are now blond and frame her chin with a sloppy cut job. The clothes that hang from her scarily thin frame consist of nothing more than light jeans and a long T-shirt. The change is simple, yet I'm unrecognizable even to myself.

While this girl has been stripped down to the barest bones of herself, her soul shattered, her heart broken a million times over, at least she's finally free.

## PHASE ONE

# NEW MOON

"EVERYONE IS A MOON, AND HAS A DARK
SIDE WHICH HE NEVER SHOWS TO
ANYBODY." — MARK TWAIN

# Chapter 1

# SENTENCED

## KINGSTON

F ootball. Playing in the NFL has always been my number one goal. My final destination. The be all, end all of my life. It's also the one thing I've always been able to control. My blessing when everything else around me seems cursed.

Or maybe it's me who is cursed. At least, it feels like I am at the moment. My head aches, I'm stiff from sleeping all wrong, and I can't for the life of me peel my eyelids apart to see where I am.

A door slams in the distance, and the fog that clouds my memory of the night before begins to clear. Images slowly filter through the haze, my grin growing with each visual of my night at one of my favorite bars in downtown Seattle.

Long red hair wrapped around my fist. A fair, freckled cheek pressed into the bathroom sink counter. Skirt pulled up around a trim waist. Me, pumping into the beautiful stranger from behind.

I'm not surprised I don't remember the woman's name. What does surprise me is the memory that pummels me next.

A bathroom door bursting open. A furious bouncer planting his body at the entrance. My head hitting tile as I'm thrown against a bathroom stall. A fist connecting with my jaw.

Then...

My grin fades, and an ugly pit grows in my gut. *Shit.* I look around to find myself in a loaded jail cell with a dozen others. The aftermath of my bad decisions slams me in the chest. The woman who'd lured me into the bathroom without an ounce of resistance from me was the bouncer's wife. Apparently, he doesn't like to share. After he tossed me to the curb outside the club, I was arrested for public intoxication. Now, here I am. My home away from home. It's only a matter of time before one of my teammates I was with last night bails me out of this shithole.

Just then, the familiar sound of steel sliding across a track gets my attention before the sound of my name does. "Kingston Scott, you're free to go."

A laugh muddled with relief shakes through me. I stand from the bench, taking one sweeping glance around the cell, and the corners of my mouth curl back into a smile. "See ya later, suckers."

Angry curse words of my cellmates fly at me as I strut toward the exit, completely unfazed. Another night in the drunk tank isn't going to be enough to alter my future. The memory of last night will be gone before I even step foot outside this place. I'm confident in that knowledge... until I spot Coach Reynolds standing at the counter with a look on his face that no fellow Seattle football player wants to see.

Disappointment.

Most other men on the team would grovel in shame at his feet, but not me. After three years playing football under the man, I know he has a soft spot for thugs like me. There has always been a silent understanding between us. I help him win football games, and he stays off my back when it comes to my personal life. But I can't help but wonder if this time is different. While I know he isn't blind to my previous misdemeanors, he's never been the one to bail me out of one. And by the look on his face as he waits for me to collect my belongings, he sure as hell doesn't look like someone who wants to do me any favors.

"Nance rat me out?" I practically spit my sour words while tearing my eyes from Coach and pushing toward the exit. "Or was it Balko? That son of a bitch." I shake my head, fuming at their betrayal. Nance, Balko, and I have always been like the three amigos, bailing each other out of whatever shit we stir up for ourselves. Apparently, whatever loyalty I thought we had died somewhere between my bathroom romp and my night behind bars.

"Does it matter?" Coach quirks a brow as his dry tone grates against my ego. "You're free to walk. Your record is clean. You get another chance to fuck it all up. Congratulations, Kingston."

Instinct kicks in, and I want to gloat. That growing pit in my stomach has already shrunk back down to nothing, and a rush of adrenaline takes its place at the thought of avoiding yet another lawful consequence for my actions.

"Are you smiling?"

Coach's enraged voice breaks through my thoughts, and my lips flatten back down as I meet his deadly gaze. I swallow my glee as he slams a hand against the glass door and swings it open, allowing me to walk out first.

I step outside, squinting and raising a hand to shield my eyes from the sun. "What time is it, anyway?"

"Noon."

I detect annoyance in his tone, and I flip him a gaze and quirk a brow. "It was just past midnight when they threw me in here. You're just getting me now?"

"Yeah, I know. Shitty of me, right?" Coach glares. "Figured I'd let you sleep it off first." He jabs a finger toward his shiny red Range Rover. "Get in."

Balko drove last night, but my guess is Coach already knows that since he's headed in the direction of my home. That asshole was probably the one who ratted me out. Annoyance stirs through me. Payback will be a bitch.

I try to ignore Coach's cool silent treatment as he drives us through the city streets toward the 520 bridge. I know the man well enough to understand just how serious his silence is. This isn't an after-the-game-we-lost kind of fury where he rips us a new one in the locker room. This isn't a screaming match on the football field when we run a drill that fails to match his expectations. This could mean something much, much worse.

I shift away as if the physical movement will erase my thoughts. Facing the outdoors, I roll down the window to feel the wind smack my face, providing alertness I should have felt last night before it all went sideways. I seem to always find myself in this dark place. Not *here*, physically, not even with Coach. He rarely interferes with his players' behavior off the field. But that doesn't erase my list of bad decisions. They're stacking up so high that I can't even see over the top anymore. Something tells me this last stunt might just be the one that makes the whole stack topple over.

Guilt isn't something I feel often, but I feel a pang of it now. Why should I feel guilty when I've only ever been trying to survive? I came from nothing and was practically raised by wolves, and I overcame it all to lead a life most others would die to have. Sure, I go off the rails sometimes, but that has nothing to do with my game. I shake my head, clearing the guilt and replacing it with my most lethal weapon. Determination.

"Tell me something, Kingston. Why do you want to play ball?"

I'm so focused on my own thoughts that I almost miss Coach's question. When I register what he asked, I turn to face him, my brows knitting in the center. "Same as everyone on the team. I love the game. And I'm the best at what I do. I've worked damn hard to get here."

Coach nods. "No one can argue any of those things. But *why* did you work so hard to get here? I want to know what drives you."

For some reason, his question throws me off guard. I stumble over my thoughts for a few seconds, coming up empty by the time Coach speaks again.

"C'mon, King. It's not a hard question. Is it the money? Is it the celebrity status? Is it the women? Pick one."

My gut reaction is to tell Coach that none of those answers are my reason, but any answer I spit out will be a lie. The truth is, I've never had to think that hard about it before. I just *know* I love football. Isn't that enough?

"I don't know what to tell you, Coach. You're asking me this for a reason, and I'm not sure I can give you the answer you want to hear. I play ball because I'm good at it. It's the only thing I've ever been good at. The adrenaline rush is a great feeling, the money is spectacular, and the women are a sweet bonus, but I'm not sure any of that is what drove me to start playing the game."

Coach nods again. "Figured as much."

That's all he says until he parks in the driveway of my Lake Washington home. An awkward silence follows as my hand slowly reaches for the door handle. I've never been one for formalities, and the tension billowing through the air only makes me want to exit the vehicle as fast as possible. Before I can make a move to exit, the engine shuts off completely.

*Shit.*

Coach shifts, turning to face me. "I think it's time you figured out why you want to play ball."

After getting my drunk ass kicked and getting thrown in jail, I thought the last thing Coach would be concerned about was my desire to play football. "Um, sure. Okay." I don't know what else to say.

Coach rolls his eyes and settles his stern gaze back on me. "Let me say it this way. I will never again do what I did for you today. Do you understand me? It's not my job to bail you out of jail. Nor is it my job to take advantage of my connections to clear you of your misdemeanor. While the crime may be minor, the publicity you managed to avoid should be considered yet another blessing in your life. If you're not careful, you're going to run out of those blessings, Kingston. No one will be there to clean up after your messes, and you won't have a home on the field to come back to."

Something twists inside me as anger and fear swarm my mind. "It will never happen again, Coach. I swear to you." I shake my head, feeling suddenly desperate to forget the events of last night.

Coach nods. "I believe that you mean that. I also expect that you can understand that I'll need to take some steps into ensuring the reputation of our team. We start practices in a little over a month, and I hope you can be there with us."

*I hope you can be there with us.* Never have words haunted me so much. Heat blasts my chest while I temper my tone. "What does that mean?"

"What do you think it means?" he fires back.

There's a fiery ball in my chest that threatens to explode. The only way I know how to diffuse it is to walk away, but I can't walk away from this. This is my life. My livelihood. The only fucking thing in my life that has ever felt right. Still, I want to do anything but continue this conversation. Suddenly, the only thing I love in this life feels threatened, and no amount of confidence I have in my career can help me. I've never felt the weight of my future so heavy on my shoulders.

"I don't know, Coach. I fucked up last night. What's new? But what does it matter? Last night has nothing to do with football."

"Last night has everything to do with football, King. That's where you seem to be lost, and it's time we set things straight."

Coach doesn't have to yell for me to feel his wrath. It's a smack in the face, and I hear him loud and clear. "What do you want from me? Some kind of agreement that I won't fuck up again? I'll do it if that's what you want."

Coach tilts his head. "I had a different idea. Well, it's Zach's idea, actually."

I frown as confusion makes its way through me. Zachary Ryan is Seattle's team captain, and he's extremely close with Coach. I guess it shouldn't surprise me that they talked, but the question slips past my lips anyway. "Zach knows about this?"

"He does, and I'm going to leave you in his hands with what comes next."

"Huh?" My eyes dart between his. "What comes next?"

"You'll find out tomorrow at five a.m. when Zach picks you up. Just have a duffel packed with some stuff to hold you over for a while. Workout gear, mostly."

"A while? How long is that, exactly?"

"Not sure yet. Let's start with one month and see how it goes from there."

My jaw drops with so much force, I can feel the stretch that comes with my shock. "One month? But, Coach—"

"I trust you'll make it work without complaint. Just be ready to go."

My mouth snaps shut as I try to make sense of what's happening, but I can't for the life of me come to any positive conclusions. "Okay." I draw the word out slowly before Coach nods for me to exit his vehicle.

"Five a.m. tomorrow," Coach repeats through his open window as he's backing out of my driveway. "We'll talk again when you get back."

He drives off without another glance, leaving me standing in the wake of my bad decisions. Whatever Coach and Zach have planned, I have a feeling I'm about to pay.

# CHAPTER 2

# IN GOOD HANDS

## SILVER

"They're almost here." My coworker, Hope, practically squeals the words as she charges into my office.

I look up from the stack of immunization records I was reviewing to find my friend's normally light skin flushed and her brown eyes big and bright. Smiling, I press my hands on my desk and tilt my head in amusement. "*They?* The campers don't arrive until Monday."

She lets out a laugh and plants herself in the nearest chair. "No, not them. The Seattle players and that creative agency who host this whole thing. They like to come in a few days early for the initial setup, remember?"

I really should remember, seeing as this will be the third year the team has held their football camp at Camp Dakota. What started out as a one-week anti-bullying fundraising event quickly grew thanks to its popularity. For one month, Camp Dakota, along with BelleCurve Creative and the Seattle football team, hosts a month-long camp. Each week, we welcome new groups of kids and Seattle players. At the end of each week, there's a scrimmage tournament to crown a team winner during the final ceremony.

"I guess I forgot. We see new groups every week. How do you expect me to remember a silly football event?"

Hope lets out an audible groan at my silence. "Seriously, Silver. How long have you lived here now?"

"At camp or in Washington?"

"Both."

I ease back into my chair and take my time to respond, choosing my words carefully. Hope has only worked at Camp Dakota for the past year, and while she's quickly become my best friend, there's still a lot she doesn't know about me. "Eight years."

Something swirls in my gut at my mention of the length of time I've lived here, but I shove it aside quickly.

"Well," Hope says, not missing a beat. "Then there's no excuse. You should be a crazed Seattle fan like the rest of us by now."

I avert my eyes and begin to clean up the paperwork spread over my desk. "Not going to happen. I've never been into sports."

"What? Why?"

I shrug. "It's just not my thing. But give me a sprained arm to sling or an open cut to clean, and I'm your gal." Hope studies me in a way that makes me laugh with unease, causing me to narrow my gaze. "What?"

She lets out a heavy sigh. "Sometimes I just want to shake you. You need to live a little. Step outside of your comfort zone. Experience new things."

Laughing, I shake my head. "I'm doing just fine, trust me."

"Maybe, but you're so career minded, it scares me."

With a big dramatic roll of my eyes, I sigh. That's the thing about studying medicine—no one outside of the field could possibly understand. "There's nothing to be afraid of. And there's nothing wrong with being focused on my career. I didn't get an advanced nursing degree for nothing. I've worked really hard to get the head nurse position here after studying under Miriam Bexley for four years. I want to do her proud. I want to do the Bexleys proud."

The Bexleys have successfully owned and run Camp Dakota for two decades. I owe them everything for offering me a job and home when I came to them with zero experience. But I'm not about to get into all of that with Hope right now. "Anyway," I say, tilting my head. "Why are we talking about this? Because I don't care for football?"

Hope lets out a groan. "No, because you aren't freaking ecstatic that some of the hottest men on the planet are about to step foot in our camp. Aren't you at least a little bit curious about them?"

"No need to be curious." I pick up one of the closed envelopes on my desk and hold it up. "I'm already up to speed on all of their medical records. Twelve Seattle players are coming this week, and trust me, there's more information in this folder than you could ever find on their trading cards."

Hope's mouth falls open, and she lurches toward my desk, reaching for the envelope.

I yank it out of reach. "Oh no," I say with a grin. "That's confidential."

She lets out a frustrated scream. "You're such a tease. I'm so jealous. You know who's coming this week. You know everything about them." Her eyes widen. "Just imagine if one of them gets hurt." She looks up at the ceiling and sighs. "You'll get to tend to their wounds." Her gaze lands back on mine before a blush spreads across her cheeks. "Maybe you should teach me CPR. Just in case."

A laugh bursts past my lips, and I stand. "You're ridiculous. These forms are just a formality, but they're of no use to me. They're bringing in a sports physician from Orcas Island Hospital to help me with the kids, but the professional players will just be here to coach. I never see them in my office."

I can practically hear the excitement deflating from Hope's chest. "Well, damn. I probably won't see them much, either, since I'm not working any of the field activities."

Hope is the activities director who's usually put in charge of team-building activities during events like this. Her disappointment hits my chest with a pang. From the moment I met her, I knew she had a huge heart. "Well, you never know. Maybe you can strut by the field every so often and lock eyes with one of these hotties. Maybe you'll score a date." I raise my brows and wiggle them to get her to laugh.

"Or maybe we can double." She waggles her brows back at me, this time causing me to break out in a smile of my own.

"Sorry. You're on your own there. I don't date the guests."

She folds her arms across her chest and studies me. "Yeah, yeah, I know your rules, but you're telling me you wouldn't for a single minute consider one of these gorgeous men, even for a little fling?"

"And what would the point in that be? Most of them will be gone in a week."

Her lids widen as she stares back at me like I'm insane. "Sex, Silver. The point is sex. It's possible to have fun with a man you don't intend to marry, especially when you're not currently having sex at all."

"Geez, you act like I'm some kind of prude. Tim and I broke up a month ago."

She gives a dismissive wave of her hand. "He doesn't count. His dick was probably as small as that tiny pea brain of his. I'm so glad Miriam fired his ass after what he did to you."

I shrug. "It's fine. I figured out soon enough he wasn't the one."

Hope tilts her head. "Because you, my friend, do not have a tiny pea brain. Your brain, in fact, is too big for your body, and it's time to give it the day off." She holds out a hand. "Come with me?"

"What?" I laugh. "To where?"

"To greet the bus, like we always do."

I burst out with a laugh. "When do we ever greet the chaperones?" I shake my head, not giving her a chance to argue. "I don't have time for this right now. There are kids who still need to turn in their immunization records. I need to make some phone calls to their parents, and..."

The look she gives me next cuts me. "Silver," she says sternly.

"Hope," I say right back.

She sighs. "I won't take no for an answer."

I give the girl credit. Out of all the years I've lived at the camp, no one has ever pushed me the way Hope has. While I try to resist her charms at every turn, I can admit that her adventurous nature has rubbed off on me a little bit.

I cringe while leaning my head back in frustration. "Geez. Okay, fine. I'll go just so you won't hold it over my head."

"Smart girl." She grins and hops to her feet. "I'll meet you out front."

After taking a minute to tidy up, I close and lock my office door. Then I cross the examination room toward the main entrance of the cabin. It's a small workspace, but it's perfectly fitting for my needs. The former head nurse, Miriam, whom I assisted, always kept me in the front room. I would greet kids and evaluate injuries, then she would come in to give the final assessment—both for me and the patients. She was always testing me, critiquing my performance, and adding to my training. The day she finally retired and left camp, it felt like someone pulling a crutch away from me. But it only took a few months to realize I could, in fact, walk on my own.

"Morning, ladies," Anderson Bexley calls out as he strolls by my office, probably on his way to greet our guests.

"Morning, Anderson," Hope and I chime back in unison.

Detecting the flirtatious tone in Hope's voice, I snap my head to her and narrow my eyes. "Obvious much?"

She shrugs, looking slightly annoyed, while her eyes are pinned on the man increasing his distance from us. "Doesn't matter. Anderson doesn't even see me."

Unfortunately, I know all too well that her feelings are justified. Anderson is just as career minded as me. We've always had that in common.

"Yeah, well, if it makes you feel better, I know he's overwhelmed right now. He's taken on a lot for his parents while his siblings are off living their lives around the world. Sometimes, I wonder if he feels stuck."

She quirks a brow at me. "Like you? Geez, you two would be perfect together."

I make a face. "Gross, no. Anderson is practically my brother. And I'm not stuck here. I *choose* to be here. There's a big difference."

The moment the words are out of my mouth, I regret saying them. I don't have to look at my friend to see the gears of curiosity churning in her brain.

"Why *do* you choose to be here, Silver? I mean—don't get me wrong. I don't know what I would do without you. But it's not like you have family tying you here. You could be a nurse anywhere. And you'd probably get paid a hell of a lot more than the Bexleys pay you. Why Camp Dakota?"

I pinch out a smile, trying to ignore the discomfort snaking through me. I could tell her that the Bexleys have done a lot for me, and that if not for them, I might not ever have gone into nursing, but that would only lead to more questions. I've learned the hard way that it's much safer for all involved to just keep it simple. "I like it here." A shrug accompanies my smile, and it works.

While Hope turns away with frustration evident on her face, she doesn't ask another question about it. We follow the winding dirt path lined with tall pine trees until we come to the large clearing, where the staff is awaiting the players' bus. I can't help but notice the undeniable energy swirling in the air. The staff's voices are more animated than normal. Their footsteps quicker. Their laughter louder.

One would think after the previous two years of the same event, the staff would be used to seeing the players, but the fanfare speaks for itself. And this is where I don't fit in with the others. As I stand here, awaiting a busload of athletes I won't even be working with, I start to get antsy. There are so many other things I could be doing right now, like inventory of my supplies or reviewing internship candidates. Miriam has been retired for a few months now, and the only assistant I've ever had recently quit to pursue other careers, which means I'm on my own until I find a fitting replacement.

I start to tell Hope I'm going to head back to work, then the sound of an approaching engine riles up the crowd. A second later, a giant motor coach painted in purple and gold, along with the Seattle football team's logo, drives through the gated entrance.

The chatter only intensifies, fading to a slight buzz only once the bus is parked and they're all trying to contain their excitement. While I'm not a giant fan of the team like the rest of them, I wholeheartedly understand their elation. Living here can become monotonous at times, so I understand how the arrival of celebrities tends to wind them up.

One by one, players step off the bus, large purple duffel bags slung over their broad shoulders. They look almost silly, like Hulk clones all huddled together as Anderson makes his way toward them with his always-present clipboard.

"C'mon," Hope hisses. "Let's get closer. I want to see if I can touch one of them."

I throw her a horrified glance as she starts to walk off. In a swift move, I clutch the back of her shirt and pull her back to me with a laugh. "Please don't be like *that*." I nod toward the gaggle of camp counselors who didn't bother to change out of their swimsuits for the occasion.

"Ugh," Hope says with disgust. "Do they always have to be so flaunty about their hotness?"

I raise a brow. "Did you just say 'flaunty'?"

She shrugs. "I did, and I'm not taking it back."

Laughing, I give my friend a little nudge. "Play it cool. Trust me. Any guy worth dating won't fall for that, anyway. They'll fall for your hotness exactly as you stand."

Hope frowns and stares down at her work uniform, which is just a pair of khaki shorts and a white polo with Camp Dakota embroidered into it. "Yeah, but no one will be able to see my hotness under this frock."

"Just wait until they see you in your cafeteria uniform."

Absolute horror registers on Hope's face as she takes in my words. Most of the regular staffers get called to take up odd jobs as needed, and Hope absolutely despises the cafeteria duties. I've never seen my friend look so mortified. "Seriously, Silver? You are the worst."

She turns back to the group of guys while trying to stifle a laugh, but even while suffering from wardrobe insecurities, she's filled to the brim with good humor.

"Holy shit." The curse flies from Hope's mouth so fast, I barely have time to register it before she's gripping my arm. "No way."

I follow her gaze and squint to see a straggler stepping off the bus. He's tall and seemingly built like the rest, but I can't see much beneath the black hoodie that's pulled over his head and the dark shades that hide his eyes.

The way Hope's jaw has practically fallen to the asphalt makes me all the more curious. "I don't understand. Why are you freaking out?"

"Is that King?" she asks, her eyes wide. "It can't be. There's no way he would be caught dead here."

I have no idea whom she's referring to. "Why not?"

"Because he's..." Her stare follows the man's movements.

Her elaboration doesn't help me make sense of her freak-out, not in the least. "Because he's what, Hope?"

"Because he's Kingston freaking Scott. The *king* of all defensive ends. A god-like masterpiece of epic proportions. Just look at him."

Squinting, I try my best to see more of the guy who now looks like he's in a heated argument with another player. I twist my lips, focusing back on the heated one. "He looks..." I try to find something positive to say. "Very..." And I'm coming up empty. "Grumpy." When her eyes bulge at me, I jump to my own defense. "I can't even see him. He's all covered up."

My nonchalance makes her wince. "I'm starting to question our entire friendship."

"Over my attraction to a *sweatshirt?*"

She lets out a laugh. "Okay, I get it. But c'mon. You're telling me you took one glance at Kingston's file and didn't feel an ounce of anything?"

I give her question some serious thought, reviewing his name over and over in my mind until something clicks. *Kingston Scott. Kingston Scott. Kingston Scott.* But nothing connects. For the life of me, I can't remember ever seeing the guy's name in the records I've reviewed. "I know nothing," I tell her honestly. "Must have skipped over him on accident."

Hope rolls her eyes while laughing. "Only you, Silver. Only you."

Grinning at my friend, I squeeze her arm. "I'm heading back to work now." When she starts to argue, I narrow my eyes, signaling that I'm not taking no for an answer again. "See you at dinner."

This time, she doesn't argue. "Okay, fine. You get back to work. I'm going to find us a couple of guys to get to know better." She winks, effectively causing my chest to heat with embarrassment.

*I don't doubt that she will.*

I make my way to the empty staff room in the main lodge and pour myself a cup of coffee. The room is quiet save for the television that someone left on. The Bexleys strictly enforce the no electronics rule around camp with this one television as our exception.

There's a cooking show playing now, and I smile when I recognize it as one I've watched with Hope before. *Desmond's*

*Kitchen* is an adorable reality-slash-cooking show that features the owner of a cooking school in Seattle alongside his girl-friend, Maggie.

I find the remote and aim to turn it off when I'm caught in what's playing out on screen. Desmond is creeping up behind Maggie, who is cutting strips of dough to make pasta. She's so focused on her task that she doesn't see Desmond kneel behind her until he places a hand on her hip.

She looks over her shoulder, and then her eyes pan down. The moment she sees him, her face morphs from confusion to shock to excitement as she registers what's happening. The volume is too low for me to hear his words, but it's enough to make her fall to her knees and tell him, "Yes!"

A bundle of emotions heat in my chest and behind my eyes, until I'm fighting back tears from the proposal playing out on the screen. It's such a beautiful moment, a sweet and thoughtful gesture, but it also makes me sad to know it's something that may never happen for me.

After taking a moment to collect myself, I grab a muffin leftover from breakfast and head to my office. I start to think about Hope and her reaction to the NFL players who arrived. It's a mystery to me how she can be so content with having a meaningless fling with a guy who will be in and out of her life within the week. Then will she do the same thing next week, when a fresh set of guys come through? She could get attached to one of them—or worse, her heart could get broken.

A pang hits my chest at the thought of seeing my friend hurt. Working at a camp makes it impossible to avoid witnessing heartbreak. It's a frequent occurrence with the coed teen crowds. If it's not a boy not noticing them, then it's a boy who cheated or a boy who was only using them for one thing. Sure, sometimes it was the girls doing the hurting, but it's a rare occurrence that a boy comes to me looking for the cure to a broken heart.

I'm still thinking about Hope when I round the corner of my office and spot Anderson chatting with the giant, angry man. Strange that I don't remember him from the roster they sent to me.

"Silver," Anderson says when he spots me, "I want to introduce you to Kingston Scott. He was a last-minute addition for this week, so I'm just getting him squared away."

Kingston is still covered up with his dark shades and hoodie like he's afraid of the sun, but the little I see is enough to send chills rippling through my body.

I step forward to close the distance between us, knowing it's my turn to say something, but finding words has never felt so difficult. From afar, it was apparent that Kingston is a tall dude, but now I'm realizing just how tall. He towers over me by more than a foot. Given the fact that Anderson is six-three and still a few inches shorter than Kingston has me doing a quick calculation in my head.

There's a sliver of light brown peeking out from under his hoodie and unshaven stubble on his cheeks. His mouth is pressed into a hard line, telling me he isn't exactly thrilled to be here. Everything about the man is such a stark contrast to his teammates who hopped off the bus and greeted the staff with nothing but smiles.

"Welcome to Camp Dakota, Kingston," I say, somehow managing to steady my voice. "I'm sure you'll enjoy your time here." Thank God Hope isn't with us now. She would laugh in my face at my formality.

"Silver is our resident nurse," Anderson adds. "She'll be working closely with the sports physician once he arrives on

Monday. Until then, she's your girl for any of your medical needs."

Kingston's brows lift above the top of his shades for a second before he reaches a hand out to me. My gaze falls to the hand he's just offered, and I hope he can't hear the way my heart is currently crashing against my ribs. While I know nothing about football, I imagine the hand he reaches out for me to take was born to hold one. "Nice to meet you, Silver."

*Holy Jesus.* Kingston's voice is like a baritone horn freshly dipped in honey, its tone still buzzing through the air long after its last note ended. I search his shaded gaze, knowing I should probably speak, but I'm coming up empty.

*What the hell is wrong with me?*

A throat clears from beside us, and I snap my head to find Anderson peering at me inquisitively. "Silver, do you mind getting him caught up on any medical release forms you'll need prior to Monday?"

"Sure thing," I manage to say, still reeling from being caught off guard, then I tilt my head, confused. "Wait. You mean right now?" I'm so flustered, I can feel my cheeks blazing.

Anderson narrows his eyes at me. "Unless you were in the middle of something?"

I give a quick shake of my head. "No, of course not. I have time now."

"Great. Make sure to show him to his cabin when you're done." Anderson backs away with a parting smile to Kingston. "Silver will be sure to take care of all your needs." He claps the man on the back before jogging off and shouting back at him, "You're in good hands."

"Is that right?" Kingston's voice is just low enough for me to hear, that same rhythmic buzz from before.

His eyes lock on mine, unleashing a flock of flutters inside of me. I don't know why, but just standing in his presence is enough to make me angry. There's just something about him that tells me he's going to be trouble.

"Well then, Nurse Silver." The side of his mouth tilts up in a cocky smirk before he opens his mouth again. "I look forward to seeing just how good those hands of yours are."

# CHAPTER 3

# BAD IMPRESSIONS

## KINGSTON

When Zach talked my ear off the entire way here, he failed to mention the bikini welcome party and the hot nurse who would be "taking care of all my needs," as Anderson put it. Instead, he went on and on about some anti-bullying charity he started years ago and how Belle-Curve Creative helped him set up an entire football sleepaway camp to raise money for his cause. He then tried to convince me how awesome my time at Camp Dakota would be, how all the kids loved the one-on-one mentoring from their favorite athletes, and how by the time I step foot back on the practice field, my past misdemeanors would be behind me.

"C'mon, man," I said to him halfway into our bus ride. "An entire month?"

"It will fly by," he said, waving me off. "Just give it a chance."

"But we're talking about four weeks. This is supposed to be my vacation time, bro. You're going to make me bunk with a bunch of kids?"

Zach laughed. "No, some of the players are rooming

together, but you'll get your own cabin. And none of us bunks with the kids. Camp Dakota provides counselors who look over the kids. You just need to be on the field this week to mentor, inspire. It'll be good."

"Give me a break with this. If all Coach wants to do is jail me up for the month, there are better approaches. Can't you put me on house arrest at home? Then at least I'll have my pool and shit."

Zach rested his head against the seat with a shrug. "That's not the point of this. Besides, the whole month idea came from Coach. And he seemed pretty dead set on it."

I gave Zach an unbelieving glare. "Coach said this was all your idea. I'm in your hands, according to him."

Zach chuckled. "C'mon, man, you know how Coach works. He was pissed and asked me for ideas. I noticed you hadn't volunteered for any of the weeks—or previous years, for that matter—so I suggested it, but I had no idea he'd make you stay for all four weeks. No one else is doing that. Well, besides me."

I shook my head in dire frustration. It felt like there was no winning at all. Even if Zach had the mind to give me a break, it was still up to Coach Reynolds. "Can you at least talk to Coach? Maybe after a few days and he's had time to calm down?"

"Tell you what," Zach said, with a reasonable look on his face. "If you put in the work this week—I mean, if you're truly there for these kids. You show up on time, you put a smile on your face, and you're a solid role model. Then I'll consider talking to Coach. Ultimately, it's his decision, and I'm going to respect whatever that decision is."

I took that conversation as a win and dropped it for the rest of the bus ride... until we arrived at camp and I got a closeup view of where we would all be staying for the week. Zach heard my bitching and moaning as soon as we stepped off the bus, which I think pissed him off, but what else was I supposed to do? Pretend I'd entered some nirvana like the rest of my team-mates? No fucking way. I entered hell, and I was more deter-mined than ever to do what I had to do to leave this godforsaken camp at the end of the week. No matter what.

Looking back on that entire conversation on the bus, I have to give it to Zach—he does the kumbaya shit well—but he's also far too naive if he believes he and Coach have the power to change me.

*Case in point.* One glance at Nurse Silver and my thoughts slipped straight off the deep end and started entertaining all kinds of stimulating possibilities. Not even the hideous maroon scrubs and gray sneakers she's wearing can ruin these fantasies. I have quite the imagination when necessary, and that long blond ponytail that sits high on her head isn't helping matters.

"Are you coming, Kingston?"

Silver's voice, tinged with annoyance, is enough to tear my eyes away from her ass and fix on her narrowed eyes instead. She already climbed the two steps to reach the entrance of the cabin while I haven't moved an inch.

Digging my mind out of the gutter, I secure my large duffel bag over my shoulder and take one step to bring me to the front entrance landing. "After you."

I don't miss the sharp warning look she gives me before turning back around and heading into her office. *Permission to stare at her ass again: denied.* So I do the next best thing and check out everything else in the tiny medical cabin.

The space is simple and boring, with a small reception desk and a single chair pressed against the wall. Save for a lone cheap painting on the back wall, there's absolutely zero personality. She leads me through a door and into an examination room, where I'm blasted with a strong scent of cleaning chemicals that will surely grace me with a monster headache by the time I leave. There's nothing much to this room either, just a long, padded table, a small countertop with a sink and cabinets above it, and a rolling stool. She moves to a door on the other side of the room and unlocks it before leading me into an office. There's not a single thing out of place. Everything looks spotless, and other than a framed photo facing her, there's not a single item of decor in the room.

Nurse Silver appears to be all business, no play. That thought puts a major damper on my mood. She sits down at her desk and turns on her computer while sneaking glances at me in between. "You can have a seat. I'm just printing some forms."

I glance at the brown folding chair that I'm certain would be crushed beneath my weight and shake my head. "I'm good."

Her eyes flicker back to her computer. "Suit yourself. I'll just be a minute."

She taps away at her computer, and I let my eyes wander around the room. There's a file cabinet to one side and a large glass case filled with medicines to the other. Curious, I step closer and peruse the contents. There are bottles and bottles of over-the-counter medicines and vitamins. The fact that Silver finds it necessary to lock them all up makes me chuckle.

I turn to look at her over my shoulder. "Tell me, when is the last time someone tried to break this lock to get their hands on a bottle of NyQuil?"

She quirks a brow at me. "You'd be surprised."

I slide my finger along the glass and point to a box of condoms on the bottom shelf. "And these?"

"Now that," she says, looking more perturbed as time goes on, "shouldn't surprise *you* one bit."

My jaw drops so fast, I can feel it ache. I'm not as offended as I am shocked by her insinuation. I turn to face her completely. "What the hell is that supposed to mean?"

The laugh that comes from Silver is filled with discomfort. "What?" she coughs out. "No, that's not what I—" She shakes her head and takes her slender fingers from the computer keys. "Maybe we need to start over." She pushes her chair from the desk, stands up, and walks over to me until she's directly under my nose. "It's nice to meet you, Kingston. I'm Silver."

When she holds out her hand for me to shake, I consider rejecting it, just to watch her squirm a little more. Little Miss Nurse deserves it after what she just insinuated. But even my asshole tendencies can't ignore the strong desire to touch her again. I wrap her hand in mine and shake.

"It's nice to meet you too, Silver. But please—" I pause, trying to fight the smile that wants to break free. "Call me King."

The speed at which her fair skin brightens to a pretty shade of pink has me thinking about all the ways I can get her to blush again. When she goes to take her hand from mine, I tighten my hold just enough to let her know we're not done with this little game. "Unless that makes you uncomfortable."

"I think I'll stick with Kingston." She pulls her hand from mine again and gestures to the glass cabinet. "Back to the—"

"Condoms."

She clears her throat. "Right. Well, I'm sure you know how teens can be. While we encourage safe sex, we have established counseling services in exchange for free contraception."

My laugh is unstoppable this time. "Counseling services? No offense, Silver." I say her name with an exaggerated flick of the tongue. "But if I was forced to get counseling every time I wanted to have safe sex as a teen, I would be fucked."

Her gray eyes widen. "Excuse me?"

God, this little nurse riles me up inside, and I don't even know why. It must be all that innocence trapped in that beautiful body. I lean down, leaving only a few inches of space between our faces. The sweet apple scent of her almost catches me off guard. "I said that I would be *fucked*." I emphasize the curse word and smile. "Because if you think for a single minute that not having condoms would have stopped my teenage ass from getting it in, then you're sadly in need of a little counseling of your own."

Silver's head tilts. "And what do you suggest? Leaving endless supplies of condoms on the front desk? That would practically encourage these kids to have sex."

I shrug. "What's wrong with that? Sex is as healthy as running a race, maybe even healthier. Think about it. You work up a sweat, it puts you in a great fucking mood, and it helps you sleep. You should try it sometime."

The way her eyes search mine like she's trying to find the humor in my response makes it seriously hard to hide the shit-eating grin fighting its way through my smile.

"Aren't you supposed to be some kind of role model or something? That's why you volunteered to come here, right? To mentor and coach kids who want to grow up to be just like you?"

I narrow my eyes at yet another insinuation. "I didn't volunteer for this shit."

She gives a quick shake of her head and laughs. "Wait. You *didn't* volunteer to be here?"

"Not technically, no."

"Care to elaborate?"

I purse my lips, pretending to deliberate over her request. "Nah, I'm good. But don't worry. I don't plan to give the little twerps any sex advice."

She lets out a breath and steps back. "Well, that's a relief," she mumbles. Then she moves to her printer and grabs a handful of papers. She flips through them, straightens them on the desk, then offers them to me. "You probably want to settle in. You can read these over and fill them out at your cabin. Just make sure I get them back today."

With a quick glance back at her, I notice a halo around her long blond hair thanks to the afternoon sun streaming through the window at her back. I might have noticed it when I spotted her among the crowd of staffers in the parking lot, but it's this moment right now that I take in just how stunning Silver is. If it weren't for the obvious annoyance at my mere existence written all over her body language, I would have probably made a move by now.

I look down at the papers, frowning, not keen on going anywhere anytime soon. I was loathing the idea of coming to this camp, but my outlook has drastically changed since meeting her. "Why do I get the feeling you're trying to get rid of me?"

She looks at me for a second as if contemplating her thoughts, then she sighs. "I'm not. But I do have a lot of work to get back to, and you really don't need me to fill all of that out."

Quirking a brow, I decide to give the woman a reprieve. As fun as her buttons are to push, she's done nothing to earn my torment. "All right, I'll get out of your hair on one condition."

A moment of silence passes while a contemplative look invades her expression. "What is that?"

"You'll need to show me to my cabin, remember?"

"I'll give you a map," she says sharply.

"I think I'd prefer if you walked me. I'd hate to get lost and accidentally run into your boss on the way. Anderson, is it?"

Her jaw drops at my subtle threat, giving me far too much satisfaction for my own good. I know I can be a bit much, but it's only a matter of time before Silver's beautiful blond mane will be wrapped around my fist while I'm easing her mouth around my cock. She'll forgive me soon enough.

She doesn't respond to my request with words. Instead, she snatches up a set of keys from her desk, pushes in her chair with a forceful shove, and walks toward the door to her office. After she locks up behind us, her steps quicken with each second that passes. Her rush to be rid of me is exhilarating, to say the least. All that anger balled up inside her. I can only imagine what she's like when she fully lets go. But even with the distracting vixen leading the way, I try to pay attention to the path she leads me on.

I didn't realize just how big the campsite was until now. There are arrows at every turn of the trail, indicating where we are, and while most of the trail she leads me down is near a giant body of water, there are some paths with nothing but woods on either side. I swear we must circle the entire peninsula of the grounds before I start to see a row of spaced-out cabins.

"What cabin number are you?" she asks while still walking.

"Uh—" I reach into my back jeans pocket and pull out a slip of paper Zach handed to me on the bus. "Twenty-four B."

A look of annoyance flashes on her face, but then it's gone after my next blink. I almost think I imagined it until she stops walking and gestures to a rustic-looking cabin set off at the end of the row. "This one is yours."

Ignoring her for a second, I look around and spot a sliver of water through the trees and an access trail nearby. There's an arrow just past my cabin pointing in the direction we were heading that reads Staff Only.

Perking up, I let my lip twitch with the makings of a smile. "Which one of those cabins is yours?"

She gives me a frustrated shake of her head. "If you think I'm answering that, then you're sadly mistaken."

"Ouch," I say with a quirk of my lip. "You really don't like me very much, do you?"

Narrowing her eyelids at me, she lets out a heavy sigh. "I don't know you, Kingston. But if first impressions are anything to go by, then you might be onto something."

"Damn. I'm going to have to work on that, aren't I?"

This time, Silver has the audacity to laugh. "I wouldn't waste your time." Then she takes a few steps back, gesturing to my new cabin. "Enjoy yourself. If you need anything, just dial four for room service."

*Room service? Shit.* I might have had this camp pegged all wrong. My own private cabin. A waterfront view. A nurse who can take care of all my needs. And now room service. I could get used to this place.

"Cool—" Before I can say anything more to her, she's walking away, shaking her tight ass behind her. God, she's sexy. And with a fiery mouth like that, I can't wait to see how she uses it on me.

I'm so busy watching her that I completely miss Zach approaching from the other direction. "You finally made it." He grins, throwing a glance in Silver's direction before settling on me. "I've been waiting for you. Wanted to make sure you got settled in okay."

Zach is a nice guy and all, but there's a reason he and I don't hang. His mere being has always rubbed me the wrong way. There's no way anyone could be that nice all the damn time.

"Just about." I hold up the papers. "The nurse gave me homework."

Zach nods. "Yeah, sorry about that. The rest of the guys submitted theirs before coming. Shouldn't take too long. Hey, when you're done, come to the field." Zach points to a trail through the woods. "Just head straight, and you'll see us."

He starts to turn when I take a step forward. "Hey, wait up a sec." I give him the most-charming grin I can muster. If I have a chance of convincing Coach to let me escape this place early, I'll need to get on Zach's good side. "I'm sorry for getting all heated when we got off the bus. This all has just kind of blind-sided me, but I think what you're doing here is great."

"No worries, man. I think you'll enjoy it once you get used to the accommodations." He chuckles lightly. "The kids make it worth it, I promise."

I nod and shove my hands in my pockets, hesitating to ask my next question, but I need to test the waters. "You meant what you said, right? You'll talk to Coach at the end of the week?"

Zach cringes a little and runs a hand through his hair. "Let's see how it goes, King. No promises, but yeah, I'll consider it." He sighs. "Look, I don't want any bad blood between us, and you'll get no judgment from me, but I respect the hell out of Coach. He wouldn't have talked to me about your situation if he didn't believe in you. I think you should look at this camp as a blessing and not as a jail sentence."

*A blessing?* What right do Zach and Coach have to tell me what I should consider a blessing? "And if I leave?"

Zach frowns for a second before shrugging. "Then you leave. I'm not going to try to stop you. This isn't a prison,

King. I just don't want you to end up in one. Neither does Coach. If you leave, then you'll have to deal with him. At least this way you get to be with your teammates and the amazing kids who idolize the ground you walk on. It's up to you."

With that, Zach gives me a final glance then takes off jogging toward the field. Meanwhile, I'm left feeling like he just put me in my place. The fact that he's giving me the freedom to walk away from this hellhole almost seems worse than forcing me to be here.

I jam a hand into my pants pocket to search for the key Anderson gave me. *Bingo.* I unlock my cabin door and push inside to find six empty bunk beds, a single desk propped under a window near the entrance, and a bathroom.

"What the fuck?" I drop my duffel bag, staring around the room, wondering what sort of hell I just entered. I don't know why I expected a little more... comfort or something. Not bare walls, crooked wood floors, and not an ounce of comfort to be seen. I knew I would be bunking alone this week since I was a last-minute add, but what the fuck is this?

It takes me two long strides to get to the pale-yellow phone on the desk, and I take them quickly. I lift the receiver, but it doesn't reach my ear. The curly cord forces me to bend down, so I'm hunched over the ancient device, listening to the long dial tone while scanning the directory. Finally, I punch the number four and wait.

"Front office. How can I help you?" chirps a friendly voice.

"Yes," I say, trying to tone down my utter dismay at what I just walked into. "I just got to my cabin, and I think someone forgot to put some items in my room."

"Oh no," the voice says. "What are you missing?"

"Everything," I growl. "Sheets. Comforters. I'll need some immediately if I'm expected to sleep here."

There's an uncomfortable silence on the other end of the line before I hear the voice speak again. "Um, well, sir, none of the beds come with sheets or comforters. You should have brought your own sleeping bag."

I blink, thinking surely I just heard the woman wrong. "Well, I didn't. Can you have room service bring something over?"

A light laugh fills the line. "Oh, sir. You are funny. You're at a sleepaway camp. There's no room service here."

*Jesus Christ.* I pull out my cell phone and gawk in horror when I realize I only have one bar of a signal. "Okay," I try again, silently cursing Nurse Silver and her evil prank. "Then can I get the Wi-Fi code so I can order some things?"

"I'm sorry, Mr. Scott. We do not provide our Wi-Fi code to guests. We believe in limiting electronics as much as possible so that you can enjoy nature's gifts that surround you. I promise, there is much to see. Will that be all?"

I stare at the phone, wondering if this lady is serious. When I realize that she is, I know there's no use in getting mad at her. It's Zachary fucking Ryan I should be angry at. Nurse Silver is right in line with him too.

I slam the phone down without another word and kick my duffel bag clear across the room. It bangs against a bunk bed ladder. After I've taken a few breaths, I toss the stack of papers on my desk and glare at them. If Nurse Silver thinks I'm filling those out, she's sadly mistaken. Zach said there's nothing stopping me from walking out of here, so that's exactly what I'll fucking do.

I'll deal with the consequences. I look around the room again, feeling firmer in my decision as time ticks on. That's right. Dinner first, then I'll be out of this hellhole in no time.

## Chapter 4

# UPPER HAND

## SILVER

"What's with the sour face?" Hope sidles up beside me in the cafeteria line as I'm spooning mashed potatoes onto my plate.

I didn't realize my thoughts were so clearly visible. Ever since leaving Kingston, I've been having trouble focusing on anything other than him. The man has no filter, no common decency, no moral compass, no—

"Earth to Silver." Hope gives my ribs a gentle nudge with her elbow. "You okay in there?"

I give her a pinched smile and shake my head. "I'm fine. It's just been a long day."

She scrunches her mouth. "You really need to take a day off once in a while, babe. It's not healthy to always be so *on*. Come to the campfire with me after dinner. We'll have some beer, mingle with some of the football players." She shimmies her shoulders at me, and I can't help but laugh.

"I still have work to do tonight, but I can meet you there after."

Hope purses her lips in disappointment then turns back to

the food she's scooping for herself. "Fine. But what kind of work do you have to do at this hour with no kids here yet?"

My eyes immediately find Kingston, who's already eating on the other side of the room. He's hunched over his plate with his brows furrowed and a scowl on his face. Zach and a few other teammates talk animatedly around him, but Kingston seems to want none of it.

In response to Hope's question, I shrug. "One of the guys has some paperwork to complete. That's all. I'm sure it won't take long for me to wrap up once he does."

A relieved smile makes its way to Hope's face. "Good. I'll bring the booze. You bring your sexy ass as soon as you can. I see a lot of opportunity here." She throws a glance over her shoulder and winks at me. "Namely, Kingston Scott over there. You know, I always knew he was one of those bad-boy types, but I think he's even broodier in person. Why are the grumpy ones always so hot? God, I bet he's a stallion in the bedroom. I'd let him take all that anger out on me whenever he wanted."

Disgust makes its way up my throat, and I can't help the warning look I give her next. "Don't even think about it, Hope. He's rude, he's arrogant, and I wouldn't be surprised if he doesn't last the week."

Hope narrows her eyes at me. "Geesh. Sounds like someone ruffled your feathers today. I've never seen you like this before."

"Yeah, well, let's just say I was provoked."

Hope's eyes light up with her grin. "Provoked, huh? Sounds kinky. Was it him? Was it Kingston?"

I nod, not trying to hide a thing. If Hope is actually entertaining the thought of getting Kingston's attention, then she should be warned. "Just trust me, okay? He's bad news."

She lets out an exaggerated sigh. "Okay, fine. He's hot and all, but he wasn't the one I was hoping to see here, anyway."

A rush of relief floods me. I shouldn't feel such intense dislike for someone as I do for him, but my blood heats as it courses through my veins. I dread the next encounter I'm forced to have with the asshole in Cabin 24B.

Hope and I take our plates to our normal seats, where most of the staff is already eating, and I try to ignore the fact that Kingston is seated in the very next row directly across from me. I can feel his presence, though. He's like this looming dark cloud threatening to spill rain at any second. To think, I have an entire week to deal with this guy. Thank God today is the most we'll ever speak. Once he's settled in, and especially once the kids get here on Monday, he'll be too busy with them to even come near me again.

Just when my comforting thoughts manage to work their magic on me, I feel an elbow in my side, followed by Hope's body scooting in closer to me. "Don't look now, but that Kingston guy has been glaring at you for the past five minutes, I swear."

A shiver shakes through me. I have to force my brain to behave and not look in his direction. It's what he wants. I know it is. And I've never felt more determined to refuse someone's wants and needs so badly.

"Ignore him. He's just mad at me because I played a little joke on him." I bite down on my lower lip to stop myself from bursting out with a laugh. I almost forgot about my little "room service" comment.

"What did you do?" she hisses, and I know she's horrified because she has some fanatical image of the man.

Shrugging, I take a stab at my roast beef then meet her wide-eyed gaze. "He was being so arrogant, and he kept making all these crude remarks. So I might have told him that if he needed anything, he could ring room service, and they'd deliver it."

Hope's jaw practically becomes unhinged as she shakes her head at me. "You are unbelievable." Laughter bursts from her. "Maybe you're not as boring as I thought. I've got to hand it to you, bestie. You sure know how to get a man's attention. And let me tell you," she says, her eyes sneaking toward his again. "You have all of Kingston Scott's attention. I'm envious."

Scoffing, I level my eyes on her. "Don't be. I meant what I said. He's the definition of a jerk. You know he didn't even choose to come here? He didn't tell me specifics, but he made it sound like it's some kind of punishment."

Hope exaggerates her sigh. "At least he spoke to you."

She's as hopeless as her name sounds, but I love her for it. "You know what?" I laugh and set down my fork. "Never mind."

I'm just starting to dig back into my food when Rosetta takes a seat on the bench across from us, effectively blocking me from Kingston's view. "Hi, ladies," she says with a bright smile.

I smile back at the cheery woman who runs the front office. She's always chipper, but like everyone else in this room, her energy seems bubblier than usual.

"Hey, Rosetta," Hope and I say at the same time.

Rosetta leans in, her sparkly eyes on Hope. "You find your future husband yet?"

She knows better than to ask me that same question, so I don't take offense.

Hope leans forward, meeting Rosetta in the middle of the table to whisper back. "Nah, Silver is shooting down my options left and right." She pouts her lips dramatically. "Can you believe it?"

The woman grins. "Who's off limits this time?"

I roll my eyes. "I was just warning her away from someone who gave me bad vibes. That's all. Hope is free to go after whoever she wants."

Hope winks at me to tell me she's just having fun with Rosetta then turns back to continue their conversation. "Kingston Scott. I guess he rubbed her the wrong way."

Rosetta stifles a giggle. "Maybe he needs to rub her the right way, then."

While my friends burst into laughter, I'm burning up inside with embarrassment.

"Oh my God." I'm absolutely mortified by my friends and their suggestive language. Why can't people see what I see? "Kingston might be insanely hot, but he's a giant jerk."

"C'mon." Hope leans into me. "He can't be that bad. Besides, you barely know him."

"I know enough."

Rosetta's laughter softens until she's got her brows bent, eyes focused on me. "You should give him a break, Silver. The poor guy is clearly out of his element here. Remember how you felt when you first arrived? You were terrified."

I tilt my head. "That's not even close to the same thing." The look I give Rosetta is enough to end my statement right there. She's one of the few people at Camp Dakota who were already working here when I first arrived, seventeen and alone.

No one knows the circumstances that brought me here, and no one has ever pried. One look at me was enough for the Bexleys to offer me a place to stay for as long as I needed. If it weren't for their generosity, I don't know where I would be right now. I wasn't terrified because I was out of my element; it was because I was running away from a nightmare I didn't know if I would ever escape. In a way, I still haven't escaped.

"I'm just saying," Rosetta continues in a softer tone. "He's clearly fighting against his own norms. We should be offering him grace at a time like this. I felt so bad for him when he called the front desk to request bedding. He thought we offered room service. Poor guy didn't even bring a blanket to sleep with."

All it takes is Rosetta and her talk of giving grace to break the dam in my head. The guilt flows straight through me, weighing me down while I fight like hell to break free from it, but I can't. I've had zero patience with Kingston, and I don't know why. Sure, he rubbed me the wrong way, but I can handle him. Surely, I've handled worse.

I pick up my half-finished tray of food and stand up, my appetite gone. "I better get back to work. I'll catch up with you ladies tonight at the fire?"

Hope grins then nods. "Yes. Don't be late."

Giving them both a short wave, I drop my tray off in the kitchen, then I quicken my pace toward my office.

Work is my lifeline when I sense that I'm losing control. Ever since Kingston stepped off that bus, that's how I've felt. I can't explain it. I've never been this wound up over someone, and I've dealt with shitty people before.

I work nonstop for the next two hours, bracing myself for Kingston's rude entrance to drop off the paperwork I tasked him with filling out. It's seven thirty when I finally glance at the clock and realize that not only is it past my office hours, but Kingston is late. I specifically asked him to drop off those papers by seven o'clock.

Frustrated, yet again, by the man who now owns my trigger button, I storm out of my office and straight to his cabin. I'm nearly there when I hear Rosetta's voice in my head. *"We should be offering him grace at a time like this."*

While I'm sure that's not what Kingston needs at this moment, I start to wonder if there isn't something to that suggestion. Rosetta's words start to invade my mind again. *"Poor guy didn't even bring a blanket to sleep with."*

I slow down in my tracks just after getting to his cabin. *Ugh.* I have been on the defensive ever since I met him. Maybe that's the wrong approach entirely to dealing with him. I breathe in slowly and release my exhale in one long stream. A second later, I've made up my mind. I know what I need to do next.

)▐◖●◗▐(

After taking the two steps up to Kingston's cabin door, I freeze, my stomach suddenly rolling over itself with nerves. But there's no time to deliberate my latest decision. I've already been tossing around the pros and cons for the past hour that preceded my retreat from ripping him a new one earlier. But before I can change my mind, Kingston opens the door, duffel bag in hand. He does a double-take when he sees me standing there, then a frown immediately pulls on his face.

"She makes night calls too?"

Just like that, I remember why I was so intent on disliking Kingston. "You really have a way with your words, don't you?"

He shrugs, looking around at anything but me. "My mouth may have a reputation, but I won't give any specific details. Gentlemen don't kiss and tell, if you know what I mean."

"I'm afraid I don't see any gentlemen from where I'm standing."

Kingston's focus snaps to me, his eyes narrowing and his nose flaring. "Is that so?"

Now it's me who feels like the asshole.

Neither of us speak. Neither of us move. I've never won a staring competition before, but I'm determined to win this one. Although Kingston and I are a few feet apart, it feels like he's pressed up against me, dominating my space and sucking every last bit of air from my sky.

"Jesus," I say, tearing my eyes away and sucking in a breath. Once I've steadied myself, I turn back to him and glare. "Why are you so intent on getting under my skin?"

One side of his mouth turns up. "It's not your skin I want to get under, princess."

I twist my face with disgust and shake my head. "That's never going to happen."

He shrugs. "Now *that* I'll agree with." Then he shifts the straps of his duffel over his shoulder again.

I squint, confused by what I'm seeing. If I didn't know better, I would think he's leaving. "Where are you going?"

"Home."

I should be relieved. "You're leaving? Why?"

"Isn't it obvious?" A flicker of pain flashes in his expression for a brief moment, but I catch it. "I don't belong here—as you so clearly pointed out with that little prank of yours."

My face burns with shame. "I'm really sorry about that. That's one of the reasons I came by to see you. You wound me up earlier, and it got the better of me. I shouldn't have tricked you like that."

"Don't do that," he says.

"Don't do what?"

"Apologize." Amusement takes over his face. "I think I liked you better before when you were calling me names and shit."

Once again, I'm completely caught off guard by his brashness. "Oh my God," I say with a laugh. "You know what? Never mind. Enjoy your journey home. Nice meeting you, blah blah blah. I'm done."

I've just turned my back on Kingston when I hear his bag land in the dirt behind me, then a hand is on my shoulder. "Whoa, wait a second. What are you holding?"

"It doesn't matter. You're leaving anyway."

"Silver," he demands. "What are you holding?"

I swallow, screaming internally at myself to not respond, to just walk away, to let the giant baby behind me fend for himself. He walks around me and waits until I'm looking right back at him. After letting out a big sigh, I lift the items in my arms slightly. "Blankets and a pillow. I heard you didn't bring anything, and I thought this could get you by until you had a chance to pick something up."

It happens in an instant, but I can feel the shift between us. In our energy. In the tension we both carry when we're around each other. It's like we were both granted a gift to start over, like a new moon marking the first lunar cycle. Maybe this is our new start.

His eyes tick between mine, and I swear I can hear the clock in his head while he decides something. "Okay then." He takes the blankets and pillow from my hands and pulls them toward himself. "I'll stay since you asked me so nicely."

Heat spreads up my neck and into my cheeks. "Don't make me regret being nice to you."

A cocky grin lifts his cheeks. "Is it that hard for you?"

"Not usually, no."

His lips spread wider. "I'll take that as a compliment."

With that, he turns back around and heads into his cabin.

"Wait a second." I follow after him, catching the door before it can close. "If you're staying, then I'll need those papers." When he gives me an annoyed look, I just shrug. "It's for liability purposes, and then you're off the hook. I'll never bother you again."

A flash of disappointment crosses Kingston's face, and there's a kick in my chest I wish I could ignore.

"Fine," he says. "I'll sign them now."

I wait in the doorway while he walks over to the desk, where the papers are already sitting. As he starts to go through them, I look around the open space, wondering why I never realized just how small these cabins are. They're big enough to fit six bunkbeds and a desk, but compared to the gargantuan male currently filling up most of the space, the size is almost laughable.

"Done," he says a few minutes later. He gathers up the papers and hands them to me with a quick shove. "Here you go, princess."

Even though I want to tell him not to call me that, I hold back the retort. I flip through the papers to make sure I have his signatures—the rest, I can examine later—then sigh with relief. "Thank you."

He gives me a nod and presses himself inside the doorway, lifting his arms so he's gripping the top frame. "So that's it, huh? We're not going to see each other again?"

I take a step back and give him my first genuine smile since meeting him. "Let's hope not." With that, I leave him with a wink and walk off, chuckling silently to myself.

I may not have had the upper hand after meeting Kingston Scott, but after a long struggle, I'm certain I have it now.

# CHAPTER 5

# UNHEALTHY OBSESSION

## KINGSTON

The large campfire is already blazing by the time I approach. As soon as Silver left my cabin earlier, I let the exhaustion from the last couple of days take me away, and I slept. I didn't know if anyone would still be here, but there they are, a mixture of staff and my teammates, all chilling in a wide circle, sipping on their beverages of choice.

There's another thing I forgot to bring with me here. Booze. I didn't know what to expect when Coach told me to pack my bags. I had no clue I would arrive at a kiddy camp with zero amenities, including a liquor bar. At the very least, I figured the accommodations would include a fucking furnished room. But it turns out the unfurnished room isn't even the worst part. I've literally been exiled to an island in the middle of nowhere, surrounded by cheery Boy Scouts who get off on the number of badges they've earned. If it weren't for the exciting back-and-forth I've had with Nurse Silver, I probably would have swum home by now.

Zach spots me on my approach and waves for me to join

him where he's sitting with his girlfriend, Monica. "Didn't know girlfriends were allowed," I say with a curl of my lip.

Monica grins and flashes her ring finger an inch from my face. "It's a good thing I've leveled up to fiancée."

"No shit," I said, not even trying to hide my genuine shock. I nudge Zach's side. "No way, dude. When did this happen?"

Zach chuckles. "Last Thanksgiving. Where have you been?"

I do a quick calculation and realize that it's been over six months, and I didn't have a fucking clue about a significant life event of a member of my own team. That's shitty. How could I have missed that?

*You've had your head up your ass—that's how.*

I shove my inner thoughts aside and focus on Zach. "Dude, I don't know. Congrats to you both."

Zach is a good sport about it, smiling back at me like he hasn't got a care in the world. "Thanks, man. We're getting married here, actually. In one month." He reaches for Monica's hand and winks at her. "This is a pretty special place for us."

It takes everything I have to hold back my utter disgust. Zach and I couldn't be any more different. "This place? This camp?"

Zach nods. "Yup. It's a long story, but the short of it is that Monica works for BelleCurve, and she helped me set up this whole football camp event two years ago. I won't bore you with the details. How about a drink instead?" He reaches into his small cooler and offers me a beer.

I look at it a long while before shaking my head. "No, man. Thank you, but I think I'm good."

As I'm saying the words, I realize how foreign they feel coming out of my mouth. The normal me would have accepted it before Zach even finished offering, but something doesn't feel right about drinking tonight, or at all. I don't know, but maybe it's the fact that I was sent to this island by Coach, who believed there was no other way to absolve me of my sins. Or maybe it's the fact that booze was one of the many factors that resulted in me being here. I just want to pay my penance, go home, play ball, and try to put all of this behind me.

*One month, or less, if I can convince Zach I'm not the total loser he probably thinks I am.*

If I can spend the night in jail, I can handle roughing it at Camp Dakota. I'll just have to find ways to make my stay more entertaining. At that thought, my eyes travel across the waving tips of the fire and catch on blond hair that's been swept up into a messy heap on her head. Silver's perfect lips are turned up into a soft smile as she chats with the girl beside her, and she doesn't look at all as intense as the woman I spent most of today attempting—and failing miserably—to flirt with.

Silver is wearing a pair of jeans and a blue T-shirt. It's nothing special compared to the group of giggly wide-eyed girls I recognize as the Bikini Welcome Committee. Their attire leaves little to the imagination, but for some reason, seeing her in something other than her nurse scrubs has all my focus. I don't know how long I've been staring when her eyes find mine across the fire, but by the surprise that glows in her expression, she wasn't expecting to see me.

If there's one thing that should deter me from entertaining any more thoughts of Silver, it's how *good* she seems to be. Resisting me was my first clue. Her naïve outlook on the condoms sitting behind that locked cabinet was my second. But beneath all the goodness, there's a spitfire of a woman who intrigues me in more ways than I can fully wrap my brain around. All I know is that I want to know more, and that's a dangerous thought.

"Is this seat taken?"

I tear my eyes from Silver's to look up at the syrupy smile of one of the bikini girls. Her dark-brown hair is curled in perfect waves around her fully painted face. Smile widening, she bats long, dramatic eyelashes that can't possibly be real.

"It is now." My response is pure instinct. I don't have to be in my regular alcohol-induced state to recognize a gorgeous woman when I see one. And her timing couldn't be more impeccable. She's just what I need to get my mind and burning gaze off the innocent wonder sitting across the fire.

I pat the empty spot on the log beside me, noticing how she inches closer than I'd anticipated. Now, this right here, is what I'm accustomed to. A beautiful girl with obvious interest, who's not at all afraid to show it. What's the point in playing games? It only delays the inevitable. And the inevitable always lands in a war of tangled limbs followed by a fully satisfied woman.

"What's your name, sweetheart?"

She doesn't tense up and glare when I lend her the endearment. Instead, she tilts her head so a layer of hair falls over her shoulder, and her smile turns flirtatious. "Vicky."

"Nice to meet you, Vicky. I'm Kingston, but you can call me King."

Vicky's eyes practically glow with delight. "All right, King it is then."

That right there is the reaction I'm used to—the way she said that with my name slipping off her tongue like she's mid-orgasm. The reaction that says, "Hello, nice to meet you. Let's fuck."

Not a second after that last thought runs through my mind, I scold myself, remembering exactly why I landed here in the first place. I don't need the temptation of a quick hump to repeat my offenses. At least, not while Coach's babysitter is sitting beside me.

"How do you like camp so far?"

It takes me a second to realize Vicky just asked me a question. I plaster on my best smile, mostly for Zach's benefit if he's listening in, and shrug. "What's not to like? And you? How do you like working here?"

Vicky scrunches her face and shakes her head. "I'm a seasonal employee. I've been working summers here ever since I was eighteen."

"And your role here is...?"

"Lifeguard." She flutters her long lashes so quickly, I think they might fly away. "If you're ever in need of rescuing, I'm your girl."

I don't know why I decide to look across the fire at that moment, but when I find Silver glancing between Vicky and me, my lips curl with satisfaction. I catch her next glance and hold it a second before winking. Silver's eyes narrow in response, and she snaps her head back to her friend, ending our silent exchange.

Disappointed, I turn back to Vicky to continue our conversation, but my mind and focus are still on Silver. I've got her in my peripheral now, and the moment she gets up to leave, I know it's my cue to leave too.

"I'm going to turn in," I tell Vicky with mock sadness. "Will I see you around camp tomorrow?"

Her eyes light up. "Of course. And if there's anything you need, you can reach me at my extension." She hands me a card with her cabin number already written on it.

I chuckle at her obvious insinuation. "Thanks, sweetheart." I stand and knock fists with Zach. "I'll catch you on the field tomorrow morning, eight o'clock."

Zach nods, drawing his fiancée into him closer. "See you, dude."

Away from the campfire, it's all dark, save for the well-lit paths on all the surrounding trails, and if I've learned anything about this place in my short time here, it's that there are a lot of fucking trails.

I don't want it to be completely obvious that I'm following Silver out of here, so I take a different route that eventually connects with the one she's on and intersects her path. When I spot her, she's standing still with her hands shoved in her pockets and her eyes aimed up at the moon. I watch her, my curiosity unspooling as I try to dissect her expression. At first glance, it appears blank, but then I see her mouth part as she takes in a long, deep breath. Her chest is rising, her lids are falling shut, and it's almost like she's asking for the sky to take her away. A chill sweeps over me. I take a step toward her and hear the snap of a stick beneath my shoe. I didn't realize how quiet it had been out here before that moment.

Silver's head snaps in my direction, her entire body jolts, she gasps, and her hand moves to her chest—all in one motion. "A little creepy, don't you think?"

That's all it takes for me to snap me out of whatever daze she had me under. I flash a smile. "I didn't mean to freak you out. Figured you'd want some company."

A small smile lifts her lips like she knows something that I don't. "That's really not necessary."

"Well, you really shouldn't be walking around here at night."

"Why? Because creepy men will jump out and spook me?" She starts to walk again. "I've been doing this for eight years, Kingston. Thank you for your concern, but I'll be okay."

Stunned by the little fact about her she just tossed my way, I take a second to let it sink in, then I'm jogging after her until I'm pacing her steps. "Wait a second. You've lived here for *eight years*?"

She seems hesitant to respond but then throws me a look. "I have. Came here when I was seventeen."

"But how? I don't even know if I'll survive a week here. How have you been doing this for that long?"

Silver shrugs. "It's my home. Just like Seattle is your home."

I don't correct her to tell her that Seattle has never felt like home to me. Instead, I keep my focus on her. "So, what brought you here at seventeen?"

"Now that," she says, "is a long story."

"I'd like to hear it."

Her face scrunches, and she shakes her head like she's confused. "And you care, why?"

Geez, this woman is impenetrable and frustrating as all hell, but something in me wants nothing more than to strip her bare, and not in the physical sense. Okay, maybe in that sense too, but the mystery surrounding Silver is eating at me.

"You did a nice thing for me earlier. People don't do nice shit like that for me."

She shakes her head, her frustration at my mere existence evident on her face. "Maybe that's because you're kind of an ass."

My chuckle comes straight from my gut and bursts out of my throat. It's at that moment when I realize why Silver is my new addiction. She's a breath of fresh air, and I love that her reactions to me are never what I expect.

"Maybe I am an ass, but that doesn't mean I can't care about things."

She's silent for a few beats before looking at me again. "And what do you care about, Kingston Scott?"

The sincerity of her question causes a strange swelling in my chest. "That's easy. Football."

"That's all? Not your friends or your family?"

I debate my response, all while wondering how the conversation shifted so dramatically. "Well, I don't have family, and my friends are the reason I ended up here, so..." I shrug. "I think I'll stick to just caring about football."

A flash of disappointment crosses her face before she tears her eyes from mine. "I'm sorry."

My face twists with confusion. "Sorry? What for?"

"That you don't have family or good friends you can care about. I've been there."

Somehow, I doubt she's ever been remotely close to the dark places I've been to in my life, but I give her the benefit of the doubt. Silver doesn't seem to be someone who bullshits her way through life, so now I'm only more curious than before. "But now you're good, right? You have all that now."

She bites down on her bottom lip like she's hesitant, then she nods. "I think so. The Bexleys are my family now, and my friends have come and gone over the years I've worked here, but Hope is a pretty good one to me now."

"Hope? Is that the girl you were sitting next to back at the campfire?"

Silver nods. "That's her." She stops walking suddenly then nods to the cabin to the left of us. "And this is me. Thanks for the company."

I glance between her cabin and my cabin, which sits just on the other side of the staff sign, and grin. "Wait a second."

She pauses and turns back around.

"You're my neighbor?"

Silver's eyes grow wide, then she laughs. "Don't get too excited about it, Kingston. I'm rarely here."

I take a step toward her, my grin widening. "Still, it's comforting to know where the nurse lives. You know, in case there are any after-hours emergencies?"

She laughs. "Why do I have a feeling I'll need to define for you what consists of an after-hour emergency?"

"Because you're smart as fuck, apparently."

Shaking her head, she turns back around and quickens her steps toward her door. "Goodnight, Kingston."

"Hey," I call after her, continuing when I realize she isn't going to turn around again. "Now that we're friends, maybe we can have slumber parties and shit."

Silver opens her door and steps inside, still not honoring me with another glance. "Don't get your hopes up."

She slams the door behind her, leaving me with the biggest fucking smile on my face. My unhealthy obsession with Nurse Silver might just help me survive this place.

# WAXING CRESCENT MOON

"THE MOON HAS AWOKEN WITH THE SLEEP
OF THE SUN, THE LIGHT HAS BEEN
BROKEN; THE SPELL HAS BEGUN." —
MIDGARD MORNINGSTAR

## CHAPTER 6

# BURIED FEARS

### SILVER

"Delivery, Miss Silver."

I look up from the paperwork spread out on my desk and smile at Marlo, the shipping-and-receiving manager. "I wasn't expecting anything on Sunday."

He gives me that look—a look that's reserved for the difficult ones of the bunch who always seem to need the unobtainable. Kingston's face flashes in my mind, and a feeling of guilt immediately follows it. I already decided that I'm moving past my initial impression of the cocky jock. He is who he is, and after he walked me home last night, I realized he isn't the total lost cause I thought he was. His intentions are in the right place, and that's all that should matter.

"One of the guys had a special request. Here." He sets the white paper bag on the desk.

"A special request?"

"Yup." Marlo shrugs. "Guy paid me two hundred bucks cash. Can you believe it? I wasn't going to turn down that offer."

"Someone gave you two hundred bucks? For what?" I

make a face, wondering who in the hell would need something that badly. It wouldn't be the first time someone has sent Marlo to run an errand, but what on earth could be so important that someone would pay two hundred dollars cash? Then I roll my eyes at my own comment when I remember who we're dealing with this week. Celebrities. Football players.

"Can't say," Marlo answers with his hands up as he takes a step back.

"Why are you giving it to me, then? He paid you, not me."

Marlo waved a hand apologetically. "I made plans with my daughter today, and I didn't want to just leave it on his doorstep. Do you mind making sure he gets it?"

I lean back and stare at the bag, curious beyond belief about the contents. "All right. Fine. I'll get it to him." I grab a pen and hover over a blank sheet of notebook paper. "What's his name?"

"Kingston Scott," Marlo says with another step back. "Nice guy."

*Of course.* I drop the pen. It won't be a problem to remember that bit of information. I wave goodbye to Marlo and wait until he's gone to look down at the white bag. It's completely open, giving me a clear view of the top of the shiny black paper box inside. It only takes a split second to recognize the gold logo on top of the packaging. I push the bag away like it's burning me.

*What the hell?*

I'm not sure why I'm surprised. Why wouldn't Kingston put in a special delivery for magnum condoms? Nothing he does should surprise me anymore.

Letting out a frustrated groan, I fold the top of the package closed so I can't catch another accidental peek at what's inside. Then I go back to work. At least I try. But my day isn't just drowned out by thoughts of Kingston. That would make my life far too easy, and it's never been easy.

When the phone rings just before lunch hour, I'm not expecting the familiar deep voice on the other end of the line that says, "Hiya, Sylvia. Happy birthday."

But the moment I hear it, my senses cease to function. I've had a mental countdown for the past eight years, each day weighted by the knowledge that although I ran and hid from my past, it would always be there to haunt me. It would always be waiting for me until my twenty-fifth birthday, the day my inheritance would be released to me.

)✦●●✦(

*SYLVIA, 8 YEARS AGO*

Long after my heartbeat stops thumping between my ears, I freeze my rocking, hold my breath, and listen with intense concentration. It's difficult to make out much past the pain that lances through my arm and the throbbing beneath my quickly swelling skin, but I can't stay here forever.

After a slow and shaky inhale, I release my hold around my bent legs and open my eyes. I've been pinching them closed so hard for so long that it takes a minute for my vision to return. Once the blurring clears, I'm faced with the aftermath of my compulsive decisions.

She's nothing but a crumpled heap on the living room floor with jagged pieces of a shattered vase sprinkled around her. Blood drips from her forehead and pools on her precious white carpet. The reality hits me, and I slap a hand over my mouth to cover the sob that slips past my throat.

I did this.

I hit her.

I *killed* her.

Using my good arm, I scoot backward, away from the crime scene, as far as I can go before an obstacle stops me—a chair, I think—but my eyes are still glued to the lifeless body beside the grand piano, so I can't be sure.

My insides feel like they're being ripped in two, with one half wanting to make a desperate dash for the door, and the other half demanding that I call 911. Then I remember what started it all.

My father's unexpected death should have been my biggest nightmare, but I quickly found out that losing him was just beginning. I could never have expected what came next.

The threats.

The legal battle.

The screaming.

The abuse.

All because of money that *she* feels is rightly hers. She was married to my father for what—two years—before he died? We were all blindsided by his death, but while I was mourning the life of my last living parent, my stepmom was furious beyond belief. He had left her nothing but a small life insurance policy and just enough money to pay off all of the debt she helped him rack up during their short marriage. The life insurance money wasn't even enough to cover the big fancy home she forced him to purchase after they got married. Not to mention the three sports cars that take up most of the space in the garage, or the expensive timeshare package they hadn't even used yet.

My father's best friend, Harvey, was the executor of his will and the trustee to my trust fund. That trust fund contains every last bit of my father's fortune—and it will go to me once I turn twenty-five. In the end, the only thing my stepmother received in the deal was me. So, for the past eight months, I've been stuck with *her*. Lucinda. The evil step-mother who belongs in a Grimm retelling of Snow White rather than in the reality she's forced me to live in. She's made it no secret that she wants every last drop of what I cannot yet claim. I never expected for it to turn violent, though.

With a quick shake of my head, I pull myself to my feet and look around. The duffel bag I attempted to leave with hours ago is sitting near the front door. My plan was to sneak away while she was still asleep, but that plan was destroyed when she stomped out of the kitchen and intercepted my exit, her face filled with a rage that terrified me.

"Where do you think you're going, you little bitch?" Her drunken snarl was enough to send me into panic mode.

The following events leading to me shattering a vase over her head play through my mind like a scratched record. I can still feel the sharp tug of my hair as she yanked me backward and the burn of my throat from my screams, not that there was a chance of anyone hearing me. Our house is set up like a fortress on hundreds of acres of woods. We no longer have the staff who took up space in our guest quarters. Lucinda could no longer afford the extravagant expenses.

She blamed me for all of it.

I scramble for my phone and tap on the last missed call. I don't recognize the number, but I know who it belongs to.

"Where are you?" Harvey snaps in a hushed voice.

"She's dead." My voice shakes as the words spill out and another sob bursts from my throat. "I tried to leave, b-but she knew. Somehow she knew. And s-she tried to stop me—"

"Jesus." The curse is a whisper, but it confirms just how badly I fucked up. "Are you sure?"

I look at Lucinda's body again and swallow past the lump in my throat.

"Sylvia," he demands. "Are you sure Lucinda is dead?"

"I-I think so. She's not moving." A shaky breath rocks my entire body. "I hit her so hard, Harvey. T-There's blood. So much blood."

"You'll be okay," he reasons quickly. "I'll take care of it."

Tears flood my eyes now as I realize just how much this changes things. "How do you know I'll be okay? What if they don't believe it's self-defense? With all the lies she's already spread about me, and the money involved, they'll think I wanted her—" I can't even say the word, but it rings loudly in my ears.

*Dead. Dead. Dead.*

"I should check her pulse."

I start to lurch forward, but Harvey screams, "No!"

"Don't touch her," he says. "The plan stays the same. Meet me at the underpass as soon as you can. I'm already here. Let me deal with Lucinda."

"But—"

"Hurry." That's the last thing he says before the line goes dead.

I'm frozen in place, staring at her lifeless body as suffocating silence fills the room. An onslaught of emotions hits me next—doubt, grief, regret, anger... The list goes on. Staying. Going. Nothing feels right.

Then I hear her moan.

My eyes stop on the woman I would have sworn was lifeless moments ago. Sure enough, she's still alive. Her eyes are still closed, but she's struggling to get up, barely raising her shoulders off the floor. The slight movement lights a fire in me that was damn close to extinguishing. My heartbeat jolts to life, and I'm once again in fight-or-flight mode. I take off running toward her.

Adrenaline charges through me, fueling my journey across the floor, including the long leap I take to clear her body to reach my exit. The plan is back on, and I'm more than determined to see it out—until I'm pulled back by my ankle by a force strong enough to send me crashing forward. My chin collides with the marble floor, my head swirls with fog, and the pain that's already shooting through my arm screams out yet again.

The grip on my foot releases, and I start to crawl forward toward my bag, toward the door. I dare a glance over my shoulder to find Lucinda still struggling to get off the floor as she moans through her pain.

"Don't you dare walk out that door," she says with an evil glare. "Not until you give me what's mine."

"If my father wanted you to have anything, then he would have left it for you. You heard the judge. My trust is untouchable."

"Not if you're dead. You're forgetting your father named a contingent beneficiary. You die, and the money goes to me."

Lucinda's threat sounds sinister enough to make my entire body shake with chills. I've never liked her, but I also never believed she would become so vindictive over money. I launch forward, trying to drown out her voice with my focus on leaving.

"If you even think about running, I will find you." Her threat rings through the empty house. "And then I'll fucking kill you. You hear me, Sylvia?" Her brown eyes blacken with her glare. "Mark my words."

I scramble to my feet again. Ignoring every ounce of pain coursing through me, I grab my duffel bag, forcing it over my shoulder. When I'm finally at the door, I stop with my hand on the knob and look over my shoulder to where Lucinda is still glaring after me. "You'll have to find me first."

## SILVER

"Harvey?" While I'm certain I recognize the voice on the other end of the line, I have to be sure.

"Yes, kid, it's me. How ya holding up?"

I swallow, my eyes darting around the room to verify I'm totally alone. A chill sweeps over me, and I press my lids together while I suck in a slow breath. All these years, and I never even imagined how this moment would go.

"Y-you're actually calling me."

A light chuckle filters through the line. "It's your twenty-fifth birthday. I think a congratulations are in order."

I bow my head. "No one has wished me happy birthday on my actual birthday in a very long time. It feels strange."

"Ah yes, I imagine that would be strange. I'm so sorry, Sylvia."

"It's Silver now," I say in a hushed whisper. "And you really shouldn't be calling me during work hours."

A light breath floats across the line, the initial humor in his tone fading away. "I know. I know. But I think it's time to get the ball rolling before…"

His hesitation breeds the festering fear in my chest. "Before what?"

"Before your stepmom—"

"Don't," I snap. "Don't call her that." It's amazing how fast the mere mention of her fills me with the rage. Lucinda is the opposite of anything a mother should ever represent. She may have scored the ring from my father, but the moment he passed away, her true colors showed she was nothing but evil.

"I'm sorry," Harvey says, his tone sincere. "*Lucinda* has petitioned the court once again to claim your trust money."

I roll my eyes. "So what? You know she won't win. She tried that same thing eight and a half years ago, remember? It's what initiated her craziness. She can't claim a cent of my trust money. It's untouchable."

"But you haven't claimed a cent. You just disappeared, which I know I helped you do, but the plan was always for you to claim your money when you were of age."

"Yeah, but that was before we knew Lucinda was capable of murder."

"She won't lay a finger on you, but she might end up getting what she wants if you don't claim your trust as soon as possible."

I snort through my disdain at his optimism. "You think she'll get over it once the money's in my bank account? No, Harvey. That woman tried to kill me. She was almost successful. She will only try harder once that money's mine. Besides, you said she went to the cops that night. Won't they arrest me the moment I make my whereabouts known?"

"Eight years later? No, Silver. That case has long been closed."

I can't see why he's so confident that I'm safe from the law and Lucinda. "I don't know. I need time to think about this."

He sighs. "I told you, we don't have time. I'm urging you to please end this. Don't you want to come home?"

"I *am* home. And I'm doing well." I swallow before I continue. "There's nothing to go back to." I know what I'm saying. He's been protecting my inheritance all this time, and now I'm telling him I'm still not ready to claim what's mine so that Lucinda can't attempt to take it away. While guilt lives and breathes inside of me every single day over this situation, I've learned how to cope with it in the best way I can.

Harvey lets out a slow breath. "Maybe not, but you should know that there's an expiration date on these things. Especially when someone else thinks that money should be theirs. Lucinda is also petitioning the court and saying that you're dead, Syl—Silver."

"What? She has no proof of that."

"Legally, after seven years, the only proof she needs is your absence. It's been eight. And if the courts can't dig up any recent history on you—jobs, school, friends, anything—and come up empty, which they will, then she'll win. Your time is up, kid. I'm preparing all the documents, and you'll need to sign off on them."

While I've gotten used to living with the guilt of leaving Harvey to deal with the fallout of my disappearance, I know I can't allow Lucinda to finally win. Not after all I've lost. My throat pinches closed. "But I'm not ready."

"Will you ever be?"

We both know the answer to that. Nothing can ever take back the horror of that year following my father's death. Nothing will ever remove the scars buried deep inside me from that night I finally made my escape.

"I imagine you've made a happy life for yourself there, and you should be proud of that. I'm proud of you, too, just as your father would be."

My throat swells as tears prick the backs of my eyes.

"But," he continues, "if you want to keep Lucinda from claiming your trust, you'll need to claim it first."

"I-I don't know, Harvey. Maybe it's not even worth it. If she wants the money that badly, maybe I should just let her have it." But even as I say the words, I know it's not an option.

"Seriously?" Harvey practically chokes on his question. "After everything she put you through? You cannot let her win."

He's right. It's not even about the money at this point. It's about principle. I swallow and shake my head, feeling torn in half. "I need a little time. The courts won't see her right away. How much time do I have?"

"One month to be safe."

A knot twists in my gut. It's not a lot of time, but it's something. "Okay."

A few beats of silence pass between us, then he's the one to break it. "I'll call back to check in on you in a few days. Whatever happens, whatever you decide, you won't be alone."

I shake my head in an effort to find comfort in his words. For some reason, no comfort comes. Deep down inside, I knew it wasn't over. I became complicit in the idea that my past would always have a grip on me. My inheritance was safe from her evil clutches, and I'd found a new home. I never felt the need to claim what he left for me, and after that night, I couldn't touch it anyway. My best bet was to stay away for good. While I knew I could officially claim my inheritance at twenty-five years old, I didn't know there would be an expiration date along with that. I didn't know the wounds of my past would split wide open and it would be me sewing it back together with the needle and thread.

"Thanks for the heads-up, Harvey. I need to go."

A heavy sigh rests on the line for a moment before he speaks again. "Okay, kid. I understand. I'll check back in soon."

I hang up, feeling sick with the tornado of emotions whirling in my chest. Eight years of buried fears are being picked up with the debris of everything I left behind. I'm not sure where I will land in the end.

# CHAPTER 7

## STITCHES

### SILVER

I try to go back to work after the phone call with Harvey, but it's pointless. It's late Sunday afternoon anyway. There's nothing much to do other than busywork, and I can't seem to get the conversation off my mind. The last time I spoke to Harvey was one month after I arrived at camp. I hoped he was calling with good news—news that would give me reason and peace of mind to return home. That was when he told me that Lucinda had filed a police report on the night I left home, and my heart sank into complete and utter darkness. It was then that I knew I wouldn't be able to go home for a very long time.

Camp wasn't completely terrible back then. The Bexleys were amazing, inviting me to the main residence on the north side of camp for family dinners and including me in their town outings and boating excursions. The Bexley brothers became my brothers, and their parents became my guardians. But during that initial month, I felt like Dorothy in the *Wizard of Oz* when her house first landed in a strange new world. Except, there were no ruby slippers in sight.

Shaking away the old memories, I gaze at the white bag Marlo brought in earlier, and I groan. I guess I can take a break and make one pit stop before I take the rest of the day off.

After snatching the bag from the counter, I head toward the field to find Kingston. It doesn't look like there's any training going on by the time I make it to the large open field where the majority of the week will be spent, but the guys all seem to be there. Some are tossing the ball back and forth, others are chatting in groups, while the rest are animated and talking to the BelleCurve film crew. I take the long way around the field to avoid the cameras and step onto the field.

"Coming for you, King!" a player yells.

Kingston takes off running in my direction, with his head turned to look over his shoulder and his eyes on the ball ripping through the wind toward him. As he starts to pivot, his eyes catch on me. I know nothing about football, but I know something is off when Kingston loses sight of the ball, even if it is for an instant. He rips his eyes from mine and continues to prepare for a catch. There's no time. He hasn't even fully spotted the ball before it smacks and scrapes against the side of his face.

I cringe as the six-foot-six-man howls and both of his large palms cover the point of impact.

"What the hell, King?" yells the player who threw the ball. He's already jogging across the field to check out the damage. "You were supposed to catch it with your hands, not your face."

Players chuckle as they gather around, while others come over looking genuinely concerned.

"Fuck you, dude," Kingston spouts back. "I think that cut me open." He curses again and starts to pull his hand away. As soon as blood starts spilling down his cheek, he slams it back in place. "Well, shit."

My steps quicken right along with my pulse as my medical instinct kicks in. I stuff the white package holding the condoms between the elastic of the back of my pants and my underwear, quickly cover it with my scrub top, then push my way through the gathering of guys until I'm right in front of Kingston.

"You got cut by a football?" one guy asks, seemingly mind-boggled.

"Is that even possible?" another guy asks.

I pick up the football like it's a weapon and examine it quickly. I toss the ball to the last guy who spoke and nodded. "It's possible, all right. If the strings draw across the skin just right, with that much speed, it can definitely tear skin." I look back at Kingston, who seems to be avoiding my eyes—out of embarrassment or anger, I'm not sure. It wouldn't surprise me if he blames me for losing his focus. "Does anyone have a clean towel?"

A guy about Kingston's size steps forward and hands me a white towel. I thank him before turning back to assess the damage. The skin around where he's cupping his face is already turning red, and more blood is starting to seep around the edge of his hand.

Eight years ago, the sight of that blood would have been enough to roll my stomach. But with the amount of activity that goes on year-round at camp, I've seen it all.

"Here," I say, lifting the towel slowly toward his face. "Move your hand away for a second."

He turns enough to signal that he's refusing my offering, and anger stampedes through me. I am not in the mood for Kingston's shit today, not after the phone call I received earlier, and definitely not while he's bleeding all over the field.

"You might need stitches," I say, trying to keep my voice calm. "Let me look at it."

He waves away my suggestion with his free hand while looking at everything and everyone but me. "Nah, I'm good."

"C'mon, King," says the guy who threw the ball. "Zach would want you to get checked out. Just let her look."

"Yeah, well, Zach isn't here right now, is he?" Kingston snaps back.

"Calm down, dude. Just listen to the damn nurse. She knows what she's doing."

"Does she?" Kingston seethes through his words while glaring back at me.

"As a matter of fact, she does," I bite back.

"You're a nurse," he spits out. "What are you going to do? Put a Band-Aid on it?"

If there's one thing that gets me fired up, it's someone demeaning the role I've worked so hard for. "I'm an APRN, which means I have a master's in nursing. Trust me, I can do far more than apply a bandage." Then I notice blood isn't just dripping around his hands now. There's a pool of it. "Which it looks like you might need." Fed up with his resistance, I step forward and get directly under his nose. "Move. Your. Hand." Each word is void of the annoyance I feel, but I know he doesn't miss the warning buried inside my tone.

His eyes widen a bit like he's shocked, or maybe he's scared. I don't know. All I care about is that he is finally obeying. As he moves his hands away, I cover the cut with the towel while taking a quick glance at it. I can't be sure until I've taken a good look, but judging by the amount of blood and how long the cut seems, Kingston is going to need those stitches after all.

As I slowly apply more pressure to the wound in hopes of stopping the bleeding, I notice how Kingston continues to look around us like he wants to be anywhere but right here with me. I don't entirely understand why. I get that maybe he's stubborn or embarrassed. But usually, his anger is aimed at me in a flirtatious way, not like this.

One of his teammates hands me another clean towel and a bottle of water. When the cloth is soaked, I uncover his face and pour water over the wound to get a quick look at the cut. I ignore Kingston's muffled growl and focus on the task at hand. It only takes a glance to confirm exactly what I was afraid of. While the cut may not be too deep, it's long and too close to his eye. He's definitely going to need some sort of stitch to close the wound.

I press the clean towel over the wound and brace myself before telling him the news. The discomfort of trying to tend to Kingston with my arm stretched as far as it will go to reach him, with his teammates staring at the both of us, and the sour look on his face is bad enough without what's about to come next.

"What's going on?" Zach asks as he weaves his way through his teammates to get to us.

"Nothing," Kingston snaps. Then he pulls away from me, replacing my hand with his to hold the towel in place. "Nance hit me in the fucking eye. I'll be fine."

"King took his eye off the ball," Nance says with a lift of his hands. "It would have been a perfect catch."

"That was a nice pass, man," another player says. "What was that? A sixty-yarder?"

Other guys start to chime in with how impressed they are, which only appears to make Kingston angrier. "Whatever. It was weak. You're second string for a reason, Nance. Now we know why."

Nance glares back at King before letting out a laugh then shaking his head. "You know what? Fuck you, dude."

"Fuck you," King shouts back.

Nance steps forward then stops himself. "I'm not dumb. I know what this is about. You should know it wasn't me who ratted you out to Coach. I wouldn't do that"

"Then you're saying it was Balko?"

Nance shrugs. "I don't know, man. Does it matter? You got off easy. Maybe you should be grateful for that instead of walking around here like you have a bone to pick with your teammates. This week isn't about *you*, King. It's about the kids."

Nance walks away from the crowd of men, and most of the guys follow suit.

Zach's hard eyes are on Kingston, but his words are aimed at me. "He needs stitches?"

I start to respond, but Kingston snaps, "No, I don't need stitches. I told you, I'm fine."

With a sigh, Zach looks at me, his eyes softening. "Silver, do you mind giving us a minute?"

I nod and move away while Zach shoos away the rest of the guys, leaving him alone with Kingston near the end zone. I expect yelling and cursing or fighting, but I'm surprised by the exchange that I can't hear. Zach is speaking calmly, but firmly, and Kingston is bowing his head, actually listening.

There's no mistaking the wrought anger dripping off Kingston when he finally gives in to whatever Zach is telling him and trudges off the field toward me. I'm standing on the sidelines, shaking off the discomfort as I realize I have to spend more time with the grumpy jock and his bad energy today. I'm not in the mood, but work is work, and this is what I was meant to do with my life. I truly believe that.

Kingston doesn't even stop when he reaches me. He just keeps on walking toward the path that leads to my office, and I'm trailing behind him with no desire to catch up. He's cranky, but so am I. Before heading out to the field, I was looking forward to spending some time away from the office. Kingston, yet again, is throwing a wrench in all that I'm used to.

He's waiting for me outside the main entrance and lets me walk inside first. He's quiet up until he gets into the examination room and stops in front of the table.

"There's no fucking way I'm letting you put a needle through my skin, princess. I just didn't want to piss my team captain off, seeing as he runs this shit show of a camp I've been forced to come to."

I close the door behind me and move to the sink, where I pull out the white bag from the back of my pants, set it on the counter, then discard the dirty towels. I wash my hands and slap a pair of gloves over my fingers. "I'm afraid you don't have much of a choice. You can't walk around bleeding all over the place, and if you don't take care of this now, you'll have a nasty scar to remind you of this day for the rest of your life."

"I'll take my chances," he says dryly.

Sighing, I turn around and lean against the counter while narrowing my eyes at him. "What are you so afraid of?"

His nostrils flare. "I'm not afraid of anything. I just don't want *or need* stitches."

"I'm telling you that you do. Don't you think I'd rather be reading a book in my hammock right now than tending to an adult baby and his temper tantrum?"

Kingston's head tilts, and his eyes blaze with fury. "The fuck you just say to me?"

I smile softly, trying to hide the fire that just burst to life in my chest, then walk toward him like his daring eyes don't bother me at all.

Kingston is a passionate man, on and off the field. And if

there's one thing I've always had a weakness for, it's men with a passion for what they do and who they are. It's why I fell for my ex, the other APRN in training. He loved the job almost as much as I did, to the point it became a competition of who got to work first and who got to tend to the next patient. But looking back, I see now that the passion was all I fell for. There wasn't anything deeper there. After he cheated on me, it didn't break my heart like I expected it to.

I step up to Kingston, our foot-and-a-half height difference causing me to lift my chin several degrees higher than normal. "Sit down, Kingston."

He dips his head slightly. "No."

It takes me an entire inhale and exhale to snuff my frustration and try again. "You are such a baby."

His nostrils flare again, and the fire in my chest roars in response. "You already used that insult. Try again."

The half growl-half scream that slips from my throat can't be stopped this time. "I just want to look at it again. There are other types of stitches, you know? Maybe you can get away with liquid, but we won't know that until you sit your butt down and let me do my job."

Kingston's eyes lock on mine for a hot minute, and I can only imagine what's going through his head right now. Maybe he wants to submit a formal complaint to Anderson. Or maybe he wants to tell me to go to hell. He is nearly three times my size. I can't do a single thing to stop him if he wants to walk right out that door. But he doesn't make a move to leave, argue, or threaten to talk to my boss. Instead, he slowly sinks until he's sitting directly in front of me, and he doesn't say a word.

Letting out a sigh of relief, I place my foot on the pedal near the floor and push down to lower Kingston's seat. He's too tall, even sitting down, so I wait until he's a couple of inches below me and release the pedal.

A smile lifts my cheeks, and I realize just how much satisfaction that gave me.

"What's that smirk for?" he growls. When I just shrug, he raises his brows. "Do you like this position, Nurse Silver?"

I stay silent, praying I don't let another emotion slip. The truth is, this entire battle has been an unexpected adrenaline rush, and I don't want him to see how much I'm enjoying it.

"You do, don't you?" The corner of his mouth tips up. "I have to say, I could get used to you being on top if that's what you prefer."

It takes everything in me to maintain professionalism while Kingston's hot mouth moves closer. I can feel each breath he releases. I can smell the blend of crisp, woodsy scents he uses to mask an entire day of being outdoors. And at this angle, with the window at his back and his piercing green eyes fixed on me, his head tipped up, I don't know how I manage to speak through the flock of flutters coming to life in my chest. He's the epitome of perfection, if only he didn't have to open his mouth.

Ignoring his comments completely, I lift my hand to move over his where he's still holding the towel. I cover his hand with mine and gently pull it away from the wound, happy to see the bleeding has finally slowed.

"Well, it looks better than I thought, but I recommend closing the wound to prevent infection. It might sting a little when I start, but it's not a terribly deep cut. It should heal quickly. What do you think?" A few beats pass until I dare another look down to find him searching my face. "What?"

His gaze snaps to mine. "Nothing. Just figuring out if I can trust you. That's all."

"What are you afraid of?"

His lids narrow slightly. "Considering how defensive you've been since I got here, you might take pleasure in causing me pain."

Biting down on my lip to keep from laughing, I shrug. "Even if that's true, it doesn't change the fact that you'll have me to thank when your pretty face looks good as new."

A hint of a smile touches his lips. "You think my face is pretty?"

"Hideous, actually. But it's in the job description to ease my patients' egos along with whatever ailments."

His laugh is soft but dripping with something that burns deep in my belly. "I'll venture to guess there's one ailment you could tend to quite well."

"I'm not opposed to pulling in HR to coach you on the no-no's of sexual harassment."

His grin widens. "You wouldn't do that. You like me, even if you want to pretend you don't. I can see right through you, Nurse Silver. Every girl needs a bad boy in her life. I could be yours."

"Bad boys aren't for me. I'm more into the sweet-and-charming type."

"Oh yeah? I can be sweet and charming too."

"Somehow, I doubt that. Now, hold still and shut up while I stitch you up."

He backs away slightly. "Aren't you going to wait for my consent?"

A giggle slips past my throat until I'm clapping a hand over my mouth while he glares at me.

"Is that funny?"

I shake my head. "No. Sorry. It's just—remember those forms you begrudgingly signed for me?"

He glares like he already knows the answer.

"That's all the consent I need. Can we just get on with this already, Kingston?"

"I really wish you would call me King."

A wave of heat climbs up my neck and into my cheeks. "That would be the day, now, wouldn't it?"

His grin transitions into a satisfying smile, then he nods. "Yes. Yes, it will be."

## CHAPTER 8

# THE BEST MEDICINE

### KINGSTON

F*uck, that hurt.*

Not the liquid stitches. That shit stung a little, like Silver warned. Silver's constant rejections are starting to frustrate me, though. It was cute at first, because she's sexy as hell, and it's refreshing to have to work a little to get a woman's attention. But Silver isn't like anyone I've ever met. There's an air of mystery to her that I desperately want to figure out. And by this point in our bickering, I would have expected her to give me some sign that I'm growing on her.

"Hey, man, how's the head?" Zach asks as he approaches me in line at the cafeteria at dinner.

I shoot him a glance and shrug. "Silver said it'll heal fine, so I'm not worried."

I catch his grin in my peripheral. "*Nurse* Silver? Isn't that who you were staring at when you missed the ball?" He claps me on the back in good humor. "Just do us all a favor and don't let her come to any of the games, okay?"

His words irk me more than they should. If only Zach knew just how easy that request would be to follow. I shrug it off and continue filling my plate while we walk down the line. "Hey," I say, thinking of something. "I hope I didn't fuck up my chances of going home at the end of this week."

Zach cringes. "Yeah, that comment you made to Nance about him being second string was pretty messed up. You can't say shit like that, dude. You shouldn't even be thinking it."

"I didn't mean it. I hate needles." I shiver, recalling my first stitch in the sixth grade after crashing my dirt bike into a pile of rocks at a construction site. My father just stood by as the doctor was jabbing me with a needle with a glare that told me I deserved every ounce of the pain. "I'll apologize to Nance. I was heated, and I took it out on him."

Zach nods. "I guess that's why you're here. You need to reprioritize that anger. Your teammates are your family, not your competition."

"I know that. I think I was more embarrassed than anything."

Zach's hand squeezes my shoulder. "Yeah, I know. Don't worry about it, okay? Let's just move on and see what the rest of the week looks like."

Relief washes through me, and I'm glad I didn't totally fuck up my chances. "That's cool of you, Zach. I guess I should be more worried about how Coach will respond to letting me leave. He was pretty pissed."

He nods. "Yeah, but he's also a reasonable man. Maybe he just needed a few days to cool off. It's not like you did anything the other guys didn't. You just got caught."

I frown. For some reason, Zach's words don't make me feel any better. "Yeah, well, I'm sure he didn't appreciate that wakeup call. And he's a good coach, even with fuckups like me."

"You're no fuckup, Kingston. You're an amazing player. Coach is terrified to lose you to something stupid. That's all."

Warmth spreads in my chest. I didn't realize that was something I needed to hear. "Thanks, man. How did you two get so close, anyway? He treats you like his own kid."

"Ah," he says. "Once upon a time, I was headed down a dark and dangerous path. He sentenced me to join the football team, and the rest is history. Let's just say, even when I don't completely understand where he's coming from, I trust he knows what he's doing."

I would never have expected that Zachary Ryan, of all people, ever had it bad. I'm quickly realizing I've had him pegged wrong from the beginning. "Well, for what it's worth, it's pretty cool what you've put together here. It's something my punk ass would have needed as a kid."

"That's exactly why I did it. Just wait until tomorrow, when the kids get here. If that doesn't light a fire in you, then all of this, this whole month sentence, will be meaningless."

While Zach finds Monica and I'm searching for a place to sit, his words echo on repeat in my mind. It sounds exactly like something Coach would say to me. I don't want this week to be a waste. I get why I'm here. I get the need to contain me somehow until the season starts so I can't damage my reputation to the point it starts interfering with the game. But that doesn't mean it will be easy for me to be good. Maybe my only chance in hell of succeeding is to play the game and hang out with other good people.

As soon as the thought crosses my mind, I search for my favorite blonde. She's sitting with her brown-haired friend, Hope, and I make my way toward them. "Mind if I join you?"

Hope's got her mouth full of an apple when her lids widen at the sight of me.

Silver shrugs, but I see the smile buried beneath her expression. It's a clear reminder of when I was in her office, squirming beneath her as she worked on my face. "You can sit anywhere you want."

I don't miss the look Hope shoots her friend while she chomps down on her apple. "Hi, Hope. How are you today?"

Hope's mouth is still full, but she manages a nod, causing Silver to laugh.

"How are you feeling?" Silver asks, turning to me.

"Thanks to the drugs you gave me, I'm feeling okay."

Silver snorts. "I gave you Tylenol for the headache."

"Well, it was helpful. Thank you."

She twists her face and cocks her head at me. "Why are you being so nice to me?"

"Because," I say, taking a stab at my broccoli and adopting a high-pitch tone. "I've decided that we're going to be friends. Not besties like you two." I wave my broccoli-filled fork between them. "But, like, friends. You know?"

Silver stifles her giggle. "Um, what is wrong with you? Two hours ago, you were telling me to go to fucking hell."

I shrug, remembering the first moment she pulled my wound together. "I was delirious from pain. I didn't mean it literally."

"Then how *did* you mean it?"

"I didn't mean it at all. Happy?"

She nods. "Yes, I am. Thank you."

Satisfied with her response, I focus on Hope now, who has successfully swallowed her last bite, and I give her my best panty-dropping smile. "So, Hope, how long have you worked at Camp Dakota?"

Hope lights up like a Christmas tree. "Almost a year now. How long have you been playing for Seattle?"

"I'm going into my fourth season."

Hope leans forward, her eyes twinkling, and I don't have to glance at Silver to know that she's listening to every word of our conversation. "Is it true that your best friend is Balko?"

I have to push down the instant anger that the mention of his name ignites in my chest. Nance confirmed my theory. Balko was the one who ratted me out to Coach. I don't know what will happen when I see him again, but the girls don't need to hear about all that drama. "We're good friends. Why? You interested?"

Hope gives me a playful look, like she's considering her response, but her expression gives it all away. Already, I can see just how different Hope and Silver are. Hope doesn't beat around the bush. She doesn't play games. And she certainly doesn't resist temptation when it's being offered to her on a silver platter.

"Maybe I am. Is he coming out here?"

"Well, he'll be here next week. I'll put in a good word."

Hope's eyes widen, her playful demeanor altering slightly once she realizes I'm serious. "Really? Just like that? What if he doesn't like me?"

I give her a quick up-and-down. Hope is beautiful. She has light-brown hair, sparkling brown eyes, caramel skin, and a banging body. "Trust me," I say, connecting with her eyes again. "He'll be into you."

Hope leans back a little and throws Silver a satisfied smile, but Silver isn't paying attention. Instead, she's eating quietly while staring out the window. For once, I don't think her behavior is in response to me. Her bright-gray eyes looked glazed over, like she's buried in deep thoughts—thoughts I would do just about anything to pry out of her.

I continue talking with Hope for the rest of dinner. I like her. Not the way I like Silver, but Hope is fun to be around and talk to, and she is a hell of a lot more enjoyable to eat with than Silver is. Once the three of us start to part ways, I watch as Silver heads off toward her cabin and switch directions to follow her. When I'm just a few feet away, I hear her sigh loudly before she stops and turns around.

"I'm really not in the mood for whatever you're doing."

"What's up with you? You spaced out all of dinner, and you're more pissy than normal."

She looks away with a quick shake of her head. "I'm having a bad day. That's all."

I point to the side of my eye, where my new stitch still stings. "Really? Your day can't possibly be worse than mine."

"It's not a competition, but yeah, I think it is," she says while smiling sarcastically.

A rumble of frustration makes its way through me. Silver's resistance is becoming quite the thorn in my side. "Let me help you feel better, then. Let's hang out. Right now."

A laugh bursts from her throat. "And what makes you think hanging out with you will make me feel better?"

*That isn't a no.* A glimmer of hope causes me to smile. "For starters, I can make you laugh. Despite what you medical types believe, laughter is truly the best medicine."

She folds her arms across her chest and studies me. "Laughter won't fix this, Kingston. No one can fix this."

The sadness buried in her tone hits me hard in the chest. I step forward, just slightly, afraid she might dash away. "Let me try. Let me make you laugh. C'mon, Silver. Give me a chance to show you I'm not as bad of a guy as you think I am."

She stares at me for an extended beat, and while I'm certain she'll reject me, yet again, I hold her stare with a silent plea for her to accept.

"Okay," she finally says. It's a cautious "okay," one filled with uncertainty and maybe a little regret. But it's an "okay" nonetheless.

"Okay." I smile back. "How about a swim?"

# CHAPTER 9

# MOON EYES

## SILVER

Feeling heavy with regret, I step out of my cabin, where Kingston is waiting for me. I should have said no. I should have been adamant and strong-willed. I should have listened to that deep sensation in my gut that told me giving into Kingston Scott was the worst possible thing for me at this particular moment in time. Or, any particular time, for that matter. But right now, I'm vulnerable. I know I'm vulnerable. And to be honest, I could use the distraction that he so kindly offered. I can't back down now.

He's standing here shirtless, wearing nothing but a pair of sea-foam-green boxer briefs. The guy is made of pure muscle, deep cuts, and skin so perfectly smooth, it almost appears fake. It's no wonder women react to him like they've got a front row seat at one of his games. I hear the way the other girls talk about him in the staff room. To them, Kingston is a god, not only for his looks, but because of his money. When Vicky started talking about his net worth earlier today, I had to exit the room. I don't need to know how much Kingston has in his bank account. I don't care.

"I thought we were going for a swim," he says with a smirk. "You're wearing a dress."

I look down at my black swimsuit cover-up then roll my eyes. "I'm used to there being kids around. I don't normally walk around in my bathing suit."

"That's unfortunate."

Pushing forward, I ignore him and sling my towel over my shoulder. "Follow me."

I lead him toward a path through the woods that dips into a shallow decline. Not a minute later, we're at a small clearing to one of the smaller lakefronts on the camp's property. A small dock juts out only a few feet over the water, and there's a hammock that I set up years ago. The staff usually gravitate toward the larger clearings, where there are rope swings, slides, and flotations available for us all to use freely, but this is the spot I frequent, due to the privacy.

At first, I questioned bringing Kingston here. I don't like to share my spot with anyone other than Hope, but it's not like Kingston will be here forever. He'll be gone in a week, then it won't matter if he knows about this spot or not. That thought alone brings me some relief.

Kingston is no different than one of the troubled youths who always wind up in my office due to reckless accidents or simply because a counselor needs to distance themselves from the ones who won't stop acting up. Kingston is a big troubled kid in that sense. Exhausting and in need of constant attention.

"So, how does this liquid-stitch-thing work? Can they get wet?"

I look at the bandaged wound near his eye and smile. "That's one benefit of liquid stitches. Yeah, they can get wet. Just don't—"

I haven't even finished getting the words out before he

takes a running leap into the water. With a loud splash, he's swallowed whole. By the time he comes back up for air, I'm laughing at the edge of the dock. After a quick assessment of his bandage, I feel confident that the impact wasn't enough to do any damage. "You sure don't waste time, do you?"

"Never. What's the point in that?" He shakes out his hair then pushes it back with his hands. He points at me with a grin. "Told you I'd get you to laugh."

"Yeah, well, if you don't mind me laughing *at* you, then I guess you succeeded."

He swims toward me and grabs hold of the ladder beneath my feet. "I'm not above laughing at myself, princess."

An icky feeling sinks through me. "I really hate when you call me that."

His brows pull together in a frown as he climbs up the ladder so he's standing in front of me. "Why are you always so difficult?"

"I have standards. The only reason you think I'm difficult is because you don't like to play by the rules."

"But it's just a name, a term of endearment, if you will."

His explanation makes me smile. "A term of endearment is reserved for someone you love. Anyone else might get the wrong idea, you know?"

A full set of white teeth practically glimmer back at me with his smile. "Yeah, well, I wish you'd get the wrong idea about now. How much wooing does a guy have to do to get you to notice him?"

Okay, Kingston wins, because this is the second time since we've been out here that he's gotten me to laugh. "Oh, I notice you all right. But I think you and I have very different definitions for what wooing is."

I don't miss the way his eyes flick down and back up my

dress. "And what would you consider wooing, Ms. Livingston?"

"I'm not going to tell you that."

"Why not?"

"Because," I say, stopping short when I realize he's continuing to inch his way into my space. His wet chest is mere inches from me. "If I tell you, you might miraculously adopt the qualities I look for in a man. It wouldn't be genuine."

"So you're looking for someone genuine. What else?"

His asshole grin causes a flash of heat to burst in my chest. I hate how I'm incapable of controlling how my body reacts to this man. I'm not into assholes. I've never been into assholes. But for some reason, *this* asshole has found a weakness in me I never knew existed.

I refuse to entertain his questioning anymore. Instead, I grab hold of my dress and yank it over my head, not looking at him again until I'm stripped down to my red, one-piece swimsuit. His eyes roam my body freely as if my just being accessible to his sight gives him the permission to ogle me, not that I'm giving him much to ogle.

"Where's your bikini?"

Laughing again, I step away from him until my toes are curling over the edge of the dock. "I don't own one." With that, I dive into the water.

"Has anyone told you that your eyes are the same color as the moon when the light hits them just right?"

It started to get dark soon after we began swimming, and

Kingston asked me to check on his stitches, so we got out and sat at the edge of the dock to do just that and never left. Nature is chirping and rustling around us now while the cool night breeze blows in, but I don't feel cold. I feel right at home, relaxed and calm. That's what being out here always does for me, and I'm always so grateful for these moments. Moments when the world disappears around me. Moments when my past isn't haunting my present. Moments when my present doesn't feel so... incomplete.

A slight smile tips my lips. "My dad used to tell me that, actually. He was obsessed with the moon." I smile at my memories. "He was always using the moon as a metaphor for the different phases of my life. If I liked a boy, or if I was upset over a mean girl in school. He used to tell me that there were different sides to people, and the sides that we see are the ones they want us to see, because everyone's hiding something."

"That's poignant as fuck."

I do a double-take to look at him and then give an airy laugh. "Well, that's my father for you. For someone so analytical, he was the biggest dreamer I knew."

"What about your mom?"

I swallow back my discomfort, reminding myself that Kingston is asking questions any normal person would ask. "I never knew my mom." I shrug to let him know it's not a big deal. I've learned over the years that the more nonchalant I am about things, the more others react in the same way.

"I didn't know my mom either."

Never have I received a response like that. My head snaps to look at him. His eyes are faced front as he leans back on his palms, his legs swinging slowly in front of him.

"Why?" I don't know why the question slips out. I hate

being asked about my parents, so I don't know why I asked him about his.

"She died when I was two. Um—" He pauses for a second, like he's trying to work up the courage. "I was an active kid. Started walking when I was ten months old and never stopped moving. One day, I was playing outside while my mom was watering the plants. I darted into the street right in front of a car." He pauses again, his eyes pointed down while his throat bobs with his swallow. "She pushed me out of the way, saved my life, but—she didn't get out of the way in time."

My heart squeezes. "Oh my God. I'm so sorry."

"Yeah." He shrugs the exact same way I would to fend off the concern others always want to give. It's their natural instinct, I suppose, but it's never helpful. "I don't remember her, only the things my father told me about her and the photos he showed me. So there's always been this emptiness there, you know? Like this big gaping hole where I know something is missing." He looks at me again, this time assessing me in a way that isn't scrolling my body to visualize me naked. "What happened with your mom?"

Very few people at camp know about my parents, and I like keeping it that way. Hope, the Bexleys, and a few other staff members who I've known since moving here know as much as I'm willing to share. They know enough to keep the rest of their questions to themselves. Kingston isn't great at understanding boundaries, so I should probably keep my mouth shut, but after what he told me, I want to tell him something in return. "She was an addict and in and out of jail for the first six years of my life before dying of an overdose." I hate the way I sound so cold telling the story, but she's always felt like a stranger to me. "Like you, I don't remember her. It's probably for the best."

96

"Jesus, I'm sorry."

I shrug and give him a soft smile. "Thanks. What about your dad? Were you two pretty close?"

Kingston snorts and shakes his head. "My dad and I couldn't be more opposite if we tried. I think maybe he always resented me for my mom's death. To him, I was such a fuckup growing up. My grades were shit if I got anything less than an A, and he hated sports with a passion. I took all kinds of odd jobs growing up to fund my own sports to play. Didn't matter, though. He told me I'd never amount to anything. In his eyes, I never did."

"What?" I laugh, despite the utter disbelief swirling inside me. "You play for the NFL. Doesn't he know how many kids come through this camp who will only ever dream of accomplishing what you have?"

Kingston grins. "Right, well, my old man doesn't see it like that. If I'm not in some high-rise corporate building, wearing a suit and tie every day while practicing law, then I'm scum. Doesn't matter that I make more money in one contract than he ever has in his entire life. Doesn't matter that I'm doing what I love, what feeds my soul. I'll never amount to what he desperately wanted me to become."

I shake my head, completely dumbfounded. "That's really unfortunate."

"Yeah, well, now it's your turn to tell me about your dad so I can feel better about mine," he teases.

Cringing, I shake my head, pushing aside the lurch of discomfort in my chest. "My dad was amazing, actually," I say softly. "But he died when I was sixteen."

"Shit. I'm so sorry."

I never know what to say to someone else's apologies over the death of my father. I believe them, and I appreciate the sentiment, but sorry doesn't bring him back. "Yeah, so I'm not sure I can help you with your feelings about your dad. At least you have one."

"Well, fuck." Kingston blows out a breath and faces forward, his head tilting toward the moon. "We're a hot mess, the two of us."

"Ah, speak for yourself. I'm doing exactly what I want to be doing."

A beat of silence passes before he speaks again. "Why did you want to become a nurse?"

"I guess the simple answer is that my father was a doctor. A surgeon. I grew up worshiping the fact that he saved lives on the daily, but it wasn't all that simple for me. When I first moved to the camp, I was given all these odd jobs. The Bexleys wanted to see what stuck. I think I tried every single position until they started connecting the dots for me. I loved being a lifeguard because of the training classes and the fact that I was helping people." I point to my swimsuit and laugh. "Hence where I got the suit." His eyes don't leave mine this time. "I was always the one accompanying the kids to the nurse's office, until eventually, Miriam Bexley asked me to work for her as her assistant."

"Bexley? She one of the owners?"

"Yup. Miriam is Andrew Bexley's wife, mother to all five of the Bexley boys, and now a happily retired world traveler. Anyway, of course, I agreed to be her assistant. The rest just happened kind of slowly, but naturally. It's funny how things work out the way they should, in ways we never would have imagined."

"I agree with that."

I smile with pinched lips. "Do you? That's not the sense I got when I met you."

He chuckles and turns back to face the water. "All I know is that I was dreading being here until I met you."

I try to ignore the rippling sensation in my chest. "You almost left yesterday," I remind him with a coy smile.

"But I stayed."

"Why?"

"Because you gave me a reason to."

His eyes drift back to mine. Even in darkness, his green eyes have the ability to suck me in and hold me to him like a magnet. Two opposite forces, connected in a way that almost feels magical. But while there's no question that I'm intensely attracted to Kingston physically, it's what comes out of his mouth that I just can't see past. Normally. *Because you gave me a reason to.* His words mix with the cool wind and shake me a little.

"I just gave you blankets, Kingston. It's really not that big of a deal."

"Maybe not to you, but it's a big fucking deal to me. No one is ever that nice to me."

I tilt my head a little, for once wanting to see past the guard of Kingston's big green eyes. "Maybe you make it a little hard for them to be nice to you. You're not exactly the warm and affectionate type."

"Be careful with those assumptions, Nurse Silver. I might just have to prove you wrong."

I wish my heart didn't just catch in my throat. I wish the damn flutters would stop erupting in my chest whenever he says something clever. I wish I didn't see the layer of Kingston Scott that I saw tonight, because now I know there's more to him than a cocky mouth and arrogant demeanor. There's a deeply buried pain, which festers and brews but he manages to contain, thanks to the many defenses he's erected over the years.

He's hiding something. Just like me.

# CHAPTER 10

# THE PLAN

## SYLVIA, 8 YEARS AGO

Headlights flicker as I approach the underpass, my duffel bag weighing down my injured arm. Everything hurts, there's a stabbing pain in my lungs every time I breathe, and I know I look like I just walked out of a boxing match.

I reach the white rented Civic, yank open the passenger door, and jump into the car as if it's about to take off without me. "Good news," I breathe, using whatever energy remains. There's not much left. After swallowing, I suck in more air. "She's not dead."

"Thank God," Harvey declares with relief. "That *is* good news." His head rolls back onto the headrest, then he lets out a loud sigh. "And how are you?"

I wince as my seatbelt clicks into place. "How do you think I am?" Snapping isn't the answer, but what kind of question was that? "Anyway, you know what this means, right?"

He bends his brows together. "We stick to the plan."

My eyes widen. "What? No. We go to the cops. We tell them everything, then I file a restraining order against her.

She'll have to stay away from me. And she'll never have a chance of claiming the money after that."

"And then what?" Harvey challenges. "It's your word against hers? Didn't you say you thought you killed her? What if she goes to the cops and tells them you're violent? You know she's been looking for any excuse to get her hands on your father's money. This is what she wanted, and now you're going to play right into her hands."

A ball of emotion builds in my throat as I shake my head. "But she attacked me, Harvey. She's in the wrong, not me. I'll claim self-defense. I'll win."

"And what if she wins? Then what, Sylvia? Then your inheritance will be as good as gone. Do you really want to take that chance?"

"So, what?" I say, blinking back the tears that threaten to spill. "I just disappear?"

I can't believe this is really happening. Even though Harvey told me he was setting up a safe haven for me to live until I became old enough to claim my inheritance, it never felt real. In fact, I rejected the idea at first. It wasn't until Lucinda's efforts became more vindictive and I was being dragged into legal mediations constantly that I decided Harvey's idea might be the only way to survive this. I couldn't stay with her anymore, and since she was my appointed guardian until I turned eighteen, it wasn't like I could move out to get away from her.

"We need to stick to the plan," Harvey says while laying a comforting hand on my arm. "I'll keep you safe, Sylvia. It's what your father would have wanted. And it will keep Lucinda away from any plot to take your father's money for herself. Trust me."

"And what if she calls the cops? She'll play the victim. Won't it look worse if I run away now?"

He bows his head. "I guess you need to make a decision. Do you go to the cops and take the risk? Or do you keep yourself safe, start over, and claim that money when you're legally able? By then, this should all blow over. The way I see it, you don't really have a choice here."

The way he puts it, I don't feel like I have a choice either.

"Okay," I finally say, though my words are so shaky and quiet, I'm not sure if he hears them. "Let's stick to the plan."

)⊂●●●)⊃(

*72 HOURS LATER*

Harvey drove all night from that underpass in Phoenix, Arizona, to a bus station in Las Vegas, Nevada. From there, he gave me enough instructions to get myself to a specific hotel in Anacortes, Washington, where my new identification and instructions would arrive. Harvey had arranged it all through a private protection program.

Now, here I am, alone in a strange hotel room, looking like a completely different person, ready to embark on an adventure that no seventeen-year-old should have to embark on. But in the six hours Harvey and I spent together in the car, debating all the ifs and buts and coulds and woulds, I came to the same conclusion as Harvey. There's simply no other safe option.

After a hard swallow, I suck in a deep breath and reach a shaky hand toward the door handle. I let the hotel door shut behind me, then I cross the deserted street toward the harbor.

It's still dark out when I reach the small building with all the transportation signs in its window.

The woman behind the glass just stares at me, her forehead lifted like she was annoyed before I got here. "Can I help you?"

Just the simple question is enough to send a flock of jitters through me. I panic and lock eyes on the first destination listed on the wall behind her. "Y-yes. One ticket to Orcas Island, please."

The woman nods and pushes buttons on her keyboard. "The next ferry leaves in forty minutes? Is that the one you want?"

"Yes, thank you." I say quietly.

"Great. That will be seven dollars and twenty-five cents."

I shuffle through my bag until I find the manila envelope. At quick glance, I see that there are quite a few hundred-dollar bills. I don't have time to ogle at the money now, so I find one of the smaller bills and hand it to the woman, who returns my change promptly. As I'm sticking my change back in my wallet, I catch a glimpse of my new ID. Harvey even managed to Photoshop my hair enough to look exactly like the color I dyed it only an hour earlier. And then I see the name I've been given and my heart feels so heavy I have to hold onto the counter so that I don't lose my balance. It's the nickname my father came up for me during one of our many discussions about the moon, when my eyes caught the light just right.

"Enjoy your ride, Ms...?"

My eyes flicker back to the woman, and I stare at her for a brief moment too long before opening my mouth to reply. The words taste foreign before they've even left my mouth. "It's Livingston," I say against my next swallow. "Silver Livingston."

# FIRST QUARTER MOON

"FOR THE MOON NEVER BEAMS WITHOUT BRINGING ME DREAMS." — EDGAR ALLEN POE

# CHAPTER 11

# FRIENDLY COMPETITION

## KINGSTON

Competition is my drug of choice. It fuels me, inspires me, and pushes me. It doesn't matter if I'm on the field or off. I need to be the best at whatever I do. Football, working out, partying, or sex. The adrenaline that charges through me before any of those activities comes purely from an insatiable need inside me.

It's day one of camp for the first group of kids, and I'm feeling that same competitive drive as I'm leading drills up and down the field. I was assigned fourteen kids for the week, and I won't deny that Zach might have been on to something with this gig. While these kids may idolize the ground we walk on, they're here to play football. Just watching my group of boys tear across the field in a race to catch the ball I'm about to lob down the center is a dopamine shot straight to my soul.

From the second the teen boys hopped off the bus and saw who was waiting for them, their reactions lit me up in a way I'll never forget. It's one thing to be in a stadium and be the reason for all the crowd noise, but in a way, this just feels... bigger.

"Hey, King."

I look over to find one of the kids, Lincoln, limping back over to me with an annoyed look on his face. I'm still learning their names, but I remember his because he caught my eye from the second we started morning drills. The kid is fierce and fast, and he has a rocket for an arm. He doesn't seem the least bit phased that he's not on track to make many friends here. He reminds me a little bit of myself.

"What happened, dude? We're just getting started."

"Got caught up in my pivot."

I look down at his feet and chuckle. "Thumpers growing too fast for that body of yours, eh?"

The corner of his mouth tips up, telling me I nailed it on the head. "Feels that way."

"Yeah." I clap him on the back and blow my whistle to signal for the rest of the team to run the drill back toward me. "I'll walk you over to the tent to get Dr. Blaine to check you out. How does it feel?"

He shrugs, the hard look on his face never letting up. "Not too bad."

"All right, tough guy." I turn toward the bleachers where Zach is just wrapping up an interview with the BelleCurve camera crew and wave him over.

"What's up?" he asks when he's close enough for us to hear him.

"Lincoln here tweaked his ankle."

"Oh no," Zach says while looking down at Lincoln's leg. "I can take him over to the medical tent."

My gaze travels over to where a ten-by-ten tent is pitched, the door flaps held open. It's set up like a small examination room with a long, padded table and plastic drawers filled with medical supplies lining one wall. Dr. Blaine is standing out front, assessing another kid's injury, but he's not alone. A bombshell blonde dressed in khaki shorts and a white Camp Dakota tank top stands at the other end, handing out water cups to the approaching players. She's got a full-on smile on her face, and I can already imagine how sparkly her gray eyes look against the perfectly sunny day.

Zach's face scrunches with sympathy before he holds out his arm for Lincoln to take.

"Actually," I say with a step forward. "I should probably go with him. You know, since I'm responsible for him. Can you finish drills with the guys?"

Zach throws a quick glance at the medical tent, and I swear I see understanding flicker in his eyes before he agrees on the exchange. "Yeah, sure, no problem."

From my peripheral, I know Silver spots me walking with Lincoln, but I ignore her for the time being. I'll let her get her eyeful. Lord knows she couldn't stop checking me out last night at the lake. She thinks she's sly, but I saw her. I chose not to call her out because I liked it too much, and I knew she would stop if I embarrassed her.

Last night, Silver and I bonded on another level. She hinted at her past, and I gave her a glimpse at mine. That is more than I offer anyone in my life, because what's the point in bringing up all that darkness? With Silver, though, it didn't feel like I was confessing my darkness. I felt like she was bringing light into it.

Dr. Blaine looks like a joke. I recognize the haughty air about him the moment we approach. He greets us with a smile that's all teeth, no personality. His dark-blond hair is slicked back with enough product to make a person choke. And his long white lab coat is a fucking laugh, given the setting we're in. This guy looks like he stepped straight off the set of *Doogie Howser, M.D.*

"Well, hey there, buddy," he starts with an exaggerated smile. "What can I help you with?"

"His name is Lincoln." I pinch out a smile, trying not to call attention to my instant dislike of this guy. "He thinks he tweaked his ankle while running drills."

"Oh, no," Dr. Blaine says, the horror on his face dialed up a few notches. He bends down to get eye-level with Lincoln. "Let's take a look at it, shall we?"

*Is that the way he thinks he's supposed to talk to kids? Jesus Christ. He's a sixteen-year-old kid, not a toddler.*

Lincoln throws me a worried look. Even he can see straight through this phony of a doctor.

I shrug and give the kid a look of genuine sympathy, because it's all I can do. Dr. Blaine takes Lincoln aside, and I meander over to Silver like I hadn't planned to all along. "Didn't know you would be gracing us with your presence today."

She shoots me a side-eyed look that I'm sure is supposed to show her annoyance, but all I see is sex eyes and fuck-me lips. I was right about how light-gray and shimmery her eyes look in this light too. She's drop-dead gorgeous, and I'm certain she's clueless about it.

"It was a surprise to me too. Doctor Blaine thought I would be more help out here on the field." She hands one of the plastic cups of water she's holding to the next kid who jogs up to the tent, then raises her brows. "See? Very helpful."

I chuckle. "In Dr. Blaine's defense, you are providing critical hydration to nearly three hundred boys and men. We are all so grateful for your services." I pluck the remaining cup from her hand and wink. "Thank you. I needed this."

She rolls her eyes, but this time, a big smile comes with it. I almost can't believe it, and if I didn't see it with my very own eyes, I wouldn't have. I made Silver smile. Suddenly, it's the only thing I want to do for the rest of my life.

I'm mesmerized, even more so after our conversation last night. I drifted off to sleep thinking about what she said about the moon and just how fitting her passion seems to be. Silver is like the moon—partially hidden, yet all I see. She's someone who seems to live her life cloaked by daylight and illuminated in darkness—always changing with each phase exposing different sides of her beauty.

I want to know more.

"Oh," Silver says with a snap of her fingers while adopting a serious expression. "Marlo dropped something off for you yesterday, and it's in my office."

*Shit.* I try not to let her see my horror, but I wouldn't be surprised if my entire face changed color before her very eyes. My friends in high school used to call me a mood ring. They swore they could tell what mood I was in by the way my pigment would change so frequently. I imagine my face is white for the horror that runs through my mind now. If Marlo gave her the package, does that mean she knows what's in it?

"Um, all right." Then I tilt my head, my curiosity getting the better of me. "Why did he give it to you?"

She doesn't give anything away if she does know. She just shrugs and takes a quick look in front of her, probably to ensure no one has approached for water. "I think he had to go somewhere and wanted to make sure you got it. That was actually why I went out to the field, but then you split your face open, and I just forgot." Her eyes move to the side of my eye. "Speaking of your eye, how does it feel today?"

"Like I cut it open."

A small smile pushes her cheeks up as her gaze travels from mine and back to my bandage, which hides where she stitched me together. "I could look at it for you later if you want. After practice. Then you can grab your, um, package."

As much as the idea of her going anywhere near my cut again makes my stomach churn, I could never pass up the opportunity to be alone with Silver again. I grin. "That's real nice of you to offer."

Her cheeks pink. "Probably nicer than you deserve."

The husk in her voice makes my cock jump. He's had his eye on Silver for as long as I have. The beast is eager to get to know her better. "Probably right. But I accept your offer."

"Great. Just stop by the medical cabin before dinner then."

"It's a date."

She lets out an exasperated breath and shakes her head, but she doesn't try to correct me, which makes my smile widen. She's already used to me, and she knows she's lost. I open my mouth to tell her how pretty she looks today, but before I can get the words out, Dr. Blaine taps on my arm.

"I'm sorry. I didn't get your name," he says, his pearly whites practically glimmering in the sunshine.

*Is this chump serious?* If he thinks I believe he doesn't know who I am, then he's more out of whack than I thought. "Kingston Scott," I say, sticking my hand out to greet him. We shake, and I make sure to add emphasis to my squeeze. "You can call me King."

The doctor's eyes widen slightly, showing the first hint of recognition since meeting me. "Well, okay then." He gestures to Lincoln, who is sitting on the examination table and holding ice to his ankle. "He definitely tweaked it, but there's no bruising, no swelling. I'm going to keep him with me so Nurse Silver and I can make sure he's taking it easy and alternating heat and ice. Hopefully, he can return to regular activities soon, but I'll be able to make a better assessment tomorrow."

I give the kid a sympathetic frown then nod at the doctor, meanwhile trying to ignore the rush of annoyance that came with the sound of Silver's name on his tongue. "All right. Thanks for checking him out, Doc. I better get back to practice." I give Silver a parting wink. "See you tonight."

With that, I flash Dr. Bonehead a quick smile, finding deep satisfaction at the confused look on his face. Hopefully, he got the message. If that wasn't a lowball attempt to stake a claim at what isn't yet mine, I don't know what is.

# CHAPTER 12

# CHECK-UP

## SILVER

"Thanks for your help today, Silver." Dr. Blaine and I just finished transporting the medical supplies back to my office for storage, and now he's lingering a little too long in the doorway.

"Of course. Glad I could be of assistance."

"Do you mind having everything set up for me tomorrow morning? I have an early appointment at the hospital. I'll jet over here as soon as I'm done, but I'm afraid it won't give me enough time to set up everything."

I nod, ignoring the appalled voice in my head that calls out his BS excuse for not having to do the heavy lifting. "Sure thing. See you tomorrow, Doctor."

He flashes me a smile and hops off the deck, onto the dirt. "Great. Look forward to it."

I'm watching the man walk away, my eyes narrowed and my chest filled with heated contempt, when the sound of footsteps approaching from the other direction makes me jerk my head toward it. Kingston is watching me with amusement written all over his face, and at the instant our eyes connect, a whoosh of warmth floods my chest.

I didn't stop him from calling this a date earlier, not because I agreed, but because I'm catching on quickly to Kingston Scott's mind games. If I had objected to the notion that we were, in fact, meeting up for a date, he would have only pushed the subject harder. The only way to shut the man up is to say nothing at all.

"See something you like?" Kingston teases.

I know he's talking about Dr. Blaine, but *yes* is the word that shouts through my mind in reference to Kingston. Yes, I see something I like, but it makes absolutely no sense as to why. Kingston has been nothing but a pain in my side since he stepped off that bus, and if I should be feeling any kind of way toward him, it should be complete and utter disdain.

Instead of answering him, I roll my eyes and step back through the doorway so he can follow me in. "This should be quick and painless," I say while leading him into the examination room. I gesture for him to hop up onto the table before walking over to the counter to get prepped.

I wash my hands, grab some alcohol wipes and a new bandage, then head back over to Kingston to find him lying down with his arms behind his head.

"I didn't tell you to make yourself comfortable."

"Well, you should have. Don't you want to make this experience a pleasurable one?"

I twist my lips to keep from smiling. "Not particularly, no. Now sit up, so I can get this over with."

A deep chuckle comes from below me before he sits up. The table is still at the same height I adjusted it to yesterday, so he's a couple of inches below me. I raise my hands to the tape that's holding the gauze to his forehead, but when I start to remove it, I see his eyelids pinch closed.

Laughing, I pull my hands back slightly. "You're such a baby."

His lids fly back open, and he pins me with his stare. "Is that how you talk to all of your patients?"

"Not all my patients flinch when I come near their face. I'm not even touching you yet."

"Yeah well, most of your patients probably didn't get the shit beat out of them by their father when they were a kid."

I drop my hands to my sides, my heart sinking into my stomach. "Jesus. Are you serious?"

Kingston looks away and shrugs like he regrets what he just told me. "I told you my father was an asshole."

A new sensation rips through my chest as I see the giant man below me in a whole new light. For the first time, I'm getting a glimpse of a side to him he masks with his anger and quick-witted mouth. There's nothing I can say to make whatever he's gone through better, even if I can relate on a similar level. It doesn't feel right to speak on it now.

I take in a slow, deep breath then release it before deciding to try again. "You can trust me. I promise to be gentle."

I don't know if he hears flirtation in my genuine promise, but a flash of hope crosses his face, then I sense him relax. "All right. Get it over with, then."

I raise my hands again, not wanting to give him another second to change his mind. "I thought football was a pretty heavy-impact sport. I would think you'd be used to getting all banged up."

"I am." His tone is gruff, and I know he's trying not to think about me removing the bandage. "It's getting cut open that has always bothered me."

"But it doesn't bother you to get knocked around on the field?"

"That's different."

"How so?"

In my peripheral, I see him look at me. "I'm defense. It's my job to attack and put a stop to the offense, not the other way around."

"So it has nothing to do with the fact that you're padded up and one of the biggest guys out there?"

His lip quirks at my question. "Maybe a little bit of that too. But I know what to expect when it comes to football."

His wound looks good, but I dab the alcohol wipe on there anyway to ensure it's staying clean. My heart clenches a little when he squirms below me. "That's the worst of it. Your stitch looks good. I'm going to put a new bandage on there, but you probably won't need it anymore after tomorrow."

He nods, then I decide to keep him talking. "What position do you play?" I know Hope mentioned it to me, but I don't know enough about football to remember.

"Defensive end."

That's all he gives me, and I laugh. "Okay. I have no idea what that is."

His lips quirk up on the side. "That's right. Miss Oblivious. I hold down the end of the line of scrimmage." He chuckles when he realizes that explanation told me nothing. "When we line up on the field opposite the other team, that's the line of scrimmage. I stand at the end of the line when it's their turn to throw the ball. My job is to keep the other team from gaining any yards toward their goal."

I try to stop my next smile, but it's impossible. "Thanks for dumbing it down for me."

"No problem."

I feel the ripple of his words as they vibrate in the air. I step away from it, creating a chasm of energy between us. He's all bandaged up. It took no time at all. For some reason, just like yesterday, I'm filled with great disappointment.

"See? That wasn't so bad. You're free to go." I turn before the words are even out of my mouth and head toward the sink to wash up.

"You headed to dinner?"

I hope he can't see the way my shoulders tense at his question. It seems that every moment with Kingston feeds an addiction I never knew I had. This isn't how I act around guys, like I'm on the playground with my sixth-grade crush, pretending not to be interested, just to grab a little bit more of his attention. But if I said I wasn't doing any of that, then I would be lying to myself. I crave Kingston's attention just as much as he craves giving it, and that's a dangerous combination.

With a quick glance over my shoulder, I'm careful not to actually meet his gaze. "I still have some things to wrap up here. I'll see you there."

"All right, then." I hear the thud of his feet landing on the floor, then his footsteps head to the door. "It's been a pleasure, as always."

The moment the front door of the cabin closes, I release a deep breath and finally relax my shoulders. My eyes lock on the calendar on the wall, and I mentally count down the days until Kingston Scott gets back on that bus and I never see him again. Four more days. I can manage four more days of his irritating charm. I have more important things I should be thinking about anyway, like the fact that my inheritance is about to go to the person who produced my need to start a new life.

My thoughts are like the line of scrimmage Kingston described for me earlier. One side as the offense, and the other as the defense, battling it out for the fate of my future. I don't know which outcome is better. If Lucinda wins, these past eight years will have been for nothing. Pride beats against the cage in my chest, telling me I should never let that woman win. But then another desire fights back, asking me what the point in all of this is anymore. Who cares if she gets the money? I don't want it. I don't need it. I'm happy here. I'm happy with my life. Maybe if I let her win, I'll win too.

I'm so lost in my thoughts as I tidy up my office and grab my keys to lock up that I almost miss the package I meant to hand over to Kingston. *Shit.* It's still sitting on the corner of my desk, untouched, and I start to question why I've really been so forgetful about it. That's not like me at all, and it's not like I haven't seen Kingston several times since Marlo handed it to me. But while I could grab it now and bring it to the cafeteria, I settle on the excuse of not wanting to hand over something so private in public.

I shake away my thoughts, lock up behind me, and start to focus on my growling stomach instead of all the heavy thoughts that have been swarming my brain. I don't need to make any decisions now. I need food.

Hope is already at our normal spot, eating, when I get in line for food. Kingston isn't that far ahead of me, but his focus is on Vicky, so he doesn't see me coming in. She sidles up to him while they fill their plates, then she follows him to a set of tables near the one Hope has claimed. Forcing my eyes away from the chatty pair, I finish choosing my food and sit across from Hope, positioning myself so I can't see Kingston unless I crane my neck. I don't want the temptation, especially not when my thoughts are teetering on the edge between vulnerable and reckless.

"Hey, friend." Hope's grin is so big that I can't help but smile back.

"Why are you so cheery?"

She shrugs and leans forward so only I can hear. "Oh, I don't know. Maybe because I was walking by the field this morning and saw you and Kingston laughing it up. How's that going?"

I roll my eyes and shake my head. "It's not *going*. Nothing has changed. He's still a thorn in my butt, that's all."

"Ugh, you're such a liar, but I'll take the bait. If you're not interested in Kingston, then what about Dr. McHottyPants?"

I choke on my mouthful of water and quickly swallow it before laughing. "Dr. McWhat?"

She's laughing harder now, and I know it's because she just scored a reaction from me. "That hot doc you get to work with on the field. He looks so young. How old is he, anyway?"

If Hope wasn't always asking about guys, then I would probably wonder what was wrong with her, but she's never been so obsessed with finding *me* a man. "He's thirty-two. I guess that is pretty young."

Hope nods her approval. "Oh, yes. And he's so good with the kids."

I don't want to ruin her fantasies by telling her that, if anything, Dr. Blaine is a condescending asshole with the kids and thinks of me as his roadie who sidelines as a water girl rather than a fellow medical professional. Perhaps I'm slightly bitter about it all, but I choose to keep that to myself for now.

"Well..." Hope says, glancing over my shoulder. "It's a good thing you're not into Kingston, I guess."

I frown, not wanting her to see the dread weighing down my gut. "What do you mean?"

She nods over my shoulder, gesturing for me to look. As

much as I don't want to, I play along to find Vicky's and Kingston's heads bowed together. They're laughing hard, and when my gaze slips down under the table, I spy Vicky's hand creeping up between his thighs. My stomach churns violently, and I turn back around to face my friend. Hope's expression is now filled with worry and sympathy, like she knows everything I won't ever speak aloud. As much as I didn't want to catch feelings for Kingston Scott, apparently I had.

"It's fine, Hope," I tell her, not trying to hide my disappointment. "He and Vicky are a better fit anyway. They're both flirtatious and outgoing, and they clearly look good together."

Hope makes a disgusted face and shakes her head. "My thoughts are not so gracious, but whatever. If you're going to have a fling with one of the guests, maybe Kingston isn't the best choice. If he's willing to choose Vicky over you, then clearly, something is obviously wrong with him."

My stomach squeezes again, and I shovel more food into my mouth to get it to stop. "It doesn't matter, Hope. Can we just drop it?"

Finally, my friend gets the hint, and she changes the subject to how amazing her day would have been since she was running errands with Anderson, but he barely acknowledged her existence.

"Just because he doesn't flirt with you doesn't mean he doesn't see you, Hope. He sees you, I promise."

Her eyes look so big and sad, it makes my heart squeeze in my chest. "How do you know?"

"Because I've known him for a very long time, and while he hasn't always been this business-oriented, he's always been a pretty serious guy. He's the oldest of all his siblings, so he's always been the one to take charge, you know? He puts a lot of pressure on himself, and he's always been a bit closed off."

"Okay, but what does any of that have to do with him seeing me?"

I lean forward and squeeze Hope's hand. "It's simple. He asks you to run errands with him. He trusts you with all of the big events. He asks about you whenever you're not around."

Hope sighs with exasperation. "That's because this is my job. He's not asking me to do him any personal favors. It's all work."

"I don't know, Hope. I think there's more to it. I see the way he looks at you."

She pouts. "Don't say stuff that will get my hopes up, Silver. Please."

Giving her a sympathetic smile, I lean back and wrap my fingers around my glass of water. "Okay, I'll shut up. But I don't think you should count him out. If anything, you should make your feelings clearer. He's the kind of man that doesn't take subtle hints well. He needs someone who isn't afraid to go after him."

At that same moment, Hope's gaze drifts away from me and back over my shoulder. "Speaking of someone who isn't afraid to go after a man."

I react before I think and turn to look over my shoulder at where Kingston and Vicky are leaving the cafeteria together. My stomach knots, and suddenly, I'm no longer hungry. Swallowing, I look back at Hope and push my tray away without saying a word.

She sees right through me and gives me a sad smile. "Well, you didn't want him anyway, right?"

I nod, but my eyes refuse to meet hers. "Right."

# CHAPTER 13

# IN THE BARN
## KINGSTON

Vicky's got an extra sway in her step now. Her flirtatious smile is supercharged, and her lashes are batting every few seconds. She asked if I had ever seen the stables where she spends her off time. Apparently, I should have lied. When she offered to give me a tour, I didn't know how to turn her down. That's not something I normally do. Under normal circumstances, I wouldn't even question jumping at the opportunity of getting a pretty girl alone, but this feels somehow... wrong. And I'm certain that feeling has everything to do with the beautiful blonde with the titanium-gray eyes and a shy smile, sitting with her back turned toward me during all of dinner.

"Here it is," Vicky says while spreading her arms and turning in a little circle. "I usually go riding in my off hours, but I come to the stables to check on my friends every day."

"Your friends?"

She gestures through the open door of the barn, where I can see the snouts of several horses, some of which are bending down to chomp on hay. "Come meet them."

Without allowing me to respond, she takes my hand and pulls me toward the open door. I follow a few steps behind her while feelings of resistance to follow her lead grow. Vicky is a beautiful woman. Back home, I wouldn't have thought twice about taking her into a bathroom stall and fucking her senseless. But I haven't even given her a chance before wanting to reject her.

We're walking past the endless stalls of horses, stopping every so often so she can pet one or feed it hay, when my curiosity gets the better of me. "I thought you were a lifeguard. You must have a lot of off time."

Vicky smiles. "Not really. The swimming spot I work at is open to the public when the campers aren't scheduled to come swim."

"Swimming spot?"

"Yeah, there are places to jump in the water all around us, but there's a bigger section of the lake we rope off for swimming. It's really neat. You should check it out. There's a big slide, a rope swing, rafts, and other recreational toys like canoes and kayaks."

"I guess I haven't gotten the grand tour yet. I had no idea this place was so... resourceful."

Vicky shrugs. "Yeah, it's got everything you could want and need."

"I don't know about that," I say dryly, thinking about the bedding situation when I first arrived at my cabin. But those thoughts are dangerous. Those thoughts lead me down the path of imagining Silver and how thoughtful she was to bring me bedding when she heard I didn't have any. A warmth fills my chest, but I snuff it out quickly. I may be sweet on Silver, but she seems pretty adamant about keeping her distance from me.

I'm so deep in my thoughts, I miss a lot of what Vicky is going on about until we arrive in an open room with a floor of hay and a mechanical bull in the center of the room.

"Wanna try it?"

I eye the giant leather seat warily then shake my head. "Nah, I'm good." I've seen the way those things operate at one of my favorite cowboy-inspired bars, where the staff of hot women jump on the bar top and shake their asses to country music. The mechanical bull rides are usually reserved for similarly hot women who let it all hang out as they get jerked around by whoever is operating the ride.

"Suit yourself." Vicky giggles. "Watch me, then." She jogs toward the bull and pulls herself onto it, hiking her short jean skirt up in the process. "Push the red button," she calls over to me.

I look to my right, and there it is—a large red button with a lever to the right of it. I don't touch the lever, but I do push the button since she asked. A second later, the machine groans as the fake bull starts to move. Vicky moves along with it, and even I can admit that Vicky rides the thing like a pro, with one hand up and her body moving perfectly with each change of direction. It's impressive, and sexy as hell if I'm being completely honest, but it doesn't stop the way my mind keeps traveling back to a certain uninterested blonde.

Vicky is laughing when the machine slows to a halt. "You need to try it."

I walk over to her while shaking my head. "You're not getting me on that thing, but I'm impressed. You ride like you can hang on to just about anything."

My flirtatious words are out of my mouth before I can catch them, and I see the flash of excitement on Vicky's face as she recognizes the tone.

She slides off the bull while I hold her waist, and she pushes straight up against me the second she's on her feet. "And what about you, King? Could you handle me the way that bull just did?" Her hand moves down my front, toward my cock.

I truly consider what she's offering. It's been a long fucking time since I've been buried in a woman. Last Friday didn't count since I was drunk out of my mind and never even got to finish. Just the thought of sinking into something tight and warm and giving my cock some needed pleasure is enough to lose myself for a second.

It isn't until Vicky's got me gripped in her palm over my jeans that reality slaps me hard in the face. An image of Silver's soft smile flashes through my mind again, and this time, a flood of guilt swarms my chest. "Fuck." I grip Vicky's hand and push it back to her before stepping away. "I just remembered, I'm supposed to be somewhere."

Internally, I'm commanding the monster in my pants to settle down while ignoring the anger that crosses Vicky's expression.

"What the hell? Really?"

I give her my best apologetic look and continue to back away. "Yeah. Rain check?"

Vicky looks completely baffled, and while I have no intention of actually cashing in on that rain check, she nods. "Yeah, sure."

I lift the corner of my mouth in a smile, turn around, and dart back toward the cafeteria, hoping to catch Silver as she wraps up with dinner.

Before I walk inside the building, I spot Hope leaving.

Her eyes widen when she sees me. "Hey, Kingston."

I stop in my tracks and suck in a breath, realizing how much energy I exerted running maybe half a mile. That has nothing to do with fitness and everything to do with the adrenaline that rushed through me when Silver entered my mind. "Hey, Hope. Is Silver still in there?"

Hope's forehead bunches together, curiosity forming between her pretty little eyes. "No, I think she said she had to go back to work." Then Hope smiles. "Like always."

I nod and start to turn around. "All right, thanks."

"Hey, Kingston, wait—"

Ignoring Hope this time, I start jogging toward the nurse's cabin. Low and behold, Silver is walking up the steps as I round the corner. "Hey, Silver, wait up."

Her head snaps in my direction, and even from this distance, I can see the way her shoulders tense. Her eyes flicker over me, lingering on my hair and my shoulder, then that guarded look I want so desperately to tear down separates us once more, and I'm left standing in front of Silver's cold expression. "It's after hours. If it's not an emergency, then I can't help you."

"I just—" *What the fuck am I doing?* Almost as soon as I start to speak, I realize I don't have a clue what I'm going to say. That I like her? That I just turned down an easy fuck because I couldn't get her off my mind? It all feels so inappropriate, considering the woman standing on the steps to her office is staring back at me like I'm nothing more than a speck of dirt she just wiped on the mat below her feet.

And just like that, my excitement to get to her dissolves with reality staring me back in my face. Silver Livingston is worth so much more than I could ever offer her, and she's well aware of it. My past is filled with nothing but misdemeanors, abuse, and using football as an excuse to expend the rage that burns inside me. Meanwhile, she's nothing but a gentle health-care worker who has to deal with someone like me, whom she clearly sees straight through.

"Um," I start again, realizing I can't say a single thing I'm thinking. I search for something, anything to excuse the fact that I just chased her down without looking like a total tool. "I forgot that package Marlo dropped off to you. Do you still have it?"

I'm not sure if I've ever seen the blood leave someone's face so fast before, but Silver's already-fair expression whitens before color fills her cheeks with a vengeance. "Yeah, of course. Wait here. I'll go get it."

She comes back out a minute later with the white paper bag in her hands and a blank expression on her face. "Here you go. Enjoy."

*Enjoy?* I take the bag from her and start to laugh through my discomfort. "Okay, I wi—"

Before I can finish my sentence and make up some excuse as to why we should hang out, she shuts the front door in my face, and I hear the lock turn behind it.

*What the fuck?*

Then I look down at the package in my hands. It's not sealed. I can see the contents through the opening of the package, which means Silver definitely saw what's inside. My heart sinks straight down to the ground.

*Well, fucking shit.*

# CHAPTER 14

# LATE NIGHT PHONE CALLS

## SILVER

I wait long after Kingston stopped knocking on my office door to wrap things up and head home. As soon as I went back inside, I locked the door behind me to shut out any possibility of another conversation. It's not like me to be so dismissive when it comes to a needy patient, but when it comes to Kingston Scott, nothing feels normal. I didn't want to listen to what he had to say after I handed him those condoms, especially after I saw the strings of hay stuck to his clothing.

He didn't know I saw what was in the bag. He didn't know that I saw him sneaking out of the cafeteria with Vicky. He didn't know that Vicky's sex pad of choice is the barn. Not that any of those things should matter. I certainly shouldn't be doing math equations in my head that result in a very vivid picture of Kingston and Vicky in a heated lip-lock.

It's dark by the time I get back to my cabin, and I head straight into the shower, to clean off the long day of arrogant men and a field of sweaty athletes. But no matter how hard I scrub, I stand no chance of scrubbing away the thoughts that are buried a little deeper. Thoughts that are constantly rising to the surface, no matter how many times I try to suffocate them. It's only been a day since Harvey called, and while I know I should be weighing the pros and cons of my next move, all I've done is choose distractions instead.

Maybe it's some sort of defense mechanism my brain has developed to protect the bad memories from damaging the fragile shell of a world I've created, but I can feel the gears slowly losing their luster. It's only a matter of time before that shell cracks.

I toss my towel over my desk chair and walk toward my dresser. I've just slipped on my panties and a tank top when the phone rings. I groan, wanting nothing more than a quiet night filled with a great book, a face mask, and good sleep. The ringing stops, but when it starts ringing again, I begrudgingly pick it up, praying it's not an emergency that will drag me away.

"Hello," I answer.

The light chuckle on the other end causes my belly to warm and the space between my thighs to buzz. "Hello, Nurse Silver. I hope I didn't catch you at a bad time."

The tone of his voice, deep and dripping of honey, brings me right back to the first day I ever heard it. I almost forgot how sexy it was until now. "As a matter of fact—"

"Don't do it," he teases. "Don't reject me again. You might think I'm equipped to handle it, but I assure you, I'm not."

I bite down on my bottom lip to keep from smiling. He can't even see me, and I'm ashamed of my reaction. He doesn't deserve my smile. "Trust me, I've always sensed your ego was on the fragile side. Which is why it baffles me that you continue to put yourself out there so boldly."

"You slammed the door in my face, Silver. I was just trying to talk to you."

I try to not let him hear my snort of a laugh. "I didn't *slam* the door, but I'm sorry. I wasn't in the mood for your antics."

"My antics?" he asks incredulously. "Is that what you call me wanting to spend time with you?"

"Is that what you wanted when you were pounding down my office door? To spend time with me?"

"Yes."

The fact that he doesn't even hesitate causes heat to rise in my cheeks while also making me uncomfortable. I know I can't take much of what Kingston says seriously, but a part of me enjoys the fact that he called me at all. It means he's not with Vicky, for one. And for whatever reason, he was thinking about me.

"Kingston," I start while carrying the phone's receiver back over to my dresser so I can find a pair of shorts. "You clearly have plenty of options. Why choose the one person who will never ever sleep with you?"

Another chuckle floats across the line, and I have to squeeze my legs together to quell the ache that shot straight to my core. "Never ever? That's a pretty bold statement."

I'm glad he can't see my face now. "Yeah, well, I'd hate to lead you on."

"Too late. I made you smile. I don't think that's a sight I'll ever forget."

This time, it's my turn to laugh. "Really? I'm pretty sure I'm glaring at you ninety-nine percent of the time, but you choose the one moment I maybe sorta smiled in your presence to cling to?"

"It was a great moment."

I sigh and bend over to open the bottom drawer.

"What are you doing?"

I freeze. The way he asked the question makes me think he can see me. "Um, getting dressed. Why?"

"I can only see your shadow, don't worry."

My head swivels to the closed blinds, my eyes widen, and I pull a couple of shades apart to peer through them. I'm greeted by a grinning Kingston, who's resting his chin on his fist as he leans against his windowsill.

"Are you freaking serious?"

He smirks. "Worried I'll see something I don't like?"

"No," I snap before yanking a pair of shorts from my drawer and slipping them on. "I'm afraid you'll like what you see too much."

I can practically hear his voice purr on the other end of the line. "I think I already like too much."

"I'm going to hang up now, Kingston."

He chuckles. "No, please don't. I'm bored. Let's hang out."

I carry the phone across the room and set it on my mattress before plopping down. "No way. I'm going to bed."

"I make a good cuddle buddy."

*Oh my God.* My face is crimson; I can see it from the long mirror on the wall across from me. But while I want to be flattered, all that crosses my mind is the visual of him and Vicky flirting at dinner. "I'm sure you do," I murmur, my bitterness on full display.

"C'mon, Silver. It's still early. We can watch a movie or something. Or play a board game."

I stifle a laugh. "I already made plans."

"With who?"

"With myself."

Kingston groans, and I can't help but wonder how that groan would vibrate between my legs. Maybe I *should* let him come over. Maybe I could use a little pick-me-up to hold me over. Maybe then I'll stop thinking about this man. Not only is he all wrong for me, but I can't stand him most of the time.

"That's not what I meant." I set the phone down and tie up my hair. "I'm reading a book tonight."

I pick up the receiver and hear him ask "Which book?"

"I'm not sure, to be honest. I just grabbed one from the bookshelf in the main lodge." I reach for it on my nightstand and flip it over. "It's an Agatha Christie novel."

"Whatever that is," Kingston says, then I hear a shuffle of fabric—I think. I can't be sure, but it sounds like he's settling in. "Fine. I won't try to come over. But you have to stay on the phone with me. I still haven't gotten used to this whole camping-in-the-woods thing."

I bite down on my lip again. "You're hardly camping. You're barely even roughing it."

"Thanks to you."

His words cause a flock of flutters to erupt in my chest. "You can stop thanking me for that."

"I'll do what I want."

"Figured as much."

A few beats of silence cross between us, and I realize I haven't tried that hard to get off the phone. I guess it's not a sin to enjoy the sound of someone's voice. Especially someone who is exceptionally good-looking. That's not something I'm willing to admit aloud, though.

"How did you wind up at this place, anyway?"

"At this camp?" I know what he's asking, but I'm stalling to figure out just how to answer that question.

"Yeah. What made Silver Livingston come to Orcas Island and decide to be one with nature?"

It's a quick decision, but I choose to tell Kingston as much of the truth as possible. "Do you believe in fate?"

"I do."

"Okay, well, I think that's what brought me here."

"How so?" The seriousness in his tone with the simple question warms me in a way I can't explain or understand.

"I wasn't happy back home, and I took the necessary steps to leave. Someone I trust worked out a temporary living arrangement with the Bexleys. But after that, my future was just kind of up in the air. I stumbled upon a career I loved, and the Bexleys gave me the opportunity to follow my dreams here on the island. It was like they took one look at me and took pity on the girl with no future. And then they gave me one."

More silence passes between us, and I wonder what Kingston is possibly thinking. I can't see his green eyes as they register my words. I can't watch his broad shoulders shift and straighten as if he slipped up and forgot who he was supposed to be for a moment.

"From my perspective, you created your own future. Maybe the Bexleys gave you an opportunity, but it was you who did something with it."

A lump forms in my throat, and I swallow over it, wondering how Kingston could see me so clearly without knowing me at all. "That is a sweet thing to say."

"It's just the truth. In a way, I did the same thing."

I hate that my gut-instinct is to dismiss Kingston's words because of his wealth and fame. But I am having trouble believing he's ever had to run away from who he was. Then I remember what he told me earlier today about getting the crap beat out of him by his father, and my stomach rolls in on itself. I feel shame for my initial thoughts. I feel heartbreak for all the things that brought Kingston pain. "How so?" As soon as I ask the question, I realize I might already know the answer. "By going against your father's wishes, even though there were consequences?"

"Yeah, that about sums it up." He clears his throat. "Do you ever feel guilty for leaving? I mean, even though you're happier now and you knew it was for the best? Does your past ever eat away at you like no matter what you do right, you can never escape it?"

My heart is beating fast as I answer each of his questions in my head. "Yes." I didn't mean for the word to come out as a whisper, but it's out now, and I know he heard it.

"I guess that's normal then. I've thought a lot about what my life would be like if I hadn't chosen football and followed in my father's footsteps. I can't picture myself in a high-rise, wearing a suit every day, and staring at a computer. I mean, good job to those who are meant for that sort of thing. I just can't picture that being me."

I smile. "For what it's worth, neither can I."

"You didn't say much about your dad," Kingston says next. "What was he like?"

My chest swells with emotion as I think about the one person in my life who left me with fond memories. "He was great," I say sadly. "He raised me as a single dad most of his life, and we had a great relationship."

"Can I ask how he died?"

The sensitive tone that comes with his question isn't lost on me. "One of his patients didn't make it. There was a malpractice lawsuit and everything. My father was suspended throughout all of it, but the first day he got back to work after winning the case, the woman's husband showed up at the hospital with a gun."

"No," Kingston whispers.

Tears are already spilling down my cheeks. I've never told this story without shedding tears and my chest feeling like a million bricks are piled on it. "'A life for a life,' the man said before he pulled the trigger. All it took was one bullet, and my dad was gone."

"Silver, I'm—"

He's sorry. I know he's sorry. Everyone who hears the horrible story is sorry. I don't need to hear it. He doesn't need to say it.

And he doesn't. "What was he like?"

I smile, just thinking about my dad's deep chuckle and wide grin that seemed to always be on display when we were together. "Happy. You hear a lot of work-life-balance stories, especially with people in his profession, but I never saw him struggle with it. Sure, he was tired at times, and he'd get called away when I didn't want him to go, but he always made special time for me. We'd go camping a lot, actually. It was one of my favorite things we ever did. We would barely bring anything with us. We'd just set up our tent, make a campfire, and sing silly songs the whole night until we finally passed out."

Kingston laughs lightly. "I would have killed to have a relationship like that with my dad."

I nod, knowing his words should make me happy to have had that, and while I am, any time I think about my life before he left this world, sadness fills me like an ache I can't mend. "Yeah, well, that was a long time ago."

A sigh floats over the line. "But look at you now. A successful nurse at a beautiful camp."

I laugh. "Did you just call Camp Dakota beautiful?"

I imagine his toothy smile in response to my question. "I suppose I did."

My chest flutters, and I don't know why. It's not like he

just complimented me, but it makes me happy that he's changed his tune, even in the slightest, about the camp. "This place is growing on you, huh?"

He groans like I just caught him in an admission he didn't mean to speak aloud. "I'll admit there's a charm to this place that I didn't see quite at first. But I'd still choose my mattress over this lumpy one."

My teeth bite down into my lip again, and I realize that I've been doing that often, like hiding my smile over the phone will hide the fact that Kingston Scott has an unwarranted effect on me. "I think you'll live." A yawn catches me midsentence, and I take it as a cue. "Speaking of mattre—"

"Don't go yet." He starts his plea before I've even finished my sentence. "I'm not tired yet, and I don't like to be left alone with my thoughts. There are too many of them."

Heat warms my chest. I'm flattered by the fact that it's me he wants to spend his time with, even if it is just over the phone. "What would you be doing if you were home?"

A beat of silence stretches between us. "You really want to know?"

The way he asks it makes me want to take back my question. "I'm sure your life is filled with constant activities."

"Constant," he repeats. "But I think of them more like distractions. I'm always doing something. Always working. If I'm not working, I'm training for work. If I'm not in the gym, I'm partying, or—"

He stops himself, and I'm grateful for the omission, even though I'm sure he was about to mention women.

"You should try to be still once in a while."

"And you should try to live a little."

We both laugh. "I guess we're both missing something, huh?"

"Yeah," he says gently, his deep voice vibrating with the single syllable. "Each other."

He's teasing. Kingston is always teasing. He's the biggest flirt I know and an asshole flirt at that, and it will take these constant internal reminders for me to keep from falling under his spell. I don't want to be another Vicky. Still, my stomach flips, my heart quickens, and for a glimmer of a second, I wonder what it would be like to be with Kingston Scott. I can't imagine it would be like any other relationship I've been in, not that I've been in many.

The truth is, I can't imagine it. I can't imagine what his active nature would do to my constant calm other than disrupt and destroy it completely. And with the ticking time bomb that is my father's inheritance weighing me down, I have enough to worry about as it is.

"There's a yoga class in the morning. You should go," I tell him.

"Will you be there?"

"I'm there every Tuesday morning at five thirty, promptly."

"What?" He practically shouts it, causing me to laugh. "Five thirty? Are you crazy, woman?"

"Hence why I'm hanging up with you. I'm going to sleep."

"Wait, no—"

"Goodnight, Kingston."

And with the click of the line, I fight the smile that burns in my cheeks and tug the comforter up to my chin. Sleep has never been a problem for me. I can nap at any time during the day. I can fall asleep within the minute I place my head on the pillow. But tonight, with thoughts of Kingston circling in my mind, I know even if I do slip into a deep slumber, he'll still fill my thoughts.

# WAXING GIBBOUS MOON

"SHOOT FOR THE MOON. EVEN IF YOU MISS, YOU'LL LAND AMONG THE STARS." — LES BROWN

## CHAPTER 15

# A NEW HOME

### SYLVIA, 8 YEARS AGO

*S*ilver Livingston.

It takes me a second to realize that the fat black ink on the white cardboard sign being held by an older brunette man is for me. I imagine this new identity of mine will take some getting used to. According to Harvey's instructions, the Bexleys know not to ask questions. In whatever private deal made with them to take me in, they agreed to the terms. They'll give me a job and a roof over my head, ask no questions, and promise not to share what little they do know with anyone.

I take a few timid steps toward the man who already has his sparkling, smiley eyes on me. He looks friendly enough, with his skin crinkling around his eyes, a thick beard shaping his face, and an easy-going stance. Still, fear terrorizes every bone and muscle in my body with every step I take toward him.

"Hello, you must be Silver." The man lowers the sign and reaches his hand out to mine.

I stare back at it, debating whether or not to accept a

141

stranger's handshake. I don't know him or anything about him other than that he owns a camp.

As if understanding my hesitation, the man lowers his hand and softens his smile. "I'm Andrew Bexley. I hear you love kids and have a great work ethic. We could sure use someone like you around my camp."

I blink back at him, seeing right through his attempt at making me feel like this is my choice and that I'm not running away from something big. He ignores my blank stare and keeps talking.

"There are plenty of jobs to choose from at Camp Dakota. We've got a barn for ridin', if you're into that. Or we can teach you if you don't know how. We've got a pool and a lake if you want to lifeguard. Or if you'd rather work in an office, we've got a main office with plenty to do. But since you like kids, maybe you'd be interested in one of the camp counselor positions." He laughs, sensing the awkwardness that comes with my lack of contribution to the conversation. "Or maybe you can try a little bit of everything to see what makes you most happy. How about that?"

This time, Andrew Bexley's jovial smile cracks me some. My father always said I had a rare ability to sense people, and I'm certain that the man standing in front of me now is one of the good ones.

"That sounds good, sir." My heart squeezes when I hear the sound of my voice. Before my life turned into a nightmare, I was bold and energetic. I spoke with confidence and drive. Now, all I hear is a girl who's got nothing left.

I fight against the tears that want to spill down my cheeks. It's a surprise I have any left.

"Please," the man says with affection in his tone. "Call me Andrew."

I nod, bow my head with my eyes pointed at the ground, and shift the heavy bag hanging over my shoulder.

"I'm going to aim to guess you're hungry. Is that right?"

My stomach roars in response to his question. "Yes, sir. I am hungry."

Andrew chuckles. "I guess the name thing will take some time. That's okay. I promise in no time, you'll realize we're all just one big family at camp. No formalities allowed."

While my eyes are still turned down, I realize I subconsciously pulled up the sleeves to my sweatshirt, revealing the yellowing bruises up my arms. I tug them down, my heart beating fast, then glance back up at Andrew. His eyes lift to mine quickly, but not quickly enough. He saw the bruises, and I saw the flash of pity in his eyes. What must he think of me?

That's the first moment guilt started to sink its way through me. It didn't take much. Just the knowledge that I'm now this man's responsibility, even if my new identification lies and tells the world I'm a year older. I'm his to employ, to give shelter, and to keep fed.

I can't believe all this is happening. Lately, my life has felt like one big circus, thanks to Lucinda. Now, I can never go back. Just the idea of that adds to the gaping hole caused by my father's death.

Andrew gently takes my bag from my shoulder before I can object. "C'mon," he says, taking a step toward the parking lot and completely ignoring the bruises. "I know a good burger joint. We'll make a pitstop there, and then we'll head home."

*Home.* Such an eerie word. I can't imagine ever feeling at home again.

## CHAPTER 16

# HUMBLE FLAMINGO

## KINGSTON

Silver is worse than a drug. She's the very essence of a high I never knew to crave. I haven't even consumed her yet, and I'm fucking gone off every thought of her, drunk off the sight of her, and wasted from the mere sound of her voice.

She's stretched out on her green yoga mat with her feet pulled into her center, her knees bouncing softly on either side of her. She lowers her chest slowly toward her feet. The moment I spot her there, I know I made the right decision to set my alarm for five in the morning. The instant my alarm went off, I didn't even question my actions. I just got up, showered myself awake, and threw on clothes before walking to the other side of camp.

I take the spot beside her, surprised to find that the class is filling up quickly. She doesn't see me yet, though, so I try to match her stretches, not even mastering it at fifty percent. As I watch her, I can't help but notice how calm she appears. Her breathing seems deep and even. Her eyes are closed, expression relaxed. And when she starts to do a slow head roll, I let my gaze slip down to take in what she's wearing. Her leggings are dark gray, her racerback sports bra is a light pink, her feet are bare, and her face is clean of makeup. I don't think I've ever seen a sexier version of her.

"What is this?" a laughing voice booms. I turn to find Hope with a full-on grin, staring right at me as she walks toward us. "The football god does yoga too? I can't wait to see this."

Matching Hope's grin, I throw my arms out wide and shrug. "Figured I'd give it a try. Someone told me I needed to practice being still." I turn to find Silver's wide gray eyes on me. "Hey there, princess. Thanks for the invite."

Her entire face darkens in color before she shakes her head like she's forcing herself to snap back to reality. "You're not seriously here right now."

Chuckling, I lean back on my palms. "What? You didn't think I would come?"

Her mouth falls open. "No. I didn't expect you to actually come. It was a joke, Kingston. I—"

She's speechless, which only widens my smile. "All that yapping you did last night, and you think I didn't listen? I'll give yoga a try for you. And then you'll go on an adventure with me. It's an even trade."

Poor Silver. Her expression is one of utter confusion, and if the yoga instructor hadn't just turned on the music to start class, I would burst out with a laugh.

Silver leans toward me, ignoring Hope, who is smiling like a Cheshire cat at us both. "We didn't make any sort of deal," she hisses. "I just made a suggestion to you—so you'd chill out a little bit."

I lean in, too, meeting her halfway. "And I made a suggestion to you—to live a little. Don't even try to deny me of this one thing after I woke my ass up at five a.m. for you."

"For me?" If a whisper could squeal, she just did. "I didn't force you to come here."

"I know, but I wanted to." For a brief moment, I let my smile fall. "I liked our conversation last night. And I care about what you say. So I'm here."

With my admission, her hard expression slips into surprise. "You are impossible."

"Impossible to say no to?"

She sighs then follows it up with a silent laugh that rocks her body. "Something like that."

"So, then it's a deal."

She rolls her eyes before letting out a breath. "Fine, Kingston. You win. But only if you stay for the entire class."

I shrug as if it's nothing. I've been through the most intense physical trainings imaginable. There's no way yoga could be that hard.

)•●●๑4(

"What the hell was that?" I yell as soon as Hope, Silver, and I are walking out of yoga. Well, *they* are walking. I'm doing something more like a limp-strut. Hope and Silver burst into a fit of giggles.

"I have to give it to you," Hope says, smacking me on the back. "You tried the whole time. And, man, your humble flamingo was the best thing I've seen in... well, ever."

Hope and Silver erupt into more laughter while my glare is pointed at Silver. "You could have told me it was the advanced class."

Silver's eyes widen with her giant smile. "But that would have taken all the fun out of it."

I limp dramatically for her to see. "You realize I'm a professional athlete? I get paid to be in top-notch physical shape. You could have broken me."

Silver's hand moves to my back, a touch that surprises me. "We both know you're not an easy man to break, Kingston Scott. I think you're going to be okay."

I hold Silver's gaze for a long moment before responding. "Well, if anyone has the power to break me, it will be you, Silver Livingston. Mark my words. But I've always appreciated a good challenge."

Silver blushes before bowing her head then looking at Hope, who's got her eyes glued on us, yet again. "On that note," Hope says with a wide-eyed smile. "I'm heading to breakfast. You two coming?"

Silver shakes her head while I say, "Yes."

When I look at Silver curiously, she gives me an apologetic shrug. "I don't usually eat breakfast. I'll steal something from the staff kitchen later. I'm going to head to the office before I need to start setting up."

She takes off before either of us can utter a proper goodbye, then I'm walking beside Hope on our way to the cafeteria.

"You like Silver," Hope says in a playful sing-song. "You really like her."

"What's it to you?" I tease back.

Hope purses her lips. "Well, I happen to be Silver's best friend, who also happens to approve of this little flirtatious thing you two have going on."

I don't know why I'm so surprised to hear Hope give her blessing. Perhaps if anyone would want me to stay away from Silver, it would be Hope. "You do?"

Hope nods. "I do. Except—"

I groan. "I knew that was coming."

"Except, I really hope if you choose to pursue my best friend that you do so without also pursuing anyone else."

*Ahh.* It all clicks together in my brain. "I'm not interested in anyone else."

Someone calls my name from across the open grass, interrupting our conversation. I look up and see Vicky grinning and waving at me from just outside the cafeteria. "Jesus," I mutter under my breath before catching Hope's knowing stare.

"You sure about that?"

With an exasperated sigh, I shake my head. "I am not interested in Vicky. Trust me."

"All right." Hope throws her hands up in defeat. "I'm not the one you need to convince."

"And how am I supposed to convince Silver of that? I've already told her."

"Silver is more of an actions-speak-louder-than-words type of girl."

I should have guessed that one. "Okay, then tell me what she usually grabs from the staff room after breakfast, and I'll get started."

Hope grins. "She's definitely a muffin girl. Normally bran or blueberry. But I think her favorite is chocolate, though she'd never say so out loud."

Knowing Hope is on my side is like an explosion in my chest. I kneel and swoop her up to swing her around in a hug. "I owe you," I tell her as I run off.

"I'll remember that!" she yells back.

# CHAPTER 17

## A LITTLE BIT WHOLE

### SILVER

I see the chocolate muffin before I see who is holding it. My stomach is growling, and it practically roars when I get a whiff of the fresh bakery item. Then I see the man who is offering it, his long arm extending it toward me, a cocky smile on his face. He knows it's my favorite, which means Hope probably told him.

"You didn't have to do that." I can feel my cheeks heat as I say the words. Obviously, he didn't have to, but he wanted to.

"I didn't want you to eat alone. Besides..." He looks around the front office where he found me when he walked in. "You said you had to set up for Dr. Blaine. Figured you could use a hand."

I take the muffin from him, praying he can't sense the shock my heart is absorbing at this very second. "Thank you. That's either very thoughtful of you, or calculated."

His smile slips into a smirk before he props an elbow on the front counter and leans into it. "Calculated how?"

"You always seem to find a way to get me alone with you."

His good-natured chuckle is almost as surprising as his

gesture. "Well, then I guess you would be right on both accounts. It was thoughtful and calculated. Do you need a hand or not?"

"Need?" I tease. "No. Want? Yes, please."

He lets out an exaggerated breath with a roll of his eyes. "Thank you, Jesus. Where do we start?"

I point at the large folded-up tent in the corner of the room. "If you grab that, I'll take the hand truck."

"Deal."

We work in silence at first, focusing on the heavy lifting then on setting up the tent. We are on our way back to the office for our second load when Kingston says, "So, I stayed through yoga. A deal's a deal."

I've already had the internal argument with myself about our little deal from this morning. I knew Kingston would come to collect, and I won't back out. Not after all he put himself through, quite hilariously, might I add. I'll never get the sight of him trying unsuccessfully to twist himself into a million different pretzels out of my mind, not even if I wanted to. So I'm going to give him this one thing without a fight.

"So, what'll it be? Are you going to teach me how to throw a football or something?"

He shrugs. "If you want, but that wasn't what I was thinking."

I narrow my lids at him, waiting for the punchline.

"Meet me at the dock tonight."

"What?" I ask with a laugh. "You're going to take me swimming? We've already done that."

He steps an inch closer to me and playfully nudges my side. "No, sassy one. Just meet me at the dock. It will be a surprise."

I don't know if I like the sound of anything Kingston

wants to surprise me with, but I bite my tongue this time, deciding to play along. "Okay. I'll be there."

And it's a done deal. Kingston helps me with the next two loads, keeping his cocky quips to a minimum. By the time we're done setting up, Dr. Blaine is making his way over to us.

"I was trying to get here earlier to help. You're a lifesaver, Silver." Dr. Blaine walks right up to me and smiles, completely ignoring Kingston, who's standing beside me.

"Oh, it's no problem. Thankfully, I had some help." I sneak a look at Kingston, who has his eyes narrowed on Dr. Blaine.

"Ah, yes, I remember you. How is the young boy doing today?"

"Haven't seen him yet," Kingston says, his tone cold and emotionless. "I'll bring him over today so you can check him out."

"Wonderful."

The entire exchange between the men is so awkward, I can feel my insides trying to squirm away from where I'm standing. Luckily, the discomfort doesn't last long, because kids and coaches start to make their way onto the field.

"I better get out there," Kingston says backing away, his gaze lingering on me. After a second of our eye-lock, I swear my insides are flipping pancakes in my stomach. Then a smile finds his lips, and he leaves me with a wink.

"That was nice of your boyfriend to help you out." Dr. Blaine doesn't ask a question, but I can sense there's one there.

Part of me wants to lie by omission to let him think whatever is on his mind. But the other part of me, the part that thinks I'm a fool to even play with that notion, is the one that wins. "Kingston isn't my boyfriend. He's just—" I have no idea what to say. No idea what he is to me or even what's going on between us. So I say the safest thing that comes to mind. "A friend."

"Good to know," he says. "Shall we get to work?"

I don't miss the satisfaction that comes with Dr. Blaine's words. It makes me more uncomfortable than the exchange between both men earlier. "Yes, of course."

)‌♦●●◑I(

"My offer still stands. I'd love to take you out for a drink if you can sneak away."

Dr. Blaine and his persistence are a newer development that started after Kingston paid a visit to our tent with Lincoln and proceeded to flirt blatantly with me the entire time, tugging my hair and leaning in to whisper compliments about my eyes or my scent. I knew what he was doing, but it didn't stop the flush in my cheeks from rising as time went on.

I give Dr. Blaine my best sympathetic frown and shake my head. "I'm so sorry. I already have plans tonight. Should I have everything set up for you in the morning?"

He gives a quick shake of his head. "No, that's okay. I'll be here to help you. See you tomorrow, then?"

I push out a smile and nod. "Tomorrow it is."

As soon as he's out of sight, I lock up behind myself and rush to my cabin to change. I throw on my red swimsuit, a tattered pair of jean shorts, a pale-blue tank top, and white sandals, then I head down the dirt trail to the dock.

Kingston is already there when I hit the small clearing leading to the water. He's sitting in a canoe at the end of the dock, a cheesy grin plastered to his face. "Your chariot awaits."

With every step closer I take, there's a buzzing in my chest that grows louder, faster, and more intense. He isn't just waiting in a canoe. The canoe is filled with all the blankets and pillows I lent him that first day he arrived, and I recognize the takeout boxes from the kitchen.

"Why does this look like a date?"

He doesn't even flinch. "It's an adventure, just as promised."

"I thought we were doing something we've never done before." I laugh, trying not to expose my nerves as they shoot off in my body. "I've ridden in a canoe before, Kingston."

His jaw gapes with mock shock. "But you haven't been in one with me."

He's got me there. Giving up my weak battle, I walk the rest of the way to him. I drop into the canoe, and as soon as I'm settled in across from him, he rows us away from the shoreline, out of the small inlet, and away from Camp Dakota completely.

"It's beautiful here." Those are the first words out of his mouth since he started rowing, and they're probably the sincerest I've ever heard him speak.

He's barely rowing at all now, and we're moving slowly around the Orcas Island coast.

"Yeah," I say, looking out at the shoreline. "It didn't take me long to fall in love with this place. In a way, it felt like I was always meant to be here."

"I can see that." He settles his gaze on me. "You fit here like one does when they grow up somewhere. It just embodies you." He doesn't realize it, but he's just complimented me in the best way.

"It took me a long time to feel like I fit in here. After my dad died, it was kind of hard to accept that I'd fit in anywhere, you know?"

Kingston tears his eyes from mine and nods. "Yeah, I get that. I've lived in Seattle for three years, and I still don't have that feeling. I figured with me playing pro ball, making enough money to do whatever the hell I wanted, and living in a city like that, I would finally grow some roots, you know?"

"Why do you think you haven't?"

He shrugs, his eyes still set on the horizon. "It's all the same shit. The money didn't change anything. The city only made the partying easier. And playing ball—it's always been my end goal, so I can't complain much. Maybe I'm not meant to ever feel settled. Maybe that's what makes me so hard."

His lip curls up at the corner, and a flutter erupts at my stomach as I take in just how drop-dead gorgeous Kingston Scott is. It's like he's made of dreams and romance books. If he weren't sitting with me right now, I wouldn't believe he's real.

"Where did you grow up?"

"Portland," he says smoothly. "And you?"

I should have anticipated the question, but I've been so focused on Kingston and all he's revealing that I didn't prepare myself. I stumble over my thoughts, until he finds my eyes from across the small boat.

"Before you moved here, where did you grow up?"

I swallow over the crashing of my heart against my ribs. "Phoenix."

I'm not telling him anything more than I would tell Hope or the Bexleys, but for some reason, the admission to Kingston feels big. He's practically a stranger. I can barely stand the guy, yet here I am, listening to him pour his heart out while I feel the tug to do the same.

"Wow," he says, his evergreen eyes sparkling in the sun. "You came a long way from home."

"Like I said, it didn't feel like home there anymore."

"And you ended up here by fate."

I sip in a shallow breath, surprised by how much he remembers from our conversation the night before. "I did."

He assesses me with his gaze then nods. "Then so did I."

I bite down on my lip, seeing the light at the end of the tunnel so I can turn the questions back on him. "You never did tell me why you came here. You said you didn't volunteer to be here. I got the impression you were forced."

There's another tug of his upper lip, but this time, it doesn't result in a smile. It's more like annoyance. "It's not important."

"It is to me." I tilt my head, waiting for him to register my seriousness. "I don't think there's anything you can say to me that will make me feel differently about you, if that's what you're afraid of." I see the rise of his brows and cut him off with a laugh. "My opinion of you is already pretty low."

He rolls his eyes before letting out a laugh. "See? That's exactly why I don't want to tell you. I'm trying to get you to like me, not despise me more."

I shove away the effects of his flattering words and try again. "Well, you're not going to win me over with lies."

He growls before finally shaking his head, signaling that he's given up the fight. "Fine. But I'm not turning this boat around, no matter how mad you get at me."

Now it's my turn to roll my eyes. "Don't worry. I can swim." He cuts me with a look so sharp, I have to laugh. "Out with it, Kingston."

"To be honest, I don't know exactly why I'm here. I'm supposed to be figuring that out. Zach thought it would be good for me after—" He peers back at me with a worried expression before sighing. "After Coach bailed me out of jail."

My jaw drops. "Jail? What did you do?"

"Public intoxication. I got thrown out of a bar, and my friends who I'd gone there with were nowhere to be found. I don't know what happened that led to me getting arrested exactly. I woke up behind bars, Coach picked me up, and now I'm here."

"Why did you get thrown out of the bar?"

His wince is almost loud enough to hear. "Pissed off a bouncer, I guess. Like I said, Silver, I don't remember much. But it was bad enough to get sentenced to this place."

"This place is not that bad." I smile back at him to show him I'm not at all affected by his story. Sure, I was a little thrown, but it's no mystery that Kingston has his demons. We all have them.

His expression calms over the next few seconds as he rows us under a bridge. "If it weren't for you, I probably would have left by now." His words are quiet, but I don't miss a single syllable.

"Because I brought you blankets and pillows."

His cheeks lift. "Maybe. But I also couldn't leave without getting to know the woman who was set on hating me so much."

An inferno of heat blasts through my body, rising up my neck and into my cheeks. He's impossible to be around without feeling a range of emotions I can't seem to make sense of. Do I like him? Do I hate him? Do I want to get to know him? Do I want him to go away? Is he hot? Is he annoying? Is he cocky? Is he charming? He seems to be all of those things, but the more time I spend with him, the more I realize that's all the armor he wears to hide what's truly inside.

A short while later, as we're coasting through Moran National State Park, Kingston unpacks the dinner he grabbed us from the kitchen—two bottled waters, roast beef sandwiches, and a couple containers of steamed veggies. We pick at our food while he tells me about the vast difference between high school sports, college sports, and the NFL.

I can't remember ever watching a football game in my entire life, so it's all fascinating to me. The impact of the sport, the training involved to keep in tip-top shape and outperform the thousands of hopefuls who would kill to take Kingston's position, all sounds so intense.

He's rowing back toward camp when he says, "Look at that." He pauses midrow and nods, gesturing for me to look to my right, so I do.

The sun is setting over the horizon, painting a canvas of pink and purple swirls around it. "Oh, wow," I gush. "That's so beautiful."

Kingston rests the paddle on his knees, and together, we watch in silence as the sun dips below the horizon. Not long after the sun slips from our view, the nightlife comes alive.

We're back in the inlet of camp when disappointment fills me. I don't want our canoe trip to end. Kingston seems to have the same thoughts, because as soon as we get to our dock, he ties a long rope to an anchor on the dock and pushes us back out into the middle of the inlet.

"What are you doing?" I laugh.

"We're not done yet." His eyes brighten with his smile as he scoots onto the blankets set out in the middle of the canoe. He props a couple pillows behind him then lies down, patting the spot beside him. "Come here."

Panic sets in, causing me to freeze in my seat. "Kingston, I can't—"

Even from here, I can see his frown. "Bullshit."

"Well, I shouldn't."

"That's bullshit too. You should, and you will."

He pats the spot again as I have another internal debate in my head. This time, my heart feels like it's joined the battle. My head loses, my heart wins, and I sink down to lie beside Kingston as the night sky darkens.

Our sides are pressed together from our shoulders to our legs, but Kingston doesn't make a move to touch me other than that. We stare up at the moon, which hangs directly above our heads, and let the silence settle around us. It's like we both needed this night. The stillness, the quiet, with nothing but water wrapping around us. At least to me, it's been a reminder of the big world that lives and breathes out there, like it's waiting for me to come home and deal with my past, once and for all. Do I make myself vulnerable, yet again, and claim my trust fund? Or do I let it all go and let Lucinda win the battle for my inheritance? She wouldn't be a threat anymore since she would have what she's always wanted. And I would be free. Truly free. Not the kind of freedom I felt when I left home that night to seek refuge. Back then, I was running to survive. But now, as I stare up at the great big moon—all I want to do is live.

"What are you thinking about?" Kingston's low voice brings a chill with it.

I can't tell him what I'm really thinking, but I can give him something. "I was just remembering when I was a kid, camping out with my father. We'd always end the night like this, with our eyes on the sky, studying the stars and the moon like it held the answer key to everything."

"Maybe it does."

My heart skips at Kingston's optimism. "Maybe. My dad sure would have liked to believe that."

"What phase of your life would he say you're in now?"

I do a double-take, failing to hide my shock at Kingston's memory of our conversation the other night. I don't need to think about his question long. I follow the cycle of the moon, like someone would a calendar. "Waxing gibbous." I bite down on my lip, knowing Kingston will find it funny.

Sure enough, Kingston's chuckle dances through the air. "You're going to need to elaborate on that one."

Releasing my lip, I smile. "*Waxing* just means that it's getting bigger, at least it appears that way. Really, the sunlit part of the moon becomes more visible. And *gibbous* refers to the shape."

"Okay, but what does all that mean to you?"

The fact that he cares so much is both flattering and unnerving. No one has ever asked me so many questions about my strange obsession with the moon before. "It's just a reminder for me that things don't always work out the way we expect for them to. And with every new phase, our situations change, we change, and it's important to let go of standards we held ourselves to at a time when our lives were different. Sometimes, we just need to reevaluate our priorities, you know?"

A beat of silence passes between us, along with a sense of calm. "I like that perspective," he says. "I guess the same goes for the standards others hold us to and prioritizing how much we care about those things too."

My heart skips a beat, and I nod. "I would agree." I turn back to face the sky. "The beautiful thing about the moon is that it's always there, always present. It's the one thing I've always been able to count on to bring me back to center. It grounds me, even when my world feels like it's falling to pieces around me. I don't know. Some people were brought up with religion as their guide. I was brought up with the moon."

I've never said those words aloud to anyone ever, and I nearly can't believe they just left my mouth. I almost expect

Kingston to laugh or to question me further, but his silence is filled with acceptance.

In my peripheral, I see Kingston turn to look at me. His eyes are focused on me for a long time before he speaks. "You said there were different sides to people, and the sides that we see are the ones they want us to see, because everyone's hiding something."

I nod, wondering what he's getting at.

"Well," he teases. "What about you?"

I turn to meet his gaze. "What do you mean?"

His gaze flickers over my face, down my neck, and back up to grip me with his eyes. "What are you hiding, Silver Livingston? Besides your disdain for me, that is."

I laugh to cover my nerves. "I don't have disdain for you."

"Really? Because sometimes, I swear you look at me like I'm a piece of garbage."

His tone is playful, but it doesn't stop feelings of horror from shaking through me. "No, I don't."

"Yes, you do."

"Don't say that. I do not look at you like you're garbage. I look at you like—" I cut myself off.

"How?" he presses.

"I look at you in a way I shouldn't, all right?" My heart is beating so fast, I can feel it in my throat.

"How is that?"

I let out a laugh, feeling ridiculous at the thoughts that are slipping past my mouth like I've completely lost my filter. There's no way I can tell him that I look at him in a way that's sinful and entirely too wrong for me to speak aloud. "If you think I'm looking at you with disdain, then you're wrong. I *hate* the way I look at you, Kingston. I *hate* the way I see past your crude arrogance. And I *hate* how you continue to prove me wrong about you, over and over again. But I don't hate *you*."

Kingston's breaths are heavier, his chest puffing out so far, it's almost distracting me from the way he turns onto his shoulder so that he's hovering over me. Then I'm so distracted by the movement that I almost miss the fact that he's lowering his head until his lips are a breath away from mine.

"Silver," he whispers.

My eyes squeeze shut, and I try to suck in a breath, but even drawing the slightest sip of air feels like the hardest job in the world. "Mmhm." It's barely a croak of a word as it enters the space between us.

His hand wraps around my waist as his body inches closer to mine. "You probably shouldn't have said that."

I haven't even had time to process his words before his mouth is on mine. Firm, hungry lips devour me like dinner wasn't enough, like he's finally feeding an addiction he's had for so long. He opens my lips with his, and my head spins while my chest buzzes. Every sensation is a vibrant one. Every nerve that fires off is like a firework illuminating the sky. This isn't the slow and gentle type of kiss I'm used to, the one that tests limits and explores unknown terrain before creeping into the promised land. No. This is the type of kiss that can delve into uncharted depths and jolt a person back to life.

I'm like an amateur dancer trying to keep up with a pro, but his choreography is too intricate for my experience. I'm always half a step behind. He's sucking on my bottom lip, then he's teasing the inside of my mouth with his tongue. He's pushing his lips to both of mine, then he's teasing my bottom lip by swiping the length of it.

It's nonstop chaos until I finally fall into rhythm with him. He's still guiding me, his hot mouth on mine, but now I can sense his next move like we've been doing this our entire lives. He sucks my lip into his mouth, and I groan. He dips his tongue between my lips, and I catch it with mine. He pushes both lips to mine, and now it's me taking his bottom lip between mine and sucking it between my teeth until he groans.

For those next few minutes while our mouths move together in perfect synchrony, I feel alive in a way I've never felt before. I feel wanted, needed, and desired in a way I never knew I craved. It's like being lifted out of my skin and hovering over a stranger—a woman consumed by a man she knows can never be hers. But her needs are stronger than her will, so much so that when his meaty fingers work their way beneath her shirt, she doesn't try to stop him.

He searches and searches, his fingers on a mission to find bare skin. I can feel the frustration in his kiss, in the rumble from his chest, when he continues to find my one-piece bathing suit instead. I wish I'd never put it on, because as much as I know this kiss is as far as we should go, I want to feel his touch on every inch of my skin.

A frustrated curse leaves his mouth as his hand slips beneath my shorts. He doesn't bother with the button, but it pops open anyway to make room for his hand. I don't know what comes over me when my legs fall apart, but it allows enough room for his thick finger to continue down until he's barely grazing my slit over my suit.

I stutter through my next breath, not sure how I'm still breathing. The sensation at the slight touch has my heart crashing hard and fast against my ribcage. He slides the same finger through me again, adding more pressure.

"You're so wet. I can feel you through your suit." He groans into my neck while continuing to swipe through me, over and over again. All I want is for him to tear every single piece of fabric from my body so that there's nothing between us, nothing to obstruct him from doing what he wishes.

"You like this, don't you?" He murmurs the words, his honey-soaked voice dripping straight down into my ear.

I don't respond. I'm too afraid to say anything at all. Afraid I'll tell him to stop. Afraid to let him continue. No matter what, I'll lose.

He's not put off by my silence. Instead, he's circling the fabric over my clit while leaving a trail of hot kisses over my shoulder and up my neck, until he's sucking on my earlobe.

"I can make you come, Silver." He says it like it's a dare. "Just like this," he growls while moving his finger faster, quickening the flames that roar in my belly. "And then I'll make you come again with my tongue," he says before darting his tongue out to swipe my neck. "And then, if you're really nice..." He applies the slightest pressure to where he's rubbing me, teasing me with his words. "I'll let you come on my cock."

A shiver shakes through me. His dirty words are more than my mind can digest. No one has ever talked to me like that before. No one has ever made me feel this... ravaged.

"Silver, let me make one thing very clear." His breathy rasp skips like rocks against my neck. "When I have the pleasure of fucking you, I won't hold back the way I'm doing now. Pleasuring you will be like an Olympic sport, where the sound of your orgasm will be my gold fucking medal. And trust me, I won't place in anything other than first."

I gasp just as my core tightens with his next swipe of his finger. I explode against his touch, my orgasm bursting through me and sending convulsions through my body. And for the first time since I can remember, the broken woman inside of me starts to feel a little bit whole.

# CHAPTER 18

# BACK TO THE BARN

## KINGSTON

Almost as soon as Silver cries out from her first orgasm, I'm making plans to give her a second. She's going to have to lose the clothes, though. There's only so much I can do through a layer of spandex. I don't expect her to yank my hand away from her promised land, prohibiting me from attempting another round.

"Stop. We can't." She breathes heavily through her words. I can see her chest heaving while she slowly opens her eyes.

My mouth hangs open as I look down at where my fingers just were, but it's almost impossible to see in the dark. "But we just did. At least, *you* just did. What the fuck, Silver?"

She covers her face with her hands. "I know. I shouldn't have let you—we shouldn't be—and I can't—"

She scrambles to her knees while I wince at the fact that my engorged cock isn't going to get any playtime. "C'mon. I want you so fucking bad. Don't tell me you didn't enjoy that."

"Of course I did," she says, tugging at the rope that's tied to the dock. "Doesn't mean it's right."

"And why is it wrong? Because you think you're supposed

to hate me? Tough shit. I see right through you, you know? You want me just as badly as I want you. You wouldn't have let me get you off if you didn't."

"I shouldn't have let you. It was a mistake."

*She's lying.* I can hear it in her voice. "The fuck it was. You had plenty of time to stop me."

I hate the fact that I can't see those pretty cheeks of hers darken in color like they always do when I start to run my mouth. Usually, I have no problem keeping up with my own snark. I can dish it all day, but something about her retreat grates on my nerves, something other than the sheer disappointment of not getting inside her. It's more than that. It's more than missing out on a great fuck. This is deeper.

The fact that Silver is too good for someone like me doesn't escape me. I've known it from the very first moment I laid eyes on her. She's beautiful, educated, witty, settled... and I'm the complete opposite of all of those things. But even while I knew that already, it didn't truly sink in until this moment right here. Silver Livingston will never be mine. What's worse, I want her to be.

I sit up and run my hands through my hair, begging myself internally to not be a douchebag about this. She pulled away. So what? Silver isn't like anyone I've ever been with before, and that's the precise reason I like her. I can respect that. Can't I?

"I'm sorry, Kingston. Maybe it wasn't a mistake, but... this is all just too fast for me. You're leaving at the end of the week, and I don't do this sort of thing. I don't sleep with men I barely know."

I ignore the fact that she thinks I'm leaving at the end of the week. I have no clue where I stand with Zach and Coach on the subject. I haven't thought much about it in days. Frankly, I'm not so sure I want to leave now.

"Then get to know me."

She lets out a quick laugh while continuing to pull us closer to the dock. "And what's the point in that? We're not a good fit, Kingston. You're this big hot-shot football player, and I'm a camp nurse. Our lives couldn't be more different. If I choose to sleep with someone, it needs to mean something. This"—she gestures between us with her hand—"is just a fling. I don't do flings. If that's what you want, then…"

"Then what?" I push her to say the words I know will send me over the edge. If she's going to reject me, then I might as well be pissed off at her to make it easier.

She doesn't answer me right away. She pulls herself onto the dock, where she's illuminated under a lamppost. I can see the glimmer of fear in her eyes, though she probably wishes it were hidden.

"Then you should go back to the barn with Vicky."

With that verbal slap in the face, she takes two steps backward then tears her gaze away to turn around and walk away. I don't try to stop her. I don't try to correct her. She's right. It would just be a fling between us, no matter how long I decided to stay at camp. But none of that matters. It doesn't matter that her words were a clear attempt at pushing me away because she doesn't trust herself to do it in any other way. What matters is the fact that I'm so fucking pissed off that I'm actually considering doing exactly what she suggests.

)✶●●●)◀(

*Knock. Knock. Knock.*

I groan and turn, but my still sleepy muscles ache at the slightest movement. I slept like shit. What's new? This camp is as good as haunted in my opinion, and my desire to call for a ride to take my ass out of here is growing stronger with every waking second. After Silver took off, I gave myself a self-guided tour around camp, raided the staff lounge until I dug up a half-gone bottle of whiskey, and finished it off. Somehow, while my mind was nothing but a welcomed blur, I made it back to my cabin and into my bed.

The knocking turns to banging, then I hear Zach's booming voice on the other side of the door. "Wake up, King, before I break this door down."

"Okay, Jesus Christ. One fucking minute." I yank the single comforter away and curse again at the fact that I'm completely naked. I tug on the nearest pair of shorts lying on my floor and yank open the cabin door. "Am I late?"

Zach's hard expression is one of the angriest I've ever seen on him. Sure, he gets revved up at games and sometimes at practice like the rest of us, but this isn't either of those things. We're at a fucking football camp, for heaven's sakes. It's not like we're about to play in the Super Bowl.

"I've been covering for you for the past two hours, King. What the hell are you doing? This isn't a vacation. You've got a responsibility to those kids. You can't just not show up for them. That isn't how your time here is going to go. Got it?"

Zach isn't saying anything cruel. Yeah, he's angrier than a pack of starved wolves, but his words hit me in the chest in a way I'm not expecting. "Got it," I murmur, not wanting him to see just how bruised my ego is after his verbal lashing.

He gives me a final cutting look then slams the door behind him.

I feel like shit, not just physically. I feel like the fuckup I have always known I am. I hate disappointing people, yet I continue to do just that. And it's the people I care about the most who seem to get hurt the most. A slideshow of ex-girl-friends, past coaches, my father, and my mother filter through my subconscious while I rush to put on clothes and brush my teeth. The last image I see is Silver's expression from last night. The one that saw right through my gutter-brained intentions and rushed away from me in the dark.

As disappointed as I was, Silver was right to stop things where she did last night. She deserves better. The best, in fact. It's no surprise that I could never be that for her. She said it best. We would be nothing more than a fling, and she's not that type of girl. While I didn't try to put a label on what we were, I can't argue with her reasoning. One week, one month, it doesn't matter. My intention was to fuck her, not to start a relationship anyway. So all I can do is honor her wishes and stay away.

A sense of deep regret fills me by the time I make it out to my morning squad and take over for Zach. I give them my apologies, but they don't even bat an eye. It's clear Zach covered for me—not just by filling my shoes, but also by giving them whatever excuse he had to. I owe him one.

The kids are full of smiles as they play a game of scrimmage. Dr. Blaine must have cleared Lincoln to join back in, because he's running around out there, looking as good as new and wearing the biggest smile of all.

I don't bother looking in the direction of the medical tent. I'm already reliving Silver's rejection every time her face flashes through my thoughts. The last thing I need is the salt of her interactions with Dr. Blaine rubbing directly onto my open wounds. In fact, I decide to make it a point not to look at Nurse Silver at all for as long as I can stand it.

At lunch, I don't object when Vicky sits across from me with her lunch tray. While I manage to avoid Silver, the death stare coming from Hope is another story. That's a look I can't escape, and it almost pisses me off, considering Silver is the one who walked away from me, not the other way around.

I eat quickly, keeping things extra flirtatious with Vicky to make a point to Silver. In case she's paying attention, she can't complain that I didn't listen to her. After I dispose of my lunch, I decide to head back to the field. So far, I'm winning the internal battle with myself and avoiding so much as a glance at Silver. It's enough that I'm afraid I'm losing before she even has the chance of becoming mine.

That's how the rest of the day goes—trying not to fuck up and somehow succeeding. As soon as practice is over for the day, I head back to my cabin—and that's when I accidentally spot Silver stacking storage boxes on a hand truck. The sight of her packing up all by herself again sends an instant shot of guilt through me. No matter how pissed off I am at her for what she said to me last night, I can't let her lug that shit around on her own.

With begrudging steps, I start toward her. I'm nearing the side of the tent when Dr. Blaine comes running up to her from the other side, a big-ass grin spread wide on his face. "One load down. One more to go."

The sinking in my chest is entirely selfish. I should be happy that he didn't leave her on her own to store everything away again. But I'm not happy. I'm not happy because it's Dr. Blaine Silver is smiling at with appreciation like *he* did *her* a favor. *What a joke.*

I back up so the side of the tent is blocking me from their view. I start to walk away, but at the sound of Dr. Blaine's voice, I pause in my tracks.

"What do you say we grab dinner away from here tonight?

I'm sure the cafeteria has some prime selections, but I know a place just down the road that can top it, guaranteed."

I'm anticipating Silver's objection like I would an opponent missing a pass during a game.

"Guaranteed, huh?" Silver asks, her voice playful and upbeat. "I highly doubt that."

"Tell you what. Why don't you be the judge? We'll go for a quick meal, and then you can make the call."

Silver lets out a breathy laugh. "I don't know. This sounds a lot like a date."

"I'd be lying if I said I didn't want it to be."

Anger flares in my chest, and silence follows. Too much of it. Silver is considering his offer. Meanwhile, I'm gripping one of the tent legs like it's my life support. *There's no way she'll agree to go with that douchebag. I have nothing to worry about.*

"I don't know, Dr. Blaine."

"Call me Matthew. Formalities aren't necessary after hours. And I insist. Unless you're worried you'll make that Kingston fellow jealous. I get the feeling he's interested in you."

The laugh that comes from Silver next might just be more hurtful than the words she spoke to me last night.

"He's not," she says, all too convincingly. "It's not like that with Kingston and me. He's just..."

*Don't say it. Don't say it. Don't you dare say it.*

"A friend."

The devil in me wants to tear straight through this tent cloth and ask Silver to repeat those words to my face. She's a liar. Pure and simple. It will serve me well to remember that while I continue to maintain my distance. It's my only option at this point.

I back away until I can no longer hear their conversation, then I head back to my cabin. I skip dinner in the cafeteria and instead satisfy my hunger with a few snack bars I jacked from the staff room last night. Then I try to succumb to my exhaustion, hoping to catch up on all sleep that was lost the night before.

Tomorrow, I'll do it all over again.

# FULL MOON

"THREE THINGS CANNOT BE LONG HIDDEN:
THE SUN, THE MOON, AND THE TRUTH." —
BUDDHA

## CHAPTER 19

# AVOIDING THE WORLD

### SILVER

He's avoiding me, but I don't think it's just me he's avoiding. For the past two days, I've watched him from afar as he coaches the kids with a little less zest than normal. Then he disappears completely—like it's all just a job and his most important duty is stamping a timecard.

He's not jogging over every five minutes for a refill on his water or tossing jealous glances my way every time Dr. Blaine so much as talks to me. He hasn't called me again or shown up outside my cabin. He hasn't even come back to the cafeteria.

I would be lying to myself if I didn't admit to missing his presence, even his over-the-top antics. But while a part of me misses Kingston Scott, I can't regret my decision to push him away. Not when my heart was starting to latch on the way it was.

To Kingston, I would have been just another notch on his belt—a meaningless fling he would have forgotten the moment he stepped back on that bus. But I knew if we took it any further, he would become so much more to me. Distance is the only answer.

In another two days, Kingston will be back on the bus, on his way to Seattle, and my life here at camp will go on just as it always did before he bulldozed his way into my life. Except, I know that isn't true either. My phone call with Harvey is another haunting reminder of why my life is anything but peaceful and why Kingston was a welcome distraction to the reality I'm about to face. I still have a decision to make, but I'll continue to avoid making it for as long as possible.

"You okay, love?" Hope is eyeing me with concern when I sit down beside her.

I shrug, too annoyed with life to pretend I'm anything but. "Yeah, I'm fine."

She presses her brows together. "Why don't you just talk to him?"

"Who?"

She narrows her lids. "Kingston. Who else would I be talking about?"

"I don't want to talk to him. It's better this way, Hope. He'll be gone in a few days, and I'll never see him again. Can you imagine how hard that would have been if we'd gotten involved?" I'm whispering across the table to her to make sure no one else can hear us.

She purses her lips, not at all convinced. "So what? You act like he did something wrong by getting you off in a canoe. He did you a favor, honey. You should be thanking him with your mouth wrapped around his—"

"Oh my God, shut up." Heat rushes to my cheeks.

"I think you should do him," Hope says with a shrug. "I think you should do him, and then at least when he's gone you'll have quite the memory to remember him by."

"No way," I hiss.

She ignores me. "It's better than always wondering how it

would have been." She pins me with a high-browed stare. "You know you've thought about it."

I look away. "I don't want to talk about this, Hope."

"Fine. Then let's talk about why you're late to dinner *again*. Did that asshole make you pack all his shit for him again?"

"It's fine. It's my job."

I don't have to look up to see Hope's incredulous expression. "No, Silver. Carting a heavy tent and medical equipment all around camp is not at all in your job description."

"But I *am* assigned to help Dr. Blaine since he's taking over most of the examinations. I feel so useless this week. Those kids can only drink so much water, you know?"

"Ugh. It's like he's punishing you because you won't go out with him."

It isn't like I haven't thought the same thing, but it doesn't feel right saying it out loud.

Hope is about to speak again when Anderson sets his tray down beside hers. She looks up at him with the sincerest wide-eyed expression I've ever seen. Despite my shitty last few days, the exchange makes me smile. I love seeing Hope smitten over Anderson. I just wish he would give her the time of day back.

"What are you two talking about?"

I try to give Hope a warning look before she starts in, but it's too late. She's talking for me before he's even sat down. She exaggerates about all the hard labor Dr. Blaine has me doing and how I would be of much better use back in my office, where I can tend to kids who need to get out of the heat, rather than handing out waters all day, every day.

"I'm so sorry, Silver. I didn't know that was how it was."

I shake my head and laugh lightly, trying to cover up how I

really feel. "It's fine. I said I would help the doctor, and I'm happy to."

"But Hope is right," Anderson says, tossing Hope a thankful look. "I'll talk to Doctor Blaine. If he needs assistance on the field, then there are plenty of staff members willing to step in. As Hope said, if kids are in need of additional care, they'll come to see you in your office." He gives me an apologetic smile. "Do you mind toughing it out one more day? I'll get someone to help you with the setup and takedown tomorrow. Then we'll make the change starting next week, when the next set of kids come in."

"That would be great. Thank you, Anderson."

He looks at Hope next. "How about you? How have the events been this week?"

Hope lights up, and I know it's because she's got Anderson's focus. I sit back and listen while my eyes float around the room, hoping to find Kingston among the dining crowd. He's nowhere. That's three nights in a row he's skipped out on dinner, and I hate to think it's all because of me.

Unable to stand wondering anymore, I slip away from Anderson and Hope without saying anything and head straight for Kingston's cabin. He answers the door after one set of knocks, and I gasp when I see him in nothing but a pair of light-blue boxer briefs.

"Oh my—" I really should tear my eyes away, but it's a little hard to manage when the solid wall of muscle standing over a foot taller than me is decorated in nothing but a tight layer of fabric. My heart is crashing through my chest, and all I can think about is what Hope suggested to me earlier.

*You should be thanking him with your mouth wrapped around his—*

"Cock."

It takes me a second to realize it was Kingston who boldly said the word, and that it wasn't all in my mind. I look up, wide-eyed, to find him glaring back at me. "What did you say?"

"I asked why you're ogling my cock, princess. Stare again, and I just might turn you in for sexual harassment."

"What? No. I—" Mortified, I shake my head, all the while regretting my decision to stop by his cabin. I take a step backward. "Never mind, this was a really bad id—"

"Shit," he says, his eyes on something behind me. Then he lunges for my hand and pulls me inside his cabin before closing and locking the door behind me. "That was a close one."

"A close one how?" Confused, I walk to the window and pull the shades apart to peek through them. "There's no one there." I look around to find him grinning. "Really, Kingston?"

He shrugs. "What? Someone could have walked by." His amused eyes transition to stern ones. "Well, are you going to tell me why the hell you're here? Or should we just strip down naked and get to business?"

I ignore the heat creeping up into my cheeks. "I just haven't seen much of you after—" I turn my face, hoping my hair covers my blush. "You know, the canoe."

"I don't know what you're talking about. What about the canoe?"

I fold my arms across my chest and glare back at him. "Don't be an ass. You know what I'm talking about. Things got... awkward, but they don't have to be."

"Nothing has been awkward for me."

"Really?" It's impossible to keep the shock and disappointment from my tone. "But you've been avoiding me."

Kingston shrugs as if nothing ever happened between us. "I've been avoiding the world, Silver. It has nothing to do with you."

"It doesn't?"

He shakes his head slowly. "Not at all. I have a lot of shit on my mind, and I'm just trying to get through my time here without fucking anything else up. My football career is riding on it. Is that all you came by for?"

The somber tone that leaks into his voice grips my heart and squeezes. His honesty, while it's refreshing, seems so uncharacteristic of him. "Yeah, that was all."

"Cool," he says, his expression indifferent. "If you don't mind, I was about to take a shower. Thanks for stopping by." He gestures for me to exit. "Just lock the door before you help yourself out." Then he turns and walks into his bathroom, shutting the door behind him.

I'm still frozen in place a minute later when I hear the spray of the water hitting the shower floor. This isn't how it's supposed to end. Not after how persistent he's been since he arrived. He's just going to brush me off like that? Like we didn't share a connection at all? We may not be a perfect fit for a million different reasons, but that doesn't erase the affection I feel for him. This ending feels so cold, so wrong, so... unfair.

Then again, isn't this what I wanted? For Kingston to leave me alone? For the pressure of falling for him to vanish completely?

Feeling dejected, I look at the cabin door, where I probably should have exited by now. But I'm not sure I want to leave. Our conversation feels unfinished, and who knows how long that will bother me.

I'm still pondering whether to leave or stay when a white paper bag catches my eye. The familiarity of it ties my stomach up in knots. It looks just like the one Marlo asked me to give to King before I accidentally saw the Magnum condoms inside. I was certain he'd wanted them to use with Vicky in the barn.

I creep toward his nightstand, knowing what I'm about to do is all kinds of wrong. An internal voice screams for me not to do it. But nothing can stop me from pulling the contents out of the bag. My curiosity has always gotten the better of me, but not to the point of stooping this low. I've never invaded anyone's privacy before, but I just have to know...

The box appears to be completely intact, and there's still a clear plastic seal across the top. The box hasn't even been opened. So many things click together at once. The fact that he hasn't slept with Vicky is at the top of my list. My words from the last night we were together haunt me. *"Then you should go back to the barn with Vicky."*

But before I can decide what to do about it, the door of the bathroom swings open, revealing Kingston wearing nothing but a towel. While he's more covered than he was when he let me inside, my racing thoughts are stuck on the fact that he's completely naked underneath. I avert my gaze, but nothing can erase the mental image now ingrained in my mind.

"Rifling through my things now?"

My lids fly open at the same moment I realize what he's referring to. I gasp as my fingers loosen around the black box. The condom box drops to the floor. "No." I shake my head. "I'm not. I just—"

"You just what?" he challenges with three long strides toward me. He bends down and picks up the box before standing up to tower over me. "I wasn't good enough for you, so you thought you'd steal from my stash. For what? Got another hot date with the doctor?"

I search his eyes, desperate to find the playful Kingston I met earlier in the week. The man with a boatload of confidence that could never be penetrated. "What are you talking about?"

"I heard you two talking the other night. You rejected me,

and then you went out with him." He shakes his head, and he laughs. "You could have just told me you were into him. I wouldn't have wasted my time."

A wave of emotion knocks me off balance. A lump rises in my throat, and tears build behind my eyes. "I've never been into Dr. Blaine."

"You mean *Matthew*?"

I ignore Kingston's comment to continue making my point, because for some reason, I feel like it's necessary. "It's not like that, and I don't know what you heard, but you're reading too much into it. He asked me out, but I didn't go." I laugh, but it feels like a cry shaking out of me. "He was so pissed off I turned him down that he's been leaving me to tear down and set up alone."

I can feel the moment that Kingston snaps. I can feel the fire that rages through him as he processes my words. "That fucking ass."

I glare back at him. "It's not like you were there to help either. You're just as bad as him." I take a step to walk past Kingston. Both of us are clearly too heated to have a civil conversation. But before I can slide by him, he's wrapping an arm around my waist and slamming me against his body.

He leans down, his nose barely grazing mine. "Let's get one thing straight." His tone is a buzzing reminder of how he made me come alive only two nights before. "It was you who walked away from me."

I can feel myself starting to shake before I even speak my truth. "Yeah, because I didn't want to be another Vicky to you. I'm no one's Vicky. And that's not something you can give me, is it?"

My heart is pounding, and I know it's because I desperately want him to give me the answer that will shut me up and put our sexual tension to rest. Instead, his heated eyes flicker between mine for a few seconds before he answers me by pulling back slightly. "And why are you so certain there even is a Vicky?"

I scrunch my face, the sight of him showing up at my office, with strings of hay still attached to him, on vivid replay in my mind. "You're trying to tell me you didn't go with her to the barn?"

He straightens, creating too much distance between us. "Yes, I went with her to the barn. But I told you I didn't fuck her. Is that what you're so worried about?"

Relief whooshes through me. "I wasn't worried—"

"Bullshit."

Flustered, I stamp my foot and try to straighten my back to gain a little bit of height to eliminate some of the gaps between us. I hate that he has this kind of advantage over me. "I'm not an idiot, Kingston. You came for the condoms that same night you were with her in the barn. I saw the straw on your clothes, and..." More words don't come. My jealousy is already ringing loudly through the air.

"No, you're not an idiot, Silver." He glares down at me. "Which is why it's hard for me to understand why you see this" —he presses the black box to me—"and you still don't get it. You still don't see it."

A few beats pass while I try to figure out what he's getting at. So what? He didn't have sex with Vicky. Fine. It doesn't change the fact that he probably wanted to. "See what? You're so defensive about this. It speaks volumes."

"Does it?" He cocks his head like it's a challenge. "But you don't care, right? You're not worried?"

I'm breathing so heavily, I can barely see straight. "That's right."

He breathes out a laugh and shakes his head. "Cool, then it probably won't matter to you that the night Vicky came on to me, I left her to look for you. When I got to you—I don't know—I guess I panicked a little. I was searching for any excuse I could possibly think of for why I was there. Then I remembered the package Marlo gave to you to give to me. That's why I asked you for the condoms. It had nothing to do with Vicky."

"If you didn't order them for Vicky, then for who?"

His jaw ticks before he rolls his eyes. "Honestly? No one in particular at that moment. Maybe I asked for those condoms for one reason, but that was before I got to know you." He shakes his head again and backs up, his hands rising in silent defense. "Take 'em with you when you leave. Obviously, I won't be needing them anytime soon." He starts to turn around, then he stops to glare at me again. "You know what, Silver? I don't think this is about me at all. You've been convinced I'm some horrible dude from the beginning, and I don't think I've given you any reason to feel that way about me. So maybe you should just admit that you're jealous of Vicky because you want me and you don't want anyone else to have me."

"What?" My mouth falls open with the word.

He chuckles and shakes his head. "I didn't think so." He turns back toward the bathroom and unwraps the towel from his waist. It falls to the floor, giving me an unobstructed view of the most defined, sculpted, delicious ass I've ever seen. I'm so caught up in the formation of it that I almost miss that he's peering back at me over his shoulder. "My eyes are up here, Ms. Livingston." Leaving me with a final glare, he slips the rest of the way inside and closes the door behind him, leaving me to my shameful thoughts once again.

# CHAPTER 20

# ONE LAST HURRAH

## KINGSTON

It's the last day of the first week of football camp, the day of the scrimmage tournament, when the kids' families come to watch the boys play. The games only last fifteen minutes each, and the winning teams move on until the final showdown. Lincoln is currently running the ball, and minus his ankle sprain earlier in the week, he's been the most dedicated player on the field. I love watching him in action. The kid knows how to dodge a tackle—that's for sure. Every time he's handed the ball, he does something with it. Five yards, ten yards, thirty yards, touchdown. He's a star, and it makes me miss playing football as a kid.

I think tournament day is the first day I haven't been obsessed with all things Silver. Her little appearance at my cabin yesterday was enough to let me know that it's not all me. She's into me, but there's not much I can do if she won't even admit that to herself. So I'm going to do what Zach brought me here to do—pump up these kids so that they can go home and have the rest of their lives to be excited about. If there's one thing I wish I'd had in my football adolescence, it's this kind of shit. If I couldn't get the encouragement from my own father, then this would have done just fine.

Everyone is cheering for everyone. Even the losing teams sit in the front row to watch the rest of the games play out. My team, the Warriors, just won the semi-final round, and they're on an unbelievable high from getting to the finals.

"All right, this is it," Zach booms with a clap on my back. "One final game. How are your boys feeling?"

I wave a hand at the huddle they've created themselves to pep talk each other. "They're making it easy. These kids are incredible, and that Lincoln kid..." I blow out a breath and shake my head, telling Zach silently what he probably already knows.

Zach nods. "Kid's got something special, yeah?"

"Hell yeah. And his work ethic is out of this world. Brings me back to those days, man. When pro ball was just a fantasy."

"That's why I love working with these kids. They remind me of what it's like to be in their shoes. Total novices on the field with only dreams and wishes and unfavorable statistics in front of them." He nods to my team in their huddle. "You realize one out of every thousand high school kids might make it to the NFL? There are two hundred and fifty kids out there. It's possible not a single one will make it."

A weight crushes my chest. "Shit," I say under my breath. "Makes me wonder how the hell I ever made it this far."

Zach raises his brows and punches my arm gently with his fist. "We're lucky sons of bitches, that's how. And there's no guarantee it will always be there for us." He points to the field. "We need that passion, that fight, that drive in us always." Then he starts to walk off, leaving me with a final wink. "Good luck, King."

For the first time since I got sentenced to this camp, I start to understand what Coach was getting at that night when he asked me why I wanted to play ball.

*I play ball because I'm good at it. It's the only thing I've ever been good at.*

I remember my response to his question like I'm rewatching our conversation play out in real time. I've forgotten what it's like to fight for a dream the way these kids are fighting for it now. *Jesus, no wonder Coach sent me away.* What happened to my ambition? What happened to my fire? What happened to my need to feel like I'm part of a team? At some point, it became a career, a job, and a paycheck. I lost sight of the rest. It became about me and only me.

The adrenaline rush is a great feeling, the money is spectacular, and the women are a sweet bonus, but I'm not sure any of that is what drove me to start playing the game.

It's not about being the best one in my position, or even the best one out there on the field. It's about the unit, the team, the singular creation that stems from individual talents who complement each other.

My mindset has shifted, and I can feel it in the lightness of my steps, the fullness of my chest, and the passion behind my voice when I sideline the guys before the start of the game.

"Treat every minute of this game like it's the Super Bowl, and you'll never be disappointed in yourselves," I say to them in our last huddle before we line up for kick-off. I stole the line from Zach. He tells our team something similar before every single game.

There's a roar from the crowd when the final game kicks off. Sixteen teams total, three games before this one, and the final two teams are hyped and ready to battle it out.

It's an intense game, but still, my gaze drifts to Silver often. Hope is working the water tent with her today, and not once have I seen her schmoozing it up with Dr. Asshole. I shouldn't care about that, but I do. I also shouldn't care that Silver never went on that date I've been so messed up about. Miscommunications can be the devil, but there wouldn't be any if Silver would stop ignoring what's right in front of her.

If there's anything I learned from our arguments, it's that Silver isn't afraid of me. She's afraid she might actually like me.

But what's the point now when I could be leaving tomorrow after all? I've finally found my stride, and I'm helping these kids achieve greatness. Better yet, I'm giving them hope for their futures. While I don't doubt the statistics Zach spouted off to me are accurate, every single kid out here has a chance of making it. Knowing that and my own journey this week with football and my feelings for Silver, I can't help but feel disappointment at the thought of packing my bags, even though it's what I begged for. It's what I still want. *Isn't it?*

I'm not sure anymore. All I know is that the Warriors are kicking so much ass that we end up winning the tournament. I don't realize Coach Reynolds is there watching the entire thing play out until he appears beside me on the ceremony stage before I accept my coach's trophy.

"Congrats, King." Coach slaps me on the back while trying to hide an amused smile. "From what I hear, you had some ups and downs this week, but all in all, you deserved this win."

I dart a look at Zach, who's giving the crowd one of his famous speeches, then I turn back to Coach. "I can't take much credit. These kids are incredible. Couldn't have done it without every single one of them."

Coach's smile appears. His real smile, not the one that didn't know if he should take my part in our team's win seriously. "That's exactly right. Those kids will never forget this week. They'll never forget the bond they shared." He squeezes my neck. "And they'll never forget that you were part of it all."

I nod, completely understanding. "I'll never forget them either, Coach."

"Good." He clears his throat. "Look. I talked to Zach after I calmed down from last weekend. You were out of line, and that shit can never happen again. With that said, you have a few weeks left before training begins, so if you want to head home tomorrow, you've earned it. You're free to leave."

A week ago, I would have lit up at the thought of getting the fuck out of here, but now, all I can do is wonder if things would be different with Silver if I had more time with her. Besides, this place has kind of grown on me. "Thanks, Coach. Your faith in me means a lot."

Coach nods. "We wouldn't be a team without you. Remember that next time you're out and about."

I chuckle. "Don't worry. I got it out of my system."

"I guess I'll believe that when I see it." He winks at me then steps forward to meet with Zach on stage to give the crowd a speech of his own.

The rest of the day flies by, between accepting my coaching award, then having one final team huddle to give everyone their trophies and one final pep talk for them to leave with. Then there were the meet and greets with the parents on the field, ending with one final mushy goodbye in the parking lot, where the campers hopped in cars with their families or on buses to leave camp.

"Hey, King," Nance calls while he's jogging to catch up to me. "You coming to the campfire tonight?" He's still feeling shitty after what happened earlier in the week, even though it wasn't his fault.

"Yeah, I'll be there, man. Might even have a beer tonight to celebrate making it through a week of this shit." Even when I say the words, I don't quite believe them. My bitterness is most likely one hundred percent to do with a certain blonde I failed to win over.

Nance gives me a sideways grin. "Nah, I don't believe you. Not with that big-ass trophy in your hands."

I look down at the gold statue I'm holding. It's the size of my palm. Then I hold it out to Nance. "Here, you have it. You deserve it more than I do, dude. I didn't even volunteer to come here."

Nance refuses it with a shake of his head. "Doesn't mean you don't deserve it. I've seen you with those kids this week. You're good with them."

"They made it easy."

"Maybe so, but you don't give yourself enough credit. They couldn't have done it without you."

I give Nance a pointed gaze then let out a laugh. "What's with the ego fluff? That's not like you."

Shrugging, he chuckles. "Maybe I still feel bad about splitting you open earlier this week. But also, it's no secret you didn't want to come here. You should know that people see the work you've put in."

"Thanks, Nance. That means a lot."

"Good." He claps me on the back. "I'm going to start packing so I don't have to worry about it in the morning. Then let's have some fun tonight, yeah?"

I nod and wave Nance off before my eyes accidentally slip to Silver, who's heading directly toward me on my path back to the cabins. Her eyes find mine, and everything about her seems to freeze except for her steps.

"Hey," I say, slowing my gait.

"Hey," she says softly.

When we're only a few steps away from each other, we both stop in our tracks and let the next few beats of silence stretch between us.

"Will you be at the fire tonight?" she asks, her words drawing out slowly like she's afraid to hear herself speak.

"Yeah, I'll probably stop by for one last hurrah. You going?"

She laughs lightly, the pinking of her cheeks showing her discomfort. "Hope would kill me if I didn't show up. So, yeah, I'll be there."

Every moment with Silver is so tempting. Instinct gnaws at me to offer to walk her there. Ego punches back and tells my instinct to go to hell. I've never had so much conflicted emotion over a woman before, and I'm not sure what to do with it all. Instead of reacting to any of it, I take the first step to continue walking. "See you then, princess."

# CHAPTER 21

# STAND STILL

## SILVER

Hope convinced me to stop by her cabin before we left for the campfire, and as soon as I arrived, she handed me a shot of something thick, sweet, and pink.

"What is this?"

"Tequila Rose. You like it? My friends in college and I used to down an entire bottle before heading to the clubs." She giggles and pours another round of shots.

I take mine and toss it back, letting the sweet and creamy liquid coat my throat. "Yum. But why are you trying to get me drunk before we even get there?"

Hope sets her shot glass down and wiggles her ass back to her closet, where she's still combing through her clothes for something to wear. "I'm not getting you drunk," she says tossing me a sharp look. "I'm giving you liquid courage to get you through this party. Maybe you and Kingston will work things out." She winks and turns back to her closet.

I frown, the reality of my own failure to trust anyone hitting me hard in the chest. Why I fought so hard to push

Kingston away has been eating at me for days, especially after our argument yesterday. "What's to work out, Hope? He leaves tomorrow."

"Stop doing that," she says. "Stop slamming the doors on your own happiness without even giving people a shot." She swivels around. "I've known you long enough to see you do this to yourself over and over again. You hold everyone at arm's length and refuse to let them get close to you. It's lucky for you that I see through your bullshit and love you anyway. Looks to me like Kingston sees through it too, but your stubborn ass won't allow yourself to see it."

"Geez, Hope. Tell me how you really feel."

There's a stern look in her eyes. "Sorry. It's time for some tough love. Your focus should be on having a great time tonight. Stop thinking about tomorrow and everything that can go wrong. Guess what? Those things will still happen if they're meant to. At least you'll have happy memories to take with you." She points to the bottle of Tequila Rose. "Help yourself while I find something to wear."

We finish off the bottle of liquor, and I get just tipsy enough to let Hope style my long hair in gentle waves and touch up my face with a light dose of makeup. After a long look in the mirror, I leave my white cotton shorts as is, lift the bottom half of my sleeveless blue blouse above my belly button, and knot it on the side. The style wins a squeal of approval and a "That's my girl" from Hope.

As we finally leave her cabin, I'm clinging to her arm like my life depends on it. I walk along the path toward the party, the anticipation of seeing Kingston one last time killing me. With one glance up at the moon, I pull in a deep breath while silently asking for it to give me courage. For some reason, I feel like I'll need it tonight.

As soon as Hope and I enter the clearing, we see that we are definitely the last to arrive. The party is going strong, with music playing, everyone laughing, drinks being passed around, and a fire blazing in the center of the action.

These type of parties don't happen often, but it's usually a given when the football players are here, especially on their last night. Next week, a new set of players will be here, and we'll celebrate at the end of that week too. By this time, after all the kids are gone, everyone is ready to let loose, including the camp staff, since most of the week was consumed with entertaining young kids.

"There's your man," Hope whispers, her eyes locked on a pair of bodies on the other side of the fire. Anderson, Zach, and Kingston are all laughter and smiles as they chat with each other.

I turn to her with a smirk. "And there's yours."

She meets my amused stare with a sigh. "I know what you're thinking. I'm such a hypocrite. Why don't I go after him? But I don't think I could be any more obvious with that man. It's hopeless."

I squeeze her arm before releasing it. "I think you're right. It's really his move at this point."

"I can't keep waiting for him to see me, Silver."

The sadness and longing in her eyes tugs at my heartstrings. "I know, babe. And I don't think you should. I think you should take your own advice and have fun tonight."

She straightens her shoulders and scans the crowd. "Okay, deal. But maybe we should just go say hi to them first."

Discomfort racks my body at the thought of approaching Kingston. "Oh no, I think that's a bad idea."

She grins and grips my hand. "Which is exactly why we're going to do it." She starts forward, yanking me along.

Delirium from the alcohol must hit my system in that exact moment, because a burst of giggles shoot through me. I've never been so nervous in my life, just knowing tonight will be the last time I get to see Kingston. As much as I've tried to fight it, I like him. I keep telling myself I don't know what on earth attracts me to him, but I know that's one of many lies. Kingston isn't just a nosey pest. He's insightful and brutally honest. And while he's arrogant as hell, he's also a gentle sort of giant when he removes that armor he thinks protects him.

That's the thing with armor. A person is no safer with it on. If anything, it hinders what comes naturally to us. Every time Kingston's walls come down, I can't help but fall for him a little more. Who knows just how deep I could fall if I'd only allow myself the chance? I hate that I have regrets. I hate that I'm considering that I might have made the biggest mistake of my life by not giving in to what I wanted.

"Where have you two been?" Anderson greets us with his charming, relaxed smile, his gaze lingering a little bit longer on Hope.

"Oh, you know," Hope teases, "Just plotting how we're going to fend off all the hotties tonight."

Kingston is close enough for me to not have to be looking directly at him to see his stare burning a hole through the side of my head. As much as I want to greet him, I know if I look at him now, I'll crumble.

"In that case," Anderson says before dipping his hand in the cooler behind him and holding two cans of beer out to Hope and me. "Bottom's up."

I love this version of Anderson Bexley. The one that always shined on family outings or on our nights off when we were younger, before Anderson made it his responsibility to run the camp like it would burn to the ground without him. In some ways, I always respected Anderson for his love for the family business, but I also miss the Anderson I knew when I first moved here. The one who never let me question my place. The one who always had my back at any sign of conflict with anything and anyone. I love when I get glimpses of that Anderson.

"Hope, Silver, I know you've met Zach here, but have you met Zach's fiancée, Monica?" It's Kingston who speaks this time.

My eyes flicker on Kingston's for a second before looking to his right. I take in the stunning brunette standing beside Zach. She's holding chocolate cake on a paper plate, which only makes me love her immediately. She's got to be at least a foot shorter than Zach, which reminds me just how small I must look standing beside Kingston.

I step forward and smile while I reach my hand out to shake hers. "Nice to meet you, Monica. I'm Silver."

She pulls one hand away from under the plate she's holding and shakes my hand. "Nice to meet you, Silver." She turns to Hope. "You must be Hope, then."

"Nice to meet you. Your dress is amazing," Hope gushes.

Monica's eyes light up even more as she looks down then beams back at my best friend. "Thank you. I made it, actually." Then she pulls out a card from her purse and hands it to Hope. "I just started an online boutique if you want to check some of my stuff out. No pressure, but if you like this, then I'm sure you'll find something else you love."

Hope's jaw practically falls to the ground. "Consider it done. There's not much I can wear here, but I'll find any excuse to dress up."

I tilt my head at Monica, familiarity clicking away in my brain. "Wait a second. I recognize you. You're with the camera crew, right?" I snap my fingers, trying to recall the name of the company she works for.

"BelleCurve? Yup, that's me. Production assistant extraordinaire." She points to a group of men standing near the fire. "That's my crew right there." Then she smiles back at me. "We'll be here all month, capturing footage of the action." She points at me in recognition. "I recognize you too. The water girl, right?"

Hope, Anderson, and I laugh at the reference, while I catch Kingston's grin in my peripheral.

"Silver is actually our camp nurse," Anderson corrects gently. "She's been here over eight years."

"Oh wow." Monica's eyes widen a little with excitement. "Hey, we could always use another camp voice in our videos. I'd love to interview you some time."

My entire body freezes while I feel like all blood drains from my body. "Um ..."

Anderson sees my panic and jumps in. "Actually, Silver doesn't really love the spotlight." There's a beat of awkward silence before Anderson starts again. "I can't believe you two haven't met by now. Silver's capable of many extraordinary things, and now water girl is one of them."

Monica laughs along with us. "Well, there's nothing wrong with that. When my sister moved to Seattle last year, she took the oddest jobs. It all builds character, don't you think?"

"I didn't mind it at all. It was nice to be on the field for a change. I don't think I've even watched a single game of football in my life."

I watch their eyes go wide on me. Then Monica is looking at Kingston and Zach with big eyes. "Well, we need to change that, don't we? You happen to know some guys who can score you great seats, if you're up for it."

"Good luck with that," Anderson mutters with a playful wink in my direction. "The only time we've ever gotten Silver to leave Orcas was when we'd boat around the surrounding islands. Other than that, I'm not even sure she's ever left the island since she moved here."

If Anderson and I were alone now, I would let him have it. I know he's only being friendly, but it feels like he's divulging too much information to people we don't even know.

"Is that true, Silver?" Kingston asks. "You've never even left the island?"

I'm thankful for the darkness so that no one close can see the color change in my cheeks. "I haven't had a reason to." I shrug and sip on the beer that's been freezing my hand. I try to act as nonchalant as possible so that someone will change the direction of the conversation. It's been on me for longer than I can stand.

Like they could all hear my wish, Monica and Zach part from our small circle right before Anderson finds a reason to drag Hope away, then it's just Kingston and me. I don't try to avoid him this time. Instead, I look up at him and sigh.

"Look, I need to apologize to you for last night. I came by to see you, to talk to you, and it didn't at all go how I hoped."

His brows pull in. "How did you hope it would go?"

Just like it always does, it feels like Kingston has sucked up all the air around us and all that's left is him and me. "I-I don't know. Better than that."

"Better how?"

I let out a disgruntled breath and tilt my head at him. "Can you give me a little credit here? You know this isn't easy for me. Nothing has been easy since the moment you set foot on this campground. It's not your job to keep pushing me off balance the moment I've gained it, you know? But that's what you do.

You push and push and push. And I-I can't even think straight around you. That night in the canoe—" I stop and look around, catching Vicky's narrowed gaze from across the fire. She can't hear me, but I decide to lower my voice anyway. "That night was... amazing and terrifying, and while I shouldn't have left the way I did, that's what I do, Kingston. I run. I've been running ever since I was seventeen, and I don't know if I can stop even if I wanted to."

He pulls his brows in tighter. "That right there. I think that's why I'm so attracted to you."

My heart is pounding, but I push down my next swallow and bat my eyes up at him. "Why is that?"

"Because while you feel like you're always running when you've never even left this place, I feel like my feet have never left the ground when all I'm ever doing is moving. I've never met someone so opposite from me that I can relate to on a whole new level. It's—"

"Unnerving?"

He leans in just slightly, enough for me to catch the scent I haven't been able to stop dreaming about ever since our night in the canoe. "More like intoxicating." He leans in farther, this time grazing my ear with his lips, causing me to suck in a sharp breath. "You make me want to stand still, Silver Livingston. But I can't do that unless you meet me halfway."

I release my breath in a whoosh before pulling back and staring deep into his evergreen eyes. "I don't think I can."

He frowns. "Why do you do that? Why do you keep pushing me away?"

"Because it's going to hurt like hell when you leave." My words fly out of my mouth so fast I have no chance in stopping them.

If this silence had a sound, it would be a blaring horn. It's too late to take my words back, so I wait while silence stretches between us.

"All I'm asking is for you to try for one night."

I'm tired of denying what my heart so desperately wants. And that's why I give in, truly give in, to what I've wanted all along. There's no sense in denying it. I'll just have to deal with the consequences tomorrow, but for tonight, I decide I'm not holding back.

"Okay."

# CHAPTER 22

# NO REGRETS

## SILVER

I'm not sure what to expect after I agree to try, but Kingston doesn't leave my side for the rest of the party. Well, for as long as we stay at the party. After our first drink, neither of us tried to grab another one. Instead, we made our rounds while he jeered at and taunted his teammates in jest over his coaching win.

I like watching Kingston with his teammates. He's no different than the crude and obnoxious man who stepped off that team bus on the first day, but it's funny what getting to know someone will do to one's perspective. Kingston is charming and playful, and he genuinely wants people to like him. And just by the things he's saying about this past week, I can tell that working with those kids meant a lot to him.

"Heard you're off the hook, dude," Nance says while holding his fist out to bump Kingston's.

I don't know why Kingston looks worriedly at me when Nance says that, or why Kingston is bumping fists with him right back like it's some secret handshake.

"Coach went easy on me this time, I guess."

Nance winks. "I'm sure nabbing that trophy today helped. For what it's worth, we all saw you bust your ass this week. You deserve it."

Kingston reaches around my waist and pulls me closer. "Thanks, man. I appreciate that."

It's not until Nance walks away that I give Kingston a confused look. "What was that all about?"

He shifts uncomfortably and looks to the side like only a guilty person would. "Nothing. I told you how Coach sent me here as a sort of punishment, right?"

I nod, still not understanding. "Yeah. And you served your time, right?"

"Not exactly." Kingston chuckles lightly. "My initial sentence was an entire month. Coach told me today that I was free to go."

My heart instantly plummets into my toes. "Wait a second? You thought you were going to be here an entire month and didn't say anything to me? What the hell, Kingston?"

I'm trying to keep my voice soft, but there's a ball of anger unraveling inside of me. Maybe knowing that simple fact wouldn't have changed my mind about giving him a shot, but who knows? All I know is that I wasn't given that bit of information to consider.

"I'm sorry. When I first got here, I didn't want to stay, so I made Zach a deal. I'd give this week my all, then he'd talk to Coach about reducing my punishment. Why would I tell you I would be here a whole month if I didn't plan on being here that long myself? It would have felt like a lie."

He's right. I know he's right. But I was stubborn and hardheaded, and wouldn't even give him a chance. Maybe if I'd allowed myself to give in to him a bit sooner he wouldn't have fought so hard to leave. Maybe we could have had more time together. Maybe—

"Hey, you okay?"

I want him to stay so badly, my insides are quaking. My eyes snap back to his, and I give him a smile. "Yeah, I'm fine. Do you want to sit by the fire or something?"

When he shakes his head, my chest squeezes. I know what time it is. I've been stealing glances at my watch ever since we got here, knowing with every passing second, we were getting closer to saying goodbye.

Kingston looks at the fire then back at me. "I should really start to pack." I open my mouth then snap it closed, then he slips his hand into mine and squeezes. "Come with me?"

My heart feels like it's flipping around in my chest when I nod and let him tug me through the crowd, toward the path in the woods that leads to our cabins. I love the way his palm practically swallows mine with his grip. It's enough for me to know that he doesn't have any interest in letting go. And I don't challenge his intentions this time. I saw what Kingston came with, and it could easily be packed within minutes.

At his cabin, he switches on the lights. "After you," he says, allowing me to enter first.

I take a sweeping step around the nearly empty cabin, and it's like a gut punch of emotion hitting me all at once. My throat closes up, and tears prick the backs of my eyes. All I can think about is the day we met. How I showed him to his empty cabin. How I stopped by with the blankets and pillows. How thankful he was for my gesture. I don't want to say goodbye to him in this cabin too.

"Um..." I back away, my eyes flickering up to catch his crestfallen expression. "I have another idea."

Our hands are still connected, and he tugs me back to him. "You're not leaving me now. Not yet."

If I don't walk away now, he's going to see what a mess I've become. I'm going to lose it. "Maybe you can pack and then meet me at my place when you're done." I give a pointed glance at his empty space. "It might be more comfortable there."

He holds my gaze for a lingering moment then nods. "Okay. I'll only be ten minutes or so."

I smile and start to pull away, but he tugs me back to him and peers down at me with narrowed eyes. "For the record, I'm not okay with letting you go. I swear to God I will bust down that door if you don't answer."

I laugh again and shake my head. "I'll leave it unlocked so you can save yourself the trouble."

Finally, he lets me go, and I can feel his eyes on me as I dart from his cabin to mine. I don't hear his door click shut, so I know he waited until I got into my cabin safely. As soon as I'm there, I rush around, tidying things up, then I hop into the shower to rinse the campfire smell from my skin and hair. I've just yanked on a pair of distressed jean shorts and a white button down tank top that's tied above my midriff when I hear a gentle knock on the door.

My quickly combed hair is still wet, and I didn't have time to redo my makeup from earlier, but somehow, I don't think any of that matters with Kingston. I cross the room and pull open the door to find Kingston there, his thick hands shoved into the pockets of his tight gray sweats. I can't help but smile at the sight of him. He's wearing a white shirt like me, and his hair is glistening from a recent shower.

As he scans me from head to toe, the heat of his eyes lights my entire body on fire. I swallow, trying desperately to regain my composure. I step back to allow him room to enter. "Come in. This is my place." I look behind me at my room, which I know looks vastly different from the one he's been staying in all week.

He takes a single step to enter, and if I thought he filled up a room before, that was because I'd never seen him walk into mine. He is incredibly intoxicating to watch, with his broad shoulders, tall stature, and ruggedly handsome face. I would hate to be his opponent—that's for sure. With his build, his ferocity when he's challenged is intimidating. I'm curious how he comes across during an actual game. Or even in bed. What would it feel like to be tackled by Kingston Scott?

My cheeks heat as I watch him as his eyes move over the room. "Damn. I should have requested a room like this."

I bite down on my lip to stifle my laugh. "I've lived here for eight years, remember? I was in my early twenties when I realized I should make it feel more like a home. That's when I started DIY'ing the crap out of everything to make it feel like mine." I gesture to the wall my bed rests up against. "I added the white-brick texture first, and then the lights and sheer curtains. I even paid to have the floors redone with my own money. And then came the furniture, little by little, until it looked like this."

He continues to pan the room, his gaze roaming over the white and blush pink tones of my decor. "I definitely did not expect this."

"Why is that?"

"I don't know. We're at a camp. Nothing here looks this—"

"Girly?"

He catches my eye and shakes his head. "I was going to say stylish." He nods in approval. "If this nurse gig doesn't work out, you've got a promising career in interior design waiting for you. You can start at my place."

I tilt my head as the thought of seeing Kingston's home sends nerves fluttering through me. "You're telling me you didn't hire a professional interior designer the moment you purchased your home?"

He smiles, almost bashfully, showing me he's been caught. "You got me. I did, but that was three years ago. My tastes have evolved."

"So, how does it look now?"

He narrows his eyes. "You should come see it for yourself."

I bat my eyes away at his flirtatious suggestion. There are so many reasons why that could never happen, and Kingston doesn't know half of it. I think about my childhood home in Arizona and how the moment I stepped on that Anacortes ferry to take me to the San Juan Islands, I never looked back. That was the last time I went anywhere, save for the surrounding islands.

Before I left Harvey's car at the bus station, he made it clear that I would have to keep a low profile. No cell phones or social media. Don't stray too far from camp. Avoid close relationships, and basically, never trust anyone. To think the time has come for all of that to end makes my stomach flop around nervously. Not that I'm any closer to making a decision. Every time I think about that ticking clock, I find something to distract me from thinking about it entirely. Kingston has been a great distraction.

"Since that will obviously never happen," I finally say, "how about you tell me instead?"

He shrugs. "There's nothing much to tell. It's the typical bachelor pad. Rec room, kitchen, and bar upstairs, where all the guest bedrooms are. Master bedroom downstairs. The furniture is so dark, though, that everything is starting to feel dated. I'd love to start over. Then again, my house is never empty enough to even think about how I'd want to approach it. I can't remember the last time I stayed at my place alone."

"Seriously?"

"Yup," he says, running a finger along my dresser. "I get restless when I'm alone."

"You don't say," I tease.

He throws me an amused glare. "It's a problem, I know. I'm working on it."

An awkward silence follows. At least, it feels awkward to me. I just invited this gargantuan man into my home, and he's perusing all of it. My movie collection, my small library of books, my open closet, and the rest of the decor that fills the room. Then his eyes are on me again.

"Do you mind if I sit?" He gestures to the bed.

I look at my bed then back at him, knowing I should probably answer quickly so that he doesn't get a full picture of just how nervous I am. I want him here so badly, but I'm struggling to figure out all the rights and wrongs that come with this scenario.

"Yes," I say on a rushed breath. "I'll get us something to drink." I start toward my small refrigerator, which is conveniently located at the other end of the room.

"I don't need anything."

I freeze midstep, lost again, not sure what to say. "Should I put on some music, or are you hungry? I might have some—"

"C'mere."

His voice is so husky, so deep, and so all-consuming that all I can do for the next few seconds is stand completely still and listen to the echoing of his words reverberate through me. I take a timid step toward him, then another, until I'm close enough for him to lean over and reach for my hands. He pulls me toward him in one swift move, then I'm sandwiched between his legs, looking down into the most addicting and hypnotic eyes I've ever seen.

"We're being still together, remember? We made a deal."

Panic drips slowly through me, and I have to focus to breathe through it.

His hands are on my bare legs then running over the jean fabric of my shorts before making their way to my exposed stomach. With a simple tug, he unties the bottom of my shirt, but he doesn't make a move to undo the rest of the buttons. Instead, he slips a finger between my shorts and my skin, dragging it teasingly from one side to the other while assessing me with his eyes.

"You're shaking."

I let out a breath, too embarrassed to speak.

"Do you trust me?"

The question is a loaded one, but for all intents and purposes, I feel confident in the nod that follows.

A small smile pushes up his cheeks. He relaxes his legs from around me. Then he unbuttons and unzips my shorts before sliding them down my legs.

"Fuck me," he murmurs as his eyes roam my bare skin, white silk panties, and exposed thighs.

He leans forward and places a chaste kiss on my stomach, right above my panty line. "Do you still trust me?" he rumbles against my skin.

When I don't answer, his lids flip up so he's staring directly back at me. "Nod for yes. Shake your head for no."

A dizzy spell hits me with my nod, and I place my fingers through his hair for leverage, gripping him at the root as he runs a finger along the length of my slit, much like he did in the canoe. I'm already so wet, I can feel the stickiness grip the fabric of my underwear. I think he sees what I know, because a look of victory flashes in his expression.

I'm so focused on the way he's staring at me, I don't even notice that his fingers have slipped beneath the hem of my panties until he starts to pull them down to join my shorts. My eyes are on Kingston, and his eyes are locked between my thighs. I think I might die from lack of oxygen when he leans in and presses his thick lips to the inside of my leg. He repeats the kiss on the other side while moving his knees between mine so I'm spread around him.

His fingers are on me again, gliding along my wetness, across my opening, slipping against my ass, then coming back to my front to do it all again. With each lap, my grip on his hair tightens. Then finally, he stops at my clit, massaging it gently, before he works his way to my entrance and slips a finger inside me.

I suck in a sharp breath—at the sensation, the fullness, and the complete euphoria that overtakes me. I appreciate his slowness and gentleness, which is not at all what I expected from Kingston. Then again, we've barely begun.

"Holy hell, I don't even need to prime you," he growls before inserting a second finger and filling me so completely, I think I might explode. "It's going to feel so good when I'm finally inside you."

He pushes deeper inside me before flicking his fingers and triggering a guttural reaction to slip from my throat. He continues to finger me, slipping in and out, teasing my sweet spot. When his hooded gaze turns up to meet mine, it's like he's wound me up as far as I will go, and I'm hit with an orgasm that completely unravels me. I'm spinning and spinning, weakening by the second.

Kingston doesn't give me a moment to gather myself. He

pulls me onto his lap, and my knees barely graze the edge of the bed. He presses me down so I can feel his bulge where I'm wet, then he's kissing me ferociously. I even hear a growl tear from his throat when our tongues collide. He's not giving me time to breathe. Passion, desire, hunger, lust—it all tangles in the air between us and strips me totally bare of my senses. I'm not going to second-guess this. I'm not going to worry about tomorrow or the fact that I'll never see Kingston again after this night. I'm giving in to what I've denied myself all week. A chance at happiness. Even if it's just for one night.

After a week of resistance, I'm crumbling like a pile of bricks. He was persistent. He found my weak spot. Then he went in for the kill. All I know is that when the dust settles tomorrow, I won't regret a single thing.

# Chapter 23

# CALL ME KING

## KINGSTON

Sex has always been just that. Sex. Even when I was seventeen years old and sliding into my girlfriend of two months, that was all it was to me. The way people talk about feelings being attached to the act, like it's all about love and trust and togetherness, was a foreign concept to me. Who has time for those kinds of feelings when the sensations take over every living part of my body?

I'm not so sure what to believe now that I have Silver in my arms. Her kiss is a bold proclamation of her true feelings toward me. I want to devour every single part of her, and I'm struggling to figure out where to start. Her lips are delectable, like the finest wine. And just the feel of her soft pussy as I ran my fingers through her wetness had me craving the taste of it. I want to bruise her lips as much as I want to fuck her relentlessly, but I also want to make sure I make her feel like the fucking goddess she is. I want to worship Silver like she's my queen. And I want her to scream my name like I'm her king.

My hands move from her thighs to her ass, and I grip both cheeks as I bite down on her bottom lip. A moan is all I hear

211

before I grind her against my erection, getting harder as her wetness soaks through my sweats. "Fuck, I'm not even inside you yet, and I'm going insane." I glide my lips from hers to her neck, scraping my teeth against her sensitive skin as I go.

I roll my hips so she can feel every inch of my desire. Her eyes flutter a little before she drops her head back and starts to move against me on her own. "That's it, princess. I want your tight pussy around me, just like that."

She continues to move, her chest pushing up into the air, and I hate that she still has a shirt on. I remove my hands from her ass cheeks and grip the material of her button-down on both sides where it's already open. I yank it apart, and buttons tear from the seams and bounce around on the floor.

She gasps, and her hypnotic gray eyes fly open, locking on mine. "What the—that was my favorite shirt."

I glare back at her before looking down at her light-pink cotton bra that lifts her generous breasts in all the right places. "Don't worry. I'll buy you a new one."

She squirms a little, but makes no move to hop off me. "I bought it years ago at a local shop. There's no way you can find a replacement."

I slide a finger where the edge of her bra meets her skin, tracing the perfect V-shape before unsnapping her bra in the back with one finger. "Then I'll find you something you like better." My eyes flip up to hers as I finish stripping the last of her clothes from her body. "Or I'll just make you forget about the shirt completely."

"What? How?"

I curl the corner of my mouth, a warning of what's to come, then I pick her up, turn us both around, and drop her on the bed.

I wish I could capture her expression and pin it to my

ceiling for every future time I jerk off to my memory of her. The bounce of her body. The shock in her eyes. The way her mouth goes agape then stares back at me like I'm a wild animal on the prowl.

With a quick pull of my shirt, it's over my head and tossed to the ground. I keep my sweatpants on, for fear I'll give in too soon and slip into her before I've had my fill of her in other ways. I kneel on the floor in front of her, wrap my arms around her thighs and yank her to me, not stopping to take a breath before my mouth is on her.

I'm devouring her juices slowly, lapping at her entrance then her clit in one slow upward swipe before she's sucked into my mouth. I don't know what comes over me, but I'm lost in her, completely trapped between her thighs, hazed in her scent, and buzzing off each drop of her sweet juices.

I wish I could say this was just sex. I wish I could say this was like every other experience that has ever given me my kicks. After all, it was all I wanted from her when I first laid eyes on her. I didn't mean to get to know her. I didn't want to care. And I definitely didn't intend for sex with Silver to become something that belonged in an alternate universe.

For the first time in my life, I want more than a quick fuck with a beautiful woman. I want to take in every single moment, every moan, every sharp breath, and every scream. I want to remember the way her wetness glimmers in the reflection of the cabin lights. I want to remember the way she stared back at me when I made her come with my fingers. And I most certainly want to remember the way she lights up with another orgasm at the speedy rhythmic flickering of my tongue.

Her scream is louder, and her head presses into the bed. Her tits push into the air, and her fingers tug so hard at my hair that it's almost painful.

I'm breathing just as heavily as she is when I stand back up and retrieve a condom from my pocket. I watch her watch me as I strip down to nothing and roll the latex around my swollen cock. It's a painful kind of swollen now. One that only Silver's sweet pussy can resolve.

When I climb onto the bed, I kneel between her legs while taking in the quick rise and fall of her chest. She looks nervous, maybe even a little scared, and that alone sobers me some. A little of the fog clears, and I grab her hand, pulling her to a sitting position so that we're face-to-face.

"You okay?" I search her expression, looking for signs of hesitation. I don't know where her nerves are coming from, but we're not going any farther unless it's what she wants. I've waited too long for this to fuck it up now.

She nods without an ounce of hesitation, but the worrisome expression is still present.

"You sure? Because we don't have to do this if you aren't sure."

She shakes her head then smiles. "I'm very sure, Kingston. I just—" Her eyes flicker between mine. "I just don't want to disappoint you. I've only been with two guys before, and they weren't—" Her eyes slip away from mine and scan the rest of my body before eyeing my dick, causing me to chuckle.

"Hey, Silver." I wait until her eyes connect with mine. "We haven't even done it yet, and you're the best I've ever had. Take that for what it's worth to you."

Her mouth crashes to mine, throwing me completely off guard. She climbs onto my lap, wraps her small hand around my length, then places me at her entrance. We take a simultaneous breath, our gazes locked on where we're about to connect. Then I'm sinking into her, inch by hungry inch. I'm filling her slowly, sensitive to the firm hug that is almost too much for me to bear, even with the damn condom separating the skin-to-skin contact I selfishly want.

I give her a minute to get used to me. I'm rocking against her while I watch every moment of her reaction—the way it morphs from the shock of how I fill her like she's never been stretched open before, to the surprise of the pleasure she feels once she's familiarized herself with the many thick inches of me.

Soon enough, the tables have turned, and she's riding me like she's desperate for it. I accept it with just as much need. My mouth finds her nipples, her neck, then her lips—biting her, tasting her. I'm all over her while she brings us both closer to climax.

"Kingston, I'm getting..."

She doesn't finish her sentence. Instead, she's filled with a gasp as she steadies her movements.

"Call me King," I growl.

I know if she does, I'll come far quicker than anticipated, but I don't care. I've been dying to hear Silver call me by my nickname from the second I spotted her.

A whimper floats from her throat into the air, and I slam my mouth over hers. I want to be as close to her as possible when she comes. Every moan, every scream, every whimper— they're mine.

I never knew sex could feel like an out-of-body experience, because I don't just feel her wrapped around my cock. She's wrapped around my heart too. And every time we connect, it only feels more intense than the last. She comes in minutes, her beautiful blond hair sticking to her skin as her tired muscles start to go limp. She's just had her third orgasm, and I can't hold back any longer.

I push her onto her back, spread her legs, and rock as deep

into her as her body will allow. With each thrust, I'm lost in her. With each breath, I'm a goner. By the time my release reaches its brink and every last drop of my buildup is pouring inside her, I know Silver is not someone I ever want to let go of. Not now. Not tomorrow. Not ever.

Long after we've both come down from our orgasmic high, we're still wrapped up in each other. Our naked limbs pretzel together while we stare out Silver's window. The moon is bright tonight, thanks to the clear sky and just enough clearance from the surrounding woods to give us the perfect view. I'm reminded of our night lying in the canoe together, where we shed some of our secrets and I learned so much about Silver.

The sex was amazing, but it's nights like that one and moments like right now, that I'm going to miss. Eventually, I speak those words aloud, knowing Silver is wide awake, just like me.

"I think this is what I'm going to miss the most," I tell her.

She lets out a breathy laugh. "What's that exactly?"

"Staring up at the moon with you."

# WANING GIBBOUS MOON

"THE MOON IS A REMINDER THAT NO MATTER WHAT PHASE I'M IN, I'M STILL WHOLE." — UNKNOWN

# CHAPTER 24

# OVER THE MOON

## SILVER

S un peeks through my open blinds, and my cheeks lift with a bittersweet smile. I know Kingston is gone. He slipped out quietly hours ago, but not before I heard him whisper goodbye. And now, it's over. My heart is heavy, and my chest aches. Even knowing I may never see him again, I have no regrets about last night. It was what we both wanted. The perfect end to an imperfect beginning.

Still, his sweet words echo in my mind.

*"I think this is what I'm going to miss the most."*

*"What's that exactly?"*

*"Staring up at the moon with you."*

Those words. Those final words before I drifted off to sleep in Kingston's strong arms are hitting me full blast now. They remind me of something my father told me when I was fifteen after I'd just gotten home from an awful double date. I thought Drake Douglas was it for me. I'd crushed on him for years before he finally asked me out, and then he spent most of our date flirting with my best friend. Turned out, he'd only asked me out to spend time with her. I was devastated, and my father was waiting for me on the front porch to witness my heartbreak.

"Oh, Sylvia," my father said gently before wrapping a firm arm around my shoulders. "No boy worth a damn will ever cause you pain like this. That boy was just a phase, an eclipse on your radar when you finally find the one and settle down. I promise."

"But how will I know when I find the one, Daddy?"

"That's easy. He'll be so over the moon in love with you that you won't even question it." He pointed to the illuminated ball in the sky that he referenced often. "You'll be his moon chariot, his one true love. And he'll be your forever moon, someone who will ground you so that you never have to search for another."

The thought of having a love so transcendent hit me hard at that moment. "Like Selene and Endymion?" There are many versions of the Greek mythology story, but the one my father told me was about Endymion, The King of Elis, who was sentenced to eternal sleep as punishment for his sins. Only the goddess of the moon, Selene, had the power to awaken him.

"Yes, Sylvia. Just like that."

Shaking thoughts of my father away, I decide it's time to face the day. I take my time rolling out of bed and getting dressed. I'm not ready to see anyone just yet. I wasn't blind to the wide eyes that kept darting to Kingston and me last night by the campfire or the hushed whispers that followed us when we left together. All I want to do today is ignore the world. I want to sit outside, where I can bask in some vitamin D and read, and that's exactly what I'm going to do.

I pluck an unread novel from my corner bookshelf and take it down toward the lake where my hammock hangs between two trees. Besides my spot at the dock, this is my favorite place to spend my time off. It's one of the only places where I can totally unwind, and Hope knows it. Not long after I've started reading, she's bouncing over to me with a bright smile and coffee in hand.

"Figured you'd need this." She winks then slips into my hammock with me. I hold the hot coffee steady while she wiggles her way beside me.

As soon as she's seated and the hammock steadies, I take a sip. "You're a good friend."

She closes her eyes and gives me a satisfied smile. "I know, but I might have ulterior motives. I want the dirty deets of last night."

I laugh. "I should have known."

"C'mon, we can swap info. You tell me how much of a god Kingston Scott is in bed, and I'll tell you all about how Vicky and her gaggle of followers reacted when you left the party last night."

I bite down on my bottom lip, my curiosity actually making me ponder her offer. Then I shake my head. "I'm not going to give you details, but I will say... It was good." Just thinking about last night makes my heart flip. "Really good."

"The best you've ever had?" Hope asks.

I nod. "Oh, yes." Then I frown as disappointment begins to cloud my memories. "He's almost too good. You think a guy like Kingston has had a lot of experience?"

Hope turns her head to face me and gives me a knowing glance. "Do you really need me to answer that? Babe, it's no secret he got around. But that was before you."

A quick sarcastic laugh bursts from me. "Right. Before and after. He's gone, remember? He got what he wanted. Did you know he was originally supposed to be here for a month?"

"What?" she says, just as shocked as I was.

"Yup, but his coach reduced it due to good behavior, I guess. Now he'll get back to his normal life and eventually forget I ever existed."

Hope sighs. "Is that really what you think?"

"I don't *think*. I *know*. He's a popular guy. He's a freaking celebrity. You saw the way the kids reacted to him. Ugh. And the way Vicky reacted to him. Just imagine him in a big city with an endless supply of women to choose from. There's no way he'll remember the easy nurse at Camp Dakota."

Hope scoots back slightly to narrow her eyes at me. "The *easy* nurse?"

I shrug. "It's true. I knew him for a week!"

With a roll of her eyes, she turns to face forward. "If you're easy, then I'm a freaking free ticket to an amusement park."

"Stop it. You know what I mean."

She shakes her head. "You amaze me. You never give yourself any credit whatsoever. Did you not pay attention this entire past week? Kingston wanted you from the moment he saw you. He didn't even give Vicky the time of day."

Hope grabs my hand and squeezes. Meanwhile, a bundle of emotions are making their way through me, clogging my throat and stinging my eyes.

"He chose *you*, Silver," she says gently. "There's no way he's forgetting you anytime soon. And I'd bet you a lot of money that wasn't the last you'll see him. He'll be back."

She lifts herself from the hammock and tilts her head down at me. "The bus is about to arrive. Want to check out the next set of players with me? King said Balko was coming."

She's so giddy, I can't help but smile, even though I shake my head. The last thing I want to do is watch Kingston's teammates step off the bus without him. "I think I'll stay here."

She sighs, but doesn't push it this time. "Okay. I'll see you at dinner. Wish me luck."

Laughing, I call out behind her, "Good luck."

I try to focus on my book once Hope leaves, but it's close to impossible with thoughts of Kingston competing in my mind. Thoughts of last night and every word of what Hope said. Even if it's true and I do see Kingston again, where would we go from there? It's not like I could ever be seen with a celebrity. The last thing I need is my face showing up in some tabloid and the world finding out who I really am. Then Kingston would know that I lied to him too. But none of that matters anymore. He lives hours away. He's got his friends, football, press, travel, and his life. I just can't see him pining away for someone he knew for a blip of time.

Kingston Scott is nothing but a fantasy—one I'm not even sure if I want. A week of him was nearly more than I can handle. Any more than that, and I would be in way over my head. But no matter how many forced feelings of rejection I try to toss toward the yearning I still have for him, I can't deny how good last night felt. And I would be lying if I said I didn't want more.

When I start to get too hot, I go back to my cabin, shower, and run quickly to my office. I should be getting new team profiles, and I want to see if any new prescriptions came in for the following week's group of kids. I like to be prepared so there are no surprises.

I'm checking off vaccination reports when my office phone rings. "Camp Dakota nurse's office. This is Sil—"

"Hey, Sylvia."

My body completely seizes up with panic the moment I hear Harvey's voice. I've left a few messages for parents to call me back, so I was expecting for one of their voices to chime back at me. I wasn't ready for his call again.

"It's Silver," I correct him. My voice hushes as I try to swim through the anxiety I'm quickly drowning in.

"It feels so strange calling you that."

I don't know where the anger that bubbles up in me comes from. Maybe it's been building all along and I've just been containing it. But who or what am I angry at? Maybe it's anger at myself for not feeling confident enough to make a decision by now. Maybe I'm angry at Harvey for barging back into my life and bringing me back to that dark place that I've successfully kept hidden for the past eight years. Who knows what will happen if I do come forward? Those who adamantly believed I was dead will know the truth. They could be angry at me for it. But it's not just them... The media could get involved too. With Lucinda still vehemently pursuing my money, there's no guarantee she'll stop once that money is officially mine. What if my exposed past hurts the Bexleys' reputation? There's so much more to consider than my father's inheritance.

"You wanted this for me, remember? You set this life up for me, and now you just want me to return it like it was all some temporary experiment."

"It was only supposed to be temporary. You know that. But Lucinda didn't let up. You would have had the court battle of your life, her word against yours."

"But she came after me. She attacked me! I was only trying to save myself that night. We should have gone to the cops and told them everything. Instead, you convinced me to hide. And now what? You want me to just act like nothing ever happened, but what happens next? What will Lucinda do? How far will she go?"

The silence that follows is eerie, to say the least. "You have nothing to worry about with Lucinda. Let me handle her."

"How?"

"I'll negotiate with her. It's what I'm good at. And I've already set up the first meeting to discuss."

Shock, rage, and fear—all of it swirls through me like a tornado set to take down an entire city. "You *what?*"

"Just hear me out, okay?" He talks fast. "Lucinda never knew I had anything to do with your disappearance years ago, so she kept in touch with me. Obviously, since I was responsible for your inheritance. Anyway, we spoke recently, and she alluded to being open to a negotiation."

"You want to *negotiate* with Lucinda?" I'm bubbling with anger, and it takes everything for me to control the eruption. "Are you crazy?"

"I was trying to get her to drop the claim against your death. She agreed that if we negotiated, she wouldn't pursue your whereabouts, which she suspects is fraudulent."

"Why would she suspect that?" I'm so angry, I can feel my voice shaking. "What exactly did you tell her?"

"Nothing, but you've been gone for eight years without a single trace. Either you're dead somewhere, or you've been committing some sort of identity fraud. It doesn't take a genius to come to that conclusion."

"Wait a second." I shake my head. "What do you mean 'identity fraud'? You set me up with a new identity so I could continue living my life. I was able to go to nursing school, no problem. And you're telling me now none of it was legal?"

A few beats of silent pass over the line. "I thought you understood."

"I was seventeen!"

"I saved your life," he growls.

I scoff. "Don't you see, Harvey? You didn't save my life. You killed me. Sylvia is gone. You should have told Lucinda I was dead!"

"And let her claim her contingency benefits on the trust? What the hell have I been protecting all these years?"

I let out a disgusted noise from the back of my throat. "So then what happens if I just claim my trust fund and refuse to make a deal with Lucinda? She'll make my life a living hell until she gets what she wants, won't she? I'll lose my new identity, and who's to say she won't open the case she filed against me that night? With me being away all this time, it will look like I ran because I'm guilty."

Harvey sighs. "Like I said, I will deal with Lucinda. Either way, you're running out of time if you're going to claim your trust. I have all the paperwork ready. The bank just needs your signature on a few things. If you don't come here—"

I shake my head, refusing the offer without needing a moment longer to process what he's telling me. "I don't want it." The words ring through the air like a bomb no one expected to detonate.

"Sylvia, you don't mean that."

"I do." I clear my throat while feeling tension release from my shoulders as my decision settles deep in my chest. "Neither option is ideal, but nothing is worth losing everything I've worked for. If the only way to keep my new identity is to say goodbye to Sylvia, then that's what I'll have to do. Tell Lucinda you were mistaken, that I did, in fact, die. Let her have the money. Let her have it all. She doesn't own me. I don't need her permission to be free." I take in a brave breath, already relieved with my decision. "I'm already free."

Harvey is already talking again, but I hang up before I hear much of it.

Abandoning the rest of my work, I don't even bother to tidy up my desk. Instead, I lock up behind me and head out past the examination room and into the main lobby of the cabin before opening the door to the outside. The moment the fresh air hits my face, I slam my lids closed and suck in a breath.

I have no doubt that I made the right decision about my future. The Bexleys and Camp Dakota weren't just my refuge. They became my family without an ounce of hesitation. Maybe the principle of it all should make me want to return home so Lucinda can't win. But the stronger forces within me know that my father's inheritance has never been a trophy. It doesn't matter how much money she has or I have—none of it will make any of us better.

I don't even notice the tears streaming down my cheeks until a familiar scent wraps around me. Specifically, Kingston's scent. My heart squeezes at the timing. With him coming and going at such a pivotal moment in my life. Maybe there was a purpose to him barging into my world. His presence became the distraction I never knew I needed.

"No need to cry, princess. I'm right here."

My lids fly open at the sound of Kingston's voice, and my insides jump while I gasp in surprise. "What the—?"

It's really him. He's standing there, looking as fresh as the first time I saw him, with a cocky smile on his face and his ever-green eyes sparkling back at me.

## CHAPTER 25

# RIDE WITH ME

## KINGSTON

She's standing there with her eyes squeezed shut, the wind ravaging her blond hair like she hopes it will carry her away, and the sadness that rains down her beautiful skin eliminates all remaining doubt I had upon returning to camp. My decision was made before I left this morning. Part of me wanted to surprise her. The other part, the darker part, wasn't sure she would be happy to see me return.

"No need to cry, princess. I'm right here."

Her eyes fly open, and the expression that transforms her face from distress to relief is the only assurance I need to know she won't resent my return. "What the—?"

I chuckle and take a step forward. She's on the top step, making us nearly the same height. "Missed me that much, huh?"

She swipes at her tears as I watch her cheeks darken a shade. "No—I mean yes. Maybe." She shakes her head, clearly flustered. "But how?"

My natural confidence is a bit buried at the moment. Suddenly, I'm terrified of how she'll react to my change of plans. "Well, while Coach relieved me of my punishment, turns out there's this thing called volunteering. Worked out since one of the guys had to bail for this week. I grabbed his spot." I shrug, doing my best to remain nonchalant.

"So," she starts slowly. "You're here for another week, and then...?"

I reach for her hand and tug until she takes a step down, far enough for me to gain some height on her. "I'm here for as long as you want me to be." I run my thumb across her wet cheek and smile. "There's some bad news, though."

She frowns, her eyes darting between mine. "What's that?"

"You're stuck with me for longer, and I happen to like your bed much more than mine." I move my free hand to her waist and squeeze gently. "Hope you don't mind the inconvenience."

Her lips tug up in the corners, and she rolls her eyes dramatically. "You know what this means, right?"

I lift my brows, waiting.

"You're going to need to fill out more paperwork."

My next laugh is filled with as much relief as humor. I cup her neck and close the gap between us, taking her mouth with mine. I'm already addicted to these lips. The entire ferry ride and bus ride back to Seattle was filled with memories of just how Silver's lips and body fit with mine and the way she moaned with her pending release, then cried out when she came. If I hadn't made the decision to come back to her, it would have haunted me forever.

"Take a ride with me first."

"Take a ride with you?" Confusion washes over her. "Wait. How did you get here?"

I bite down on my bottom lip and lift my set of keys. "I drove."

She stares at my keys like I've smuggled drugs into camp.

"You drove here." She looks back up. "Why didn't you come on the bus that got here earlier today?"

"Because," I say with a shrug. "If I'm going to spend another second here, then I might as well check out the island, maybe all of the San Juan Islands while I'm at it." I leave out the fact that Balko was on that team bus, and I wasn't ready to face him. "I looked it up, and there are great places to go hiking and sight-seeing." I scan her face, hoping I'm not saying too much. "And I thought I could take you out tonight."

"Out?"

"On a date." The words coming off my tongue are so foreign. I think the last time I asked someone out was in high school, and my intentions were less than honorable.

Everything about her seems to melt right there. A smile blossoms on her face, and she tilts her head up slightly. "Do I have time to change?"

My smile is so big, my cheeks hurt. "Yes. I'll grab you in an hour."

We part ways, Silver jogging off toward her cabin and me heading back to my car to grab the last of my things. I already managed to haul a few loads before seeing Silver. This time, I'm prepared. I enter my cabin, but emptiness doesn't greet me now. I brought my own bedding, so much of it that I ended up pushing two of the bunk beds together. After tossing my final duffel bag to the floor, I take a quick shower, change into a pair of white shorts and a light-blue button-down, then head over to Silver's just as she's stepping outside.

Instantly, my mouth gapes. She's wearing a gray dress that looks like a two-piece in the front but connects on the sides. The top is bunched together below her breasts, and the connecting wrap skirt starts just above her belly button. A simple rose gold necklace hangs from her neck, and a black fedora sits on her head.

"Wow."

She looks down at herself then back to me. "Is this okay? You didn't say where we were going."

I step up to her, unable to stop my hands from gripping her waist, and take another sweeping look at her. "It's perfect. You're perfect."

She tilts her head and smiles. "Careful, I might start forgetting who the real Kingston Scott is."

I brush my lips along her cheek then whisper in her ear, "Don't worry. I won't let you forget." My hands slip down to grip her ass, causing Silver to inhale sharply. "Ready?"

Her eyes are wide on me when she nods. With a smile, I thread my fingers with hers and lead her toward the parking lot.

"This is your car?" Silver doesn't hide her shock when she spots the gunmetal-gray Jaguar convertible in the parking lot. The top is already down, revealing the bright-red interior.

"Yes, it is. She's a beauty, isn't she?"

Silver nods. "F-Type?"

Now it's my turn to look shocked. "How the hell did you know that?"

She chuckles. "I had a white one like this in high school." She tosses me a look, revealing an entirely new side to Silver that only makes me more curious. "I miss her."

"Her?" I grin. "You named your car, didn't you?"

She shrugs, her eyes gleaming with entirely new light. "Sheeba the White Tiger."

I shake my head, still reeling with shock. "Well, then"—I toss my keys to her—"maybe you should drive."

"Really?" She looks at the keys then shakes her head before

tossing them back to me. "No. I couldn't even if I wanted to. I haven't driven in eight years."

"Eight *years*?" I decide not to push it for now and move toward the passenger door to open it. "We can fix that later. Get in."

She slips into the seat, her skirt hiking up to reveal her smooth and shiny legs. Damn, she's sexy, and she's completely oblivious to it. I make my way around to the driver's seat and smile when the engine roars to life. I love my car for the obvious reasons—it's sporty, fast, expensive, and fun. It's also the perfect ride for a cruise around the scenic byways. The fact that I have Silver by my side makes it even better.

I take off for the main drive of camp and exit through the electric gate. Once we're out on the road, I gun the engine, and we whiz past thousands of acres of evergreens, miles of farm-land, and beautifully manicured lavender farms. I continue toward Eastsound, the commercial district, and on past the waterfront park before returning to Horseshoe Highway. We've just entered Moran State Park when I hear her speak.

"Where are we going?"

Silver's voice carries with the wind, and I turn to look at her, shook by how natural she looks sitting beside me. I could get used to this. To her. To us. The way a tendril of blond wraps her chin. The way her silver eyes brighten with the expo-sure of the day. For someone who hides from the rest of the world so well, to me, she's clearer than anyone else in my life.

"I don't know," I say honestly. "I was just going to keep driving until we got hungry."

She smiles then nods ahead. "Follow the signs to Mount Constitution Road."

I do as she says, turning down another road after another mile, then I follow that uphill for another five miles. "This is a great place to hike to if you get the chance," Silver says, just as a tall stone tower peeks out between the trees.

I park and turn to Silver. "What is this place?"

"It was built in the thirties as a watchtower. The view from the observation deck is incredible. Let me show you." She opens her door before I have time to even exit the car, and I have to jog to catch up with her.

"Hey, I was going to open that for you."

She nudges me playfully. "You were too slow. C'mon."

Something about her is different today, and I can't help but wonder when she last left the camp. As if she can read my mind, she shoots me a look over her shoulder. "Besides the odd bar I visit with Hope, I haven't journeyed away from camp in a while."

"Why is that?"

We've just entered the stone tower, and she's taking me up the first short flight of stairs. "I don't know, honestly. Ever since I got the head nurse position, I haven't really made time for stuff like this. I forgot how much I loved it. Hiking around here is so beautiful. The beaches are magical, and the whales..." She sighs. "Just wait until you get a good orca sighting. It's incredible."

I reach for her hand. "It's a good thing I have my own personal tour guide."

"It's the perfect time of year to go now that the salmon runs are strongest. Lime Kiln Point State Park on San Juan Island is the prime watch spot."

"Take me there."

Silver pauses a moment to meet my gaze. "I will."

"Tomorrow." I know I'm pushing my luck, and she's most likely thinking the same thing, because she narrows her eyes at me like she doesn't believe my request.

She smiles with a hint of humor in her eyes. "Don't you have camp duties?"

"I mean after all that."

I love the way she looks at me now, like she can't believe what I'm asking. "Okay." She nods. "Tomorrow, then."

We continue up about five more short staircases until we exit onto the observation deck and move to the edge.

"It's a perfect day for this." Silver spins slowly to take it all in. "Look, you can see Mount Baker, Canada, and Mount Rainer. Oh, that's the Olympic Mountain Range over there. Wow. I almost forgot about this view."

The way she gushes has me staring at her more than anything else. My arms catch her waist midturn, and I hold her to me, her back to my front. I dip my mouth to her neck with a smile. "This is going to sound cheesy, but I don't know if I can take my eyes off of you long enough to see a damn thing."

Her cheeks darken in color, and she twists her neck to look at me. "You're one big cheeseball today, aren't you?"

"I am. I can't help it."

"Why is that?"

"Because I like you," I say easily.

"You must like me a lot if you came back to camp for me."

I detect her flirtation and raise her with a glare. "Maybe I came back for the kids." I shrug. "Maybe I want to win another trophy." I turn her by her waist and close the gap between us, bending her back slightly at the edge. "Or maybe I just don't want you to know how crazy I am for you."

Her breath catches as her eyes flutter before locking back on mine. "That's a sweet sentiment, Kingston, but you don't know me."

"I like what I know, and I want to know more. I want to know everything." I lean down, bringing my face close to hers.

"Starting with how your lips taste on the observation deck of a watchtower."

I press my lips to hers, hyperaware of the slight hesitation that follows our connection, followed by a mouth that's just as starved as I am for her. I'm also fully aware of the way she's gripping my shirt like she never wants me to let her go.

"Damn," I whisper against her lips when we start to part. "I like you too much." I shake my head, internally cursing myself for being so weak. "Too much. I'm not used to this."

She bites down on her bottom lip. "You're not used to liking *anyone*, or just me?"

"Maybe a little of both. You went from being the hot nurse I wanted to fuck to the woman I can't stop thinking about, and I don't even know how it happened. I think you slipped me something when I wasn't looking."

She laughs, so I push my lips to her neck just below her ear and feel her entire body shiver.

"You've completely hypnotized me."

"Are you sure that isn't the sex talking?"

I hear the tease in her voice, but I also hear the fear. I shake my head, knowing she can't see me. "I'm talking about you. Your laugh, your smile, your eyes, your touch. I adore everything about you, and I know I haven't even grazed the surface." Smiling, I step back and tug her toward me. "And that's what this week is for. I think I've seen enough here."

"Where to next?"

I push my hand into the pocket of my shorts, pull out my keys then dangle them in front of her face. "I think it's time I give you a driving lesson."

# CHAPTER 26

## TICKETS

### SILVER

Kingston is here. The shock still hasn't worn off, but now I have a bigger problem than I did during the first week of dealing with Kingston. Another week, maybe more, with him only means more time to grow these feelings that have already taken root. My plan was to detox him from my system once he was gone. I would have been okay. But now that he's here, wanting to spend time with me and whispering sweet words in my ear, I know I'm falling too hard, too fast.

Kingston tells me to just drive, so I stick to the side streets, familiarizing myself to the feel of a powerful engine in my control. I almost forgot the adrenaline rush I got when I drove along the main roads back home. With the wind in my hair and the music blasting from the speakers, I can't help the ridiculous smile on my face as my confidence returns.

"Driving looks good on you."

I don't dare take my eyes off the road to glance at him. "I miss this. I forgot how much I missed driving."

"Why'd you stop?"

I swallow, feeling the happiness of this moment slowly dwindling when I begin to think of what I lost during my journey here. "Where would I go?" I shrug. "I have everything I need back at camp."

I can almost feel Kingston's disapproval. "C'mon, Silver. You can't possibly believe that. You're young. There are bigger mountains out there to hike, bigger oceans, too. You're telling me you don't want to see the world? Go on vacations?" There's a moment of pause that seems to lighten the moment. "Or maybe attend a Seattle football game or two? I happen to have an in with the team if you ever want to pop by to see me in action."

Just the thought of going to any large public event gives me chills. I try to play it off with a smile. "The last time you tried to play football in front of me, you nearly lost an eye. For your benefit, I think I'll stay at camp."

He sighs, and even though the wind is loud around us, I can hear it like a needle drop. "All right, then I guess we better enjoy today. Want to see how fast you can go?"

I grin, pushing all my anxious thoughts aside, and focus on the road ahead. I apply pressure to the gas and fly down a road with nothing but farmland on either side. It's such a beautiful day. The sun is out, there's a slight breeze, and the weather is warm but not too much. By the time we enter a woodland section of town, trees shade us from every direction, and everything feels so perfect.

Then I hear the siren. Dread fills me as I instantly release the gas and shoot a worried look at Kingston, who's got his head tossed back in a laugh. Horrified, I glance at the rearview mirror to see a cop right behind me.

"How are you laughing?" I ask as I slowly apply the break and start to turn onto the side of the road. "I was going sixty in a forty-five. Am I going to get a ticket?" Then another thought floods my every vein. "Oh my God, what if he arrests me for reckless driving?" I'm not okay. My heart is pounding, and my insides are quaking so hard, I think I might vomit. It's not the thought of getting arrested that terrifies me. Harvey warned me long ago that if I want to remain hidden, I can't have so much as a speeding ticket in my name.

I'm parked on the side of the road with the cop car's lights flashing behind me. I turn to Kingston, who is still laughing. "I can't get a ticket."

He takes one look at me, and his smile fades. "What? It's not a big deal, Silver. It's just a ticket. No one's going to jail."

I know that in Kingston's mind, I didn't do anything a normal person wouldn't do. But this is different. I'm not a normal person. I'm a lie, and one ticket could ruin all of that.

"You don't understand." My voice shakes. "I cannot get a ticket."

All humor leaves Kingston's expression now, and he just nods before looking over my shoulder. I turn to look toward the sound of approaching footsteps to find a stern-faced cop with his eyes on me. He stops at my door and looks down. "License and registration, miss."

That's it. No mercy. He's not even going to ask me why I was speeding. I hesitate for a second before reaching into my purse to grab my ID.

"Here, sir," Kingston says, reaching past me. "This is my car, so you'll want my registration. Here's my ID too."

The man gives Kingston a disapproving look, then he takes the registration card and ID from him.

"I'm new to the area. Here for a football charity event at Camp Dakota. My girl here was showing me around. We were thinking about finding a watch point to see the orcas. You don't happen to know of any good spots, do you?"

I don't know why Kingston just keeps talking, until I watch the look on the cop's face change with recognition while he stares down at the cards in his hand. "Kingston Scott," the officer says. "As in defensive end Kingston Scott?" His eyes shoot to Kingston's. "You play for Seattle?"

And there it is. Kingston's charming megawatt smile. "That's me. You're a football fan, huh?"

The cop completely loses his cool, breaking out with a smile of his own. "Are you kidding me? I've been a Seattle fan since my pop sat me in front of a Sunday Night Football game when I was two. You've been one hell of an asset to the team these past few years."

"Thank you, sir."

I watch Kingston in awe as he looks genuinely flattered by the officer's words. He has the man eating out of his hands.

"You should come to a game sometime," Kingston adds. "Just tell me when you can make it, and you'll have two tickets waiting for you at will call."

"No way. That's awesome of you, King. I'll tell you, it's not every day we run into celebrities around here." At that moment, the cop remembers there was a reason he pulled me over. He looks down at me and narrows his eyes. "Young lady, these are residential roads. We can't have you speeding down them and injuring someone out here, or yourself and your friend, for that matter." He nods at Kingston. "You've got precious cargo here, and I expect you to take it easy from here on out."

I nod quickly while biting down on my bottom lip at him using the term "precious cargo" to refer to Kingston. "Absolutely, sir. I'm so sorry about that."

Kingston hands the officer a slip of paper with his name on it. "Just text me when you want those tickets, Officer...?"

"Donald Moore." The cop smiles. "I look forward to seeing you in action next season. Thank you." He looks back at me with a point of his finger. "Drive safe."

Office Moore hands the papers back to Kingston then walks back to his car. After he zooms off, I eye Kingston. "Wow. That's all you have to do, huh?"

He shrugs, his cockiness totally illuminated. "You could say thank you for saving your ass."

I scoff and shake my head. "I can't believe that. I would have gotten a ticket, or worse, if you hadn't name-dropped yourself."

Kingston laughs. "What did you want me to do? Sit back and watch you get a ticket? No fucking way."

I'm still shaking, and I don't want to drive anymore. I don't want to get out of the car here either in case another car zooms by, so I pull into what looks like a private drive and put the car in park. "Lesson's over." Without waiting for him to respond, I hop out of the car then walk around and tug open the passenger door. "Get out. You're driving."

Kingston grins up at me without budging. "No way. You're taking us to dinner."

I shake my head and reach for his hand. "I'm not taking you anywhere. I'm not getting behind the wheel again."

I try to tug him out of the car, but he tugs back on me harder, sending me falling into him. With a chuckle, he grabs me by the waist and lifts me onto his lap. My knees dig into the seat on either side of him, and the next thing I know, he's pulling my head toward him with one hand while the other shifts my already-bunched skirt higher.

Our mouths crash together. Every ounce of my adrenaline

rush feeds into the kiss while he steadily grows harder beneath me. The way I want Kingston is beyond anything I've ever felt before. I could kiss him forever and never tire of the way his lips hunger for mine.

I reach between us to unbutton his shorts then help him wiggle them down his legs enough for me to roll on the condom that magically shows up between his fingertips. Kingston pushes my panties aside before I ease my way down around him, burying him inside me until I'm so stretched full, I feel like I could burst.

The first time he entered me the other night, I didn't know if I would ever find my breath again. Once I did, I knew I'd never breathed so fully. Today only reinforces those thoughts and feelings, and it terrifies me.

He reclines the seat, pushing himself deeper inside me. I ease up and down around him, moaning at the girth of him firmly planted between my thighs. He's all muscle and strength, even when he lets me take control.

I feel my orgasm build quickly and powerfully, then my entire body is shaking. I cry out with my release at the same time Kingston grunts and curses below me. I feel his warmth, even through the condom, and I wonder how good he would feel without the layer of latex blocking our connection. The desire to feel him bare is so strong, I can feel the danger in my thoughts.

"Holy fuck, woman." Kingston says the words through his heavy breaths, then he laughs. "You are sinful when you ride me."

I smile and lay my head on his shoulder. "I can't help it with you."

"Thank God for that." Kingston kisses my head and whispers, "Silver."

My eyes squeeze shut, and I try to suck in a breath, but even the slightest sip of air feels like the hardest job in the world. I'm so afraid he's about to tell me bad news. "What?" It's barely a croak of a word as it enters the space between us.

"Do you remember when you were telling me all the things you wished you hated about me?"

I nod, remembering that conversation vividly.

"Do you want to know what I hate?" His hand wraps around my waist.

I go still before whispering, "What?"

"That I'll never be good enough for you. I finally have you, and I just know I'll fuck this up somehow." His eyes search mine. "I really don't want to fuck this up."

His words are so genuine, so sincere, but I don't have the heart to tell him that his intentions are useless. Our futures are inevitable, no matter how hard he tries to make something more of what we are. He can never know the truth about my past, and we can never have a future. So, instead of answering, I push off him and stand outside the car. "You ready to head to dinner?"

The hurt and confusion on Kingston's face is clear. "Yeah, okay. Let's go."

# CHAPTER 27

# OPEN WOUNDS

## KINGSTON

Our naked bodies are tangled together when Silver's alarm starts to go off early on Monday morning. Silver stirs, and I shut the alarm off quickly, praying to steal a few extra minutes before I have to leave her bed. It's the first day of camp again, only this one is starting much differently than the week before it. I've got my girl in my arms and a future to look forward to. For once, that future involves more than just football. While it felt good to volunteer to coach for another week, it's no secret to Zach or any of the guys who were here last week that I'm here for Silver. There was no way I was going to spend another second of my vacation at home when I could be with her.

Last week, my mission was to survive camp. That was it. Do my due diligence, get the coach to relieve me from the rest of my punishment, then get the hell out of dodge. Now I have a new mission—make Silver Livingston fall in love with me. Simple as that.

I'm not clueless when it comes to the beautiful blonde with the sparkling gray eyes and bashful smile. I know she's hiding something from me. She isn't holding back because she's afraid I'm going to leave. She's holding back because she's afraid I'll stay. I don't have the slightest clue why, but one thing is certain: Silver is hiding something.

I slide down her warm body and sink beneath the covers until my face is buried between her thighs. Her satisfied moan is all the fuel my confidence needs to feast. I slip a finger deep inside her as I work her furiously with my tongue, flicking and sucking her between my teeth. I'm relentless in my pursuit of her pleasure. It's an addiction, I suppose. I want to command her orgasms like they're the finale to my symphony and each breath she releases is a part of the masterpiece. I can practically hear the applause when she reaches that final note as she comes on my tongue, her legs shaking with a vibrato that lingers long after the piece is over.

Her breasts are heaving, and she's staring down at me with amused shock on her face. "That was quite the alarm."

Smiling, I climb back up to her. Hovering over her body, I place a kiss on her lips. She pushes up to kiss me again, then she spreads her legs and grabs my ass, pulling my thick cock against her entrance.

I groan at the sensation of our bare skin connecting. "I want you so bad just like this."

She shudders against me and kisses me hard. "Me too." Her eyes lock on mine, and we both breathe out the words we know so well together. "But we shouldn't."

It physically hurts to tear myself off Silver. As much as I want to bury my cock between her legs, neither of us want to be late. So we settle for a quick shower together, bruising kisses, and a promise to reconvene after dinner.

When I enter the field, I'm on such a big high that I almost forget Balko's on this week's roster. Then his smug smile greets me at the fifty-yard line.

He's flipping a ball in the air and catching it when he nods at me. "There's the man I've been looking for. You been avoiding me, King?"

I avert my eyes to see Zach staring between the both of us as if assessing the situation. Zach is aware I figured out Balko was the one who told Coach that I'd landed behind bars that night, and he's no dummy. He can spot the difference between my attitude with Balko then versus now. I should ignore him. Life is too good to let Balko get under my skin.

"Been busy, dude."

Balko shakes his head with a laugh. "All right, well, I'm here now." He winks. "I hope you're ready to get into some trouble."

One glance back at Zach, and from the annoyed glare he's wearing, I know he heard Balko. He gives me a pointed stare, and I shake my head to tell him that I'm not playing into Balko's game. One week ago, I would have welcomed the invite to get into some trouble. I would have done the inviting. But everything is different now.

"Look, I think it's best we stay away from each other this week, okay, dude? No one needs to be getting into any trouble."

Balko rears back and looks at me like he's confused. "What the hell is up with you? Is this about what happened at that club?"

"No, it's about what happened after. You ratted me out to Coach, dude. That was so fucked up. After all the times I've bailed you out."

Balko lets out a disgusted laugh and shakes his head. "I was too fucked up to drive. What else was I supposed to do?"

"You could have called anyone else. Why Coach?"

Balko lifts his arms and shakes his head. "I don't know. I was completely out of my head, as were you. He got you off without a scratch on your record, didn't he?"

"That's not the point."

Balko scoffs, rolls his eyes, and walks off, muttering, "Whatever."

Zach nods for me to greet the team of kids I'll be coaching this week, and we all split up to start our day. And just like that, I'm back in action, walking the kids through drills and play calls that fill my adrenaline rush as much as theirs. I'm good at coaching. I never would have realized that if I hadn't come here. Crazy to think how much my perspective has changed in one week.

I don't see Balko again until dinnertime, but I do my best to steer clear from him even then. I grab my food, find Hope and Silver in their normal spot, and head toward them. They greet me with smiles, and I give Silver a kiss on the cheek.

"You weren't on the field with the good doc," I say to her, confused. I won't lie and tell her I was disappointed when I saw one of the male camp counselors helping Dr. Blaine.

"I forgot to tell you." She sets down her water. "Anderson thought my time was better spent at my office, so he asked Grover to help out at the tent."

As much as I loved staring at Silver from across the field every day, I'm glad she's no longer servant to that asshat.

"So, you're back, huh?" Hope's grin is big enough for both of the girls. "Smart move, King."

I match her grin with one of my own. "Well, thank you, Hope. I think so too. Figured she couldn't stay away from me the first week. This week, she's bound to fall in love with me."

I wish I could read Silver's mind now. Her expression slips

from her shy smile to something that resembles fear. I want to know what she's so afraid of—distance doesn't have to be an issue. And we have all the time in the world to know everything we need to know about each other.

I reach for Silver's hand under the table and squeeze it. She looks back at me, and I give her an encouraging smile. I don't need her pulling away from me now. "What's going on in that beautiful brain of yours?"

She smiles back, and that's all it takes to lighten the mood. "Trust me, you don't want to know. It's a mess in there."

I don't care that a dozen of my teammates and young kids could be staring at us. I lean in and place a tender kiss directly on her lips before breathing her in and whispering in her ear, "I'm determined to find out everything beautiful and messy about you, Silver Livingston."

Her response is quiet and subtle, but I don't miss the way she leans into me.

"Is this seat taken?"

My entire body stiffens when I hear Balko's booming voice.

Before anyone has the chance to respond, he takes a seat beside Hope and sticks his hand out to shake hers. "Hi, gorgeous. What's your name?"

I almost forgot Hope asked about him last week. And I told her I would put in a good word.

"Hope Winston Davies." She takes his hand, and they shake. "And you are?"

I want to laugh at Hope playing coy.

Balko doesn't miss a beat. "Balko."

She tilts her head, amusement flashing in her eyes. "Nice to meet you, Balko."

It doesn't take much to ruffle Balko's feathers, and the fact that Hope doesn't let on that she knows who he is does just that. He turns to me, then his gaze slips to Silver whose body is still leaning against mine. His eyes flicker with mischief.

"Well, hello there." Balko reaches his hand across the table. "And you are?"

The urge to smack it away from her is strong.

Silver takes his hand. "Silver. Nice to meet you."

His gaze moves to me then back to Silver. "I take it you and my friend King here are well-acquainted?"

Silver sits up and darts a look at me. "Oh no, we're just—"

Heat explodes in my chest at what Silver is about to say. I look down at her with narrowed eyes, just daring her silently to say the word. *Friends.* I'm furious, and she hasn't even finished her sentence. *Go on,* I taunt in my head, *say it.*

"Friends?" It's Balko who speaks up, not Silver. "Trust me," Balko chides. "You don't want to be this guy's friend. He holds grudges."

"Grudges?" Silver asks with an uncomfortable laugh. "What are you talking about?"

"Nothing," I snap, nailing Balko with a warning look. "He's just messing with you."

Balko's eyes widen, and I see he has no intention of backing down. "Am I? Because one second, you're ditching me at a club to fuck the bouncer's wife in the bathroom, and the next minute, you're getting tossed out of the club and arrested. Then you give your best friend the silent treatment? I'm not the bad guy here, King. You are."

I can feel Silver's eyes on me as she pieces together the exact reason why I got sent to camp. I told her I'd gotten arrested, but I left out the part about the bouncer's wife. That part didn't seem to matter. But the guilt that flows through me now, matched with the way Silver's heated eyes are glued to the side of my face, makes me think I fucked up big time.

Everything from that moment on happens so fast, I can't seem to stop the domino effect after Balko pushed the first one over. Silver gets up from the table. Hope follows her. Balko sneers at me like he's just won a victory. Then I lunge for him from across the table.

)▪●●●▪(

## SILVER

I've been back in my office for less than ten minutes when the front door bangs open, and loud, angry voices enter. Instantly, I recognize the voices as belonging to Kingston and Zach.

"I can't believe you pulled that shit in front of the kids. What the fuck, King?"

"It wasn't me. You know Balko was poking at me. He wouldn't let up. What was I supposed to do?"

"Walk away," Zach explodes. "You were supposed to walk away. Now I need to figure out how I'm going to deal with this. These kids had cell phones out, pointed at you two idiots. If they can manage to get a decent signal, this will be all over social media by morning."

"Who the fuck cares? We're teammates. We bicker. No one got hurt."

"No one got hurt?" Zach booms again. "You're bleeding all over the damn place."

I shoot out of my desk and toward the front of the cabin, my heart racing, not just because of the fighting, but because Kingston is hurt. As soon as I push open the examination room door to the front reception area, I gasp at the sight of

Kingston holding his eye—the same eye he busted open last week. Just like Zach said, there's blood everywhere.

"Oh my God. What happened to him?" I don't know why I ask Zach instead of Kingston, but at least Zach answers.

"Balko happened to him. Can you check out his eye? I think he split open his stitch."

Nodding, I quicken my steps the rest of the way to Kingston and latch on to his free hand. "Come with me."

"Stay away from Balko until I figure out what I'm going to do with you two." It's Zach's final demand before I close the door to the examination room.

I save my questions for now. My main concern is getting his eye looked at and restitched as fast as possible. But first, I need to stop the bleeding. Kingston is silent, but his steady eyes stay on me as I work. At least he isn't arguing with me nonstop. That's a drastic contrast to the week before.

"You gonna say anything to me?"

I ignore the obvious reason for his question and shrug. "Sure. What do you want to talk about?"

"You're not even going to ask how this happened?"

"Don't need to," I say easily. "You and Balko party together, and you blame him for having to come to camp in the first place. He gave me the dirty details. I walked away. And then you decided to start a fight in the middle of a cafeteria with teenage boys watching their role models go at it like toddlers. Sound about right?"

The fury coming off Kingston creates heatwaves circling in the air. "So you're pissed at me?"

I shake my head. In the ten minutes I had alone after leaving the cafeteria, I made up my mind. While whatever happened with Kingston in the past still sucked to hear, I couldn't be upset with him for that. Do I wish he was the one who told me the whole story? Sure. Do I wish Kingston didn't have the playboy past he seems to have? Of course. But none of those things change the way I feel about the Kingston I know now. And none of those things matter in the grand scheme of things. Not with the identity crisis on my hands.

I ignore his question and continue working on resealing his stitch. When I'm done, I rinse my hands in the sink then grab a fresh bandage. I've just finished applying it when he asks the question again. "Are you pissed at me?"

"Pissed at you for sleeping with the bouncer's wife and for hiding that small fact from me? Am I pissed at you for getting into a juvenile brawl in the lunchroom and potentially getting yourself kicked out of here? Or am I pissed at you for allowing Hope to think that Balko was decent enough of a guy to date her? It's a lot to unpack at the moment."

"I can't for the life of me think of any scenario where telling you the details of what happened that night would be at all useful information for you. I never lied to you about who I was and what I was about before I met you. As far as Hope, she's a big girl who can make her own decisions. But it's nice to know you care that I could get kicked out."

I sigh and stare back at Kingston as he holds me between his legs. "I'm not pissed at you for any of that. I'm just—"

He searches my eyes with his. "You're just what?"

"Confused."

His hurt expression that flashes like a high beam has my heart racing. "Confused about me?"

It doesn't take much to weaken in Kingston's presence, but his vulnerability melts me completely. "No. I'm not confused about you or the way I feel about you. Not at all."

"Then what is it? If it's not me, then what?" He cups my face and leans in so his forehead touches mine.

"We live two completely different lives."

"Stop focusing on that," he pleads. "Just be with me right now. Stop looking for anything and everything to use to keep that damn wall up. I'll knock that shit down every single time."

"It's a little hard to focus on right now when I fall for you more and more each day. I don't want to get in so deep that I can't climb my way out when it's over."

"You say *when* like it's inevitable."

"Isn't it?"

Kingston shakes his head slowly, rolling his forehead against mine. "We're only just getting started."

# THIRD QUARTER MOON

"SOMETIMES YOU DON'T FEEL THE WEIGHT OF SOMETHING YOU'VE BEEN CARRYING UNTIL YOU FEEL THE WEIGHT OF ITS RELEASE." — UNKNOWN

## CHAPTER 28

# CLOSING IN

### SILVER

A dozen beautiful wildflowers were waiting for me on my nightstand when I woke up this morning, along with a note asking for me to be ready to go see the orcas after work today. By the time five o'clock rolled around, Kingston was waiting for me outside my cabin, and the flutters in my chest became more persistent. I can't ignore this anymore. Not him. Not these feelings. My caution isn't helping either of us.

We took the ferry to San Juan Island and drove to the famous Lime Kiln lighthouse, where a small group of people has already gathered. Some are at the balcony of the lighthouse, while others are a bit more daring, finding closer viewing spots on the rocky bluff.

"Do you see them?" I grip Kingston's hand excitedly as we near the action.

"Holy shit, they're really here."

The way his eyes sparkle in amazement makes me smile.

"Want to get closer?" I point to the bluff, and he gestures for me to lead the way.

We climb out onto the rocks, eventually stopping at a large one we can share. Kingston wraps his arms around me from behind as we stare out at the killer whales at play. "We're lucky, you know? The pods don't always come this close. Some people visit from far away just to spot an orca and leave disappointed."

"I didn't have any doubts."

An orca leaps out of the air at that moment, and the sight is so majestic, it reminds me of the first time I came out here with the Bexleys not long after I moved to camp. We got quite the show that day, and it seems like we're getting one now.

"Why do they slap their tails like that?" Kingston asks.

I wish I'd brushed up on my orca knowledge before coming out here. I didn't know he would have so many questions. "It's one way they communicate. It's all about the energy of the tail. It could be a signal to warn for predators, or it could be part of a mating ritual. I'm afraid I don't know much more than that."

"I know some stuff." Kingston is laughing before he's even reached my ear. "Did you know that orcas are known for having extremely large penises? One was recorded at eight feet long."

I roll my eyes. "If that's true, that's disgusting."

"I thought it was pretty cool."

"Of course you did. I can't unhear that. I'll blame you for my nightmares tonight."

Kingston squeezes me from behind. "Who says you'll get any sleep tonight? All this penis talk is giving me a few ideas."

I throw my head back onto his chest and laugh. "And here I thought orca watching sounded like a romantic idea."

"This is romantic," he insists.

I shake my head. "Nope. Sorry. Not romantic." I sigh and

turn around to face him. "But if you want to try again, say with dinner, then I'll happily allow it."

He glares down at me with a playful smile on his face. "I think you're getting spoiled. I let you drive my car, I take you orca-watching, and now you're demanding dinner. Next thing I know, you're going to be asking me to make whale noises in the bedroom."

I'm dying with laughter by the time we leave the scenic bluff and I'm back in Kingston's car. It's not until we arrive at the Friday Harbor House that I realize Kingston does, in fact, have more planned for tonight.

"Don't worry," he says before I can argue. "We'll be back at camp before we start work tomorrow. I just want one night with you away. The menu at the restaurant here looks amazing too. Let's check in to our room then grab some dinner?"

He asks me like I could possibly say no after he clearly went to some effort to find us the perfect getaway. My heart is melting before my next words are even out of my mouth. "I think that sounds perfect."

And it *is* perfect, from the quaint harbor-view room with sweeping views of the marina to the impeccable dinner served to us downstairs. But nothing beats the bath Kingston draws for me when we get back to the room, especially when he manages to squeeze into the tub with me.

I'm fitted between his legs, my back against his front, as he runs soapy hands up both of my arms. We're staring out the large window, where all we can see are the marina lights below and the sky lights above.

"So, what phase is the moon in now?"

I don't even have to think about it before I answer. "Waning crescent. The illuminated part of the moon is decreasing, which can be looked at in different ways. The optimist would say that the moon is only one cycle away from rebirth. It's a time to cleanse and start fresh."

"And what would the pessimist say?"

My heart squeezes as I feel the truth in my words before I even speak them. "That the darkness is closing in. A new cycle doesn't always mean a new beginning. It can also mean the end." I swallow, feeling much too close to this topic to continue. I gave up my birth name to continue the charade. It felt like the best decision out of all the choices given. Still, I can't help but wonder what would have happened if I accepted the trust money, signed those papers, and reclaimed my name. Does Lucinda truly have the power to haunt me for the rest of my life? Turning down my trust was, in a way, me taking back the power in the situation. But a part of me wonders if I gave up too much too soon. Because of that, the end is near with Kingston too.

"You are so tense." Kingston starts to massage my neck, his magical hands somehow making me feel like putty beneath him. "Just relax, babe. There's nothing to worry about when you're with me. Not a damn thing."

I sigh and let his words comfort me, then I'm closing my eyes while hyperaware of the way his strong hands continue to knead and relax me. Over my shoulders, my neck, my arms, my chest. He lingers on my breasts for a minute, palming me and giving extra care and attention to my hard peaks. All the while, he's growing harder beneath me.

I'm getting too hot, so I unplug the drain with my toe and start to climb out of the tub. Before I can get far, Kingston's arms wrap around my waist and bring me down on his lap. Water splashes around us, and our laughter echoes around the room.

"You're crazy," I say to him with a teasing glare.

"Crazy about you."

I gasp when I feel his dick nudge against my entrance. He's shifting my hips, lifting them then setting me back down until I can feel him pushing inside me. He's bare, and even though I'm on birth control, we haven't discussed this. As much as I want to feel him, I know we're not ready for all that comes with it.

"Kingston, where are your condoms?"

He growls and pulls back slowly. "In my pants on the bed."

"I'll go get them."

I tear myself away from him, step out of the tub, and walk into the bedroom, where his pants lie on the bed. I'm leaning over and feeling into his pockets when I hear Kingston's wet feet slapping the tile floor of the bathroom behind me. "Don't move," he warns.

I grip the condom wrapper and tear it apart with my teeth before he takes it from me. A second later, he's pushed up against me, kissing my neck, my hair, and my back. He picks me up and places me on the bed on my knees. Before I know what's happening, he's bending me forward so fast, my palms slam into the mattress. Then he's pushing into my entrance with a thrust so eager, I can see stars burst behind my lids.

"Holy shit." I absorb the shock as he drives into me from behind, pushing deeper than I've ever felt him before.

"You feel so fucking good."

I swallow at the intensity of his width pushing into me. It's always like this, too much at first, then complete bliss once I'm used to him. But this is something different. More. I already feel like I could come.

Kingston's fingers reach between my thighs and massage my clit. That's all it takes for me to be a goner. I come so hard, I fall forward onto my elbows before he flips me onto my back and enters me again. His hands grip my wrists and push them onto the bed, and his mouth lands on my neck, sucking and biting while another climax rockets through my body.

I'm nearing my third orgasm by the time Kingston warns me of his pending release. He's got me riding his lap, my muscles weakening by the second. His middle finger is penetrating my ass enough to make me feel like I'm about to explode. Two seconds later, Kingston thrusts into me once, twice, three times. Then he's filling me with every last drop of his arousal.

"Silver." It's a drowsy whisper a few minutes later, when we're wrapped in each other's arms.

"Hmm," I mumble, unable to find the strength to conjure up any words.

"I'm over the moon for you."

Those words. It's like an earthquake shakes through me as I remember what my father said to me all those years ago, and it's all I can do not to repeat them back to him. But doing so would be unfair to us both. He can't be my Endymion. Not when I'm imprisoned beneath the same moon as him.

I frown and look up to find his eyes completely closed. "Goodnight, Kingston."

## CHAPTER 29

# HAMMOCKS & SEAPLANES

## SILVER

The sun beats down on my face as I lay in my hammock. A book rests open on my bare stomach while I give in to the gentle breeze rustling the surrounding trees. Quiet mornings like this are rare, and I'm relishing every single moment. It's Sunday morning, and Kingston is having breakfast with his team before this week's group of guys head out on the team bus. After Balko and Kingston were forced to apologize to the entire camp of kids and talk about how wrong their actions were, Kingston spent the rest of the week earning his keep.

I've loved watching the more serious side of him this week —the side of him that wants to prove he's here for the right reasons. Namely, his love for football. That love is evident in the way he mentors those kids. When we meet up at lunch and dinner, he's got some proud story about how well one of his players did that day. Other than that, everything has felt... normal.

My hammock shifts, and my first thought is that it's the

wind, but then I'm sinking deeper as if additional weight is pressing on it like it does when Hope joins me. But this isn't Hope. It's not her scent, her touch, or her small body hovering over me. And these certainly aren't her plush lips kissing mine.

"You looked so angelic laying here. I couldn't resist joining you." His words are soft against my lips, my cheek, and finally, my ear.

"How did you find me?" I bite back a smile with my teasing words. I didn't tell Kingston where I would be, but I knew he would find me. He always finds me.

He kisses me in that spot between my neck and my shoulder that drives me wild. "I inserted a GPS tracker on you last night when you were sleeping."

A giggle slips past my throat, but not from his words. He's sliding my skirt and panties from my hips down my legs.

"Where did you insert it exactly?"

He shakes his head, bringing his mouth to the slight bit of cleavage that's showing. "I'm afraid that's top secret. I can't tell you. But I can show you." He grips the fabric of my midriff top at the bottom and slides it over my breasts then my hair, leaving me completely naked for him.

He dives down and latches on to my nipple. I draw in a shocked breath and moan. "What has gotten into you?" It's a silly question, really. There isn't a second that goes by that he doesn't make me feel wanted.

His hand covers the breast he just kissed, kneading it, while his mouth moves to my other breast and gives it equal attention. My head presses back, and my back arches slightly as I give in to his touch.

It's so natural how my legs spread around him, and he slowly grinds his erection over my center like we've been doing this all our lives. One thing I've learned about Kingston is that he isn't shy about where he has sex. One thing I've learned about myself... apparently, I'm not shy either.

A flotation in the lake. Check.

The staff room after hours. Check.

My office desk. Check.

My examination table. Double check.

I'm not surprised that Kingston is getting us both completely naked in the hammock now too. "Someone could walk down here and see us," I whisper, but it's too late. He's removed the last of his clothes and is rolling a condom over his thick length.

"Let them." He lowers himself back to me and kisses me roughly, like this is more than the sexual comfort we've been for each other this past week. He kisses me like he needs me, like he'll die if he can't have me, and I return his lip-lock with just as much vigor, because no matter where we are or what the consequences might be, I want him too.

By the time he pushes inside me, I'm already worked up. I'm just waiting for his powerful thrust that usually comes with his usual eagerness. But that's not what comes next. Instead, I can feel Kingston try to balance us both in the hammock while he pushes inside me. While that blissful feeling of complete fullness satiates me like it always does, there's something different about this time.

He's careful and gentle, and even while he stretches me open so I can take every inch of him, he's in no rush. There's no thrust, no quick pumping of his hips to get me off in record time. It's then that I notice the shake of his arms as he holds on to the roped edge of the hammock with a white-knuckled grip. I almost burst out with a laugh when I realize he's struggling to hold his balance while he buries himself deeper and deeper inside me. Any thought of laughter is cut off by the way his entire body vibrates.

"Holy fuck," Kingston groans. "I didn't anticipate how challenging this would be."

"We can go to my cabin."

He gives a firm shake of his head. "No way. This feels too good."

My heels dig into the weaving on either side of him as I surrender to this new sensation. Slow, rhythmic, and close, it's like he's afraid to move too fast, or we'll both go tumbling. I drag my eyes up his body, over his tight abs and bulky chest, to his massive arms and thick neck, finally landing on his gorgeous eyes that blend in with everything I love about this island, even more so with him on it.

My orgasm rolls through me like I'm watching a colossal storm in the middle of the Atlantic in slow-mo. It teases me from afar until finally building to towering heights above me. I'm just a shadow in its presence. A victim to its inevitable doom. Then it captures me, crashing over me and sweeping me away without a life raft in sight. All that's left of me are scattered pieces that now belong to the sea—to him. And I know I'll never be whole again.

Hours later, we're zipping down the walkway toward the path in the woods that leads to the camp's private marina.

"Why are you taking me to the marina?" I ask with a laugh, but the truth is, I don't care. What I care about is that

Kingston wants to spend this time with me, and I'm not taking that fact for granted.

"I haven't seen it yet," he says, giving me a wink. "Don't worry. We're not getting in another canoe."

My neck and cheek burn with a blush.

He squeezes my hand. "Thought maybe you could give me the tour."

We exit the path and arrive at the small marina where several small boats are moored to the dock. "There's not much to tour," I say with a wave of my hands. "This is it. We offer water activities to the campers. Skiing, wakeboarding, rafting, you name it. But only when accompanied by a staff member."

"You're staff, right? Can we take one out?"

My eyes grow wide. "I mean, I'm more like family, so I know Anderson wouldn't mind, but..." I laugh through my discomfort while staring at him, waiting for him to tell me he's joking. "Are you serious?"

He shrugs, not finding his question the least bit funny. "Why do you seem so amused?"

"Because—" I struggle to come up with a legitimate reason for my shock and amusement. "I just wasn't expecting the request."

"C'mon," he says, tugging gently on my hand. "Live a little. Maybe we'll see more orcas."

A swarm of butterflies fly freely in my chest when he unleashes his mischievous smile. He knows he's got me. He knows exactly what he's doing to me. "Fine, but I need to tell Anderson we're going."

Kingston adopts the biggest, cheesiest grin, sending a rush of adrenaline shooting through my body. "That's my girl."

I try not to let him see how all my insides melt at the sound of his endearment, and I rush off to the boathouse, where I punch in the code and grab a set of keys to one of the compact speedboats. I shoot Anderson a quick message while I'm there: *Taking a boat for a cruise with Kingston.*

His reply is almost instantaneous: *Just you two?*

Me: *Yes. Shouldn't be long.*

Anderson: *Where are you going?*

Me: *I'm not sure. A quick cruise around the island maybe?*

Anderson: *I'll have my phone on in case you need me. Text me when you're back.*

My stomach flips at how easy that was. Anderson, more than his brothers, has always acted like an older brother to me. He tends to get protective when it comes to the guys I go out with. He's also been my biggest cheerleader. And while I know he wants me to be cautious with Kingston, he must also approve of him.

Me: *Will do.*

I lock up the boathouse and join Kingston on the dock. "That one," I say to him while pointing my finger at the boat near the end of the marina.

He nods, wrapping his arms around me from behind. The way his entire body envelops mine like a protective blanket gives me an unexpected sense of comfort. I can't remember a man ever making me feel safe just with his touch, not that it's ever been that easy for me to feel that way in general. I guess I never thought I could. After losing my father and the abusive aftermath with Lucinda, I kind of thought I was broken.

His mouth comes down on my ear, and when he breathes out, I feel it all over my body. "Lead the way, Captain."

I bite down on my smile. Kingston has learned what makes me weak for him, and he has no qualms about using that knowledge against me. At the same time, I'm learning a few tricks to use against him, as well.

Kingston loves when I'm the first to grab his hand. He gets the cutest, most child-like grin when I do it. He loves when I slip on one of his shirts in the morning. It inevitably ends up back on the floor. He loves when I'm on top more than any other position while he controls the pacing of my hips. He loves the way I run my tongue around the outer shell of his ear and moan, and the way my cheeks always seem to burn when he makes one of his crude comments.

It's funny how well we seem to fit. Then again, there's a part of me that still questions how true that connection is. Is it just sex? Is it more? I'm not sure I'll ever be able to answer those questions—not when I'm carrying a lie that could change everything.

Almost as soon as we're cruising away from camp, Kingston moves behind me and takes control of the wheel. He seems to know where we're going as he steers us around the San Juan Islands.

When I was younger, boating was one of my favorite things to do with the Bexleys. Usually, it was Andrew Bexley at the wheel, but other times, it would just be the Bexley brothers, me, and a few of their girlfriends. We would always find a place to turn the engine off and dive into the water near Oak Harbor, but we never ventured out past that point. When Kingston steers the boat around the island and directly toward the Orcas Island Airport, my heart begins to pound. I realize he has more up his sleeve than he let on.

I turn my neck to shout over the wind. "Why do I get the feeling you're up to something?"

Kingston smiles and places a kiss on my cheek. "Because you're smart."

There are so many emotions swirling through my heart and mind. Excitement and fear dominate them all. "Okay," I say, feeling my entire body shake. "But you should know right now... I'm not getting on a plane."

He chuckles. "We'll see about that."

We secure the boat at one of the sanctuary docks, and Kingston takes my hand. I half expect him to drag me forward, but he stops and looks at me while squeezing it. "There's somewhere I want to take you. And don't worry, I already cleared it with Anderson." He winks.

My heart is pounding. It's been eight years since I left the islands. I had no plans on changing that today. "Kingston—"

He interrupts with another squeeze of his hand. "Do you trust me?"

I blink up at him. Saying no to him is difficult enough, and when he asks me like that, I can't seem to remember why I wanted to say no to begin with. "Of course, but—"

He tugs me closer and brings his head down to mine so our foreheads touch. "But?"

I shake my head. Every doubt I have melts away with his gaze. "Nothing. Have your way with me." I say it with mild playfulness and a hint of sarcasm, but Kingston's giant smile is back, making my heart flutter again.

He scoops me up and takes off jogging, causing me to burst with a fit of laughter. Kingston is just as insane as I thought on that first day I met him, but somehow, I've fallen head over heels for him anyway.

We approach a grassy area, where a row of seaplanes are parked. A man is walking toward us, his eyes pinned on Kingston. Clearly, he was expecting him. "Kingston Scott," the man says. "It's a pleasure to meet you. I'm Captain Nick Bellfonte, and I'll be your pilot today."

The two men shake hands like they've been bros all their life, and I tune out most of the casual banter having to do with football and what Kingston is doing in town. Instead, I stare at the beautiful red-and-white beast of an aircraft that's about to carry my fate on its wings.

Fear has me wanting to run straight back to the boat, but my curiosity grounds me to my spot. Then a few minutes later, Kingston is helping me aboard.

"I can't believe you got me in this thing," I say as soon as we're strapped in and headphones are covering our ears.

He chuckles from across the aisle and squeezes the hand he's still holding. "You should know by now, Silver. If you tell me you haven't ever done something—or even in a while—I'm going to make it my mission to get you to do it."

I vaguely remember Anderson mentioning to Kingston that I haven't left the San Juan Island area since I moved here. He listened. My heart catches in my throat, and I'm not sure if it's because of Kingston's sentiment or because we're finally floating over the water and gaining speed to take off into the air.

I still have no idea where we're going or if Kingston even has a destination in mind. My eyes are glued to the water beneath us and the air that starts to separate us from my home for the past eight years. High above the straits of San Juan, Kingston begins to point out landmarks I've only heard of before now. We pass by Anacortes, Port Townsend, and Whidbey Island. Then we enter the Puget Sound waters, where Kingston's hometown of Seattle lies.

When the pilot steers us inland, I shoot Kingston a wide-eyed look. "Where in the world are you taking me?"

He winks, then, as if he can sense my nerves, he tightens his hold on my hand. "I've lived in your world for the past two weeks. Now, it's time I show you mine."

I don't know what's racing faster, my heart or my mind. All I know is that I'm terrified and excited in equal measure, and I've never felt so alive.

## CHAPTER 30

# ALL I SEE

## KINGSTON

"We're home," I say to Silver with a wink. We've just landed in my backyard, also known as Lake Washington, and Captain Nick is securing us to my private dock before we can jump off. I watch Silver's eyes dart from mine to my home.

"This is your house?"

I nod, feeling pride swell in my chest more than it ever has before when referencing my home. I've worked damn hard to get where I am in my career, but it's easy to lose sight of where I was before all of this. "This is it. My little slice of heaven." *And I want to share it all with you.*

"Isn't it a little"—she looks around as if to make a point—"big?"

"That's what she said."

"Kingston," she scolds, but I see the amusement in her eyes when she smacks my chest.

"The house isn't all that big actually," I say with a shrug. "It was the property and privacy I wanted. That's a little hard to get in this area without spending all of my earnings."

She looks at me for a second. "You forget I've lived in a two-hundred-square-foot cabin for the past eight years. Anything bigger than that is a mansion in my book."

"Ah, c'mon." I tilt my head, remembering all the little hints she's given me about her past. Her old car. Her father being a surgeon. "I'm sure before Camp Dakota, you were living it up. Eight years ago isn't *that* far in the past."

She loses whatever trace of amusement she carried moments ago and averts her gaze. I've noticed the sharp shift in posture and expression every time I mention her father. Because I know she holds her past close, I haven't asked too many questions. But that's all part of why I wanted to bring her here. I figured if there was any place she could finally feel safe enough with me to rip down her walls, then it would be away from Camp Dakota, somewhere we can be alone. I don't want to push her. All I want is for her to trust me.

It was Wednesday night when I realized that I'd spent more time fully committed to pursuing Silver than I have with any woman ever. I can't remember the last time I pursued a woman, period. Casual relationships, one-night stands, and weekend flings are more my style. But if someone were to ask me if I ever saw myself settling down, I would shock the hell out of them and tell them yes. Marriage, kids, dogs, cats, the works. I want a family—big or small, doesn't matter. I want a chance to do things right, to give my kids a life they deserve, where they're loved without threats, conditions, or rules...

At the same time, relationships have always terrified me for those same reasons. I always thought it was because I wasn't ready to settle down, but after meeting Silver, I know that wasn't the problem at all. I just hadn't found *her* yet.

I thank Captain Nick and start up the dock, my arm locked

around Silver's waist. "This was the first home I ever purchased, and honestly, it was meant to be the ultimate bachelor's pad. I remodeled it as soon as I moved in. You'll see."

She's quiet as we approach the pale-yellow two-story house with decks spanning the entire back side of the house on each level, and I think it's because she's taking it all in. Large surrounding trees. Garden spaces that I've failed to keep up with but somehow still look beautiful. A large firepit with six red Adirondack chairs around it. She stares at the small waterfall and creek that runs through the property.

"Just looking at all this space has me wanting to take up gardening." She waves her hand at nothing in particular. "It's like one big natural canvas out here. It's beautiful."

"See, that's exactly what I wanted. Like I said, the house itself isn't big, and there's a lot of wasted space. But that's the good thing. There's room to grow here, you know?" My gaze flickers over Silver. I'm unable to help the way I envision how she would fit in here. It's crazy to even think about, considering how little we still know about each other. But somehow, I just know she fits into my life in every single way.

We step onto the bottom deck, and I push my key into the door. "You hungry?"

"Starved."

"Me too. I'll order us something, and then I'll give you the grand tour, ending in my bedroom, of course."

She rolls her eyes, but she can't keep the smile off her face. "You had to throw that one in there, didn't you?"

"Would you rather I acted like I didn't want to roll around my sheets naked with you? It's a California King, and compared to the one back at camp, the mattress is like floating on a cloud. You'll thank me in the morning."

Shock transforms her face. "Morning? We're spending the night here? But..."

I can almost hear all the excuses Silver sorts through in her mind about how she has to get back to camp, but I know before she responds that she'll come up empty. Neither of us have to be back at camp until Monday morning. Anderson is fully aware of our plans. The boat is safely secured at the airport dock. And I'm certain I can easily combat any argument she comes up with.

Her panic morphs into confusion before finally becoming acceptance. "I didn't bring a change of clothes or anything."

"Don't worry. You're not going to need any."

She laughs and pushes her palms into my chest. "I hope you have a spare toothbrush."

My chest feels like it could burst with her words. "I do."

"Next time, warn me before you kidnap me."

I scoop her up so she's eye level with me and her feet are dangling over a foot above the patio deck. "No can do," I tease, burying my mouth in her neck. "Kidnapping you is far better for my ego than letting you reject me."

"I wouldn't have rejected you."

I raise my brows questioningly. "You wouldn't have?"

She smiles and chews her bottom lip. "Well, most likely, I would have put up a fight first."

With a roll of my eyes, I set her down. "See? Look how much time I saved us." I open the door to my living room. "Make yourself comfortable while I order food."

She nods, a small smile playing on her face, then she crosses over the threshold in a moment that feels significant, like she's crossing over from her world and into mine. Now, how do I make her want to stay forever?

"Wow, your office is so... empty." Silver is holding a glass of red wine while I give her the grand tour. So far, she's in love with the vaulted ceilings and skylight in the great room, the floor-to-ceiling windows featured in almost every room of the house, and the large brick fireplace in the family room.

"That's because I'm never in here. My job doesn't require much office space anyway. My real office is in the detached studio."

She furrows her brows confused. "You have a second office?"

I grin and signal for her to follow me across the hall, out the door to a covered walkway, and over to the four-hundred-square-foot mirrored room where all my exercise equipment can be found, along with a giant mounted television and a surround-sound stereo system. "This is my real office. Well, this and the six-hundred acres of forests, hiking trails, and water-front parks right next door."

Silver gives the room one giant, sweeping gaze before settling back on me. "Okay, so then why do you have that office in there?"

I shrug. "To fill the room, I guess. I already have a guest room. I can't imagine ever needing two. The most logical thing to do was to make it an office." I grin and shrug. "I told you this house has a lot of empty space. Room to grow, remember?" I don't give her time to respond to that. Instead, I ask her, "What would you do with it?"

Her eyes widen slightly. "Me?"

I narrow my eyes, trying to keep my amusement at bay. I love how easily flustered Silver gets. "I'm not asking you to move in, Silver. Not yet anyway. I'm just asking what you would do if the space was yours to do something with."

She relaxes a little, sets her wine glass on the window ledge, and then looks as if she's thinking about it. "Maybe a library like the one at camp. That used to be my favorite room in the world. I remember the days when I practically lived there in my off time. Partly because I was too quiet and scared to get to know anyone else. Partly because I just loved to bury my nose between the pages of a good book. Well..." She laughs. "They weren't all good, but I read them anyway."

I watch Silver get lost in her story, my chest thundering at the raw emotion behind her words. It's another rare glimpse into the past of Silver Livingston, and I don't want to miss a single beat.

"You don't spend time there anymore?"

She shakes her head, looking wistful. "Nah, now I love being outside as much as I can."

"In your hammock?"

Her pink cheeks darken a few shades as her eyes meet mine. "It used to be such an innocent place."

I smile. "Sorry about that. I'm sure you have other favorite spots, though."

She nods, staring pointedly back at me. "The lake would be one of them."

Images of all the things I've done to Silver in and on that lake are enough to make my insides heat. "You're saying I've stolen what's left of your innocence?"

"Oh no, you didn't steal anything. I happily gave that away." She sticks her tongue out enough to bite down around it with her teeth while dipping her hands into the pockets of her cotton dress. She twists playfully, and I can't stand how adorable she looks right now.

I reach forward, gripping the fabric at the front of her dress, and use it to tug her forward. She fumbles toward me, landing against my chest just as I'm leaning down and capturing her beautiful lips with mine. Hooking my arm around her waist, I pull her closer to me and deepen the kiss.

Who am I right now? I don't even recognize the man I've become with Silver in my arms. It's like she's hypnotized me and I'm still trying to figure out why and how while never wanting the feeling to end. I lift her and hook her bare legs around my waist, then I walk us toward the nearest mirrored wall and murmur against her lips, "Kidnapping, stealing. If you're not careful, I just might trespass right into that chained-up heart of yours."

"Mhmm. Clever." The corner of her mouth curves into a smile as she loops her arms around my neck. "Make sure you don't vandalize it when you get there."

"You said *when*." I suck her bottom lip between my teeth and release it with a pop. "That's quite optimistic of you. And I would never dream of damaging that precious organ. Believe it or not, you're in good hands with this thief. I take care of my precious jewels." I wink, but the doubt that flickers across her expression gives me pause. "You do believe it, don't you?"

She tilts her head, narrows her eyes, and smiles lightly. "C'mon, Kingston. You're a heartbreaker, aren't you? Why should I believe you wouldn't do the same with me?"

My heart squeezes, and I reel back an inch. "Are you serious? I thought you weren't going to do this—doubt me."

Her jaw slacks, and she shakes her head. "I'm sorry. I don't doubt you. I just—" She frowns and searches my eyes as if she'll find the answers to her worries there. "I don't know how this works, okay? The only long-term relationship I've ever been in was at camp, and it wasn't like this. It was simple and boring and predictable and safe." Her gaze slips into something that squeezes my heart yet again. It's like she's pleading for me to understand something she hasn't yet told me. "It's like you came into my world and completely flipped it upside down."

"And that's exactly how I feel about you. It's crazy to think I've only known you for two weeks. I feel like I've known you my entire life."

She shakes her head. "For now, maybe. But what happens when you're back in Seattle—full-time with football, traveling for games, and women are throwing themselves at you left and right? I'll still be at Camp Dakota, sticking bandages on little knees and following up with vaccination reports."

"Is that what you want to be doing?"

Her eyes glaze over for a second. "I thought it was. I've never really considered work outside of Camp Dakota."

"Why not?"

"I guess I didn't know that I could dream that big." She lets out a frustrated laugh and sighs. "Why are we even talking about this?"

"Because," I say, unable to stop the heat of emotion that's swelling in my chest. "You still have your walls up with me. What do I have to do for you to let me in? You talk about how different our worlds are, how far apart we live. It's like your mind has already been made up."

She squeezes her eyelids shut and shakes her head. "I'm sorry. It's not that I don't want to see beyond the short term. Believe me, I want to."

"Then why don't you?"

She blinks, and I swear I see moisture in her eyes. "It's that I *can't*, okay? There are things you don't know. There are reasons why I ended up at Camp Dakota and with the Bexleys." She pauses, the distress on her face making me feel completely helpless. "And there are reasons why I can never leave."

Her words are so final, so cutthroat, I can feel my heart cracking at the impossibility in her tone. To her, we have no future. To me, that's all I see.

## Chapter 31

# BAGGAGE

### SILVER

Kingston doesn't push the subject any longer. Our food arrives, he takes my hand, and leads me to the living room fireplace I told him I loved so much. That's where we eat our takeout—sushi bento boxes from a place he highly recommended. Conversation flows into all his favorite food joints around the area to how he maintains his healthy-eating regime during football season, but he never once circles back to our earlier conversation. The fact that he's avoiding the subject should bring me relief, but all I feel is guilt.

Even though we've moved on to safer topics of conversation, my lie of omission haunts me well past dinner, to when we're finally in his bathroom, getting ready for bed. We're brushing our teeth in the side-by-side sinks, and all I can think about are all the scenarios that come along with telling him everything. Even if I were to tell him the whole truth, that doesn't change my situation. I'm still the teen runaway who will soon be pronounced dead. I'm still the girl who nearly killed her stepmom in self-defense on the night she ran away.

But how much is my secret worth? Is it worth the risk of losing Kingston?

*No.* The answer is simple, but it terrifies me just the same.

"I'm going to hop in the shower." He nods toward the closed door leading into his bedroom. "Make yourself comfortable. I'll be out in a minute."

He leans in to kiss me softly, his lips lingering as if he wants to say more, but he doesn't. I watch his reflection as he turns the valve. Water instantly begins to pour down like rain from the square silver showerhead. He strips down to nothing, revealing every naked inch of the gorgeous man I've spent the past week freely exploring. But what I've learned about Kingston Scott goes beyond the physical, beyond the great sex, and beyond the crude jokes. I've learned that there's more to him then he lets on, but it doesn't take much to see all the other caring, sweet, and charming layers to him. Somehow, I've managed to fall in love with all of it.

Steam is already billowing around him in the shower. Soap suds foam in his hair as he scrubs his way through it before dragging his hands over his neck then down his front. My heart is beating a million times a second when I make the decision to strip down and step into the shower behind him.

The hot water has an instant calming effect to my nerves. While my heart is still pounding furiously within the confines of my ribs, my confidence breaks free like it's wanted to since I met Kingston. I slip my hands around his waist. The way he jumps in surprise tells me he didn't hear or see me coming. I take another step forward and press my front to his back, the ache between my thighs coming to life at the mere thought of Kingston being inside of me again. And then my hand drags down his sternum, to his hard abs, and finally straight down the length of his hardening cock.

He makes a noise in the back of his throat that resembles a groan before leaning forward slightly to rest his palm against the shower wall. His shaft grows thick and heavy in my grip. The fact that he's coming to life with each of my slow strokes only adds to my confidence. I'm working him steadily while allowing my other hand to explore the terrain of his body until my own body is quaking with a desperation to make him come.

I slide around him and sink to my knees. My hands move up his thighs, to his hips, and then back down again. When I dare a glance up at him, I'm not expecting the dark hunger in the green eyes above me. He's bigger than life as he stares back at me as if daring me to take him in my mouth. My tongue darts out as my mouth waters at the sight before me. Every inch of him is beautiful, and I'm taking this moment to revel in it.

Droplets slide over his hair, cheeks, and lips, and I follow one of them as it slips over one pec, down the middle of his stomach, then begins to roll down the beast between his thighs. My fingers wrap him at his base, and I lift him slightly before placing my tongue on the underside of his shaft. His thighs tremble, fueling my already insatiable desire. But it's not until he's sinking between my firm lips that I truly know what it feels like to be at the helm of so much power.

Watching Kingston react to my mouth around him is almost as much of a turn-on as being in control of his pleasure. I test his patience, working him slowly, until those dark eyes open on me again. Then I know what he wants without him even having to say it. I force myself deeper, my jaw stretching until he hits the back of my throat while my hand still grips several inches of his base. Then I'm stroking him into my mouth, pulsing against the tip of him while gradually picking up speed.

His curses and groans fill me with an adrenaline rush I

don't know what to do with. Desperate for my own pleasure, I spread my knees, place two fingers at my clit, and massage it in a slow circle until I'm on the verge of detonating.

As if Kingston can sense my pending orgasm, he grunts and slips his dick from my throat. In one swift motion, he's hauling me off the tile floor and wrapping my legs around his hips. Another groan escapes him as he slams his mouth into me. My back hits the wall of the shower. My fingers dig through his sopping wet hair. And then he's entering me quickly, roughly, pounding me into the wall once before our eyes fly open and lock on each other.

"Fuck," he says, his breaths coming quickly. "No condom."

I swallow, knowing the exact reason for his curse. But when he starts to pull out from inside me, I push back against him and shake my head. "It's okay. I want you like this."

He lets out a breath. "You sure? There's no turning back."

"I don't want to turn back. Only forward."

He doesn't question my words again. Instead, he hoists me up so my legs are hooked around his forearms and his palms are gripping the outside of my thighs. Then he buries himself inside me over and over again. The sensation is all too real as he hits me deeper than he's ever gone before. The friction, the speed, the strength—it all contributes to building the blaze that torches through me.

I've been with two other men in my life, and it's never felt like this. Like my entire body will explode with another single second of contact. I could come up with a million excuses why. I had been dating those men for several months prior to our ever becoming intimate, so maybe things got stale before we ever touched like this. Or maybe, deep down, I chose them because they were safe in a way that ensured I would never get emotionally invested. With Kingston, everything is just... *more.*

"Are you close?" he rasps.

"Yes." I breathe out the word as my pending release takes over my every sensation. I can feel it in his tremble that he's close too. My lips move to his ear. "Come with me." I'm already losing control of my release when I plead with him to join me, but he's right there with me without missing a beat.

He pumps into me, filling me with every last drop until both of us are spent. We're both catching our breaths, and I expect him to put me down, but he stays inside me as we cling to each other. Then he presses his lips to mine, connecting us in every physical way possible. And I know it's up to me to bridge the gap emotionally. The question is... will he accept me when he knows everything?

)●●●●●●(

He wasn't kidding when he compared his bed to floating on a cloud. It's lush and big enough to fit an entire family. After our shower, we didn't bother getting dressed. We dried off and sank beneath his fluffy covers before I curled up in his strong arms. Even after our intense shower sex, it's clear he's still guarded with me.

It's quiet for several minutes before I work up the courage to speak. "Kingston, I—"

"It's okay," he says, cutting me off.

I'm thrown off by the cold indifference of his tone now compared to earlier this evening. "What's okay?"

He averts his gaze and unthreads his hand from mine. "It's okay if you don't want to tell me whatever it is you're hiding. I should have never pressured you to tell me. It's really none of my business, and it's also okay if this"—he gestures between us in reference to the sex—"is all you want this to be."

My heart feels like it's crumbling with his words. "Is that what you think? That I just want you for sex?"

He shrugs. "If it's not, then what are you doing with me if you expect it all to be over soon? You got what you wanted, we had our fun, and you'll end it when you want to. It doesn't have to be a big deal."

Confusion and frustration billow through me. "Wasn't that all *you* wanted in the beginning? I thought you were coming and leaving in a week. I didn't expect for you to come back."

"Maybe I shouldn't have." His Adam's apple bobs, and he blinks before detangling his legs from mine so our bodies are no longer connected at all.

A chill hits me deeper than just my bones. Suddenly, I feel the loss of him before it's even happened, and I'm devastated.

"Don't say that. I was so happy you came back." I scoot toward him, closing the gap between us and pressing my hand to his chest. "I'm with you now because I'm crazy about you. The way I feel when I'm with you is unlike anything I've ever felt before. I told you this is new for me."

He sucks in a breath and releases it in a rush. "Don't you think this is new for me? I don't meet women like you in my world. But the moment I saw you, something changed in me. I just didn't realize what it was right away. I've never been in love before. I don't—" He stops when he realizes what he just said.

A flock of flutters take off in my chest. "You're in love with me?"

He blows out a breath and slams his lids together. "I didn't mean to say that." He opens his eyes again and sighs. "To be honest, I don't know what this is, Silver. It's more than lust, but I don't know what love is supposed to feel like. I don't know if all these crazy feelings I have for you will pass. All I know is that I don't want them to... and I can't imagine that they will."

I swallow over the lump of emotion quickly building in my throat. How I managed to fall so hard for Kingston is something I can't even work through in my brain. Maybe I need to stop trying. "I feel the same way about you."

He shakes his head, and it breaks my heart that he's denying my words without a second thought. A tear slips from my eye. *Did I really mess this up so badly?*

"I do," I say again, gripping his hand in mine.

"That's impossible if you can't even trust me with your secrets."

The impact of his words is crushing to my soul. If I lose Kingston, it will be my fault and my fault alone. I can't let that happen. "It's just," I start, desperately searching for the right words. "I come with baggage that's not easy to explain. I wouldn't dream of putting that on anyone."

"Who doesn't have baggage? I've told you the shitty way I grew up, about my mother's death, and I've been honest with you about my past relationships. None of us are perfect. The trick is to find someone who accepts us for all we are, isn't it?" He places his forehead against mine. "I want your imperfections, your fears, your dreams. I *want* your baggage. Don't you get that?"

I lay there for a minute, letting his words soak in. And then finally, after a slow exhale, I utter the words I never thought I would say aloud. "I ran away from home when I was seventeen years old, and I've been hiding ever since." My insides are swirling with a full range of emotions—relief at speaking those words aloud, panic at the fact that I actually did it, and fear of how he'll respond.

Kingston's jaw goes so slack, I can almost feel the shock radiating through him. "You what?"

I'm eyeing him cautiously, half-expecting him to pick up the phone and call the cops. "I left. I disappeared. One day, I was a senior in high school on the verge of graduating, and the next day, I was a runaway."

He reels back slightly. "But why? What would make you want to do that?"

I haven't even told him the worst part, and I'm already trembling. "I felt like I had to at the time... I felt like it was my only choice." Still, I'm choosing my words carefully.

He sits up, totally alert, his attention completely on me. "Your only choice for what?"

Two words come to mind when I think of how to answer him. "To survive."

He blinks and grasps my hand in his. "Because of your dad's death?"

I shake my head and swallow, stumbling around in my mind for more cautious words. I'm afraid there aren't any.

"Then who in the hell made you feel that way?" His voice is quiet, but the undertone is boiling with anger.

I open my mouth then snap it shut again until I think of another around-the-bush way to get to the point. "Have you ever seen *Cinderella*?"

He nods, not showing any signs of amusement.

"You know the evil stepmom?"

He nods again, and this time, his expression adopts a look of understanding.

"Well," I continue, "let's just say my stepmom made the Disney version look like an angel. Lucinda was an entirely different brand of evil." My eyes move up to his, as I'm finally feeling brave enough to meet his gaze. "So I escaped."

"What did she do to you?" It's Kingston who is shaking now, all while wrapping me tightly in his arms. "Did she hurt you?"

I hesitate for a second, then I nod. "She did more than hurt me. I changed my entire identity because of her."

# PHASE EIGHT

# WANING CRESCENT MOON

"YOU ONLY GROW BY COMING TO THE END OF SOMETHING AND BY BEGINNING SOMETHING ELSE." — JOHN IRVING

# CHAPTER 32

# UNEXPECTED ARRIVAL

## SILVER

I told Kingston everything that night in his bed. From the moment Lucinda married my father, to her behavior after his death, to the nonstop legal battle for my inheritance, to the night of my escape that Harvey had planned, and then finally to my arrival at Camp Dakota. He held me throughout my entire story, hugged me tighter when I cried, and kissed me deeply when I told him about my most recent decision to let Lucinda pursue my presumption of death and take whatever she wanted. Then we made sweet, slow, tender love.

When I awoke in his arms the next morning, I felt free. Truly free. He'd allowed me to unload everything I'd kept tucked away inside me for eight years, and I would be forever grateful.

I listened to his soft, rhythmic breathing and watched as his long lashes fluttered softly against the tops of his cheeks, allowing myself to truly feel what I'd been wanting to feel since I met him. It didn't matter how long we'd known each other or all the things we were still learning. I knew his heart, and it was enough for me to make a decision right then and there. I was in love with Kingston Scott.

Nearly two weeks later, we're back at camp, and I'm more in love with Kingston than ever. Though neither of us has spoken those three delicate words, I feel it building to the verge of rupturing through us every time we're together.

Hope calls us the honeymooners since we can't keep our hands off each other when we're away from the kids, but I just feel at peace.

"See you tonight?" I ask against his lips.

He nods before deepening the kiss. "I'll swing by your office when practice ends. Some of the guys mentioned heading to a bar in town if you're up for it."

I shrug. "Sure. I'll see if Hope wants to come. Her and your kicker, Paulie, seem to be hitting it off."

Kingston grins. "I'm pretty sure tonight's outing was her idea."

I roll my eyes, not at all surprised. "I should have known better."

"What kind of best friend are you?"

"Apparently, the kind that's in la-la land over some guy." I roll my eyes.

"Good to know. I'm sure he feels the same about you."

"You think?"

He nods without saying a word and kisses me again, this time squeezing my ass while he does it.

Our goodbyes always seem to linger longer than they should. "Are we still going to your place tomorrow?"

"Yup," Kingston says with a grin. "We're driving and taking the ferry this time, though."

I pout in mock disappointment. "No seaplane? What kind of date is this?"

He tightens his grip around me and lifts me off the ground before burying his mouth in my neck. "The kind where you bring some stuff to permanently leave at my place."

I let out a nervous laugh. "That sounds an awful lot like moving in with you?"

He sets me down and shrugs, his eyes shining. "I consider it more like frequent sleepovers. You'll stay with me when you don't have to stay here."

I tilt my head, forcing a smile. "I love living here."

"I know you do, which is why I'm not proposing that you move in—yet." He winks. "But with football season approaching, it just makes sense for you to have a key and be there waiting for me in bed naked when I get home from a long, rough day on the field."

He bites down flirtatiously on his bottom lip, making me blush.

I glare back at him, trying not to give in and laugh. He's like a big kid sometimes. "Is that so?"

He nods slowly, his gaze dropping down my neck to my chest then rising again. "Have I mentioned how worked up I get after a game? If you're there, you'll only benefit from all that tension."

My body heats at the dark images that start to play through my mind. I've seen how passionate Kingston gets while coaching the scrimmages. And I've already benefited from how he chooses to release all that energy inside me. I can only imagine how much more intense he gets after a real game.

"I'll come to you when I can," he continues. "But if I can't and you have the time off, I want you to know my house is your house."

My stomach flip-flops at what still feels like him asking me to move in with him, albeit, cleverly. "That sounds fair enough."

The corners of his mouth turn up in a victorious smile. "Good. I'm dying to show you all my favorite places. There's this restaurant in the park near my house that reminds me of Tavern on the Green in Central Park. It's beautiful, and the food is to die for. Sometimes they play these outdoor movies where we can bring food and wine..."

My smile slips as Kingston speaks about all of the wonderful things he wants to do with me. Public things. He may know all my secrets now, but that doesn't change the fact that we can never have a normal relationship. "All of that sounds amazing," I say, staring back up at him regretfully. "But won't me spending all that time in Seattle eventually expose us —or me? You're a famous athlete with cameras in your face everywhere you go. What if the media starts to dig into my past? I still don't know how all of this will play out with Lucinda and the money. I still don't know if it's over."

He bends his brows, sympathy written all over his face. "What if you called Harvey and talked to him? Stop letting these people control you, Silver. You've done nothing wrong. This Harvey guy should have never encouraged you to run away in the first place."

"But I could have killed Lucinda that night. For a few terrifying minutes, I thought I did."

"But you didn't. Hurting her was never your intention. You were defending yourself against an abusive thief. That's all. A law professional would use that to your advantage and fight for your justice. He should have never encouraged you to just disappear."

My heart beats faster at the way he talks about Harvey. "He was only trying to protect me." I search Kingston's expression, waiting to see understanding break through his concern. "They were best friends, through thick and thin, since college," I add, hoping he'll see it my way. "While my father pursued his medical degree, Harvey pursued law. They'd meet for beers when their noses weren't struck in books. They graduated around the same time, and then they started their professional careers just a block away from each other. When I was growing up, especially after my mom died, Harvey was always around, always there for me when my father couldn't be. It's why my father trusted him. He knew Harvey would protect what was mine. He only started to distance himself after my father married Lucinda. He didn't like her much either, but no one could persuade my dad away from her."

Kingston's face relaxes some. "Well, whatever you decide, just know you're not alone. If you want privacy, I'll make sure you get it. If you want to tell all of social media you won the impenetrable heart of Kingston Scott, I'm down for that too." He winks, lightening our heavy conversation.

I laugh, grateful and relieved for his support. "It won't bother you that we can't be seen together?"

He deflates a little and frowns. "To be honest, yeah, a little. But it's not forever, right? You said you're giving up your inheritance to get Lucinda off your back, and that should end all of this. I'm sure you could speed up the process by just talking to Harvey, but if you don't feel comfortable doing that, then that's fine. We'll wait as long as we need to. Besides," he says with a shrug. "I like keeping as much of my private life as private as possible." He brings his forehead down to mine. "All that matters is that when you're with me, you're safe."

There's a fluttering in my chest, and warmth spreads through me. I squeeze my arms around him. "I feel safe with you."

The buzz of our kiss lingers on my lips long after he's walked away as I consider my hesitation.

Back in my office, I'm all smiles as I start my monthly inventory. Unless a kid shows up and needs to be tended to, this will be all I'm doing today. It's quiet in my office, save for the acoustic pop music playing from my office speakers. I'm so in the zone at work that I jump at the sound of the chimes from someone entering the reception area.

Laughing at my ridiculous reaction, I make my way through the doors of my office and into the examination room, then I'm opening the door to the front room. At first, I think Andrew Bexley is back from his overseas trip and that it's him standing there with his back turned to me. But why would he be staring up at the acrylic Orcas Island landscape that he painted on the wall? My gut churns as an uneasy feeling works through me. That isn't Andrew Bexley—or anyone I know from camp, for that matter. Maybe it's a parent of one of the boys.

A droplet of relief hits my veins, and I'm trying to convince myself that's the case, even though deep down, I know it's not true. "Hello," I say gently, my hand still gripping the doorknob behind me. "Can I help you?"

The man turns in a slow pivot, revealing the face of a man who, for so many years, I thought was my savior. "Hello, Sylvia."

# CHAPTER 33

# THE TRUST

## SILVER

"Harvey?" I don't know why I'm asking it like it's a question. There's absolutely no mistaking my father's old best friend and the man who's been responsible for keeping my inheritance safe all these years.

Sure, Harvey's skin has aged from what my memory recalls —deep creases line his forehead and beside his eyes; there are bags beneath his bottom lashes and sprinkles of gray throughout his black hair—but no matter the time that has gone by or the situation we find ourselves in today, I can't help but see my father when I look at him.

The panic that shot through me the first moment I saw him quickly dissolves into a rush of emotion. He shouldn't be here, but I can't deny how nice it is to see a familiar face again.

"Well," he says. "Don't I at least get a hug or something?"

Maybe it's the familiarity of the playfulness I remember when I was a kid before we lost my dad too soon. Maybe it's the lull of his deep tone as I try to process a piece of my past entering my present. But his request is the trigger that snaps me. I walk forward, a smile breaking out on my face as a sob escapes me.

"I'm sorry," I say when I wrap my arms around his neck. "I can't believe you're really here."

He hugs me tightly, and I wish it was a warm embrace that brings me back to my childhood, but too much has changed since that hug meant anything good. I stiffen and back away, leaving a few inches between us before taking another good look at him. *He looks tired.* I push that thought away.

"It's been a long time," he says, his gaze taking in the much-different version of me. "You've grown up a lot. You look well."

I take the compliment with a heavy heart. "Thank you. I've been happy here. The Bexleys have been wonderful to me."

"I'm so glad. Are they here? I'd love to speak to them and thank them in person."

"They're retired now, and they travel a lot. I can let them know you stopped by."

His cheeks push up slightly as he looks down at my scrubs. "A nurse. I should have congratulated you years ago. Better late than never, right? You've certainly managed to make something of yourself. Your father would be very proud."

Emotion swells in my chest. "You think so?"

He nods, his expression so sincere, I feel the sting in the backs of my eyes. "Yes, Sylvia. He always knew you would join the medical field somehow. Even as a little girl, all you wanted to do was help. And your stuffed animals never once complained about the service you gave."

I laugh at the very vivid memory of my lineup of my first patients. "I suppose I owe them a debt of gratitude."

"Ah, I can make that happen. Your storage locker is still in Arizona, waiting for you."

My smile fades at the thought of yet another thing from my

past that I pushed to the side like it never existed. While it's nice to reminisce with Harvey, I'm struggling to hold my anxiety at bay. He shouldn't be here. It can't be good that he is.

Awkward silence fills the air. It seems we've run out of ice breakers, and now all we're left with is the elephant in the room.

"Why are you here, Harvey?" I ask gently, even though I know he could perceive it as rude. "I already told you, I made my decision. I don't want the money."

"I know, but I was hoping I could persuade you to reconsider."

"What?" I laugh at his ridiculous request. "Why would I?"

"Because," he says, and I can tell that he's choosing his words carefully. "Lucinda is no longer a problem."

"What? That makes no sense. After all these years, she's suddenly not a problem?"

"Let's just say, I made her an offer she couldn't refuse. It's a done deal. We need to end this thing, Sylvia. It's time."

I'm so confused and caught off guard. I still feel like I'm missing something. "And how do you see this all working out for me, Harvey? There's still the issue of identity fraud. If you transfer twelve million dollars into my bank account, don't you think someone is going to start asking some questions?" I don't need him to respond. I shake my head and continue. "I've thought about this a lot. I've obsessed over it and ran every possible scenario through my mind. And I'd rather be considered dead than wind up behind bars."

Harvey's frown deepens into a glare. "You can't possibly mean that. Don't you want your identity back? You can't be Silver Livingston for the rest of your life. And this—" He waves his hand around in one sweeping gesture. "This isn't a home."

He used to be so familiar, so calming, a friendly presence to my chaotic world. Now, he just feels like a stranger. "This is a home. *My* home. I have a life, a career, friends, and a—" I swallow before the word *boyfriend* slips past my lips. I don't want Kingston brought into all of this.

"Fine," Harvey says, his patience seemingly tested. "You want to keep this life? Then you need to play along. I'm closing the trust account. All you have to do is sign on the dotted line saying the money is in your hands."

"And if I don't?"

He narrows his lids, and his entire body goes still. "Then you'll be contacted for identity fraud."

"Then I'll tell them it was you who set it up."

Harvey chuckles. "You'll never be able to prove it." He picks up a black briefcase from the floor, sets it on the reception table, and proceeds to pull out a stack of legal-sized papers. He doesn't offer them to me. Instead, he lays them on the counter beside his briefcase, along with a business card. "Read up, and I'll be back with the document you'll sign tomorrow."

So cold, so unlike the Harvey I remember. That night, he was so insistent that I leave, hellbent against letting Lucinda have any chance of getting that money he said belonged to me. Maybe Kingston was right about Harvey. Maybe he never had my best intentions in mind when he convinced me to leave. But then why? Why encourage me to leave then push me to reemerge now? It makes no sense.

Harvey doesn't say another word as he picks up his briefcase and walks out of the cabin. Letting the door slam shut behind him, he leaves me with a stack of legal documents, my shaky limbs, and an entirely new perspective.

I don't know how long I've been standing there before the cabin door opens again, revealing Kingston.

His smile slips when he sees me. "Silver?" Then he looks

behind him, out the closing door, and points. "Who was that man that just left?"

I blink once, twice, then I swallow, trying to contain my wits long enough to tell Kingston what just happened. "That was Harvey."

Kingston frowns. "Your father's best friend, Harvey?"

I nod.

"Seriously? What did he want?"

I look down at the legal paperwork, still not ready to touch it. "He wants me to sign off on the transfer of funds. He's dumping the money into my account tomorrow. And he didn't ask this time."

Kingston grabs the papers from the counter and glares down at the top sheet.

"Something is off with Harvey. I don't understand why he's pushing this on me when I told him I already made up my mind."

Kingston is still examining the document, not giving anything away in his expression. "You said Harvey was loyal to your dad, right? Maybe he's just sick of dealing with Lucinda. Maybe he just wants this to be over." Kingston flips a few pages, and his eyes practically bulge out of his head. "Your father left you twelve million dollars?" He snaps his head up to gawk at me. "Silver, this isn't the kind of money you just let sit there. You need to claim this. People do some bad shit for unclaimed money like this."

I cower a bit as I begin to truly see how naïve I've been all these years. "I don't think I had any concept of what that dollar amount meant at the time. I was young. My dad had just died. It wasn't like I had all these lavish plans. It was just money."

Kingston furrows his brows. "Have you ever asked for an accounting of the money Harvey's been holding on to?"

I squish my face. "What? No. Why would I need an accounting when I didn't even touch it to begin with?"

"So you and Harvey never discussed how to handle your money while he was put in charge of it?"

I shake my head, still confused. "I guess I didn't really think much about the money other than that I didn't want Lucinda to have it, especially after what she put me through. I didn't really care about anything else at the time."

The worry etched into Kingston's face has me worried too. "But you said there were legal battles before Lucinda became violent. Who paid for all of that?"

"I don't know."

"And your room and board here. Harvey must have used some of your trust to cover the Bexleys' expenses."

"I have no idea. We never discussed the logistics of it all."

"What about nursing school? Who paid for that?"

"Me. I saved up some money working here, and I took out a loan for the rest. It wasn't worth the risk to reach out to Harvey. I guess in the back of my mind, I never wanted to feel dependent on the money. I wanted to know I could survive on my own."

He grows quiet, and my heart sinks.

"Why do I feel like I'm missing something big here?"

Kingston takes my hand and squeezes it. "I'm sorry. I'm not trying to question your relationship with Harvey or anything you two have worked out. But—"

I raise my brows, waiting for him to finish. "What?"

"You trust Harvey, right?"

I start to nod, to tell him I would trust Harvey with my life, but that doesn't feel true anymore. "I don't know. He's never given me a reason not to."

Kingston drops the hand still holding his papers. "Then

you're probably not missing anything. This could just be Harvey ready to let go of the last piece of your father, and for some reason, this is how he thinks he needs to do it. Who knows?" He releases my hand and cups my chin. "How about we go grab some dinner and then take a closer look at this stuff? You should know exactly what you're agreeing to *if* you sign on that dotted line."

I can't help but smile despite how I'm feeling. Through the thick fog of emotion that just blew through my world, Kingston's heart and soul are as clear as day. At the end of this nightmare, somehow I know he'll still be standing with me, and that just might make it all worth it.

# CHAPTER 34

# STALEMATE

## KINGSTON

"Everything seems legit." Silver turns the last page of the legal document and shrugs. "Maybe we're just being paranoid."

I take the papers from her and set them on the nightstand. The hope in her voice makes me want to be hopeful too. Maybe it's years of negotiations and contracts with sports teams, agents, PR firms, and companies offering endorsement opportunities. The list is endless, and there's always someone trying to squeeze their own agenda into things. It's conditioned me to be hyperaware of every legal document that passes my way. It's why I have a legal team and a publicist I pay to watch out for my best interests. Silver has none of that. Her innocence is as beautiful as it is heartbreaking, which is why I can't push my opinions on her. She'll need to see it for herself. Perhaps she's already starting to.

"It's not paranoia to want to thoroughly review legal documents. You need to know what you're signing." I frown, because while my gut is still unsettled over the whole situation, Silver is right. Everything seems legit. Harvey handed her the initial trust document signed by Harvey and her father, a bunch of bank statements, the initial trustee acceptance form, tax forms from the last eight years, and more paperwork for closing the trustee bank account. Physically, it's hard to deny that Harvey was here for the exact reason he stated—to unload the trust now that she's of age, so he can be done with it.

"Hey." I rub Silver's back while speaking to her gently. "This is a big deal. Take your time, okay? That's the only way you'll feel good about your decision. No one is rushing you to do anything."

"Harvey is."

I glare, just thinking about the guy. I wish I'd shown up at her office sooner so I could have gotten a good look at him. I'm sure I would've been able to tell if he was being sincere or not. "Tell Harvey to fuck off."

Silver raises her brows at me. Okay, so Silver won't tell him that.

"Tell him you need some time to figure out your next step. This isn't just about Lucinda anymore. Even if he has taken care of her—whatever that means—there's more at play here. Let's say Lucinda isn't a threat anymore. You know what accepting this money means."

Silver blinks back at me, and my chest squeezes at the sight of fear in her eyes. "The Nursing School at University of Washington won't understand. They could pull my credits, degree, my certifications, the hundreds of hours I trained at the Orcas Island Hospital, all of it. I could lose everything."

I shake my head with adamant protest. "You won't lose everything. Not even close. You've got the Bexleys and Hope. You've got me." I swallow. The way my feelings have grown for Silver in such a short amount of time has been the biggest blessing in my life.

"What about my job, Kingston? If I lose my certifications, then I lose my job. That's not just hurting me. That's hurting the Bexleys too."

"You're not going to lose anything. The Bexleys will understand. They already knew they were taking in a runaway, right?"

She nods.

"Then you shouldn't doubt that they'll be there for you when this all blows up. We'll figure this out, Silver. I promise."

She bows her head, and it kills me to see her so riddled with anxiety over this when she's done nothing wrong.

"You were seventeen. You had just lost your father. You were given very bad advice from someone you and your father trusted. You were scared." I cup her chin and look deep into her eyes. "This isn't on you. *You* are in control here."

Silver sighs then nods, her jaw set firmly in place. "You're right. I know you are. It's just hard to step outside of the fear I've been trapped in for so long. I mean, Harvey was adamant that Lucinda would be a living hell or kill me to get what she wanted. But now he's not worried about her and wants this all over and done with? It just doesn't make sense."

"It makes sense to me. Lucinda wanted money, and he probably gave it to her. I wouldn't be surprised if your trust fund has been drained thanks to his business ethics. Harvey was getting paid as trustee, right?"

Silver nods and pulls out the trust agreement. "Yup, right here. He's entitled to one percent of the total trust, plus any out-of-pocket expenses."

"That shithead just got a free vacation to Orcas Island."

Silver shakes her head. "That's the least of my worries, Kingston."

"I know. I'm sorry."

She curls up into me, and I wrap my arms around her. "What should I do?" she whispers, the cry in her voice breaking my heart.

"I think you should rest, and then we'll talk more after the scrimmage tomorrow. My lawyer friend is looking over everything. I don't think you should even talk to Harvey until we hear back from him. Trust me, if something is off, Simon will find it."

Silver nods before pressing her lips to my bare chest. I love having her in my arms like this at night, so much so that I can't imagine ever sleeping without her again. I think back to our talk earlier in the day about moving in together. Even the fact that she considered it gave me all the assurance I needed to know that we were both on the same page. We've come so far, yet I know she still has a lot to figure out on her own. I've never been a patient man, but with Silver, I feel like I can do just about anything.

She falls asleep in my arms, and I'm just about to also, when my cell phone starts to blink with a call. Silver handed over the Wi-Fi password earlier so I could call Simon. I slip out of bed and take the call outside to not wake Silver.

"Hey, bud, thanks for calling me back."

"No problem, King. It's always a pleasure, my man."

I sigh with relief, hoping beyond hope that Simon can deliver some news that helps Silver make her decision. "Did you get everything I screenshotted to you?"

"Yup. I read through the documents, made a few phone calls with a PI buddy of mine to dig into some of the names you mentioned, but I noticed that there's no accounting for the funds. Do you mind sending that to me?"

I scrunch my face in concentration while I try to think back to the financial documents that were included. "I think I sent you those bank statements."

"Yeah, I got those. But I'm talking about an accounting of the funds that this Harvey guy has been responsible for. I noticed a lot of receipts and deposit slips, but there should be an actual tally of all the incoming and outgoing funds from the time he was assigned the trust to now. The bank will want that if he's trying to close the trustee account. There also isn't any proof that I can see that he actually transferred the money into her account. Is that something Sylvia—I mean Silver—can find?"

"He didn't give that to her."

There's a rustle on the other end of the phone before Simon speaks again. "That's a little strange. The bank will want to audit how the money has been handled up until now, and Silver will need to sign off on it. He can't move forward without that signature."

"Well," I say with a shrug. "I guess we have a stalemate. Silver won't be making decisions anytime soon then."

Simon chuckled. "Make sure she doesn't. It's like this guy patchworked the documents to give her only the stuff that won't raise any brows. I've seen this shit before. He gets her all comfortable with one document and then slips her another, and she won't even blink twice about it. You don't have any other info on this guy, do you? House address, license plate, anything?"

"I can ask Silver, but I doubt it. It's been a long time since she's seen the guy, and he could have moved by now."

"All right, no worries. I'll put a rush on everything, and you'll hear from me tomorrow. Until then, let Silver know not to sign anything."

"She knows. Hey, thank you, man. I appreciate you jumping on this."

"Anytime, King."

The eerie feeling that swarms me after Simon hangs up the phone has me as alert as if I've just sucked down a bucket of coffee. What he said triggered the unease in my stomach and tightened my chest.

"Uh oh." I look up to find Zach grinning at me as he's walking by with Anderson. "She kick you out?"

Normally, I would grin and toss him some cocky retort about how I'm just giving Silver space before the next round, but I give him a small shake of my head. "Nah, it was a long day, that's all. She's already asleep."

Anderson frowns as if he can sense something is off. "Is she okay?"

I hesitate a second too long, causing Anderson to step toward me, with Zach on his trail. "What's going on? This doesn't have anything to do with the man in the suit who visited her at her office today, does it?"

I freeze. "Wait. You saw him?"

Anderson nods. "Security alerted me as soon as the guy drove through the gates. By the time I got to them to check it out, he was already leaving. I was going to ask Silver about him. Didn't look like someone's parent."

"No, it wasn't someone's parent." Suddenly, I'm more eager than ever to check out that footage to see exactly what this guy looks like. And then something Simon asked me sparks in my brain. "Hey," I say to Anderson. "Is there any way I can get that footage? You said you saw him drive through the gates? Did you catch a license plate number, by chance?"

Anderson steps forward again, his expression hardening.

"Uh, sure, if you tell me what the hell is going on. Is Silver okay?"

I take in a slow breath while averting my gaze. How much of this will Silver want me to tell these guys? None of it, probably. But Silver can't do this alone. And if she trusts me to help her, then she'll understand what I have to do next.

"I'm not sure, actually." I look back at the cabin, where Silver rests behind those doors, then face the guys, my decision made. "Can we talk somewhere in private?"

# CHAPTER 35

# SCRIMMAGE

## SILVER

My alarm wakes me up, but the gloom peeking through the blinds has me pushing snooze several times before I finally stretch and throw myself in the shower. It's scrimmage day, so I know Kingston is already out on the field. The crack of lightning followed by a low growl of thunder tells me there might be a pause in the day's events, though. Not to mention all the accidents that tend to happen when the rain starts to fall. It's inevitable. A kid runs too fast, slips on a patch of concrete or catches himself in a mud puddle, and the next thing I know, there's a lineup of bloody arms and twisted ankles.

The day hasn't even begun, and I'm already dreading it. Then again, maybe it's not the weather that has me down. I'm toweling myself dry when I walk back into my bedroom and see the legal documents sprawled out on the floor below my bed like I knocked them off the nightstand at some point in the night. Maybe it's a sign—a sign that I should burn the papers and tell Harvey to move on with his life, the way I intend to.

At some point in the early hours of morning, I awoke to a

deep-breathing Kingston, his strong arm wrapped around me, and a long string of memories that haunted me. I couldn't shut them off. It was like a dripping faucet, with each drop quickly pooling around me and drenching the soil below until I was slipping deep beneath the earth's surface, lost, and finally buried alive with nothing but darkness surrounding me.

I don't know why it's taken me eight years to consider that Harvey has been the one controlling the faucet. Watching me. Waiting for me to just disappear. But I see it now. The cautious way he spoke to me about his plan to help me disappear until I could claim my inheritance without Lucinda interfering. Why *didn't* he help fight for me to keep my name rather than encourage me to give up my entire life? What was he so afraid of? Or better yet... what did he want me to be afraid of?

I pull on a pair of gray scrubs, pull my hair up into a quick messy bun, and collect the paperwork from the floor. I ignore the rolling of my stomach and head to work with Kingston's voice replaying in my head. *You are in control here.*

It's a slow morning in the office. Only a few kids come by with stomachaches and headaches, so they're in and out quickly. Since the camp is closed next week for Zach and Monica's wedding, I have no prep work to dig into. And since I finished inventory yesterday, my office is too clean to even straighten.

There's too much quiet time for me to be in my thoughts, so when the phone rings before I leave for lunch, I freeze so fast, I can feel my heart jump straight into my throat. That could be Harvey, but I'm not ready to talk to him yet. I stare at the phone one last time before busting out the front door to join Hope in the cafeteria line.

"How's the scrimmage?"

She beams back at me. "It's good. Kingston's team didn't do too hot, but I guess he can't win 'em all."

I frown. The distraction of last night probably didn't help his odds. "Are they out of it?"

She nods. "Yup. He seemed okay about it, though." She tilts her head. "I think. I don't know. Something feels off with everyone today. Maybe it's just the weather."

I look around, searching the cafeteria and then the line of players walking through the entrance. No trace of Kingston. "Hopefully his ego isn't too bruised." I smile despite the gnawing feeling in my chest. "He's been on such a high of winning all month."

Hope grins. "That boy is certainly competitive. It's hilarious how serious he takes the game. Hey, speaking of the game." Her eyes twinkle, and she leans in excitedly. "Since you leave the island now"—she winks—"are we going to get to Seattle to watch some games this season? You've never come with me before, but you can't avoid them anymore."

I smile. "Kingston's going to get me season tickets, and I wouldn't dream of asking anyone to come with me but you."

Hope squeals and wraps her arms around me. "Have I ever told you how much I love being your bestie?"

I hug her back as guilt swarms through me. There's so much I need to tell her. But not just her, Anderson and the rest of the Bexleys too. If there's anyone besides Kingston that I can trust, it's them. If I do sign those papers, there will be no turning back. They're going to find out everything. I just want them to learn the truth from me first.

Lunch ends, and Kingston still hasn't come to the cafeteria. I look around and realize that Anderson and Zach are missing too. The three of them have become closer over the past few weeks, so I don't think too much of it, other than that I really wanted to talk to Kingston again after everything that went down yesterday.

I've just started on the path to my office when Kingston jogs up to me, looking like he's just run a few miles. "Hey," he says before wrapping his arms around my waist, dipping down, and kissing me square on the lips. "Did I miss lunch?"

I laugh lightly, wondering what has him all worked up. "Yeah. Where have you been?"

He blows out a breath. "I'll tell you everything tonight. Have you heard from Harvey yet?"

I make a face. "No, thank goodness, but I've been avoiding phone calls today. I probably shouldn't do that in case it's a parent or something, but I'm not ready to talk to him yet."

"Good." Kingston's tone is so firm, it makes me quake a little under my skin. "Simon called me back last night. He's still digging into things, and he suggested not signing anything until he's done."

I nod vehemently. "I won't. When will you hear back from him?"

"Soon, hopefully. I keep checking my phone." He takes a step back. "I'm going to grab a quick lunch and then get back to it."

"Okay. I'm going to see if things pick up. If not, I'll hopefully catch the end of the scrimmage for the ceremony."

Kingston winks and jogs off, leaving me with a fluttery belly and a hefty dose of relief to help me through the rest of the day.

It's another slow afternoon in my office, to the point that I lock up around five in the afternoon and head to the field to catch the tail end of the final scrimmage. Hope is at the bottom of the bleachers, standing with a group of other staff members and cheering for the final team. I join her while searching the sidelines for Kingston. He's standing with his team while they cheer on the remaining teams.

A sigh escapes me, and I realize how hyperaware I was of his absence today. To think after this game, he'll be gone for good. While I thought this day would be filled with sadness and longing for how much we've grown together over the past four weeks, I'm filled with only anticipation for our future. Once the looming cloud of Harvey disappears for good, we'll be able to explore so much more in our relationship. Just the thought makes me smile.

"Silver, there you are."

I turn to find Rosetta weaving her way through the crowd to find me. "Hey, Rosetta, what's up?"

"A parent is here to talk to you. He couldn't find you, so he called the front desk and said he'd wait for you outside your office. It sounded pretty important."

*Ugh.* My insides coil. Most of the parents I come into contact with at camp are amazing, but every now and then, I have to deal with the difficult ones whose child would never do something so stupid as to slip and fall while running somewhere they weren't supposed to, and they want to toss blame on the camp or me for not paying better attention.

"Great," I mutter before turning to Hope. "Guess I better head back."

She cringes. "Do you want me to come? I can pretend like I'm your manager."

Laughing, I shake my head. "Thanks, but I'm good." I pinch out a smile at both of them. "Do you mind finding Anderson? He might need to join us if this gets out of hand."

Rosetta and Hope promise to start searching, and I take off for my office, but no one is there, not even on any of the surrounding paths. I push my way inside, thinking someone will be standing there at reception, but the room is empty. Annoyed, I continue through the examination room and walk straight into my office. It isn't until I'm near my desk that I realize something is very wrong.

I didn't have to unlock my door to get in. I always close and lock my office door when I leave. It's a habit I don't even have to think about, but this time, it was already open.

I swivel around to find Harvey inside, examining my office like my entrance didn't surprise him in the least. "Harvey," I say, my heartbeat thundering in my chest. "If you're here about the trust, I'm not ready to sign anything. You'll need to give me some more time."

Harvey chuckles. "Not even a hello. I came all this way." He pouts, but amusement is written plainly on his face.

I sigh, feeling a tinge of guilt for the way I've reacted to his presence. For all I know, he has a job to do and I'm only slowing down the process. Of course he's annoyed. And he did travel a long way. "I'm sorry." I shake my head. "It really is nice to see you again. If circumstances were different, I wouldn't be so—"

He raises his brows. "Afraid?"

An uneasy laugh shakes through me at his strange choice of words. "No, you don't scare me. *Tense* is probably a better way to put it. It's been eight years. You have to understand how this will affect my life moving forward. I just need to figure out a game plan."

His expression is unchanging, causing a wave of chills to roll over me. "I've given you a month. Longer than that if we're counting the nine years I've been managing your account since your father died. You're telling me that you forgot what would happen when you turned twenty-five?"

I shake my head. If he meant to make me feel like an idiot

with that comment, then he did. "I didn't forget. I just... stopped thinking about it, I guess."

"You stopped thinking about twelve million dollars?" His eyes darken for just a second before they flash with something new, something I can't quite distinguish. "Just think. Years ago, you were an innocent young girl dealing with a tragedy that shook us all. Except you came out the winner, didn't you?" He waves a hand around the room. "Look at this life you've built. I can see why you wouldn't want to change a thing."

I swallow and step back slightly so I'm leaning on my desk. "I've been very happy here, but believe me when I say I want nothing more than to end this too, Harvey. Eight years is a long time to carry a lie. I just want a normal life. I've been afraid of my own shadow for far too long."

His eyes shine as he points to my desk, where the papers sit in a neat sack. "Good. Then let's get to it, shall we? Sooner you sign, the sooner you can move on."

I gnaw on my bottom lip, debating a response. The thought is so tempting, to just sign my old name and be done. But I know it won't be that easy. "Harvey," I start slowly. "Signing those papers will expose me. I could lose everything. What if the money isn't worth it?"

The laugh that bursts from Harvey's throat makes every last hair on my body stand straight. "You'll be twelve million dollars richer, minus what I've had to spend to manage your account." His eyes turn cold. "And you're worried about losing what exactly?"

My body locks up, my mind immediately thrown into defensive mode. "Try my career, for one. I love my job. I love the Bexleys. I worked so hard to create a life for myself here after you made me leave my home."

Harvey glares back at me, and I swear I can see steam

blowing out of his red ears. "After I *made* you leave your home? I saved your life, you ungrateful bitch."

I gasp, but he blows right through the derogatory remark and continues on.

"Lucinda would have killed you for that money. She almost succeeded."

The man in front of me isn't the same sweet, caring man who took a risk that night to remove me from a violent situation. He had my back then. He cared about me. He cared about honoring my father's wishes and keeping me safe. Didn't he?

"We should have gone to the cops that night. We could have told them what happened."

"I wasn't there, Sylvia. How was I to know you didn't try to kill your stepmother? Just because I didn't question you doesn't mean the cops wouldn't have."

"That's bullshit, and you know it." I'm fuming now, my voice starting to rise in volume. I can't hold back. Not after what he just called me. "Your job was to protect my assets, which you could have done by taking me to the cops that night."

"Like I told you then, it was smarter not to risk it. Hiding you was what your father would have wanted."

"No," I say with a shake of my head. "My father would have wanted justice. My father would have wanted me to live out my life under the name he gave me." I wave my hands. "You threw me to the wolves, and I survived." I shake my head. "No, I've thrived." I glare back at him. "And now that you think it's time to rescue me, you're realizing that I've already adapted, haven't I? You're desperate for me to close the trustee account, aren't you? Why, Harvey? What are you afraid of?"

He takes a quick step forward—too quick. I stumble backward, afraid of what he'll do next. He wraps his hand around the edge of the door, glares back at me, and slams the door behind him. The sound of it ricochets off the walls.

I start to move forward to open it back up and leave, but I halt when the door clicks locked under his grip. His head slowly turns back toward mine, a black handgun rises from his pocket, then before I can even blink, it's aimed for my head.

"Sit the fuck down and shut up. I tried to do this the nice way. I'm done."

# CHAPTER 36

# SEARCHING FOR SILVER

## KINGSTON

All day had felt like an intense waiting game. I think I slept for three full hours before meeting Anderson and Zach on the field that morning to continue discussing our game plan. Before that, we spent nearly three hours in the security cabin, watching footage of Harvey's every move once he entered the grounds. From the moment he stepped out of his car and looked around like he was hyper-aware of his surroundings, I knew for sure that something was off about the guy. But it wasn't his arrival that creeped me out the most. When he was leaving the medical cabin, he turned to face the closed door then glared at it for a few long seconds before finally walking away. That chilled me to the bone.

"Simon said the license plate will help a lot," I told Anderson first thing this morning. "He'll call as soon as his PI has anything. He knows how time sensitive this is."

Just before lunch is when I got the next phone call from Simon. Anderson and Zach followed me down to the lake, away from the scrimmage noise, where I put him on speaker. "Hey, Simon. What's up?"

"Still digging," he said. "My buddy is trying to locate this Lucinda woman, with no luck so far, but if anyone will find her, it will be him. But the license plate opened up a bunch of interesting things I think you should know."

My heart started beating fast, and my eyes looked between Zach's and Anderson's to make sure they were listening. They were. "Tell us."

"Well, for one, Harvey Michaels doesn't have his own law practice anymore. However, he maintains the same office space he's had for twenty years. And he still sees clients, but his license to practice law in the state of Arizona hasn't been renewed in nearly seven years. This guy is shady. I'm telling you that much."

I hung up with Simon and just stared at Anderson, whose face had gone white. "What do you know about this guy? Did you get a hold of your parents?"

Anderson scrunched up his face. "I did this morning, yeah. My dad said he didn't work with anyone named Harvey Michaels. He worked with a witness protection program. They called him up, said they were a government entity willing to pay for him to provide food, shelter, and safety to a minor, no questions asked. My dad says the money was good, and at the time, he simply couldn't refuse. Figured he could put her to work too. Two months into the whole deal, my parents wanted to adopt her, but she was set to turn eighteen in May, so it wouldn't have been worth the time and paperwork. Anyway, my dad said he didn't notice anything shady. He got paid, but only until she was eighteen. Said he didn't even bat an eye when the money stopped coming."

*Damn. The Bexleys really do love Silver.* Not that I questioned that fact, but from what Silver has told me and what

Anderson just told me, Andrew Bexley and his wife seem like standup humans.

The ceremony just started, and I'm searching for Silver everywhere throughout the crowd. She's always out here by now. I spot Hope walking toward the crowd, and I work my way over to her. "Hey, Hope."

She stops and snaps her head in my direction with a soft smile. "Hey, King. Your team did great today. Sorry about the loss."

Jesus, I'd almost forgotten about losing the scrimmage until she brought it up. "It's okay. Can't win 'em all, right?"

She perks up, her eyes shining. "That's what I told Silver at lunch."

"Speaking of Silver, have you seen her?"

Hope nods. "Oh, yeah. She ran back to her office to meet someone."

Unease snakes through me. "Who did she go to meet?"

Hope shrugs. "A parent of one of the kids. Someone probably forgot their meds or something. Happens all the time. I can't find Anderson, so I was actually about to go check on her and see if she needs backup. We'll come find you, okay?"

I nod and watch her leave, the gnawing in my gut digging deeper and festering inside me. Three things happen next: Simon calls me back, Zach begins to make his final motivational speech to the excited crowd, and Anderson approaches but is interrupted when he gets a call on his walkie-talkie.

I watch him walk off to answer his notification while I accept my call. "Hey, Simon."

"You ready for this?"

The warning tone in Simon's voice is like a Taser to my soul. This isn't going to be good. "No, but go ahead."

There's a crackle of the walkie-talkie as Anderson walks farther away to listen in.

"Lucinda Grant, wife to the late Dr. Martin Grant, was just found dead in the outer banks of Lake Pleasant nearly an hour ago."

My heart sinks. Lucinda's death shouldn't affect me like this, but Harvey said he "took care of her." Is this what he meant? Was there foul play involved? "What was the cause of death? Do you know?"

"The initial gut check from detectives on the scene? Homicide. They can't make a call yet, but the woman's wrists had markings like she'd been tied up before she went in. You think this Harvey guy had something to do with it?"

There isn't a shadow of a doubt. "I do."

"Okay." Simon is tapping something on the other end. "I'm giving police in the area an anonymous tip. It will at least put Harvey on their watchlist to investigate if they find that her death was at all the result of malicious intent."

Anderson is jogging toward me, the look on his face ringing all the alert bells in my brain. "Hey, Simon. I need to go. I'll call you back."

"Wait, King. There's one more thing."

"What's that?" My heart pounds as I'm torn between Anderson's frantic expression and the urgency coming over the line.

"I didn't trust the papers you sent me, so I dug up what I could under public records. Did you know Lucinda was named as the contingent beneficiary of the trust? Apparently, she had been pursuing proof of Silver's death in order to claim that trust money."

"Silver mentioned something like that." I can't stop the bitterness that comes with my words.

323

"Okay, but then two weeks later, she winds up dead? Something is very suspicious with that."

The speed at which this puzzle is clicking together makes me sick to my stomach. "Thank you, Simon. Call me when you learn more."

I shove my phone in my pocket when Anderson gets close enough for me to hear him.

"Harvey is here."

I blink. "What?"

Anderson stops in front of me and nods. "Security was making rounds and didn't catch it on the cameras at first, but he's here."

"Where?" I demand, but I'm afraid I already know.

He nods toward the path leading to Silver's office. "At the medical cabin. Apparently, he walked in first, and then Silver walked in ten minutes later. Neither of them have come out."

Panic quickens in my chest. "How long ago?"

"Security says maybe ten minutes ago, but they weren't sure. We were talking as they reviewed the footage." Anderson looks to be examining my expression. "Don't worry, man. You said Silver didn't want to sign those papers. She's stubborn as hell, man. She won't sign anything if she doesn't want to."

"The last thing I'm worried about are those papers." I start off on a jog, and Anderson is right on my heels as I tell him what Simon just told me.

"You're scaring me."

I wish I wasn't scared myself. "We just need to get to Silver, okay? I don't know if this guy is dangerous, but I don't have a good feeling about him."

"You think he'll try to hurt her?"

I quicken my steps, pushing the horrifying possibilities out of my mind. "Over my dead body." Something else crosses my mind, and my heart sinks farther into my chest. "Hope went to check on Silver."

"What?" The yell bursts from Anderson as fear and anger lance across his expression. It's like lightning striking, and every single thing is illuminated. *He's in love with Hope.* Hope has made it no secret with me that she has a thing for Anderson, but in no way have I seen him reciprocate those feelings until now.

I stop about a hundred feet from the cabin, where we're still tucked beneath a blanket of trees. I'm about to take off again at a sprint when Anderson yanks me backward toward him. "Wait a second and think about this. What if this guy is dangerous? We can't just charge in there. We need a plan."

I shake my head. "We don't have time for a plan. Look." I nod toward the front of the cabin. "Hope just walked inside."

# CHAPTER 37

# FREE

## SILVER

Tears squeeze out from my eyes as Harvey's gun nudges against my temple. "Sign it."

I grip the pen as Harvey uses his free hand to wrap around mine and push the pen onto a paper I've never seen before. At a glance, I can see that it's some sort of accounting document, but that's all I can make out.

"Why are you doing this?" My breath shakes violently with each word.

He jams the barrel into the side of my head again, this time so hard, my temple aches with excruciating pain. "I think the question is, why are you being so damn difficult? All you have to do is sign, and I'll be on my way."

"I don't understand. What is this, Harvey?"

"It's the final summary of accounting that says all money has been distributed fairly according to the terms in the trust. Spoiler alert. You're getting nothing. Looks like this will work out for both of us. You don't want the money, and I do. Seems like a fair trade to me."

I try to pinch back more tears, but my efforts are useless. He sees my fear. He sees my defeat. What options do I have? For the second time since I've known Harvey, he's giving me a choice between what he wants me to believe is life or death. Now, though, I know life isn't that black and white. I'm determined to find the gray.

"But why? Why are you doing this? Even if the money doesn't matter to me, this isn't what my father wanted."

A cynical laugh bursts from Harvey. "What about what I wanted? I knew your father for decades longer than any of you, and what did he leave me? A job. He gave me a job to babysit money that neither you nor Lucinda deserve. Neither of you had to work for a cent."

"That's how inheritances work, isn't it?" There's a gun pointed at my head, yet I can't help myself. He's delusional. How could I have never seen it until now? "It's not like you're not getting paid. Between the will, insurance, and my trust, your payout is generous."

"Compared to twelve million dollars? I don't think so."

I'm trying to understand how it all got to this point, but none of it makes sense. "If you wanted my money then why did you help me leave home so that we could keep it safe from Lucinda?"

"I wasn't helping *you*, you stupid bitch. I was getting you out of the picture to make sure Lucinda couldn't get to you and the money. You were on the verge of cracking. I could feel it. So I conjured up the whole escape plan and then tipped Lucinda off that night. I didn't know you two would nearly kill each other, but it all worked out to my benefit. Scared the shit out of you, didn't it?" He chuckles again.

My blood boils. "If you wanted me out of the way, why

come after me to claim the money? You could have claimed I was dead like Lucinda was planning on doing."

He drops his head back and rolls his eyes so hard I think they might get stuck. "If I had done that, then Lucinda would have been first in line for your inheritance, not me. Keep up, Sylvia. This was the only way. If Lucinda became trust bene-factor by default then she would have wanted full accounting of the money. I don't think she would have approved of the seven million I've already drained from the account for my own personal usage."

My jaw drops, though I'm not sure why anything surprises me at this point. "You stole my money?"

"What does it matter to you anyway?" he asks. "You haven't even thought about it for the past eight years while it's been my life's work to keep accounting for your father's debt, his real estate, ensuring your privacy was secured, not to mention that bitch Lucinda, who never quit reaching for more and more and more."

"So, you're going to take what's left of my money and then what? You don't think Lucinda will come looking for that money? You won't get away with this."

Harvey's lips curl up in an evil smile. "Lucinda won't come after me. I've made sure of it."

A chill sweeps through me at his ominous tone.

He jabs the gun to my head again. This time, the searing pain feels like it's tearing me apart from inside out. "Stop," I wail.

"Sign, and then it will all be over."

There's no fighting the man with a gun. After a shaky breath and a tear-filled moan, I do what Harvey wants. I sign away every last penny of my inheritance.

I drop the pen, fully expecting him to remove the gun from

my temple, but when he grips the back of my head, my blond hair sinking through his fingers, I know signing those papers wasn't the end. Not even close.

Harvey tugs on my hair hard, my head snaps back, and I wail.

"Silver?"

My heart sinks at the sound of Hope's voice.

"Silver, are you okay?"

I hear footsteps getting closer. I look at Harvey, who's got his eyes locked on the door, then he raises his gun just as the door opens.

"No, Hope! Run!" I scream it as loud as I can, but she's completely exposed in the doorway. Her eyes move from me to the gun. Her expression changes with each emotion charging through her, finally landing on the knowledge that her life is about to come to an end. Everything happens so fast.

Hope moves toward me.

I lunge toward Harvey.

Harvey pulls the trigger.

Hope screams.

Harvey pushes me back hard, and I crash into the glass medicine cabinet before falling into a heap on the ground.

Hope is crying, moaning, but still alive, and this gives me enough adrenaline to look straight up into Harvey's eyes as they glare down at me. I know right then that no matter what happens to me, Harvey Michaels will not win.

The gun that just shot Hope is now staring down at me, but not for long. I roll to the side, swiping my leg out under his, causing him to fall to the ground. His gun falls too. I scramble for it and reach it before he can. Then I push myself off the ground and aim the gun directly at Harvey's chest.

"I'd tell you to say hi to my father for me, but we both know you're going straight to hell. Enjoy the ride, asshole."

A bang ricochets through the air, blasting my eardrums to smithereens. As I watch Harvey's life fade right before my very eyes, there's only one thing I feel. Free.

# CHAPTER 38

## LIFELESS

### KINGSTON

Anderson and I are halfway to the medical cabin from the woods when a gunshot bursts through the air, stunning us both. "No, no, no, no."

I sprint the rest of the way then yank open the front door. Before I even have the examination room door open, there's another gunshot, and it's like my own life is fading before my very eyes. I expect the worst—Hope and Silver dead with a menacing Harvey standing over them with a weapon. But that's the opposite of what we see.

"Hope!" Anderson spots her before I do, and I watch in my peripheral as he runs to where she's trying to sit up. She's crying, and her arm is soaked with blood. "I've got you. You're going to be okay."

I turn my full focus on Silver, who is standing over a man's seemingly lifeless body. She's holding a gun, her knuckles white, and her eyes wide like she can't believe what she just did.

"Silver." I run the rest of the way to her. She's shaking hard, even as I remove the gun from her grip and set it on the desk. "Are you okay?" I look her over, checking for any sign of injury. Her hair is wild, the side of her head looks bruised, and there are blood spots on her arms and legs. Other than that, though, she looks okay.

She's still staring down, so I follow her gaze. I don't have to check the man's pulse to know he's dead. And I don't have to ask her who she just shot. I know that man is Harvey Michaels.

Finally, she looks up, her eyes connect with mine, and it's like a dam bursts. She completely crumbles into my arms, sobbing while I hold her against me. "Shh, you're okay," I say softly.

"Hope." She stretches her neck to look around me to find her best friend in Anderson's arms. "Hope, thank God you're okay. I-I'm so sorry."

Hope looks just as teary-eyed as Silver, but she's got nothing but love and forgiveness written in her expression. "You weren't the psycho who shot me. Who the hell was that, Silver?"

"I'll tell you everything, I promise. But we need to get you to a hospital first."

"I called an ambulance. They're on their way," Anderson says before dropping his phone in his pants pocket and then pulling his shirt off to hold it to Hope's arm.

Silver's gaze drops to where Hope was shot, where there's a pool of blood seeping through her clothes. "Oh no." She takes a step away from me and starts toward Hope. "Let me take a look at you first."

I know better than to try to stop her even though she should be resting and seeking help right along with Hope. Instead, Anderson and I move into the examination room with the girls and listen to Silver explain everything to Hope and Anderson while she tends to Hope's wound. I haven't told her yet that I had to divulge some of her story yesterday in order to get Anderson to release the security footage to me, but everything will come out eventually.

Silver starts at the beginning, ending on how it all concluded minutes ago. We hear a siren blaring in the distance, and I'm still in complete shock at the turn of events. "You're telling me this Harvey guy conjured up a plan to hide you from Lucinda, and then waited eight years just to steal your money?"

She looks at me for a long second and nods. "That about sums it up, except he's been taking money from the trustee account this whole time. He mentioned seven million, but I haven't looked at any of the numbers." She sucks in a deep breath and her brows push together. "Are you sure Lucinda is really dead?"

I bow my head and nod. Knowing Silver, she'll blame herself. Sure, Lucinda was evil and wanted money that didn't belong to her, but it sounds like Harvey really played her up as someone to be terrified of.

"I guess it's really over then." Silver looks around the room as the siren's blare grows louder.

Hope grabs Silver's hand and nods in the direction of the open door to her office where we can still see Harvey's lifeless body. "It's over, babe. He'll never hurt you again."

## CHAPTER 39

# JUST LIKE THE MOON
### KINGSTON, 3 DAYS LATER

Memories from that awful day play out in my nightmares every night. I can't escape the moments of panic when I thought Silver could be dead. It wasn't up to me to save Silver from Harvey, as much as I wanted to. I know that's why memories of that night play on in my mind. That power was completely out of my hands.

It's Silver's sweet voice that wakes me this time. "It's just a dream," she whispers. "I'm here."

"Jesus," I say, pulling myself from the depths of my slumber. My heart beats like crazy in my chest. "Again?"

Silver nods, the tableside lamp casting a glowing halo around the crown of her head. It's fitting. She's my angel. She may have saved herself that day—and Hope, for that matter—but it was me she saved from an unfulfilling life. In the end, I will always be grateful for the day she was finally set free.

"Maybe you should see someone," Silver says, concern knitting her brows. "About the dreams."

I shake my head and pull her close. "No, I'll be fine. I just feel guilty for not getting to you sooner. Please don't worry about me." I kiss the side of her head. "It's time for me to be the one to take care of you."

She sighs and melts into my arms. "I'm just sorry I put you and Hope and Anderson through all of that."

"Yeah, well, everyone is fine. Better than fine. Hope managed to make it out of the hospital the next day with a clean entrance-exit wound from the bullet. If you hadn't pushed Harvey out of the way, who knows where that bullet would have gone."

"Ugh, don't say that."

I smile and tighten my hold on her. "You're a hero, babe. Stop blaming yourself for what that asshole did."

"Then you need to stop having nightmares about all the awful what-if scenarios."

"Deal."

She sighs and looks up at me with lifted cheeks. "Anderson still won't leave her side, you know?"

"See," I say, giving her a little nudge. "Hope is probably happy she took a bullet. Watch, they'll fall in love and live happily ever after, and she'll have you to thank."

Silver rolls her eyes. "Don't count on it. As much as I want those two to be together, I know Anderson. He's a hard nut to crack."

"Yeah, because he's been carrying the weight of keeping the family business afloat. With the money you're donating to the Bexleys they don't have to worry anymore. Maybe it's enough to take some stress off Anderson so he can focus on his love life."

"I hope you're right."

"Of course, I'm right. Speaking of being right. Simon

called me late last night and confirmed that Lucinda's death was ruled a malicious homicide."

Thanks to Silver's takedown of Harvey and all the information she was able to provide regarding her history with the guy and Lucinda, it was easy for officials working on her death to tie the crime to Harvey. All in a day's work.

"Wow," she breathes out. "It really is over, isn't it?"

"Well, you still have to deal with the University of Washington about your false identity, but other than that, I'd say so."

My tease earns me a glare, even though I know she appreciates the levity I force on her. If it weren't for my bad jokes, she'd worry herself to death. No matter what happens, Silver has made it clear that she's ready to deal with whatever the ramifications are, even if that means another round of school to regain her credits. Nursing is her life's passion, and she respects the medical field enough to do whatever it takes to make things right.

"Everything is going to be fine," I remind her. "I promise." I reach for her face, cupping her in my palms and pulling her down to my lips in a slow, heated kiss. My heart is still crashing against my ribcage, and I pour every ounce of that adrenaline into loving her, as I will for the rest of my life.

"I love you," I murmur against her lips.

She sinks into me, her body molding into mine until finally whispering back, "I love you too."

I roll her over onto her back, making use of my California king bed, and spread her knees wide. After insisting that she was okay, Anderson was the one who convinced Silver to leave camp for a while, demanding that she take some time off. I convinced her to play house with me for the short term.

I groan at the feel of Silver's naked body beneath mine. We

didn't bother dressing after a full three rounds of sex last night, and my dick is more than happy about that. I draw my tongue down between her heaving breasts then over to a hard, blush-tinted nipple. I cup her breast in my palm and dip down to taste her before swirling my tongue in a way that always make her moan. And when I tease her with my teeth grazing her sensitive peak, I push two thick fingers between her pussy lips and watch her arch her back and gasp like she's been awakened.

God, she's beautiful. I'm a voyeur as I watch her absorb the pleasure my fingers give her. The way her body shakes as she comes. The way the walls of her cave squeeze back as a high-pitched moan slips from her throat. I catch her moan with my next kiss, drinking in every last syllable while I remove my fingers and replace them with my cock.

She pushes my arm, and I help her flip us both over. Her small palms move to my chest. Her thick blond locks fall around her face and shoulders. And then she's moving her hips and riding me like she's in a race for more. I grip her ass to pull myself deeper, meeting each roll of her hips with thrusts of my own until I can feel her tense up with another climax.

"King, I'm coming," she warns on a breath.

My heart catches in my throat. "Did you just call me King?" I growl, the intensity of my pending eruption building to new heights. Still, I'm afraid I imagined her sweet voice calling me by my nickname.

"I did," she says, a smile blossoming on her face. "And I kind of liked it." She pushes her mouth against mine, slides her lips to my ear, and whispers, "Because you're *my* King."

I'm flying high from her words. "It's about damn time." I squeeze her chin, pulling her mouth to mine. "You're my queen, Sylvia Grant. My everything. Forever."

"Forever." She nods. "I like the sound of that."

Her release takes over and I'm right there with her. We're soaring together, high above the world—an unstoppable force, just like the moon. In a journey that will last a lifetime.

# CHAPTER 40

# THE WEDDING

## SILVER, 5 DAYS LATER

The royal blue dress I bought specifically for tonight is sitting on Kingston's bed when I return from doing my hair and makeup. I almost forgot how adorable it is until I slip it over my head and take a look at myself in the long mirror against his wall. It might be too short for a wedding, but the rest of the dress classes it up a bit, with its lace crochet flower bodice and full sleeves over a sweetheart neckline underlay. The tulle skirt is pleated just enough to give me a good swish when I move my hips, and the high waist works perfectly with the white strappy sandals I pair with it. I've never worn high heels and I'm not about to start today.

I look up just as Kingston struts in wearing white pants, a white button-down dress shirt, and a blue suit jacket that matches the color of my dress. I smile as I take a long look at him. "You peeked at my dress, didn't you?"

There's a twinkle in his eyes, but he shrugs as if to tell me he's innocent. "Maybe we just think alike."

I step forward, sliding my fingers down one of his lapels

and biting back a smile. "This isn't prom. We don't need to match."

"Then I guess you don't want this either." He pulls a clear box from behind his back, revealing a wrist corsage that somehow manages to be even more beautiful than my dress.

I gasp. "You didn't."

His cheeks lift in a silent but cocky reply. "I did. I kind of guessed that you missed your senior prom with all the running away you did, and I was too busy getting wasted to remember mine, so I figured tonight could be ours. What do you think?"

I blink back tears and watch Kingston open the box then carefully slip the flower arrangement over my hand. "I love it. Thank you."

He grips my hand in his. "You ready to go?"

"I'm ready."

He leads me out to the deck. In the next few seconds he takes to lock the door behind us, I find my gaze sweeping over the tall pine trees paired with the perfect view of Lake Washington at the bottom of the slope. Sometimes it feels weird to walk outside to a different view than the one I've been used to since I started living at Camp Dakota, but today it makes me smile.

It's only been over a week since leaving camp, but I already feel like a new person. Whenever I thought about what it would be like to actually be free, I didn't realize how much weight would lift from my body and soul. I'm weightless now —happy and overwhelmed with all the possibilities that are open for me to explore.

Once upon a time, I thought I'd never want to leave Camp Dakota, even if given a choice, but I don't know if that's true anymore. And that's the beauty in today. I have options to consider that I never dared to dream of before.

And then there's Kingston. While he's gone during the week for personal training to prepare for the football season a good chunk of the days, he's been nothing but attentive and charming. I love how he leaves me little notes for when I wake up and he's not there, and I love how he's always talking about the future like there's no question I'll be a part of it. Deep in my soul, I know we have what it takes to make it forever.

"Wait a second," I say when I spot a bright blue seaplane sitting at the end of the boat ramp. "Is that for us?"

Kingston comes up behind me and gets close to my ear. "Your chariot awaits, my love."

Every inch of me turns to goo at his words. I look at him with narrowed eyes and a hint of a smile. "I guess I should have questioned why we were cutting it so close on time. The wedding starts in two hours."

"It was a surprise."

I roll my eyes and follow his lead as he walks me down to the dock. "I still don't love surprises, King."

"Well, I think you'll like this one."

I frown a little, not fully understanding. We've ridden on a seaplane before. I'm not sure why this is such a big deal—and then we get close enough for me to see the side of the plane and the letters scrawled across the side.

## OVER THE MOON

My first thought is that it's a coincidence, but when I look at Kingston and he's wearing a giant grin, I know it's most definitely on purpose. "What did you do?"

I'm in shock before he says a word, because I think I know, but I'm too shocked to allow myself to believe it.

He stops before we reach the plane and then turns to me, a

sweet smile on his face. "I know it's a lot. I probably should have aimed for a necklace or a rose or some shit like that, but I figured if I was going to get you anything it might as well be practical."

My eyes bulge and my heart begins to race. "Kingston, you did not buy me a plane."

He looks over my shoulder, directly at the plane and then back at me. "Well, it's a seaplane." He starts talking again before I can argue. "Once you get a legit license, you're welcome to one of my cars. Until then, I figured this was the fastest, safest mode of transportation for you to get to and from work."

When I don't say anything right away, I can see his smile fall. "It's for both of us. I can come to you, or you can come to me. I've got pilots on standby, and to be honest I think it's pretty badass."

I turn to look at the seaplane again, my chest swelling with emotion and my eyes welling with tears. When I look at Kingston again, I wrap my arms around his neck and jump to reach his height, knowing he'll catch me. He does. He always does.

"I think it's perfect."

"You do?" His worry fades into a smile.

I nod. "I do. However..." I bite down on my bottom lip to keep from smiling. "What are we going to do about that reputation of yours? You've turned into one big romantic."

"Maybe." He sets me down and kisses my lips. When he pulls away, he winks. "But only for you."

I grin and turn my entire body to face the plane. He wraps his arms around my waist and rests his chin on my head. "What do you think of her?"

I laugh. "Her?"

"Yup, Over the Moon is a her." He tightens his hold and brings his mouth to my ear. "Because that's how I'll always feel when I'm with you."

)𝕻𝕺𝕺𝕺𝕲𝕴(

Zach and Monica's wedding is a stunning affair set with the water and forest of pine trees as the backdrop. Complete with an arched gazebo with flowing white sheets, real logs being used as benches for the endless rows of guests, and candle arrangements that line the aisle where the wedding party enters —it's all a dream.

I barely got to know Monica before her wedding, but when her father walked her down the aisle and she welled up as he gave her away, it took everything inside of me to keep from sobbing. It was beautiful, but also heartbreaking in a selfish way, because I know I'll never have that. I think, in that moment, Kingston knew what I was thinking because he reached for my hand and squeezed. To think the woman dressed in white one day could be me is almost impossible to imagine, but that's the thing about Kingston—he's made me realize that nothing is impossible.

We're at the lively reception now waiting for the bride and groom to change into outfits before they cut the cake. Kingston's just stepped away to go to the restroom when I hear a familiar squeal.

"There you are." Hope dashes toward me and wraps her arms around my neck. "I've missed you."

Warmth spreads in my chest at the sight of my best friend. "It's only been a week."

She pouts. "Yeah, well, while you've been living the life

with your hot celebrity boyfriend, I've been holed up in the staff room watching cooking show reruns."

"I thought Anderson was keeping you company."

Hope shrugs and I can see the fleeting look of disappointment. "Yeah, he checks on me often, but his initial concern has worn off. He's back to putting his every waking moment into work. He's on this new mission to change the name of the camp from Camp Dakota to Camp Bexley."

I frown, even though I love the idea of the name change. "I'm sorry, Hope. I really don't understand that man. He's impossible it seems. But hey..." I wiggle my brows at her. "You look gorgeous. Where did you get that dress?"

"Isn't it amazing? It's from Monica's shop."

The gold open-back lace dress with a high neck and long lace sleeves really is stunning. It accentuates Hope's curvy frame in a way that will make any guy do a double take at the sight of her.

"Well, it's a perfect fit." I shoot a glance around the dance floor and surrounding tables. "There's bound to be a hottie for you somewhere. Did you notice how many of Zach and Kingston's teammates showed up?"

Hope points at me and bursts out with a laugh. "Since when do you recognize Seattle players?" Before I can respond, Hope's eyes latch onto something over my shoulder and her jaw completely drops, catching me off guard.

"Oh my God, they're even more gorgeous up close, don't you think?" She grabs me by my shoulders and turns me to face the same direction she's looking in. "Look."

It takes me a second, but I spot the familiar couple immediately. "Yeah, I didn't realize Desmond was the best man until I saw him up there with Zach at the altar. And you're right. They're definitely beautiful."

Kingston walks up to catch the tail end of our conversation. "Desmond and Zach have been friends since they were kids. They used to play ball together, but Desmond quit when he realized he wanted to go to culinary school."

Anderson approaches with two glasses of champagne and hands one to Hope. "Your hand was empty. Figured you might want this."

I think I die a little inside at the exchange, especially when Anderson gives Hope a wink as she's accepting the glass. Her expression reveals how utterly stunned she is by his gesture, and I hope this isn't the beginning of another round of pining that Anderson can't return. Hope has loved him too long and too hard to make it through more disappointment.

"Do you want to meet them?" Kingston asks, breaking up the moment.

"Meet who?" Anderson's brows bend in.

Hope perks up and nods. "Yes, please."

A minute later Kingston is walking back over to us with the stars of the cooking reality show, Maggie and Desmond. Maggie looks like some type of model with her exposed long legs, flawless skin, and the overall way she carries herself. She's tall too, but Desmond is taller. He matches her charm, but differently. His long brown hair is tied back in a bun while he fills out his gray suit in a similar way Kingston does, fully with no regard to the hearts they might break tonight at just the sight of them.

"Desmond, Maggie, this is my girlfriend, Silver, and my good friends, Hope and Anderson."

Desmond claps Kingston on the back and gives him a side eye before grinning. "I didn't think I'd ever hear you say those words. Your girlfriend?"

I blush and Kingston shrugs. "What can I say? I think she's

the only woman I've ever chased who didn't want to get caught?"

"Not at first, no," I add. "But running has never been my favorite sport, anyway. He wore me down eventually. Figured I might as well give him a shot."

Maggie steps forward with a smile. "Well, what Desmond meant to say was that it's nice to meet you all."

All the attention turns to the bride and groom when they exit the wedding party tent and enter the party. Monica and Zach are dressed down slightly, Monica in a breezy off-the-shoulder lace dress with frilly scalloped edges. It's playful and sweet, just as she seems to be in what little I know about her. Zach is in off white slacks and a white button down with the sleeves pushed up to his forearms and the top two buttons undone.

Their faces are radiant as they take in the loud cheers that welcome them, and then they're walking toward the cake, but stopping to talk to their friends and family on the way. When they finally get to us, Monica's eyes catch on Hope first.

"Is that my dress?" Monica gasps and weaves the rest of the way to a laughing Hope.

"It is! I fell in love with it online and knew it would be perfect for your wedding."

"Well, it looks perfect on you. I'll need to get your phone number. I have so many samples sitting around. You'll love them."

Hope's jaw drops. "Oh no, you don't have to do that."

Monica shakes her head. "Hush, I want to. Desire, my wedding planner, said you were such a big help with the wedding. I'm so grateful."

Hope tilts her head, accepting the compliment. "Well, it was my pleasure. You look stunning, by the way. Your wedding dress was phenomenal, and this—" Hope shakes her head, appearing amazed. "Did you make them both?"

A quick laughs bursts from Monica. "Oh no. I was too nervous about planning the wedding to design my own dress, too. But thank you."

Zach steps forward and takes Monica's hand. "Cakes, it's your time to shine." He nods toward the most beautiful wedding cake I've ever seen. It's a tower of cake with what looks like chocolate dripping down the sides of it and strawberries decorating the exterior.

They walk off and Hope sidles up to me with a grin. "Is it weird that I just fangirled so hard over the bride?"

I laugh. "No. I think she fangirled right back."

We watch Zach and Monica as they finally cut the cake and feed each other bites of a chocolate covered strawberry with devilish looks in their eyes.

"Smash that cake in his face, Mon!" Maggie screams. Everyone laughs.

Monica looks over at Maggie and winks, and then picks up a handful of chocolate cake in her fist and smacks it square on her new husband's forehead. Zach stares back at her wide-eyed like he did not expect for her to do that. She's laughing so hard that she doesn't see him grab his own fistful of dessert until his hand is raised. "Oh crap!" She squeals and starts to turn, but he pulls her back by her waist and wipes his cake-filled palm down the side of her face. The entire room is howling.

The rest of the reception is a full-on dance party. The booze flows harder, the voices grow louder—everyone is having too much fun to leave. Most of the guests are staying in the surrounding cabins, anyway, so there's really no excuse to call it quits.

Kingston and I are wrapped in each other, slow dancing to

a fast song, when I spot Anderson on the edge of the dance floor appearing frustrated. I follow his gaze to find Hope dancing with one of the wedding guests. While the entire scenario makes me sad for Anderson, I'm not at all about to get in the way of Hope's temporary happiness to alert her of the update. She's given Anderson plenty of chances before this to step up. Now, it's his turn to put in the work.

Kingston leans down to reach my ear. "Thirsty?"

"Yes!"

He tugs me to the bar where Zach, Monica, Maggie, and Desmond are already congregating along with another couple who I haven't had a chance to meet yet. Hope and her new guy are approaching, too. Zach introduces Kingston and I to the couple, Gavin and Chloe, and that's when I notice the double stroller to the side of Chloe. I peek down and smile at the twin boys dressed up in baby tuxedos. Their eyes are closed, but they're fidgeting like they're awake.

"Oh my gosh," I say, holding my hand to my chest. "They are precious."

Chloe smiles down at them like a proud momma, and then leans over to lift one of the boys from the stroller. "They are very precious." She nuzzles his cheek with her nose and adopts a cutesy baby voice. "They're also quite the handful."

"They're so tiny," I gush. "How old are they?"

"Eight months. This is Thor." She nods over at her husband, Gavin, who is picking up their other baby. "And that's Parker."

I laugh in recognition. "Marvel names?"

Chloe nods toward Gavin. "My husband has always been obsessed with comics."

"Give me my baby," Monica says playfully while shoving her arms out.

Chloe laughs and hands him over to her. "Be careful what you wish there, Mon. Soon enough, this will be you."

Monica leans in closer to Thor. "Whenever it happens, I'm ready. At least you have a babysitter in the meantime."

Maggie chooses that moment to swoop in to join the conversation. "Wait a second. I'm the older sister. First, you get married before me, and now you're trying for babies before me? At least wait until after my wedding so that we can have our babies at the same time."

Desmond and Zach's focus is on us now. "Wait. What?" they ask at the same time.

We all burst into laughter while the guys catch on to the conversation.

Kingston chuckles. "Sounds like you guys better check for holes in your condoms when you get home."

Monica's eyes widen like she hadn't thought of it. "Great idea, King."

Zach walks to stand behind her and kisses her cheek before whispering something in her ear that makes her blush. She melts and offers Thor back to Chloe. "Looks like we're calling it a night."

There's a mixture of ahs and laughter before they make their rounds to say goodbye to their guests.

I manage to pull Kingston back on the dance floor for another slow song, because I can feel that our time is winding down. My arms are wrapped around his waist and he's smiling down at me while we barely move from side-to-side.

"What about you?"

I tilt my head, not understanding his question. "What about me, what?"

"Are you going to poke holes in my condoms one day?"

I throw my head back and laugh. "Considering we stopped

using those, probably not." My skin heats, because I know that he didn't mean it literally. "But one day, I could see myself getting off birth control." I search his eyes, realizing this is one of the many conversations we've yet to have. "How do you feel about kids?"

"Well..." He tightens his hold around me. "I've always secretly wanted a big family of my own."

I pull back slightly, surprised. "Really?"

He nods. "Yeah, it sucked being an only child. I want three kids. Minimum."

The pure excitement that flashes in his eyes makes me smile. "Well, then I hope your future wife is prepared to handle all the mini-Kingstons that will be running rampant."

His lids narrow, and he swoops down to press his mouth to my ear. My heart is pounding like crazy. "You say that like I won't make you my wife one day. Sylvia Scott. I think that has a nice ring to it, don't you?"

The giddiness that explodes through my body is almost too much to handle. But I manage to lean back slightly to hold his gaze. "I don't know," I tease. "I kind of think *Nurse* Sylvia Scott sounds better."

He winks and presses his lips to mine. "That sounds like a damn good compromise."

# EPILOGUE — ANOTHER NEW MOON

## SILVER, 7 MONTHS LATER

If anyone would have told me eight months ago that I would be hanging out in a VIP beer garden in Tampa Bay getting ready to watch my boyfriend play in the Super Bowl, I would have choked on my laugh. Hope, Monica, Maggie, Desmond, and I flew in yesterday, and I'm a wreck with nervous flutters, not just because this is the biggest game of Kingston's career, but because this past week has been the longest I've been apart from him since we've been together and I can't wait to be back in his arms.

I'm standing at a high table waiting for Monica to return from the bar. Hope is walking around with Desmond and Maggie, drinking and laughing like she's on cloud nine. After her injury and getting her hopes up over Anderson, she deserves some serious fun.

"Here." Monica slides a shot glass in front of my nose. "Figured you could use one of these too."

I take it and laugh. "Thanks. Why am I so nervous? I'm not even playing."

"Girl." Monica shakes her head like she's been through this before. "Welcome to my world. It's intense every season, especially during playoffs, but the Super Bowl is on a whole other level. Does Kingston get all quiet and in his head before games, too? Zach becomes so focused, I barely recognize him sometimes." She bounces onto her toes and grins. "But it's all worth it when the season ends. Promise."

I throw my head back and laugh, already feeling buzzed off the one vodka. "Oh my gosh, yes. I never realized how superstitious he was until these past two weeks, too. Kingston talks to himself in the mirror, pumping himself up."

Monica clutches my arm with her laugh. "That's almost as bad as Zach sleeping with his lucky football. He's had it since he was in high school and it gets tucked into bed right beside him like a little baby."

I'm laughing so hard that tears are forming in my eyes. Monica holds her shot in the air, gesturing for me to take mine with her. We toss them back, and suddenly I'm feeling courageous.

"Speaking of off-season," I say. "Do you think it's bad that I want to stay in Seattle with Kingston? I mean, Anderson is going to give me my job back as soon as I'm certified again but being away from Kingston when he travels is already so hard. I just—" I chew on my lip. "I love him so much and I hate the idea of working so far away when he finally has time off."

Monica's entire expression softens, and a smile lifts her cheeks. "Take it from someone who almost blew it with my soulmate for overthinking—do what's in your heart. You can be a nurse anywhere, right?"

"I can." My pulse is racing just thinking about making a detour on the path I thought I was set on for life. "And now that I'm back at the university making up some of my face-to-face credits, I'm finding out all of these nursing opportunities I'd never considered before. But I'm worried I'm only considering anything outside of camp because of Kingston, and I can't be that girl, you know? I don't make decisions based on men."

Monica laughs, grabs my hand, and squeezes. "It's okay to base some decisions on the man you love. And I have it on good authority that Kingston is madly in love with you, too. Whatever you decide, my guess is you and Kingston will find a way to be together. You support each other's careers and that's hugely important. The rest will fall into place."

"You think so?"

"I know so."

Her response is so heartfelt, so affirmative, that it leaves me with nothing but excitement for the future. "Thank you for talking with me about this. I can't really mention anything to Hope yet. She'll convince me to come back."

Monica squeezes my hand again. "You can talk to me about anything, anytime. You have my number. Besides, we're SeaPlayer Chicks. We stick together."

"Wait," I say with a laugh. "There's a name for dating a Seattle football player?"

Monica laughs as if she's just handed me the key to a secret society. "There's a whole new world when you're dating a Seattle player." She winks. "Just wait until you marry one."

)‡��†‡(

"We won!" I scream the words at the top of my lungs while the Seattle crowd around us goes absolutely wild.

"Holy shit, we won!" Hope squeals before wrapping her arms around me.

"By three freaking points," Maggie says while shaking her head in amazement.

I've gone to enough games with her by now to know that she isn't the rowdiest of fans even though she loves football. Her fiancé on the other hand is hooting and hollering so loud his face is beet red. But after a neck-and-neck game, we'd all been clinging to each other like our lives depended on it. Seattle won by a field goal in overtime and I thought I was going to fly out of my body with excitement.

I think we laugh, cry, and scream nonstop until the officials call the end of the game, and then we're weaving our way down to the field for the celebration. We're mixed up in a large crowd of fans, media, and players when I finally spot Kingston. He's wearing the biggest smile I've ever seen on his face, and I swear his eyes are wet with tears. The overwhelming emotion of it has me crying all over again.

At the same time I spot him, Zach swoops Monica up in his arms and kisses her smack on the lips. My heart swells, and I want nothing more than to get to Kingston to do the exact same thing. I start walking in the direction I last saw him, when he slips back into the crowd and I lose him again.

"Did you find him?"

I didn't realize Hope was following me until I hear her voice. I shake my head and pout. "Yes, but I lost him again."

"I'll help."

She tugs me toward the front of where the crowd is congregating, but everything is happening so fast. By the time we get to where I thought I might have saw him last, Coach Reynolds is speaking into the microphone and all the players are standing around him. So, we stop and listen to the speeches and cheer like crazy for Zach when he accepts his MVP award.

When Zach leans into the microphone after making his MVP speech and echoes throughout the stadium, I completely freeze. I don't know why, but something deep in my gut tells me this isn't normal protocol.

"Really quickly," Zach says. "I need to shoutout my buddy and the best defensive end in the league, Kingston Scott. Not only did he have the best season of his career with 82 tackles, 21 sacks, and 17 passes defensed, but he played his best game of his life today. I want to bring him up here really quick to give him the mic."

My heart is exploding like fireworks in my chest when Kingston grabs the microphone and beams out at the crowd. I miss him so much that seeing him so close yet so far away is almost unbearable.

"A hell of a season, am I right?" Kingston raises his hands like a conductor leading a symphony of crazed fans. "We couldn't do this without you guys here." He waves a hand over the crowd. "And you." He points to the camera. "This entire season has been a dream for me, and one of the reasons why is standing here somewhere." His gaze travels over the sea of people. "Where are you, Silver?"

I love that while I'm Sylvia again, legally, my friends all still call me Silver. But hearing Kingston say my name now in front of millions of people sends a wave of heat through my body.

Hope raises her hands beside me. "She's right here!"

Kingston sees Hope first and then his eyes lock on me. He smiles, and every ounce of nervousness I'd been feeling melts away. "There you are."

Just then, Monica, Maggie, and Desmond come to stand

beside me. I don't know what is going on or why my heart is racing or why I feel like I'm floating on a bubble until Kingston speaks again.

"It didn't take me long to figure out that you're the love of my life. You make me feel like the man I never dared dream to be and I would never want to do this life without you."

I'm shaking so hard I can't stop the tears from sliding down my cheeks.

"Right here, right now, in front of the world, I need to ask you a very important question."

My hands move to my mouth and I can feel my eyes widen as they stare back at him. "Is this real?"

It's just a whisper, but the Hope's arm around my waist tells me she heard me. Meanwhile, Kingston grabs the microphone and hops off the stage. The crowd parts enough to allow him to walk right up to me with a smile. Hope hands him a gray velvet box while he hands her the microphone to hold. He winks and that's when I realize *she knew this whole time.*

"Sylvia, Silver, Livingston..." Kingston's smile is so hopeful I want to burst. He kneels in front of me, and I'm so emotional that I can't think of anything but to grip his face in my palms. All I want to do is say "Yes!" before he's even asked.

"I can't imagine completing a single phase of life without you by my side. The dark, the light, let's navigate it together. What do you say we make this *forever*-thing official? Will you marry me?"

I burst into tears as he opens the ring box. I haven't even looked at the sparkly jewel before I'm falling to my knees, pushing my lips against his, and saying, "Yes. A million times, yes."

His arm wraps around my waist and we kiss, unable to keep

the smiles from our faces. When he pulls back he slips the most beautiful vintage-looking ring I've ever seen on my finger. The rose gold band almost looks like a crown. Diamonds decorate the ornate shape and a gorgeous oval moonstone sits in the middle.

"I can't wait to spend forever with you, Kingston." I swipe at my tears.

He wraps me in his arms and brings me to my feet, then leans me back and kisses me while the world watches. To think, less than a year ago, I was hiding from the world, perpetually stuck hidden on the dark side of the moon. Now, I'm living my life loud and proud, finding my forever, and getting engaged on national television. I've found my way into the light with Kingston Scott.

With him, I've found my forever moon.

## THE END

*Thank you so much for reading Silver and Kingston's story!* Curious about Hope, Anderson, and the rest of the Bexley brothers? Find out more in an all-new series of standalones, starting with Weight of Regret. Keep reading for a peek inside!

**Want to find other books in the BelleCurve series?**

*Up in the Treehouse (Chloe and Gavin's story)*

*Under the Bleachers (Monica and Zach's story)*
*Through the Lens (Maggie and Desmond's story)*
*Over the Moon (Silver and Kingston's story)*

**Looking for another bingeable series?**

*Check out the sports romance readers are raving about,*
*Center of Gravity!*

# Dear Reader,

I hope you enjoyed Silver and Kingston's story! If you have a few minutes to spare, please consider leaving a review on Amazon, Goodreads, and BookBub. Reviews and sharing your love for our stories mean the world to an author. Just a few lines goes a long way!

You can also connect with me on social media to be sure and never miss a new release, event, or sale!

Subscribe: geni.us/KKAllenNewsletter
Instagram: Instagram.com/KKAllen_Author
Facebook: Facebook.com/AuthorKKAllen
TikTok: Tiktok.com/@k.k.allen
Website: www.KKAllen.com

**Join Forever Young**
Enjoy special sneak peeks, exclusive giveaways, enter to win ARCs, and chat it up with K.K. and special guests.
**Facebook.com/groups/foreveryoungwithkk**

# Weight of Regret

## Excerpt

## Prologue

He's a whisper in the night when I'm all alone and buried under my covers, with nothing else around save for my thoughts.

I always think of him. Anderson Bexley. The man who gripped me at first sight with an amber-eyed glance. But it was his heart that kept me.

It was easy to fall for the man who carried his responsibilities like they were badges of honor—and fall I did. Deeper and deeper into the sweet abyss of dreams fueled by simple moments few and far between.

If only he had fallen with me.

With my hands raised, fingertips reaching out to his shadowy form, I call out to him, desperate for him to see me. It's my own voice that responds in layered echoes as I fall. Because that's what I do. I spiral helplessly and hopelessly into a bottomless pit of agony.

He never catches me.

*Bang.* Lightning cracks, ripping me straight from the depths of my slumber as a scream shreds my throat. I sit up, gripping my quilt tightly to my chin. My lungs gasp for air as if I'm sucking from a straw, but only at first. My panic always subsides, but the nightmares live on whether I'm asleep or awake. Though, the storms seem to trigger me most.

After a near-fateful shooting left me with a bullet wound in my arm last year, memories of that horrid day have served me a cold dose of reality. This life could be over in the blink of an eye... and I'm still chasing a man who sees me as nothing more than a doting, loyal employee.

Footsteps creek against the old wood outside my door, and then there's an urgent knock that's almost as familiar as my recurring nightmares.

*It's him.*

I can visualize Anderson's scrunched brows and his tightly closed fist as he alerts me of his arrival.

"Hope," he calls from the other side of the door. "Are you okay?"

There was a time when I would find any reason to believe that Anderson Bexley loved me back, even just a little. Even now, I have to fight the glimmer of hope in my heart that wants to believe there's more to this late-night visit than the mere coincidence of him hearing me scream during his routine rounds of the campground.

My breathing couldn't possibly come quicker as my feet pad against the worn wood. I wrap my hand around the chipped brass doorknob and squeeze like it's a stress ball. While constant disappointment has conditioned me to expect nothing in return, my heart beats for him still.

A twist of my wrist—a gentle tug—and I'm staring back

into golden eyes shrouded in a dark cloud of worry. A furrowed brow and a downturned bearded mouth greet me.

"Nightmares again?"

My sigh releases with a quick, airy laugh. "It's just the storm. I'll be fine." My faux nonchalance isn't lost on him. While Anderson may not love me back, he certainly knows me well.

He takes a step toward me, like he expects me to invite him in, but I close the gap in the door an inch instead. The slight move causes him to look down at my attire—a short, yellow silk camisole top and matching shorts. Not something I'd normally wear in front of my boss, but here I am.

While I'm not shy when it comes to my body, something about the change in temperature between us gets my heart racing a little too hard. Anderson's throat bobs, and his eyes stick a little too long on all the parts of me I'm desperate for him to touch.

*It means nothing.* I silently scold myself for encouraging that desperate woman inside me who has dreamt of Anderson Bexley since the moment we met three years ago—a dream that felt so close to becoming a reality once upon a time.

His gaze locks back on mine. "I can stay." There's a kick inside my chest at his insistence. "Let me stay. At least until you fall asleep." He darts a look behind him. "The weather isn't getting any better for another few hours. And..." His eyes search mine.

My heart lobs into my throat. "And what?"

"And I wanted to talk to you about something." He lets out a breath. "Something important."

With a release of the knob, I take a step back to allow him entry. One step, and his large frame fills the space. He dominates my senses, triggering a cage of wild butterflies to awaken after weeks of hibernation.

He closes the door behind him, shakes out of his soaked jacket, and hangs it over the wooden chair at my desk. Clearly, he's no stranger to my cabin, considering he stayed here to nurse me back to health after I took a bullet in the arm—a nightmarish incident caused by a psychopath who had trespassed onto our campground. Luckily the bullet only left me with temporary nerve damage. Still, the wound, like my nightmares, will haunt me forever. But it was during those short few weeks afterward that I would have sworn his feelings for me were stronger than he'd ever let on.

He never left my side. Morning, noon, and night, it was me who held his attention. More than work, more than the guests, more than his nonstop family issues, and more than any other employee at camp. For a moment in time, his broody armor fell away, and I got to see the broken man beneath the mask. And deeper I fell.

But the moment I healed enough to go back to work, whatever was beginning to sizzle between us stopped cold. Because that's what Anderson does. He cares for people. He cares for me too—just not in the way that I want.

That's the problem with unrequited love. It doesn't give back, even when you think you're on the verge of something spectacular. It's like looking into a one-way mirror, knowing in the depths of your soul that you're standing in front of *the one*, but he never sees you in return. Still, you try. It's an addiction. A trap. And the deeper you fall, the harder it is to climb your way out.

Anderson reaches my oversized cream chair in the corner of the room, turns around, and opens his mouth, slamming it closed again, like he doesn't know what to do or say next.

I take a tentative step forward. "Is everything okay?"

His jaw ticks. "When were you going to tell me about Seattle?"

Heat blasts me from within, encasing me in an inferno that I don't know how to escape. "How did you hear about that?" My voice is small, shaky. Of all the reasons Anderson could have come here, I hadn't expected that.

His expression darkens. "So, it's true. You're leaving?"

The rapid staccato of my heart has me fighting for my next breath. "I-I haven't decided anything yet. It was just a job offer, but—"

"Is it what you want?" It's not like Anderson to interrupt anyone. "You applied, so it must be what you want."

I can feel the hurt and anger rippling off his body.

"Someone sent me the job description, and it sounded interesting. You know how much I love the project management side of things. So I applied. I didn't think I would actually get an interview."

"But you did."

My nod comes with a hard swallow. "I did."

"So you snuck off to interview."

"I didn't sneak off anywhere. I went on my day off. But yeah, I went."

Silence stretches like taffy between us, lengthening and winding in one sticky knot. "Did you accept?"

"Not yet. I'm not sure if I will."

"Why not? Clearly, you're unhappy here."

My shoulders fall with my sigh, and I tilt my head, imploring eyes desperately trying to get him to see me. *Why doesn't he ever see me?* "This camp is my home, Anderson. It's the first home I've ever truly had. I'm not unhappy, but there are things I want that I'm not getting here." *Like you,* I want to scream.

Living on a small island off the coast of the Pacific Northwest comes with endless perks. It also comes with its burdens, and those are the ones I'm fighting off right now. I'm not getting any younger, and it's starting to feel like my life has stalled, in a sense.

"You recently got a raise. All your medical is paid for, not to mention your room and board." He waves his hand as though he's provided me with the best digs in the world. "You're one of my best senior staff members, Hope. If you're going to leave, I would appreciate some notice."

My jaw drops. "Is that all you care about? Notice? Is two weeks sufficient, or do you need more?" My sass, like his anger, is out of character.

Anderson takes a step in my direction, his eyes flashing with emotion that appears to carry more fear than anger. "You could have at least told me what you were considering. Instead, I had to find out from chatter in the dinner hall after you'd left."

It had been a mistake to tell my coworkers. The island is small, but the camp is smaller. Gossip travels fast.

"I'm sorry." I chew on my bottom lip, trying to choose my words carefully. "It didn't feel right telling you when I hadn't even made up my mind. There's a lot to consider."

"Like?"

I throw my arms up. "I don't know. All the pros and cons, I guess. Give me a break, okay? If I do choose to leave, it's not like I won't help you find someone to replace me."

"No one can replace you."

His gruff voice is filled with so much emotion, my throat thickens with my next swallow. "That was a sweet thing to say."

"Well, it's true." He blows out a breath and pans his eyes to the ceiling. "Which is why you should take the job."

My breath halts in my lungs as my heart clenches with its unrelenting grip. "Why do you always do that?" I slam my palms to my side. "You say something sweet, and then you take it away like you meant something completely different. Do you want me to stay? Or do you want me to take the job?"

"I want you to be happy." His gaze settles back on me. "I want you to feel fulfilled and valued. You shouldn't have any regrets, and if you don't take this opportunity, then you just might." His face relaxes. "You'll always have a job here if it doesn't work out."

Why do I feel like Anderson is pushing me away before I've even made up my mind? "That's kind of you, but there's still a lot to consider. Seattle is a big city." I wrinkle my face. "There's traffic, skyscrapers, and fast food." Another troubling thought comes to me. "And where would I even live?"

"I'm sure the pay they're offering you is more than triple what I'm able to pay you here." The bitterness isn't lost in his tone.

Instinct draws me closer. I'm well accustomed to the tall, brick walls that surround Anderson. After chipping away at them over the past three years, I'm dying to take a wrecking ball to them to finally break through.

"I don't work at Camp Dakota for the money."

"Camp Bexley," he corrects.

Frustration rolls over me in waves. "Sorry. I'm still getting used to that."

Despite the intense moment we're sharing, I can admit the camp's name change is a huge accomplishment of his—one of many since Anderson took full control of the family business. He's proud, as he should be.

"Well, if you aren't going to fire me, then I think we should end this conversation now. I'm not making any decisions tonight."

Anderson's rock-hard stance remains unchanged, but his throat bobs, making me desperate to know what's going on under that thick skull of his.

He must finally accept my request because he nods, jaw tight, and sits down in the oversized chair. "I'll stay until the storm passes."

With a sigh, I walk over to the floor lamp to switch it off. As I do, I catch sight of my reflection in the wall mirror. Anderson is there, too, his eyes roaming my backside and locking on my ass. When I pause a second too long, it must alert him, because his eyes shoot up just in time to see he's been caught, before I switch off the light.

When I slide beneath my covers, I know sleep will be impossible. I'm too worked up, and with Anderson only a few feet away, guarding me like he's the protector of my nightmares, I find myself reading more into the situation than is probably true.

"Anderson." His name is a shallow whisper.

"Hope."

My heart beats faster, and I squeeze my eyes shut tight, trying to work up the nerve to speak again. "There's plenty of room next to me." I scoot over and lift the comforter lightly, not sure if he can see me with the dim light of the sky streaming through the cracks in the blinds.

I'm used to his rejection, and I'm ready for it. But for some reason, no words come, just the rustle of his clothes against the chair as he stands, then the slow and deliberate footsteps that bring him to the edge of my bed.

My breath catches in my throat when I hear the clank of his

belt as he unbuckles it. The sound of leather sliding slowly against his belt loops comes next. But it's the thud of his jeans hitting the wood floor that sends my blood pumping straight to my heart.

When he climbs in beside me, I turn onto my side to face him. He didn't even hesitate at my invitation, and now here he is mere inches away. This is why my feelings for Anderson Bexley are and will always be so fucked up. He gives me an inch, and I become desperate, rabid, to take a mile.

"You should take the job, Hope." His voice cracks on my name.

My chest squeezes. "I don't want to leave *you*."

"Everyone leaves."

His words are like a vise on my heart, clamping and squeezing the life out of me every time he speaks. "I won't."

"Well, you should. You deserve so much more than I could ever give you."

I scoot toward him, placing my hand on his chest, my eyes pleading with his. "All you have to do is ask me to stay." My heart is pounding so furiously I almost miss the hand that slides around my waist and pulls me toward him.

With his eyes squeezed shut and a long release of a sigh, his forehead leans against mine. Our lips are only inches apart, and the buzz I've always felt between us only grows stronger.

"Please, Anderson. Say something."

All he has to do is say the words and give me one small clue that this thing between us isn't entirely in my imagination.

"I can't ask that of you."

His words feel like a slap in the face. Frustration blows through me. With as much time as I've given him to meet me halfway, I finally feel as though I'm at my breaking point. How can he be this close to me, and this close to losing me, and not give me anything in return? At this point, I have nothing else to fear.

"Well, then don't." I bring my lips closer, inviting him in. "Show me."

Everything goes hot—my body, the air, our tangled breaths. It's like the calm before the storm, when everything stills before the warning comes in a violent rumble.

It's Anderson who closes the distance, merging our lips in an achingly slow caress. When the shock subsides, I match his movements—slow, shaky, and timid, yet there's an eagerness brimming beneath the surface that's palpable.

A groan slips from his mouth to mine, awakening a bundle of unspoken feelings within me, and I can't hold back anymore. My tongue dips between his lips. My hand snakes beneath his cotton shirt and drags up his chest. My front presses closer to his. And he reciprocates with every move—kissing me harder, pulling me flush against his body, and slipping his rough hands beneath my silk shorts.

We find a natural rhythm, our exploring hands daring to reach unexposed territory, our kiss deepening with each passing breath, and my heart rate tripling.

"Make love to me." It's just a whisper against his lips, but the moment the words are out of my mouth, I know it's the wrong thing to say. In the silence that follows, I'm starkly aware of the weather outside that has turned eerily calm.

Anderson freezes, his entire body tensing, and then he pulls away faster than I can even blink. "I can't do this." He stands, pulls on his jeans, and begins to refasten his belt. "You should take the job, Hope." Anderson turns toward the door.

I can't breathe, but somehow, I manage to think fast enough to leap out of bed and race across the room to plaster my body against the door, blocking his exit. "You're pushing me away." Emotion claws its way up my throat. "Why do you always push me away?"

He shifts his gaze, turning his head with it in a blatant attempt to avoid facing the hurt that he's caused. "You're meant for so much more. More than this camp can ever provide you." He faces me again, the hardness in his eyes revealing his unbreakable stance on the matter. "Take the opportunity. Take it while you can."

My chin quivers with each word. "And if I don't?"

His amber eyes flash a warning I can't quite decipher. "Then you're fired."

I take a step to the side at that biting remark and watch him open the door and step back into the night. Then I leave him with a final threat that I hope haunts him for the rest of his days.

"You're going to regret this, Anderson Bexley."

## Chapter One

The dock is rickety under my weight when I leave the boathouse—a stark reminder that I have loads of work left to do on the renovations I set out to tackle two years ago. After a generous donation from someone close to our family, everything I ever dreamed for this place began to come to fruition. But in my mad dash to expand and renovate every section of camp, it appears I overlooked the marina.

Lanterns light a clear path for my exit, but I don't head in that direction. Instead, I walk to the edge of the dock and stare out over the moonlit water. This is where I do my best breathing after a long day of work. Whether I'm tending to guests, training employees, drafting contracts for vendors, or filling in for missing staff, moments like these are cherished ones.

It's a perfect fall evening. Clear skies. Quiet night. Our last guests of the fall season left earlier today, which means staff gets the next month off to do as they please—three weeks longer than normal. But with camp renovations winding down, I want to get the place prepped and ready for new guests in the winter. Some staff will use the time to head home to their families, and others will take off for vacations. No one stays when camp is closed.

I've been looking forward to this in-between time more than all the previous ones. Maybe it's the fact that I've been running a million miles an hour over the past years to take my mind off more personal matters. Or maybe because I can finally dedicate the next month to the massive branding overhaul I've been working toward for the past two years.

Come to find out, while drowning myself in my work has been helpful, it hasn't taken away the emptiness I still feel when

I think about all the people I've lost along the way to building the camp's success.

Like Hope.

"Hey, stranger."

The unexpected voice causes me to swivel away from the water, my heart rate rocketing in my chest. The sight of a blonde with silver eyes and a familiar smile shocks me still.

"Shit, Silver. I wasn't expecting you." I walk forward, swooping my sister up in my arms and squeezing her tight. "God, I missed you."

"I missed you, too, doofus."

She tousles my hair and pulls back with a tilted head. "Looks like my sisterly intuition kicked in at the right time. You look like shit, Bexley."

My groan leaves me before I can process my emotions, but it serves me right to be all up in my feels when Silver happens to stop by. She knows me better than anyone else in our family, probably because she's more of an adoptive sort of sister. My family took her in when she was seventeen and needing a home. She was heaven-sent, coming to us at a time I think we all needed it, and she grew on us all—me, the most.

When my brothers all took off to abandon the family camp, Silver stuck around, loyal to a fault. Well, until recent years had her altering her course. I couldn't be happier for her. It's been two years since she's worked as our head camp nurse, but she still pops by on occasion.

"I was just heading to get a drink. Want to join me?"

Silver grins. "Absolutely. As long as I can have my old cabin."

"No can do. They're all being refurnished this week, but I can put you up in something better." I wink.

She gasps and jumps a little. "The new site is all ready?"

"It is," I tell her.

"I can't wait to see it all."

I pause for a second, realizing something is off about Silver's arrival. "Wait. Did you walk here from the parking lot?"

She nods. "I drove."

My mouth falls open while my fingers press into my chest in mock horror. "Oh, my. No seaplane this time?"

She rolls her eyes and nudges me from the side. "Hush. I happen to enjoy the drive and the ferry ride. Besides, I had to stop by Orcas Hospital to see one of my old mentors, so I made a day of it. With Kingston out of town, our house gets a little lonely."

A vague picture pops into my mind of Silver and her NFL star husband's obscenely large home in Seattle. "I can imagine. Well, you picked the perfect time to visit. I could use your help with a few things."

She stuffs her hands into her pockets and shrugs. "Sure. Put me to work. You know I love getting my hands dirty." She grins up at me.

"All the major renovations are done. No dirty work needed besides a few tune-ups here and there." I frown when I remember the creaky marina and mentally add that to my to-do list. "I'm talking more about marketing." I wave my hand around, gesturing to the camp. "I built it, and now I need for them to come. Marketing is a beast I am far from comfortable with. I haven't had to think about it much over the past year since we've always been booked out so far in advance, but now with the new adult site, I'm kind of feeling lost."

The silence that follows makes me dread saying anything to Silver. I can almost hear Hope's name in her thoughts, considering they're best friends and all.

"Have you reached out to her?" Silver's voice is quiet,

gentle, and I hate that I'm the reason for her timidness.

Bitterness rumbles in my chest. "I'm sure you know the answer to that."

"I do, but I figured I'd talk to you about it for once. You know, if you want to."

An image of Hope crosses my mind, but it's not the image I'd grown to adore that I'm seeing now. This one is eerily like the sadness on her face when I told her I'd fire her if she didn't take the job in Seattle. I pushed her away in the cruelest, coldest way possible, and now I've lost her forever.

*"You're going to regret this, Anderson Bexley."*

I still hear her final words. They're a haunting whisper whenever I'm alone with my thoughts.

"I don't think we should go there," I say quietly.

"But it's been a whole year. You two were so close, and you worked so well together. If anyone can help see you through this marketing stuff, it's definitely her."

We take the path that leads toward the newer side of camp that Silver has yet to see completed. While I was excited to show her, all I can think about now is the woman who got away. "There is absolutely no way Hope will consider helping me after..." I shake my head. "Never mind. Can we drop it? I have something I want to show you."

I steer her down a newly lit path into a territory that used to be nothing but woods for miles. My brothers and I had ventured back into these woods when we were younger and had a heyday building forts, shooting BB guns, and running our bikes over the same hills so many times that we created trails.

It was during those happy days that everything felt normal between us all, before life happened and reality tore our family apart.

When I hear Silver gasp, I know she spots the surprise I had in store for her. "Anderson Bexley, you put in a restaurant?"

I chuckle and tug her toward the swinging doors. "More like a little saloon. But yes, a restaurant. It's like a real resort now. Complete with a glamping area filled with luxury tents, five-star cabins, and…" I wave my hand out. "Tada! A bar."

Her gray eyes are so wide and unbelieving, it hits me straight in the chest. "I can't believe you've been keeping this from me. This is everything you and your brothers dreamed of back in the day." She wraps her arms around me. "You did it."

I feel a hollow ping. The fact that I did it without the help of my brothers is a gloomy thought that I wish I could douse along with the reminder that I'd lost Hope. It's all one dart in the chest after the other.

"So, what'll it be?" I walk around the curved bar and grin. "Are we getting a little drunk tonight?" I hold up a bottle of wine. "Or a lotta drunk?" I hold up a bottle of Jack Daniels.

Silver tosses her head back and laughs. "I think Jack will take care of us tonight." She sits on a stool across from me and slaps her palms on the counter. "I'm so proud of you, Anderson. Please tell me the guys know about all the work you've put in."

While Silver is the most supportive member of my family, she's too sweet and innocent for the truth at times. "You know the deal. Jamison's caught up in the corporate life in Seattle, Benson's traveling the world and crashing on couches for a living, and Cayson's got it made in the Air Force. This place isn't their dream anymore. They couldn't care less."

Silver's mouth forms a pout. "It all just feels so wrong. Surely, they miss this place. I didn't even grow up here the way you boys did, and I miss it every day."

I pour out a shot of whiskey over ice, top it off with some

club soda, and slide the tumbler to her. "Yeah, well, we sheltered you from a lot. When you showed up, I think we all wanted to heal, so we tried."

Silver nods. "You boys put on a good show, I guess. And I was too caught up in my own baggage to realize things were so off."

I sigh. "Yeah, well, you were here when things changed faster than any of us were ready for. In the blink of an eye, it felt like I lost everyone." I smile at the ray of light shining right in front of me. "Except for you. You stayed. You saved me, Silver."

She places her hand on mine. "And you saved me. What you all did for me back then is something I'll never be able to repay."

I raise my brows, telling her precisely how wrong she is. "You repaid us plenty. But now, the success of this place is on my shoulders, and it's beginning to weigh me down. I need your help." I give her all the irresistible charm I can muster with a batting of my lashes and a pouty mouth. "Please help me figure out what the fuck I need to do next to get an entirely new type of customer to vacation here."

Silver's soft smile is the most genuine thing I've ever seen in my life. "You know I'd do anything for you. I still think you should call Hope, but if you don't feel comfortable doing that, I have another idea. You'll just have to trust me."

I raise my arms as another glimmer of light dances in my chest. "You have all my trust. Tell me what I need to do."

### 

Keep reading here: https://geni.us/WeightofRegret

# More K.K. Allen Books

**Up in the Treehouse**
Haunted by the past, Chloe and Gavin are forced to come to terms with all that has transpired to find the peace they deserve. Except they can't seem to get near each other without combatting an intense emotional connection that brings them right back to where it all started... their childhood treehouse.

**Under the Bleachers**
Fun and flirty Monica Stevens lives for food, fashion, and boys... in that order. The last thing she wants to take seriously is dating. When a night of flirty banter with Seattle's hottest NFL quarterback turns passionate, her care-free life could be at risk.

**Through the Lens**
When Maggie moves to Seattle for a fresh start, she's presented with an unavoidable obstacle—namely, the cocky chef with a talent for photography and getting under her skin. Can they learn to get along for the sake of the ones they love?

**Over the Moon**
Silver Livingston has spent the past eight years hiding from her past when the NFL God, Kingston Scott, steps off the bus to mentor a football camp for kids. Kingston wants to be anywhere but at Camp Dakota... until he sees her. The intoxicating woman with the silver moon eyes, the reserved smile, and the past she's determined to keep hidden.

**Dangerous Hearts (A Stolen Melody, #1)**
Lyric Cassidy knows a thing or two about bad boy rock stars with raspy vocals. In fact, her heart was just played by one. So when she takes an assignment as road manager for the world famous rock star, Wolf, she's prepared to take him on, full suit of heart-armor intact.

**Destined Hearts (A Stolen Melody, #2)**
With stolen dreams, betrayals, and terrifying threats--no one's heart is safe. Not even the ones that may be destined to be together.

**British Bachelor**
Runaway British Bachelor contestant, Liam Colborn, is on the run from the media. When he gets to Providence to stay with his late brother's best friend, all he wants is a little time to regroup from his time on a failed reality show. That is, until he meets the redheaded bombshell nanny who lives in the pool house.

**Waterfall Effect**
Lost in the shadows of a tragedy that stripped Aurora of everything she once loved, she's back in the small town of Balsam

Grove, ready to face all she's kept locked away for seven years. Or so she thinks.

## A Bridge Between Us

With a century-old feud between neighboring families with only a bridge to separate them, Camila and Ridge find themselves wanting to rewrite the future. It all starts with an innocent friendship and quickly builds to so much more in this epic second chance coming of age romance.

## Center of Gravity (Gravity, #1)

Lex was athleticism and grace, precision and passion, and she had a stage presence Theo couldn't tear my eyes from. He wanted her...on his team, in his bed. There was only one problem... He couldn't have both.

## Falling From Gravity (Gravity, #1.5)

Amelia was nothing like Tobias had expected. Even after all the years—of living so close to her, of listening to her giggle with his sister in the bedroom next to his—he hadn't given much thought to his sister's best friend, until a secret spring break trip to Big Sur changed everything.

## Defying Gravity (Gravity, #2)

The ball is in Amelia's court, but Tobias isn't below stealing— her power, her resolve, her heart. When he wants a second chance to reignite their connection, the answer is simple. They can't. Not unless they defy the rules their dreams were built on and risk everything.

## The Trouble With Gravity (Gravity #3)

When Sebastian makes Kai an offer she can't afford to refuse, she learns taking the job will mean facing the tragedy she's worked so hard to shut out. He says she can trust him to keep her safe, but is her heart safe too?

**Enchanted Gods**
As powerful forces threaten the lives in Apollo Beach, Katrina can't escape the evocative world of mythological enchantment and evil prophecies that lurk around every corner. If only she wasn't cursed.

**Find them all here: www.kkallen.com**

# ACKNOWLEDGMENTS

Are you as over the moon for Silver and Kingston as I am? If so, there are people to thank for that. People I would be lost without.

First, let me just say THANK YOU to those of you who are as addicted to this BelleCurve world as me. It's been so much fun getting to know these characters and revisiting them with each book. I don't know if I'll ever be done writing in this world, but I am incredibly excited to tell you more about the spin-off series coming in 2022. All I have to say is GET READY for the Bexley brothers.

To my momma! All it takes is a simple phone call about legal jargon and you are always such a knowledgeable resource. Thank goodness for your many years in law. Weaving in Silver's backstory was no easy task, but you made it so much easier. Love you to the moon and back.

To my family and friends who supports me on the daily, I love you!

My next shoutout goes to my incredible Alpha team! These ladies read while I write to catch plot holes and inconsistencies to make sure my books are the best stories possible. To Cyndi, Sammie, Renee, and Patricia. Thank you so much for always guiding me in the right direction. Adore you babes so much.

To my Beta team who swooped in with their eagle eyes and gave me invaluable feedback while giving me all their feels while reading. Emily, Lindsey, and Brenna. *Over the Moon* wouldn't be what it is without you.

A special huge thank you to Erin Patrick Allen, RN, my medical Subject Matter Expert. I'm always so afraid to dive into a subject I know nothing about and having you as a resource for Silver's nursing background was the biggest help. Thank you, babe. I loved getting to write the caring, smart, and GOOD character that Silver is.

Some of you one-clicked this bad boy purely because of the beautiful cover. That's what happens when you pair Regina Wamba's photography with Okay Creations' graphic design skills. MAGIC every single time.

To my editor, Stefanie, from Red Adept. You are amazing! Thank you for all the helpful and glowing notes. Silver and Kingston thank you, too. And Lynn, thank you so much for always managing to work with my schedule. I am so appreciative.

As always, a huge thank you to my street team, Angsters, my reader group, Forever Young, my Instagram team, Booksters, and to every single blogger who supported this release in any way. I'm so appreciative of everything you do. Your love for books is why I get to write full time. *Sobs* Thank you!

Lindsey, I would be lost without you. Thank you for keeping me in line like a good boss should ;)

To my publicist, Dani, and the entire Wildfire team. Thank you so much for everything! Thank you for helping *Over the Moon* get seen in a sea of amazing books.

To my constant cheerleaders who always have my back and lift me when my spirit is seriously lacking, Harloe Rae and Heather Orgeron. You beeches mean the world to me. I can't wait until our reunion soon!

I dedicated this book to my bestest friend in the world and

to her momma, Anna, whose birthday happens to fall on *Over the Moon's* release day. When I think of how I fell in love with reading, I think of you both. Tasha, who shoved all of her Sweet Valley High books at me. Anna, who laughed at us for not being more rebellious. I'm so glad we got to have those shots together in Vegas. You are missed every single day.

Finally, thank you to every single reader who took a chance on *Over the Moon*. Your reading options are endless and I will never forget that.

Thank you XOXO,
K.K. Allen

# *Shop*
# EXCLUSIVE

* Signed Books
* Book Boxes
* Book Inspired Drinkware
* Collectors Items & Swag

# FREE
# Shipping
on orders over
# $100

## www.KKAllen.com/Shop

# ABOUT THE AUTHOR

K.K. Allen is a *USA Today* bestselling and award-winning author who writes heartfelt and inspirational contemporary romance stories. K.K. is a native Hawaiian who graduated from the University of Washington with an Interdisciplinary Arts and Sciences degree and currently resides in central Florida with her ridiculously handsome little dude who owns her heart.

K.K.'s publishing journey began in June 2014 with a young adult contemporary fantasy trilogy. In 2016, she published her first contemporary romance, *Up in the Treehouse*, which went on to win the Romantic Times 2016 Reviewers' Choice Award for Best New Adult Book of the Year.

With K.K.'s love for inspirational and coming of age stories involving heartfelt narratives and honest emotions, you can be assured to always be surprised by what K.K. releases next.

www.KKAllen.com

Milton Keynes UK
Ingram Content Group UK Ltd.
UKHW011308210923
429112UK00004B/240

9 798985 906332